CATALINA
—
THEN AND NOW

W. SOMERSET MAUGHAM

CATALINA
—
THEN AND
NOW

Original Illustrations by
Michael Charlton

HERON BOOKS, LONDON

Published by arrangement with
William Heinemann Ltd., London

© *Illustrations, Edito-Service S.A., Geneva, 1968*

CONTENTS

Catalina   1

Then and Now 253

CATALINA

I

IT was a great day for the city of Castel Rodriguez. The inhabitants, wearing their best clothes, were up by dawn. On the balconies of the grim old palaces of the nobles rich draperies were spread and their banners flapped lazily against the flagpoles. It was the Feast of the Assumption, August the fifteenth, and the sun beat down from an unclouded sky. There was a feeling of excitement in the air. For on this day two eminent persons, natives of the city, were arriving after an absence of many years, and great doings had been arranged in their honour. One was Friar Blasco de Valero, Bishop of Segovia, and the other his brother Don Manuel, a captain of renown in the King's armies. There was to be a *Te Deum* in the Collegiate Church, a banquet at the Town Hall, a bull-fight and when night fell fireworks. As the morning wore on more and more people made their way to the Plaza Mayor. Here the procession was formed to go out and meet the distinguished visitors at a certain distance from the city. It was headed by the civil authorities, then came the dignitaries of the Church, and finally a string of gentlemen of rank. The throng lined the streets to watch it pass and then composed themselves to wait until the two brothers, followed by these important personages, should enter the city, when the bells of all the churches would ring out their welcome.

In the Lady Chapel of the church attached to the Convent of the Carmelite nuns a crippled girl was praying. She prayed with passionate devotion before the image of the Blessed Virgin. When at last she rose from her knees she fixed her crutch more comfortably under her arm and

1

hobbled out of the church. It had been cool and dark there, but when she came out into the hot breathless day the sudden glare for a moment blinded her. She stood and looked down at the empty square. The shutters of the houses round it were closed to keep out the heat. It was very silent. Everyone had gone to see the festivities, and there was not even a mongrel dog to bark. You would have thought the city was dead. She glanced at her own home, a small house of two storeys wedged between its neighbours, and sighed despondently. Her mother and her uncle Domingo, who lived with them, had gone with all the rest and would not be back till after the bull-fight. She felt very lonely and very unhappy. She had not the heart to go home, so she sat down at the top of the steps that led from the church door to the plaza and put down her crutch. She began to cry. Then suddenly she was overcome with grief and with an abrupt gesture fell back on the stone platform and burying her face in her arms sobbed as though her heart would break. The movement had given the crutch a push, the steps were narrow and steep, and it clattered down to the bottom of them. That was the last misfortune ; now she would have to crawl or slither down to fetch her crutch, for with her right leg paralysed she could not walk without it. She wept disconsolately.

Suddenly she heard a voice.

"Why do you weep, child?"

She looked up, startled, for she had heard no one approach. She saw a woman standing behind her and it looked as though she had just come out of the church, but she had just done that herself and there had been no one there. The woman wore a long blue cloak that came down to her feet, and now she pushed back the hood that had covered her head. It looked as though she had indeed come out of the church, since it was a sin for women to enter the house

2

of God with uncovered heads. She was fairly tall for a Spanish woman and she was young, for there were no lines under her dark eyes, and her skin was smooth and soft. Her hair was very simply done with a parting in the middle and tied in a loose knot on the nape of her neck. She had small delicate features and a kindly look. The girl could not decide whether she was a peasant, wife perhaps of a farmer in the neighbourhood, or a lady. There was in her air a sort of homeliness and at the same time a dignity that was somehow intimidating. The long cloak concealed the garment underneath, but as she withdrew her hood the girl caught a brief glimpse of white and guessed that that must be the colour of her dress.

"Dry your tears, child, and tell me your name."

"Catalina."

"Why do you sit here alone and cry when all the world has gone forth to see the reception of the Bishop and his brother the captain?"

"I am a cripple, I cannot walk far, Señora. And what have I to do with all those people who are well and happy?"

The lady stood behind her and Catalina had had to turn round to speak to her. She gave a glance at the church door.

"Where have you come from, Señora? I did not see you in the church."

The lady smiled, and it was a smile of such sweetness that the bitterness seemed to fade from the girl's heart.

"I saw you, child. You were praying."

"I was praying as I have prayed night and day since my infirmity fell upon me to the Blessed Virgin to free me of it."

"And do you think she has the power to do that?"

"If so she wills."

There was something so benign and so friendly in the lady's manner that Catalina felt impelled to tell her sad story. It had happened when they were bringing in the

3

young bulls for the bull-fight on Easter Day and everyone in the town had collected to see them being driven in under the safe conduct of the oxen. Ahead of them on their prancing horses rode a group of young nobles. Suddenly one of the bulls escaped and charged down a side street. There was a panic and the crowd scattered to right and left. One man was tossed and the bull rushed on. Catalina running as fast as her legs would carry her slipped and fell just as the beast was reaching her. She screamed and fainted. When she came to they told her that the bull in his mad charge had trampled over her, but had run wildly on. She was bruised, but not wounded; they said that in a little while she would be none the worse, but in a day or two she complained that she could not move her leg. The doctors examined it and found it was paralysed; they pricked it with needles, but she could feel nothing; they bled her and purged her and gave her draughts of nauseous medicine, but nothing helped. The leg was like a dead thing.

"But you still have the use of your hands," said the lady.

"Thanks be to God, for otherwise we should starve. You asked me why I cry. I cry because when I lost the use of my leg I lost the love of my lover."

"He could not have loved you very much if he abandoned you when you were stricken with an infirmity."

"He loved me with all his heart and I love him better than my soul. But we are poor people, Señora. He is Diego Martinez, the son of the tailor, and he follows his father's trade. We were to be married when he was finished with his apprenticeship, but a poor man cannot afford to marry a wife who cannot struggle with the other women at the market place or run up and down stairs to do all the things that need to be done in a house. And men are but men. A man does not want a wife on crutches, and now Pedro Alvarez has

4

offered him his daughter Francisca. She is as ugly as sin, but Pedro Alvarez is rich, so how can he refuse?"

Once more Catalina began to cry. The lady looked at her with a compassionate smile. On a sudden in the distance were heard the beating of drums and the blare of trumpets, and then all the bells began to ring.

"They have entered the city, the Bishop and his brother the captain," said Catalina. "How is it that you are here when you might be watching them pass, Señora?"

"I did not care to go."

This seemed so strange to Catalina that she looked at the lady with suspicion.

"You do not live in the city, Señora?"

"No."

"I thought it strange that I had not seen you before. I thought there was no one here that I did not know at least by sight."

The lady did not answer. Catalina was puzzled and under her eyelashes looked at her more closely. She could hardly be a Moor, for her complexion was not dark enough, but it was quite possible that she was one of the New Christians, that is to say, one of those Jews who had accepted baptism rather than be expelled from the country, but who, as everyone knew, still in secret practised Jewish rites, washed their hands before and after meals, fasted on Yom Kippur and ate meat on Fridays. The Inquisition was vigilant and, whether they were baptised Moors or New Christians, it was unsafe to have any communication with them; you could never know when they would fall into the hands of the Holy Office and under torture incriminate the innocent. Catalina asked herself anxiously whether she had said anything that could give rise to a charge, for at that time in Spain everyone went in terror of the Inquisition, and a careless word, a pleasantry, might be a sufficient reason for arrest, and then weeks, months, years even might go by before you could prove your innocence. Catalina thought it better to get away as quickly as possible.

"It is time for me to go home, Señora," she said, and then, with the politeness that was natural to her, added: "So if you will excuse me I will leave you."

She cast a glance at the crutch that was lying at the bottom of the steps and wondered if she dared ask the lady to fetch it for her. But the lady paid no attention to her remark.

"Would you like to recover the use of your legs, child, so that you can walk and run as though you had never had anything the matter with you?"

Catalina went white. That question revealed the truth. She was no New Christian, the lady, she was a Moor, for it was well known that the Moors, Christian only in name, were in league with the devil and by magic arts could do evil things of all kinds. It was not so long ago that a pestilence had ravaged the city, and the Moors, accused of having caused it, confessed on the rack that they had done so. They perished at the stake. For a moment Catalina was too frightened to speak.

"Well, child?"

"I would give all I have in the world, and that is nothing, to be free of my infirmity, but even to regain the love of my Diego I would dono thing to imperil my immortal soul, for that is an offence to our Holy Church."

Still looking at the lady she crossed herself as she spoke.

"Then I will tell you how you may be cured. The son of Juan Suarez de Valero who has best served God has it in his power to heal you. He will lay his hands upon you in the name of the Father, the Son and the Holy Ghost, bid you throw away your crutch and walk. You will throw down your crutch and you will walk."

6

This was not at all what Catalina expected. What the lady said was surprising, but she spoke with such calm assurance that the girl was impressed. At once doubtful and hopeful, she stared at the mysterious stranger. She wanted a moment to collect her wits before she asked the questions that were already forming themselves in her mind. And then Catalina's eyes nearly started out of her head and her mouth dropped open, for where the lady had been there was nothing. She couldn't have gone into the church, for Catalina had had her eyes fixed on her, she couldn't have moved, she had quite simply vanished into thin air. The girl gave a great cry, and more tears, but tears of a different kind, coursed down her cheeks.

"It was the Blessed Virgin," she cried. "It was the Queen of Heaven, and I talked with her as I might have with my mother. Maria Santissima, and I took her for a Moor or a New Christian!"

She was so excited that she felt she must tell somebody at once, and without thinking she slithered down the stairs on her backside, helping herself with her hands, till she got her crutch. Then she hobbled back to her home. It was not till she got to the door that she remembered there was nobody there. But she let herself in, and discovering she was hungry, got herself a bit of bread and some olives and drank a glass of wine. It made her drowsy, but she sat up determined to keep awake till her mother and her uncle Domingo came back. She couldn't think how she could wait to tell them her wonderful story. Her eyelids drooped and in a little while she was fast asleep.

II

CATALINA was a very beautiful girl. She was sixteen, tall for her age, with breasts already well developed, very small hands and feet, and before she was crippled walked with a sinuous grace that charmed all beholders. She had eyes that were large and dark, shining with the glow of youth, black hair naturally curling, and so long that she could sit on it, a brown soft skin, cheeks of a warm rose and a red moist mouth; and when she smiled or laughed, which before her accident she did often, she showed very white even small teeth. Her full name was Maria de los Dolores Catalina Orta y Perez. Her father, Pedro Orta, had sailed for the Americas to make his fortune soon after she was born and since then no news had been heard of him. His wife, Maria Perez by birth, did not know if he was dead or alive, but she still hoped that one day he would return with a coffer full of gold and make them all rich. She was a pious woman and every morning at Mass said a prayer for his safety. She grew angry with her brother Domingo when he said that if Pedro was not long since dead he was living with a native woman, or perhaps two or three, and had no intention of leaving the half-caste family he had undoubtedly produced to come back to a wife who had by now lost her youth and beauty.

Uncle Domingo was a sore trial to his virtuous sister, but she loved him, partly because it was her Christian duty, but also because notwithstanding his grave faults he was lovable and she could not help it. She remembered him too in her prayers, and she liked to think that it was due to their efficacy and not only to the fact that he was getting on in years that he had abandoned at least the worst of his wild ways. Domingo Perez had been destined to the priesthood, and at the seminary of Alcalá de Henares, whither his father sent him, took minor orders and received the tonsure. One of his fellow pupils was Blasco Suarez de Valero, the Bishop of Segovia, whose arrival in the city that day the inhabitants were celebrating. Maria Perez sighed when she thought how different the careers of the two had been. Domingo was a bad boy. He got into trouble at the seminary from the very beginning, for he was headstrong, turbulent and dissipated, and neither admonition, penance nor beating served to tame him. Even then he was fond of the bottle and when he had had too much to drink would sing lewd songs that were an offence to his fellow seminarists and to the masters whose business it was to instil into their young minds decency and decorum. Before he was twenty he had got a Moorish slave with child, and when it appeared that his misbehaviour must be exposed ran away and joined a troupe of strolling players. With them he wandered about the country for two years and then suddenly turned up at his father's house.

He professed repentance for his sins and promised to amend his ways. He was evidently not meant by Providence to enter the priesthood, and he told his father that if he would give him enough money to keep him from starving he would go to a university and study law. His father was eager to believe that his only son had sown his wild oats, and indeed he had come back mere skin and bone, so it did not look as though the life he had led had been an easy one, and he let himself be persuaded. Domingo went to Salamanca and stayed there for eight years, but he pursued his studies in a very desultory fashion. The pittance he received from his father obliged him to live in a boarding-house with a group of other students and the food was only just sufficient to keep them from dying of hunger. In after years he used to regale his boon companions at the taverns he frequented with stories of the horrors of that establishment and of the cunning shifts they were put to to supplement their meagre fare. But poverty did not prevent Domingo from enjoying life. He had a glib tongue and charm of manner, and he could sing a good song, so that he was welcome at any entertainment. It may be that the two years he had spent with the strolling players had not taught him to be a good actor, but they had taught him other things that now came in useful. They had taught him how to win at cards and dice, and when a young man of fortune came up to the University it did not take him long to scrape acquaintance with him. He constituted himself his guide and tutor in the ways of the town, and it was seldom that the newcomer was not a good deal poorer for the experience he acquired. Domingo at that time was a personable fellow and now and then was lucky enough to excite the passions of women addicted to venery. They were not in their first youth, but in comfortable circumstances, and Domingo thought it only just that they should relieve his necessities in return for the service he rendered them.

The period he had spent as a strolling player had inspired him with the desire to write plays, and every hour he could spare from his amusements he devoted to this occupation. He had considerable facility, and besides writing a number of comedies, would often indite a sonnet to the object of his profitable attentions or write a set of verses in honour of a person of note which he would then present in the hope of receiving in return a present in cash. It was this knack he had for stringing rhymes together that finally led to his undoing. The Rector of the University by some ordinance he had passed had aroused the anger of the students, and when a set of indecent and scurrilous verses at his expense was found on a tavern table it was hailed

10

with delight. In a very short time copies were passed from hand to hand. It was bruited abroad that the author was Domingo Perez, and though he denied it, it was with such complacency that he might just as well have admitted it. Kind friends brought the verses to the attention of the Rector and at the same time told him who had written them. The original copy had disappeared, so that Domingo could not be convicted by his handwriting, but the Rector made discreet inquiries which convinced him that this bad and dissolute student was responsible for the insult. He was too astute to bring a charge that might be hard to prove, but, determined on revenge, took a more subtle course. It was not difficult to discover the scandal Domingo had caused as a seminarist at Alcalá, and the life he had led during the eight years he had spent at the University was notoriously profligate; Domingo was a gambler and it was well known that gambling was a common source of profanity; witnesses came forward who were prepared to swear that they had heard Domingo utter the most horrid blasphemies, and there were two who had heard him say that to believe in the Articles of Faith was first and foremost a matter of good breeding. This in itself was enough to make him a proper subject for inquiry by the Holy Office, and the Rector put the information he had received into the hands of the Inquisitors. The Holy Office never acted in haste. It collected evidence with secrecy and care and until the blow fell the victim seldom knew that he was suspect.

Late one night, when Domingo was in bed and asleep, the alguazil knocked on his door and when he opened it arrested him. He gave him just time to dress and pack his scanty baggage and his bedding roll, and conducted him, not to prison because he was in minor orders and the Inquisition took pains to avoid scandal to the Church, but to a monastery where he was incarcerated in a disciplinary

11

cell. There under lock and key, allowed to see no one, allowed to read nothing, without even a candle to light the darkness, he remained for some weeks. Then he was brought up for trial before the Tribunal. It would have gone hard with him but for one fortunate circumstance. Not long before, the Rector, a vain and irascible man, had quarrelled violently with the Inquisitors over a question of precedence. They read Domingo's verses and laughed with malicious delight. His misdeeds were evident and could not be passed over, but they perceived that by tempering mercy with justice they could put an affront on the indignant Rector that he would resent but would have to bear. Domingo admitted his guilt and professed repentance; he was then sentenced to hear Mass in the audience chamber and to be exiled from Salamanca and the immediate neighbourhood. He had had a fright. He thought it well to absent himself from Spain for a while, so he went soldiering in Italy and spent some years there gambling, cursing when the dice or the cards played him false, fornicating and drinking. He was forty when he returned to his birthplace, as penniless as when he left, with a scar or two which he had got in drunken brawls, but with many recollections to entertain his idle hours.

His father and mother were dead and his only kin were his sister Maria, abandoned by her husband, and his niece Catalina, then a pretty child of nine. Maria's husband had dissipated the dowry she brought him on marriage and she had nothing but the little house in which she lived. She supported herself and her daughter by doing the difficult and skilful needlework in gold and silver thread which decorated the velvet cloaks of the images, images of Jesus Christ, the Blessed Virgin and patron saints, that were carried in the processions of Holy Week, and the copes, chasubles and stoles that were used in the ceremonies of the

Church. Domingo had reached an age when he was ready to exchange the adventurous life he had led for twenty years for a settled one, and his sister, wanting the protection of a man in the house, offered him a home. When this story opens he had been living with her for seven years. He was not a financial burden on her since he earned money by writing letters for the illiterate, sermons for priests who were too lazy or too ignorant to write them for themselves, and affidavits for suitors before the law. He was ingenious also at making out the genealogies of persons who wanted declarations of purity of blood, by which was meant that for at least a hundred years their ancestors had not been tainted with Jewish or Moorish blood. The little family would thus have not been so badly off if Domingo had been able to break himself of his bad habits of drinking and gambling. He also spent good money on books, chiefly volumes of verse and plays, for on his return from Italy he had taken once more to writing for the stage, and though he never succeeded in getting anything produced he found adequate satisfaction in reading his compositions to fellow topers in his favourite tavern. Having become respectable he resumed the tonsure, which was a safeguard amid the perils of life in Spain at that time, and dressed in the sober habiliments which became a scholar in minor orders.

He grew very fond of Catalina, so gay, so vivacious and so pretty, and watched her grow into a beautiful girl with a satisfaction in which there was nothing of desire. He took her education upon himself and taught her to read and write. He taught her the Articles of Religion and attended her first communion with all the pride of a father; but for the rest he confined his teaching to reading verse to her, and when she was old enough to appreciate them the plays of the dramatists who were just then getting themselves so much talked about in Spain. Above all he admired

Lope de Vega, who he declared was the greatest genius the world had ever seen, and before the accident that crippled her he and Catalina used to play the scenes they most admired. She had a quick memory and in course of time knew long passages by heart. Domingo had not forgotten that he was once an actor and he taught her how to say her lines, when to be temperate and when to tear a passion to tatters. He was by this time a skinny, loose-limbed man, with grey hair and a lined yellow face, but there was still fire in his eyes and resonance in his voice; and when he and Catalina, with Maria their only audience, acted a striking scene, he was no longer a withered, drunken, elderly ne'er-do-well, but a gallant youth, a prince of the blood, a lover, a hero or what you will. But all this ceased when Catalina was trampled by a bull. The shock kept her in bed for some weeks, during which the surgeons of the town did what their poor science suggested to bring life back to her paralysed limb. At last they admitted that they could do nothing. It was an act of God. Her lover Diego no longer came to the window at night to make love to her through the iron grille, and it was not long before her mother brought home the rumour that he was going to marry the daughter of Pedro Alvarez. Domingo, to divert her, still read plays to her, but the love scenes made her cry so bitterly that he had to stop.

III

CATALINA slept for some hours and was awakened at last by the sound of her mother bustling about in the kitchen. She seized her crutch and hobbled in.

"Where is Uncle Domingo?" she asked, for she wanted him to listen to what she so urgently wanted to say.

"Where do you suppose? At the tavern. But if I know him he'll be back for supper."

As a rule, like everyone else, they had their only hot meal of the day at noon, but they had eaten nothing since morning except a hunk of bread spread with garlic that Maria had taken with her, and she knew Domingo would be hungry; so she lit the fire and set about making the soup. Catalina could not wait a minute longer.

"Mother, the Blessed Virgin has appeared to me."

"Yes, dear?" Maria answered. "Clean the carrots for me, will you, and cut them up."

"But, mother, listen. The Blessed Virgin appeared to me. She spoke to me."

"Don't be silly, child. I saw you were asleep when I came in and I thought I'd let you sleep on. If you had a nice dream all the better. But now you're awake you can help me to get the supper ready."

"But I wasn't dreaming. It was before I went to sleep."

Then she related the extraordinary thing that had happened to her.

Maria Perez had been good-looking in her youth, but now in middle age she had grown stout as do many Spanish women with advancing years. She had known a lot of trouble, two children she had had before Catalina had died, but she had accepted this, as well as her husband's desertion, as a mortification sent to try her, for she was extremely pious; and being a practical woman, not accustomed to cry over spilt milk, had found solace in hard work, the offices of the Church, and the care of her daughter and of her wilful brother Domingo. She listened to Catalina's story with dismay. It was so circumstantial, with such precise detail, that she would not have been unwilling to credit it if only it hadn't been incredible. The only possible explanation was that the poor girl's illness and the loss of her lover

15

had turned her brain. She had been praying in the church and then had sat in the hot sun; it was only too probable that something had gone awry in her head and she had imagined the whole thing with such force that she was convinced of its reality.

"The son of Don Juan de Valero who has served God best is the Bishop," said Catalina when she finished.

"That is certain," said her mother. "He is a saint."

"Uncle Domingo knew him well when they were both young. He can take me to him."

"Be quiet, child, and let me think."

The Church did not look with favour on persons who claimed to have had communication with Jesus Christ or His Mother, and discouraged these pretensions with all its authority. Some years before a Franciscan friar had caused a great to-do by healing the sick by supernatural means, and so many people had resorted to him that the Holy Office had been obliged to intervene. He was arrested and never heard of again. And through the gossip of the Carmelite Convent for which she did work now and again Maria Perez knew of a nun who asserted that Elias, the founder of the order, appeared to her in her cell and conferred singular favours upon her. The Lady Prioress had forthwith had her whipped until she confessed that she had invented the story to make herself important. If then friars and nuns suffered for making such claims it was only too likely that the Church would take a serious view of Catalina's story. Maria was frightened.

"Say nothing to anybody," she told Catalina, "not even to Uncle Domingo. I will talk to him after supper and he will decide what had better be done. Now in heaven's name clean the carrots or we shall have no soup to eat."

Catalina was not satisfied with this, but her mother bade her be quiet and do as she was told.

Presently Domingo came in. He was not drunk, but neither was he sober, and he was in high spirits. He was a man who liked to hear himself talk and, while they had supper, for Catalina's benefit he held forth loquaciously on the events of the day. This affords a suitable opportunity to tell the reader how it came about that the city was in a turmoil of excitement.

IV

DON JUAN SUAREZ DE VALERO was an Old Christian, and unlike many of the most noble families in Spain whose sons, before Ferdinand and Isabella united the kingdoms of Castile and Aragon, had married daughters of rich and powerful Jews, he could trace an ancestry unspotted by misalliance. But his ancestry was his only wealth. He owned a few poor acres a mile from the city near a hamlet called Valero, and it was to distinguish themselves from other persons called Suarez rather than to give themselves importance that he and his immediate forebears used the hamlet's name as part of their own. He was very poor, and his marriage with the daughter of a gentleman of Castel Rodriguez brought him little to enlarge his circumstances. Doña Violante bore her lord a child every year for ten years, but of these only three, all sons, survived to adolescence. They were named respectively Blasco, Manuel and Martin.

Blasco, the eldest, from his infancy showed signs of unusual intelligence and fortunately of piety as well, and so was destined to the priesthood. He was sent at a suitable age to the seminary of Alcalá de Henares and in due course attended the University. He took his degrees of Master of Arts and Doctor of Theology at so early an age that it was evident he could look forward to high distinction in the secular clergy. Promise of high preferment was made him. But on a sudden, saying that he wished to live out of the world so that he might devote himself entirely to study, prayer and meditation, he announced his intention of entering the monastic order of the Dominicans. His friends sought to dissuade him, since the rule was austere, with a midnight office, perpetual abstinence from meat, frequent disciplines, prolonged fasting and silence; but nothing served and Blasco de Valero became a friar. His gifts were too great to be ignored by his superiors, and when it was discovered that besides a fine presence and great learning he had a voice both powerful and melodious, and a fiery eloquence, he was sent here and there to preach; for St. Dominic had been ordered by Pope Innocent III to preach to the heretics and ever since the Dominicans had been noted as missionaries and preachers. On one occasion he was sent to his old University of Alcalá de Henares. He had by then a considerable reputation and the whole city flocked to hear him. His sermon was sensational. He put forth all his resources to convince the vast congregation of the importance of preserving the faith in its purity and of utterly exterminating the heretics. In tones of thunder he commanded the laity, as they valued their souls and dreaded the rigour of the Holy Office, to report whatever came to their notice that might savour of the sin and crime of heresy, and he impressed upon them in menacing words that it was the religious duty of each one of them to inform against his neighbour, the son against his father, the wife against her husband, for no ties of natural affection could absolve a son of the Church from conniving at an evil which was a danger to the State and an offence to God. The result of the sermon was satisfactory. There were numerous delations and in the end three New Christians, convicted of having cut the fat off their meat and changing their linen on the Sabbath, were burnt; a goodly number were sentenced to perpetual imprisonment, with confiscation of their possessions, and many more were scourged or subjected to penalties pecuniary or otherwise.

The friar's forcible eloquence had made so deep an impression on the authorities of the University that he was shortly afterwards appointed Professor of Theology. He protested his unworthiness and wished to be excused from accepting this responsible position, but his superiors in the order commanded him to undertake it and he was obliged to obey. He acquitted himself of his duties with credit, and his lectures were so popular that though he lectured in the largest hall at the disposal of the University, there was not enough room for all who wanted to listen to him. His reputation grew to great heights and after some years, being then seven and thirty years of age, he was made Inquisitor of the Holy Office in Valencia.

Though still sincerely conscious of his unworthiness he accepted the post without demur. Valencia was a seaport where foreign ships, English, Dutch and French, often put in. Their crews were not seldom Protestants and so were proper objects for the Inquisition to deal with. Moreover they frequently attempted to smuggle in prohibited books, such as translations into Spanish of the Bible and the heretical works of Erasmus. Blasco de Valero saw that he could do much useful work there. But besides this, there were great numbers of Moriscos at Valencia and in the surrounding country; they had been forcibly converted to Christianity, but it was common knowledge that with the great majority their conversion was but skin deep, and they adhered to many of their Moorish customs. They would not eat pork, they wore in their homes clothes which they

19

were forbidden to wear, and they refused to eat animals that had died a natural death. The Inquisition, supported by royal authority, had succeeded in stamping out Judaism, and though the New Christians might still be regarded with suspicion it was becoming more and more rare for the Holy Office to find occasion to prosecute them. But the Moriscos were a different matter. They were industrious, and not only was the agriculture of the country in their hands, but all the trading; for the Spaniards were too idle, too proud and too dissipated to engage in menial pursuits. The consequence was that the Moriscos were growing richer and richer, and since they were exceedingly prolific were increasing in numbers. Many thoughtful persons foresaw the time when the whole wealth of the country would be in their hands and they would outnumber the native population. It was natural to fear that then they would seize power and reduce the shiftless Spaniards to servitude. Somehow it was necessary to get rid of them at all costs and several plans were devised to effect this. One was to turn them over to the Holy Office and bring them to trial for their notorious heresies and then burn so many at the stake that the remainder would be harmless. Another, and less troublesome one, was to deport them; but the government had no wish to increase the power of the Moors across the Straits of Gibraltar by adding several hundred thousand hardy and industrious men to their population; and so the ingenious suggestion was made to send them to sea in unseaworthy ships under the pretence of landing them in Africa and then scuttle the ships so that all would be drowned.

No one was more concerned with this problem than Friar Blasco de Valero, and perhaps the most famous sermon he preached during his sojourn in Alcalá de Henares was that in which he proposed that the Moors should be transported *en masse* to Newfoundland, the males young and old having been previously castrated, so that in no long time they would all perish. It may be that it was this sermon which caused him to be given the high and honourable post of Inquisitor at the important city of Valencia.

Friar Blasco undertook his new duties with confidence, fortified by fervent prayer, that there was before him the opportunity to do great work to the honour of the Holy Office and the glory of God. He knew that he would have to contend against vested interests. The Moriscos were vassals of the nobles, to whom they paid tribute in money, kind or service, and it was to their advantage to protect them; but the friar was no respecter of persons and he decided that he would allow no one, however great, to interfere with his duties. Before he had been many weeks in Valencia it was reported to him that a powerful nobleman, Don Hernando de Belmonte, Duke of Terranova, had prevented the officials of the Holy Office from arresting some wealthy vassals who contrary to the law wore Moorish dress and used baths, so he sent his armed familiars to seize the Duke, fined him two thousand ducats and sentenced him to perpetual seclusion in a convent. It was a bold stroke to attack at once one so highly placed, and it terrified the most stout-hearted. When, however, it became evident that the Inquisitor was determined to exterminate the Moriscos the authorities of the city went in a body to remonstrate. They pointed out to him that the prosperity of the province depended upon them and it would be ruined if he continued in his course. But he berated them sharply, threatened them with excommunication, and so forced them to submission and humble apology. He succeeded before long by punishment and confiscation in reducing the Moriscos to misery and destitution. His spies were everywhere and it went ill with any Spaniard, lay or ecclesiastic, who laid himself open to suspicion. Since in his sermons he continued to impress upon the people of Valencia the obligation to denounce anyone who in jest or anger, ignorance or carelessness uttered a thoughtless expression, it was not long before everyone in the city lived in fear.

But the Inquisitor was a just man. He was careful to fit the punishment to the crime. For example, though as a theologian he condemned fornication between the unmarried as a mortal sin, it was only if people declared it was not a mortal sin that it concerned him as an inquisitor, and then he sentenced them to a hundred lashes. On the other hand he punished the assertion, equally heretical, that the married state was as good as celibacy with no more than a fine. He was also a merciful man. It was not the death of the heretic that he desired, but the salvation of his soul. On one occasion an Englishman, master of a ship, was arrested and confessed that he was a member of the reformed faith, whereupon his ship was seized and the cargo confiscated; he was tortured till his strength failed, and then consented to become a Catholic; it was with heartfelt satisfaction that the Inquisitor thus was able to condemn him to no more than ten years in the galleys and perpetual imprisonment. Two or three further instances may be given of his merciful disposition. Ever since the death of a penitent as the result of two hundred lashes, he had insisted on the scourging being limited to one hundred. When torture was to be applied on a pregnant woman he postponed its infliction till after her confinement, and it was his tender heart, rather than regard for the law, that made him take the utmost care that torture should cause neither permanent crippling nor broken bones, and if occasionally an accident happened and someone died as the result of its application no one could have more bitterly regretted it.

Friar Blasco's term of office was highly successful. In

the course of ten years he celebrated thirty-seven *Autos de Fé* at which some six hundred persons were penanced and over seventy burnt either alive or in effigy, thus not only rendering a service to God, but also edifying the people. A less humble man than he might have looked upon the last of these celebrations as the crowning glory of his career, for it was held in honour of Prince Philip, the King's son. The various ceremonies were conducted so properly and provided the royal prince with so much entertainment that he sent Friar Blasco a present of two hundred ducats with a letter in which he congratulated him on the improving spectacle and exhorted him to continue thus to serve God to the glory of the Holy Office and the advantage of the State. The zeal and piety of the Inquisitor had evidently made a deep impression on him, for when shortly afterwards Philip the Second died and he ascended the throne he lost no time in appointing Blasco de Valero to the bishopric of Segovia.

He accepted this new dignity only after spending a whole night on his knees wrestling with the Lord, and left Valencia amid the lamentation of great and small. He had won the admiration of the highly placed by his zeal, the austerity of his life and his scrupulous honesty; and he was worshipped by the poor for his charity. He received a handsome salary as inquisitor, and the canonry at Malaga to which he had been appointed was accompanied by a considerable income; but he spent every penny on relieving the necessities of the needy The confiscations of the wealth of convicted heretics and the fines inflicted on penitents brought large sums into the treasury of the Holy Office, and these moneys served to pay the great expenses of the organization, but it was not unusual for the inquisitors to keep considerable amounts for themselves. Even the saintly Torquemada thus accumulated an immense fortune, which he spent on building the monastery of St. Thomas Aquinas at Avila and enlarging that of Santa Cruz at Segovia. But Blasco de Valero never countenanced this practice and left Valencia as poor as when he arrived.

He never wore anything but the humble habit of his order, he never tasted flesh, nor wore linen or used it on his bed, and regularly disciplined himself, on occasion so severely that blood was splashed on the wall. His reputation for sanctity was such that when his habit became so worn that he was obliged to provide himself with a new one people paid his servants money to be given fragments of that which he had discarded so that they could wear them as a charm against the pox great and small. Before his departure several influential persons made so bold as to try to extract from him a promise that when at length the Almighty called him to Himself they should have the privilege of burying his body in the city where he had laboured so fruitfully. They were assured that they could bring enough influence to bear on Rome to obtain if not his canonization at least his beatification, and to have his bones in the Cathedral would be a glory to the city; but the friar, divining their thoughts, sternly refused to commit himself.

He was escorted for three miles beyond the city gates by a great company of ecclesiastical dignitaries, the magistrates and a number of fine gentlemen, and when they parted from him there was not a dry eye in all that distinguished gathering.

V

IT is unnecessary to deal at such length with the other sons of Don Juan de Valero.

The second son, Manuel, was several years younger than his brother and though far from stupid was neither so intelligent nor so industrious. He was more interested in the sports of the field than in the acquisition of learning. He grew into a handsome, stalwart man, with great strength of body and an uncommonly good opinion of himself. He had dash, courage and ambition. He was a great hunter and could ride horses which others found unmanageable. From his earliest youth he had played at bull-fighting with the other lads of the town and when he was old enough never missed a chance to jump into the ring and play the bull. At the age of sixteen he managed to be allowed to fight a bull on horseback, and to the admiration of the public killed it with one thrust of his lance. He had long decided upon a career of arms, for at that time in Spain, if you did not go into the Church, there was no other way to advance yourself. Though poor, Don Juan de Valero was highly respected, and it chanced that one of the nobles of the city was distantly related to the great Duke of Alva; and so one fine day, with a letter of recommendation in his pocket, young Manuel rode off to seek his fortune. He reached the great man at a favourable moment, for, banished from Court, he was then confined to his Castle of Uzeda. He was taken with the gallant bearing of the youth who sought his favour when he was in disgrace, and when shortly afterwards he was recalled by Philip II to assume command in the war with Portugal he took him in his suite. The Duke defeated Don Antonio, the King, and drove him from his kingdom. He seized a great treasure at Lisbon and gave his soldiers permission to sack the city and its suburbs. Manuel acquitted himself bravely in battle, and later, in the looting, picked up a good many valuable objects which he promptly converted into ready money. But Alva was old and near his death, and since the young man was eager to continue his military career he gave him letters to such of his old captains as had served under him in the Low

25

Countries and who were now under the command of
Alexander Farnese.

For twenty years Manuel fought with distinction to
regain the Northern Provinces for the King of Spain. He
proved himself not only courageous but astute, and he was
advanced first by Alexander Farnese and then by the
generals who on his death replaced him. He was as unscrupulous as he was intrepid, as ruthless as he was able,
and as devout as he was brutal, so that in due course he
was given important commands. It had not taken him long
to discover that when you serve your country you are
unlikely to be rewarded for having deserved well of it
unless you ask for what you want. This he had no hesitation in doing, and since by the loot he acquired in captured
cities, by the extortion he practised on the merchants of
the towns he administered, and by the granting of favours
in return for hard cash he amassed considerable sums, he
was able eventually to substantiate his claims in a manner
that made it hard not to acknowledge them. He received
the coveted order of Calatrava and proudly wore its green
ribbon. Two years later he was created Count of San
Costanzo in the Kingdom of Naples with the right to
dispose of the title as he chose. It was the thrifty habit of
the Spanish Kings so to reward the deserving, and since
they could sell their titles to rich commoners who desired
thus to ennoble themselves the Crown was able to provide
financially for those that had served it well without expense
to the treasury. But the Knight of Calatrava had invested
his money judiciously and had no need to do this. He had
been wounded several times, the last time so severely
that only his strong constitution enabled him to survive.
His wound gave him a reasonable excuse to leave the King's
service, and he determined to go home and marry into a
family of the old aristocracy of his native town, which with

26

his rank and fortune he had little doubt he could do, and then go to Madrid where he could use his energy and gifts for intrigue to achieve his inordinate ambition. Who knew but what, if he played his cards well, cultivating the right people, he might in the end rise to great heights? He was at this time forty years old, a fine figure of a man, with bold black eyes, a handsome moustache, an air of insolent virility and an agile tongue.

VI

OF the third son, Martin, even less need be said. Every family has its black sheep, and the family of Don Juan de Valero was no exception. Martin, the youngest of the three and the last child that Doña Violante bore her husband, had neither the fiery zeal that had enabled Blasco de Valero to reach eminence in the Church nor the ambition and dexterity that had brought fame and fortune to Don Manuel. He seemed content to devote himself to the cultivation of the few beggarly acres by the produce of which his father and mother kept body and soul together. At that time, owing to the constant wars and the attraction of America for the young and adventurous, there was a shortage of labour in Spain. The Moriscos, who were clever and industrious, had never been numerous in the region, and by then all but a very few had been forced to leave it. Martin was a sad disappointment to Don Juan, and though his wife urged that there was a certain advantage in having a son who was strong, active and willing to put his hand to any sort of work, he continued to chafe.

But a greater blow was in store for him. At twenty-three Martin married, and married beneath him. True, his bride was an Old Christian, the testimony was convincing that for four generations there had been no intermarriage with persons of Jewish or Moorish blood, but her father was a baker. Consuelo was his only child and would inherit whatever he had, but the fact remained that he was a tradesman. Some years passed, and Consuelo had children, and then still another blow befell Don Juan; the baker died; Don Juan heaved a sigh of relief, for now the bakery could be sold and the stigma of this connection with a menial occupation might be lived down. But no sooner was the baker decently buried than Martin informed his parents that he proposed to move into the city and run the shop himself. They could hardly believe their ears. Don Juan stormed, Doña Violante wept. Their son pointed out to them that if they had lived somewhat less meagrely than before it was owing to the dowry Consuelo had brought him; this was now spent; he had four children and there was no reason why he should not have four more; cash was scarce in Spain and he could not expect to get more for the business than would support them all for a few years, and then they would have nothing to look forward to but starvation. He put forward the ridiculous argument that there was nothing more disgraceful in baking bread than in ploughing a barren field or pressing olives.

Martin installed his family over the shop. He got up long before dawn to bake the bread and then rode out to the farm and worked there till dusk. He prospered, for his bread was good, and in a year or two was able to hire a man to take his place on the farm, but he never let a day pass without going to see his parents. He seldom came without bringing them something, and soon they were able to eat meat every day that the Church allowed it. They were getting on in years, and Don Juan could not deny that the presents his son brought were a comfort to his old age.

28

Though there had been some surprise in the city when the son of Don Juan de Valero thus demeaned himself and the boys in the streets called after him mockingly *Panadero, Panadero*, which means Baker, Baker, his good nature and his unconsciousness that he had done anything odd presently disarmed everyone. He was charitable, and no poor person ever came to his door asking for alms without being sent away with a loaf of new bread. He was pious, went to Mass every Sunday, and confessed regularly four times a year. He was now a hale and hearty man, thirty-four years of age, somewhat corpulent, for he liked good food and good wine, with an open red face and a cheerful, happy look.

"He's a good fellow," people said of him, "not very intelligent and not very cultured, but kind and honest."

He was pleasant of approach, fond of a joke, and in course of time, when he was able to take things more easily, men of respectability often came to his shop for a chat, and indeed it became a sort of meeting-place where one could see one's friends and have a talk.

It was fortunate that he had taken upon himself the charge of his parents, since Friar Blasco had never in the twenty years he had been away sent any money to help them, for everything he had went in charity, while Don Manuel never sent them anything since it never occurred to him that anyone could make better use of his money than he could himself. They were thus in their old age entirely dependent on Martin. They were still ashamed of him and could not but regret that he had made such a miserable business of life. It was a constant irritation that he seemed quite content with it. They treated his plebeian wife with the stately courtesy which they felt their own self-respect demanded of them, and grew fond of their grandchildren.

29

But their fondest thoughts went to the two sons who had brought honour and glory to their ancient name.

VII

IT is not hard to imagine with what joy Don Juan and Doña Violante looked forward to seeing them after a separation of so many years. The friar had written at rare intervals, and since neither Don Juan nor his son the baker was handy with his pen, or would in any case have trusted himself to write with the elegance due to a learned ecclesiastic, they had got Domingo Perez to answer his letters. This he had done with complete satisfaction both to them and to himself, for he took pride in the elegance of his style. Don Manuel, on the other hand, had never communicated with them except when he was intriguing to get the order of Calatrava and was obliged to offer proof of his unsullied ancestry. Here again the good offices of Domingo were requisitioned and he prepared a genealogy, duly sworn to by the magistrates of the city, in which he traced the origins of the family, without a single admixture of Jewish blood, to Alphonso VIII, King of Castile, who married Eleanora, daughter of King Henry II of England.

The occasion of the coming of Don Juan's two sons was not only the return of Don Manuel, after his long service in the wars, and the elevation of Friar Blasco to the episcopacy, but also the celebration of their parents' golden wedding. The two brothers arranged to meet at a town some twenty miles from the city and make their solemn entry together. It was pleasing to Don Juan to think that the grandeur of the reception arranged for them would in some measure counterbalance the long disgrace of poor

Martin's degradation. It was of course impossible for him to house his two sons and their suite in his tumble-down grange, and it was arranged that the Bishop should be lodged in the Dominican convent, while the steward of the Duke of Castel Rodriguez, his master being absent in Madrid, offered Don Manuel an apartment in the ducal palace.

The great day arrived. The noblemen of the city rode forth on their horses, the magistrates and the clergy on mules; Don Juan and Doña Violante with Martin and his family followed in a carriage lent them by a person of rank; and presently the anxiously-expected visitors were seen making their way along the dusty, winding road. The Bishop in his Dominican habit, on a mule, rode side by side with his brother on a charger. Don Manuel wore a magnificent suit of armour inlaid with gold. After them came the Bishop's two secretaries, members of his own order, and his servants, and then the captain's in sumptuous livery. Having greeted the important personages who had come to meet them and listened to some eloquent speeches, the Bishop asked for his father and mother. They had been hanging back modestly, but now came forward. Doña Violante was about to kneel and kiss the episcopal ring, but the Bishop, to the admiration of the onlookers, prevented her and taking her in his arms kissed her on both cheeks. She began to weep and many of those present were so affected that tears coursed down their cheeks. He kissed his father and then, while the two old people turned to their second son, he asked for Martin.

"*El panadero*," someone called. "The baker."

Martin made his way through the crowd with his wife and children. They were all in their best clothes, and the jolly, red-faced, corpulent man looked well enough. The Bishop greeted him affectionately, Don Manuel with a

31

certain condescension, and Consuelo and the children knelt on the ground and kissed the Bishop's ring. He graciously congratulated his brother on the number and healthy appearance of his offspring. In their letters to him Don Juan and Doña Violante had told him of their youngest son's marriage and of the children as they were born, but had never dared to inform him that he had become a trades-man. They watched the meeting with apprehension. They knew the truth would have to come out soon, but were anxious that nothing should happen to mar the joyful occasion. After much disputing it had been arranged who should ride on the right of the two distinguished sons of the city and who on the left, and though a good deal of ill feeling remained, the procession was formed and the cavalcade made an imposing entry into the city. As they passed through the gate the church bells were set ringing, crackers were exploded, trumpeters blew their trumpets and drummers beat their drums. The streets were crowded and there was a great shouting and a clapping of hands as they passed through on their way to the Collegiate Church where a *Te Deum* was to be sung.

The service was followed by a banquet, and the Bishop's hosts noticed that though it was a Feast Day he neither ate meat nor drank wine. When it was over he intimated his desire to be for a short time alone with his immediate family, so Martin went to fetch his mother, who had gone with his wife and the children to the baker's house. When he returned he found his brother Blasco alone with his father, but he had only just got into the room with Doña Violante when Don Manuel strode in. His brows were knit, his eyes black with anger.

"Brother," he said, addressing the Bishop, "do you know that this Martin, son of a gentleman of ancient lineage, is a pastry-cook?"

Don Juan and his wife started, but the Bishop merely smiled.

"Not a pastry-cook, brother. A baker."

"Do you mean to say that you knew?"

"I have known it for years. Though my sacred duties prevented me from taking the care of my parents that I wished, I have watched over them from afar and have constantly remembered them in my prayers. The prior of our order in this city has kept me informed of their condition."

"Then how could you let him bring such shame upon our family?"

"Our brother Martin is a virtuous and a pious man. He is a respected citizen and charitable to the poor. He has taken good care of our parents in their old age. I cannot blame him for taking a step which was forced upon him by circumstances."

"I am a soldier, brother, and I put my honour before my life. This has ruined my plans."

"I very much doubt it."

"How do you know?" blustered Don Manuel. "You do not know what my plans are."

The shadow of a smile lightened for an instant the Bishop's austere features.

"You cannot be very worldly-wise, brother," he replied, "if you are unaware that there is little of our personal affairs that remains hidden from our servants. You forget that we spent two days under the same roof on our way hither. It has reached my ears that you did not come here only to fulfil a filial duty, but also to choose a wife from among the nobility of the city. Notwithstanding the avocation which our brother has chosen to follow, with the title which His Majesty has been pleased to grant you and the money you have won in his service I think you will have no difficulty in achieving your object."

33

Meanwhile Martin had listened without any sign that he was in the least ashamed. There was something very like a grin on his good-humoured face.

"Do not forget, Manuel," he said now, "that Domingo Perez has traced our descent from a King of Castile and a King of England. That should assuredly carry weight with the family whom you are proposing to honour by taking their daughter to your wife. Domingo told me that one of the Kings of England made cakes, so perhaps there is no great disgrace in a descendant of kings making bread, especially as it is by common consent the best bread in the city."

"Who is this Domingo Perez?" the soldier asked sulkily.

That was not a very easy question to answer, but Martin did his best.

"A man of learning and a poet."

"I remember him," said the Bishop. "We were at the seminary together."

Don Manuel tossed his head impatiently and turned to his father.

"Why did you allow him thus to disgrace us?"

"I did not approve of it. I did everything in my power to prevent it."

Don Manuel now turned sternly on his younger brother.

"And you dared to go counter to your father's wishes? They should have been a command to you. Give me one reason, only one, why, flinging decency to the winds, you demeaned yourself by becoming a baker."

"Hunger."

The world seemed to crash to the floor like a pile of masonry. Don Manuel smothered an exclamation of angry disgust. Once more a faint smile trembled on the Bishop's lips. Even saints retain some small measure of humanity, and during the two days they had spent together the Bishop had come to the conclusion that he had little love for his military brother. He blamed himself for it, but all his Christian charity was insufficient to overcome his feeling that Don Manuel was a coarse, brutal and domineering fellow.

Fortunately this family reunion was interrupted by persons who came in to tell them it was time to go to the bull-fight. The two brothers were placed in seats of honour. The municipality had spent enough money to get good bulls and the fight was worthy of the occasion. When it was over the Bishop with his attending friars retired to the Dominican convent and Don Manuel to the quarters that had been prepared for him. The people of the city wandered back to their homes, or to the taverns, to talk about the exciting day, and Domingo Perez eventually found his way back to his sister's house.

VIII

AFTER supper, as was his habit, Domingo went upstairs to his room. In a little while Maria followed him. From the floor below she could hear him reading in loud and dramatic tones, and when she knocked at the door he did not answer. She went in. It was a small bare chamber containing nothing but a bed, a chest for his clothes, a table and a chair. There was a shelf filled with books, and books were lying on the table, on the floor, on the chest. The bed was unmade and on it he had flung his cassock. He was in shirt and breeches. The table was littered with papers and there was a great pile of manuscripts in one corner of the room. Maria sighed when she saw the untidiness which she had never been able to cope with. He took no notice of her entrance, but went on declaiming the speeches of a play.

"Domingo, I want to speak to you," she said.

35

"Don't interrupt, woman. Listen to the glorious verses of the greatest genius of our day."

He ranted on. Maria stamped her foot.

"Put down that book, Domingo. I have something very important to say to you."

"Go away. What can you have to say to me that is more important than the divine inspiration of the phœnix of the age, the incomparable Lope de Vega?"

"I will not go till you listen to me."

Domingo threw down his book in vexation.

"Then say what you have to say, say it quickly and begone."

She told him then Catalina's story, how the Blessed Virgin had appeared to her and told her that the Bishop, Don Juan's son, had the power to cure her of her infirmity.

"It was a dream, my poor Maria," he said when she had finished.

"That is what I told her. She declared that she was wide awake. I cannot persuade her otherwise."

Domingo was disturbed.

"I will come downstairs with you and she shall tell me the story herself."

For the second time Catalina narrated the incident. Domingo had but to look at her to be certain that she firmly believed every word she said.

"What makes you so sure you were not asleep, child?"

"How could I have fallen asleep at that hour of the morning? I had only just come out of the church. I cried, and when I came home my handkerchief was wet with my tears; could I have dried my eyes in my sleep? I heard the bells ringing when the Bishop and Don Manuel entered the city. I heard the trumpets and the drums and the shouts of the people."

"Satan has many wiles to beguile the unwary. Even Mother Teresa de Jesus, the nun who founded all those

36

michael charlton

convents, was for long afraid that the visions she had were the work of the devil."

"Could a demon assume the mildness and the loving kindness of Our Lady when she spoke to me?"

"The devil is a good actor," smiled Domingo. "When Lope de Rueda got impatient with the members of his troupe he would say that if he could only get the devil to play for him he would willingly give him in payment the souls of all his company. But listen, dear heart, we know that certain pious persons have received the grace of seeing with their own eyes the persons of Our Blessed Lord and His Virgin Mother, but they have received this grace as the reward of prayer, fasting, mortification and a life devoted to the service of God. What have you done to deserve a favour that others are accorded only as the result of long years of self-immolation?"

"Nothing," said Catalina. "But I am poor and unhappy, I prayed the Blessed Virgin to succour me, and she took pity on me."

Domingo was silent for a while. Catalina was determined and self-willed, and he was afraid. She had no notion of the risks she was incurring.

"Our Holy Church does not regard with indulgence individuals who claim to have communications with heaven. The country is infested with persons who declare that they have been granted supernatural privileges. Some are poor deluded creatures who honestly believe what they say; many are impostors who make these pretensions either to gain notoriety or to make money. The Holy Office rightly concerns itself with them, for they cause disturbance among the ignorant and often lead them into heresy. Some the Holy Office imprisons, some it scourges, some it sends to the galleys and others to the stake. I beseech you as you love us not to divulge a word of what you have told us."

"But, uncle, dear uncle, all my happiness is at stake. Everyone knows that there is no more saintly man in the kingdom than the Bishop. It is common knowledge that even pieces of his habit have a miraculous power. How can I remain silent when the Blessed Mother of God herself told me that he can cure me of the infirmity that has robbed me of the love of my Diego?"

"It is not only you that are concerned. If the Holy Office takes it upon itself to make an inquiry, it may well be that the case against me will be re-opened, for the Holy Office has a long memory, and if we are put into the prison of the Inquisition this house will be sold to pay for the cost of our maintenance and your mother will be thrown into the street to beg her bread. Promise me at least that you will say nothing till we have had time to reflect."

There was so great a dismay, so deep an anxiety, in Domingo's expression that Catalina yielded.

"Yes, I will promise you that."

"You are a good girl. Now let your mother put you to bed, for we are all weary after the events of the day."

He kissed her and left the two women to themselves, but from the stairs he called his sister. She went out.

"Give her a purge," he whispered. "If she has a good movement of the bowels she will be more reasonable, and we can persuade her tomorrow that the whole thing was no more than a very unfortunate dream."

IX

BUT the purge had no effect—at least not the desired one. Catalina continued to assert that she had seen the Blessed Virgin with her own eyes and had spoken with her.

She described her attire with such accuracy that Maria Perez was filled with amazement. Now it happened that the next day was a Friday and Maria went to confession. She had had the same confessor, Father Vergara, for many years and had confidence both in his benevolence and his wisdom. So after she had received absolution she told him Catalina's strange story and much of what Domingo had said.

"Your brother has behaved with a discretion and good sense the more admirable because these qualities could hardly be expected in him. This is a matter that must be treated with caution. We must do nothing in haste. There must be no scandal and you must order your daughter not to speak to anyone of this thing. I will reflect upon it and if needful consult my superior."

Maria's confessor was also her daughter's, and he knew them both as only a confessor can know his penitents. He knew that they were simple, honest, guileless and God-fearing. Even Domingo had not been able to corrupt their innocence or impair their candour. Catalina was a sensible girl, with a good head on her shoulders, and if she had not borne her injury with resignation, she had certainly borne it with courage. She was too ingenuous to invent such a story for any ulterior motive and, he was convinced, of too material a temper to imagine a spiritual event. Father Vergara was a Dominican and it was in his convent that the Bishop and his suite were lodging. He was a simple man of no great learning and Maria's story of her daughter's adventure troubled him so much that he felt bound to report it to his prior. The prior after some thought came to the conclusion that the Bishop should be informed of it, so he sent a novice to ask if it would be convenient for him to see him and Father Vergara on a matter that might be of importance. In a little while the novice came back to say that the Bishop would be pleased to receive them.

He had been given the most commodious cell in the convent. It was separated by a double archway with a supporting column into two parts, one of which served as a sleeping apartment and the other as an oratory. When the prior and Father Vergara entered they found the Bishop dictating letters to one of his secretaries. The prior explained on what errand they had come and then left Father Vergara to repeat exactly what his penitent had told him. The friar started by telling the Bishop how good and pious the two women were, how blameless their lives, then went on to describe the accident that had caused the unfortunate Catalina to lose the use of her leg and the attentions of her lover, and finished by repeating the story of how the Blessed Virgin had appeared to her and told her that the Bishop could cure her of her infirmity. As an afterthought he added that Domingo Perez, her uncle, had exacted a promise from her to keep the episode a secret until the matter had been well considered. By the time he had come to an end the Bishop's face had assumed an expression of such severity that the friar, his voice faltering, sweated at every pore. Silence fell.

"I know this Domingo," said the Bishop at length. "He is a man of evil life and one with whom no one who values his salvation should associate. But he is not a fool. When he exacted a promise of secrecy from his niece he acted with prudence. You are the child's confessor, Father?" The friar bowed. "You would be well advised to refuse to give her absolution until she promises that she will not speak of this affair to anybody."

The poor friar stared at the Bishop in confusion. Was he not by common consent a saint? Father Vergara thought he would have welcomed the opportunity to exercise his miraculous powers and thereby not only glorify God, but bring many sinners to repentance. The Bishop's eyes were cold. You might have thought that he was controlling his anger only by an effort of will.

"And now if you will permit me I will go on with my work," he said, and then turning to the secretary: "Read over the last sentence I dictated."

The two friars sidled away without another word.

"Why is he vexed?" asked Father Vergara.

"We ought not to have spoken to him about it. I am to blame. We have offended his humility. He does not know how great a saint he is and does not look upon himself as worthy to perform a miracle."

This seemed a very reasonable explanation and since it only redounded to the Bishop's credit Father Vergara made haste to tell his brother friars all about it. Soon the convent was buzzing with excitement. Some praised the Bishop's modesty, others regretted that he had not taken occasion to do something that would so greatly add to his renown and to the credit of the order.

Meanwhile, however, the story reached another quarter. The church in which Catalina had prayed and from which, if she was to be believed, the Blessed Virgin had come was attached, as has been mentioned, to the Carmelite Convent of the Incarnation. The convent was richly endowed and for a good many years the Lady Prioress had been in the habit of giving Maria Perez work to do, partly from charity and partly because she was very skilful in the difficult and laborious handicraft she exercised. Maria had thus come to be on friendly terms with many of the nuns. Since it was a convent of the mitigated order they enjoyed a good deal of freedom and it was not seldom that one of them came to her house for a meal and a talk. Two or three days after Maria's confession she had occasion to go to the convent and after doing her errand began to chat with the nun who was her most intimate friend. Swearing her to secrecy she told her of her daughter's strange experience. The nuns were great gossips and such a story was bound to be an event in the pious but monotonous routine of their lives, so that within twenty-four hours every inmate of the convent heard it and eventually it reached the ears of the Lady Prioress. Since this lady plays a not unimportant role in this narrative it is necessary here, even at the risk of boring the reader, to tell her history.

X

BEATRIZ HENRIQUEZ Y BRAGANZA, in religion Beatriz de San Domingo, was the only daughter of the Duke of Castel Rodriguez, a grandee of Spain and a Knight of the Golden Fleece. He had great wealth and great power. He managed to retain the confidence of the morose and distrustful Philip II and filled with distinction important positions in Spain and Italy. He had vast estates in both countries, and though his duties forced him to sojourn here and there he loved nothing better than to dwell with his wife and children, for he had three sons and a daughter, in his native city with its salubrious air and noble prospects. It was from there his race had sprung, and it was through the successful repulse by one of his ancestors of the Moors who were besieging the city that his family had first become eminent. There none was greater than the Duke of Castel Rodriguez and he lived in a state that was almost royal. Throughout its history the members of his family had made great alliances, so that he was related to all the grandest nobles in Spain. When Beatriz, his daughter, was thirteen he looked round to find a suitable mate for her and after reviewing various possible candidates settled on the only son of the Duke of Antequera who was descended, on the wrong side of the blanket, from Ferdinand of Aragon. The Duke of Castel Rodriguez was prepared to give his daughter a magnificent dowry and so the matter was arranged without difficulty. The young people were betrothed, but since the boy was only fifteen it was decided that the marriage should not take place till he had reached a suitable age. Beatriz was allowed to see her future husband in the presence of the parents on both sides, their uncles and aunts and other more distant relatives. He was a squat little boy, no taller than herself, with a mass of coarse black hair, a snub nose and a sulky mouth. She took an instant dislike to him, but she knew it was useless to protest and so contented herself with making faces at him. He responded by putting out his tongue at her.

After the betrothal the Duke sent her to finish her education at the Carmelite Convent of the Incarnation at Avila where his sister was prioress. She enjoyed herself. There were other girls, daughters of noblemen, in the same situation as herself, and a number of ladies who for one reason or another boarded in the convent, but were not subject to its discipline. The mitigated rule of the Carmelites was not strict and though some of the nuns devoted themselves to prayer and contemplation, many of them, while not neglecting their duties, went out and about to see their friends and sometimes stayed away for weeks at a time. The parlour was always filled with callers, male and female, so that there was a cheerful social life; matches were made, the state of the wars discussed, the gossip of the city exchanged. It was a peaceful, harmless existence, with modest diversions, and to the nuns a not too strenuous way to attain eternal happiness.

At the age of sixteen Beatriz was taken away from the convent and went down with her mother, and a host of attendants, to Castel Rodriguez. The Duchess was in poor health and had been ordered by the doctors to live in a climate less severe than that of Madrid. The Duke, occupied with affairs of state, unwillingly remained behind. The time was approaching when the marriage of Beatriz might take place, and her parents thought it well that she should learn something of the conduct of a great establishment. So for some months the Duchess devoted herself to teaching her daughter the social observances which she could not be expected to have learnt in the convent of the Carmelite nuns. Beatriz had grown to be a tall girl of great beauty, with a clear skin unblemished by smallpox, features of classical regularity and a lithe, slender figure. The Spaniards admired a greater opulence of form than she then possessed and some of the ladies who came to pay court to the Duchess lamented her thinness, but the proud mother promised them that marriage would soon remedy that defect.

Beatriz at that age was gay, passionately fond of dancing and aglow with animal spirits. She was mischievous and wilful. She was even then of an imperious temper, for she had been spoilt and had very much her own way all her life, and from her earliest years had realized that she was born to great station and that the rest of the world must submit to her caprice. Her confessor, not a little disturbed at this desire for domination, spoke to her mother of it, but the Duchess was somewhat cool toward his admonition.

"My daughter was born to rule, Father," said she. "You cannot expect from her the servility of a laundress. If there is an excess of pride in her disposition her husband, if he has character, will doubtless modify it, and if he has not, then her sense of what is due to her will be of assistance to him."

At the convent Beatriz had taken a great fancy to the
novels of chivalry which some of the lady boarders were
fond of, and though not permitted to read them by the
nun who had charge of the pupils she managed now and
then to snatch a glance at one or other of those inter-
minable romances. On coming to Castel Rodriguez she
found several in the palace and, with her mother often
indisposed, her duenna complacent, she devoured them
with avidity. Her young imagination was inflamed and
she looked forward with distaste to her inevitable marriage
with the boy whom she still saw as a scrubby, black-browed
and uncouth urchin. She was well aware of her beauty and
at High Mass with her mother missed none of the admiring
glances that the young blades of the city cast on her. They
would gather on the steps of the church to see her come
out, and though she walked with eyes modestly cast down,
the Duchess by her side, followed by two footmen in livery
carrying the velvet pillows on which they had knelt, she
was conscious of the excitement she caused and her ears
caught the praises that the young men in the Spanish
manner uttered as she passed. Though she never looked
at them she knew them all by sight and it was not long
before she found out their names, what families they belonged to, and in fact all there was to know about them.
Once or twice the more venturesome serenaded her, but
the Duchess immediately sent out her servants to drive
them away. Once she found a letter on her pillow. She
guessed that one of her maids had been bribed to place it
there. She opened it and read it twice. Then she tore it
into little pieces and burnt it in the flame of her candles.
It was the first and only love letter she ever had in her
life. It was unsigned and she could not tell from whom it
came.

Owing to her bad health the Duchess thought it enough

to go to Mass on Sundays and on feast days, but Beatriz went every morning with her duenna. It was very early and not many people attended, but there was a young seminarist who never failed. He was tall and thin, with decided features and dark passionate eyes. Sometimes, going on an errand of mercy with the duenna, she passed him in the street.

"Who is that?" asked Beatriz one day when she saw him slowly walking towards them reading a book.

"That? Nobody. The eldest son of Juan Suarez de Valero. *Hidalguía de Gutierra.*"

That may be translated as gutter nobility, and was the scornful term applied to gentlemen by birth who had not the means to live according to their station. The duenna, a widow and vaguely related to the Duke, was proud, devout, censorious and penniless. She had lived at Castel Rodriguez all her life till, when Beatriz left the convent, the Duke had chosen her to attend his daughter. She knew all about everyone in the city, and though so pious was not above a tendency to speak evil of her neighbours.

"What is he doing here at this time of year?" Beatriz inquired.

The duenna shrugged her thin shoulders.

"He fell ill at the seminary from overwork and his life was despaired of, so he was sent home to regain his health, which through the mercy of God he has done. He is said to be very talented. I presume that his parents hope that through the influence of the Duke your father he will obtain a benefice."

Beatriz said no more.

Then for no reason that the doctors could discover she lost her appetite and her high spirits. She lost her fresh colour and grew pale. She was listless and would often be

found bathed in tears. She, whose gaiety, charming wilful-
ness and irresponsibility had given life to that grim, magnificent palace, now was mopish and dejected. The Duchess
was at her wits' end, and fearing that the child was going
into a decline wrote to her husband to ask him to visit
them so that they might consider what was best to do. He
came and was shocked at the change in his daughter. She
had grown thinner than ever and there were dark smudges
under her eyes. They came to the conclusion that the best
thing to do was to get her married at once, but when that
was proposed to Beatriz she was seized with shrieking
hysterics so that they were more alarmed than ever and for
the time dropped the subject. They dosed her with medicine, fed her with asses' milk and ox-blood, but though she
obediently swallowed everything they gave her nothing
served. She remained wan and despondent. They did
what they could to distract her. They hired musicians to
play for her; they took her to a religious play in the
Collegiate Church; they took her to bull-fights: she continued to fail. The duenna had become greatly attached to
her charge, and since Beatriz no longer cared to read the
romances which had been her greatest entertainment, she
knew no other way to amuse the sick girl than by telling
her the gossip of the city. Beatriz listened politely, but
without interest. On one occasion she happened to mention
that the eldest son of Juan Suarez de Valero had entered
the Dominican order. She went on chatting away about
one person and another till suddenly Beatriz fainted. She
called for help and Beatriz was put to bed.

A day or two later, when she was better, she asked permission to go to confession. She had for several weeks
refused to go, saying she did not feel well enough, and the
Duchess's confessor, who was also hers, had agreed that
it was better not to insist. Now, however, both her parents

tried to dissuade her, but she was so urgent, she cried so
bitterly, that at length they yielded; so the great carriage,
used only on state occasions, was brought out, and accompanied by the duenna she went to the Dominican church.
When she returned she looked more like her old self than
she had looked for many weeks. There was a faint flush
on her pale cheeks and her fine eyes shone with a new light.
She knelt at her father's feet and asked his permission to
enter religion. This was a great shock to him, not only
because he did not want to lose his only daughter to the
Church, but because he was unwilling to forgo the important alliance which he had planned; he was, however, a kind
and a devout man, and he answered without harshness that
it was a matter not to be undertaken lightly, and in any case
out of the question while she was in such poor health. She
told him then that she had spoken of it with her confessor
and that the scheme had his full approval.

"Father Garcia is no doubt a very worthy and a very
pious person," said the Duke, with something of a frown,
"but his profession has perhaps prevented him from knowing how great are the responsibilities attached to noble
birth and high rank. I will talk to him tomorrow."

So next day the friar was summoned to the ducal palace
and ushered into the presence of the Duke and Duchess.
They knew of course that he would not reveal anything
that Beatriz had said to him in the confessional, and they
did not attempt to find out whether she had given him any
reason for taking a step which was so unwelcome to them;
but they told him that though she had always followed the
observances of the Church she had been light-hearted, fond
of every kind of amusement and had never shown any
inclination to the life of a religious. They told him of the
great marriage that had been arranged for her and the
inconvenience it would be, the ill feeling it might cause, if

it were broken off; and finally, with all due respect to his habit, they suggested that it was unwise of him to approve of her wish when it was so obviously due to her mysterious illness. She was young and her constitution was sound; there was no reason to suppose that when she regained her health she would be of the same mind. They found the Dominican strangely obstinate. He thought that Beatriz's desire was too strong to be opposed, and that her vocation was real; he went so far as to tell these great personages that they had no right to prevent their daughter from taking a step that would bring her peace in this world and happiness in the next. This was the first of many discussions. Beatriz remained firm in her determination and her confessor supported her desire with every persuasive argument at his command. At last the Duke agreed that if at the end of three months she still wished to enter a convent he would give his consent.

From then on she grew better. Three months passed, and she joined the community of the Carmelites of Avila as a novice. Arrayed in all her finery of satin and velvet, wearing her jewels, she was accompanied to the convent by her family and a number of the noblest cavaliers of the city. At the door she bade them all a gay farewell and was admitted by the portress.

But the Duke had made plans of his own to deal with the situation. He decided for his own honour and to the glory of God to found a convent at Castel Rodriguez to which his daughter could come as soon as she had finished her novitiate and where in due course she would be prioress. He owned property in the city and he chose a site just within the wall which was suitable to his purpose. There he built a handsome church, a cloister, and suitable edifices for conventual life, and laid out a garden. He employed the best architect he could find, the best sculptors, the best painters, and when everything was ready Beatriz, now known as Doña Beatriz de Santo Domingo, came to stay at the palace, with several nuns from Avila who had been chosen for their virtue, intelligence and social consequence. The Duke had decided that no nun should be eligible unless she were of noble birth. A prioress was chosen with the understanding that as soon as Beatriz de Santo Domingo was of a suitable age to take her place she should retire. The duenna, on the Duke's somewhat urgent persuasion, had entered a convent at Castel Rodriguez at the same time as Beatriz had gone to Avila, and was now ready to join her old charge. Mass was said by Father Garcia, the Blessed Sacrament was enthroned, and the nuns took up their abode in the new foundation.

At the time with which this narrative is concerned Dona Beatriz de San Domingo had been prioress for many years. She had won the respect of the citizens of Castel Rodriguez and the admiration, if not the love, of her nuns. She never forgot her great rank, but neither did she forget that her daughters were of noble birth. In the refectory they sat in their proper order of precedence, but when, as sometimes happened, there were disputes on this point Doña Beatriz dealt with them firmly. She was a strict disciplinarian and however well born a nun might be she did not hesitate to have her whipped if her orders were disobeyed. But so long as her authority was unquestioned she was affable and even indulgent. The convent was under the mitigated rule of Pope Eugenius IV, and provided that the nuns performed their religious duties she saw no reason to deprive them of the privileges they had been thus accorded. They were allowed to visit their friends in the city, and indeed, if the reason were good, to go and stay with their relations in other places for quite long periods. Many visitors, both lay and clerical, came to the convent; several ladies, as at Avila, lived there for their pleasure; so that there was a good deal of agreeable intercourse. Silence was only obligatory from Compline until Prime. Lay sisters did the menial work in order to give the nuns more time for their devotions and for occupations of more honour. But with all this liberty and with these temptations to worldliness no breath of scandal had ever tarnished the good name of these virtuous women. The reputation of the community was so great that there were more applicants for admission than the prioress could do with, so that she was able to be very particular in her examination of candidates.

She was a busy woman. Besides her religious duties she had to supervise the economy of the convent and keep an eye on the behaviour of the nuns, and on their health, bodily and spiritual; the foundation had been richly endowed both with houses in the city and with lands, and she had to deal with the factors who collected the rents and with the farmers who farmed the lands. She visited them frequently to see that everything was well and that the crops were in good condition. Since the rule allowed her to own private property the Duke had turned over to her several houses and a handsome estate, and on his death she had inherited much more. She managed it to such advantage that she was able to give away every year a considerable sum in charity. What remained over she spent on beautifying the church, the refectory and the parlour, and on building oratories in the garden to which the nuns could retire for meditation. The church was magnificent. The vessels for the sacred offices were of pure gold and the monstrance was studded with jewels. The paintings over the various altars were heavily framed in gilt wood elaborately carved, and the images of the Saviour and of the Blessed Virgin had great cloaks

51

of velvet, richly embroidered with gold (by Maria Perez), and their crowns blazed with stones, precious and semi-precious.

To celebrate the twentieth year of her profession Doña Beatriz built a chapel to St. Dominic, for whom she had a special cult, and hearing from one of the sisters, a native of Toledo, that there was a Greek there who painted pictures that wonderfully exalted the devotion of the worshipper, she wrote to her brother, the present Duke, to order one for an altarpiece. Being a businesslike woman she gave him the exact dimensions. But her brother wrote back to tell her that the King had ordered from that very Greek a picture of St. Maurice and the Theban legion for his new church at the Escorial, but when it was delivered was so dissatisfied that he would not have it placed. In these circumstances the Duke thought it would be indiscreet of her to give that painter a commission, and so sent her as a gift a picture by Lodovico Caracci, an artist celebrated in Italy, which by a happy chance was of precisely the right size.

The late Duke, her father, when constructing the convent had arranged an apartment for her to occupy when she was lady prioress which was as elegant as was fitting to the office and her rank. There was a cell on one floor to which no one was admitted but the lay sister whose business it was to keep it clean and in order, and from it a small stairway led to an oratory on the floor above. Here she performed her private devotions, attended to affairs and received visitors. It was severe, but stately. Above the little altar at which she prayed was a great crucifix with a figure of Christ, carved in wood, almost life-size and painted with great realism; while over the table at which she worked was a picture by a Catalan painter of the Virgin in glory. Doña Beatriz at this time was between forty and fifty, a tall, gaunt, pale woman, with hardly a line on her face, and great sombre eyes. Age had refined her features and thinned her lips so that she had the calm and severe beauty of a knight's lady on a Gothic tomb. She held herself very erect. There was something imperious in her air which suggested that she looked upon no one as her superior and few as her equals. She had a grim, even a sardonic sense of humour, and though she often smiled it was with a sort of grave indulgence; when she laughed, which was seldom, you had the feeling that it was with pain.

Such then was the woman to whose ears it came that the Blessed Virgin had appeared to Catalina Perez on the steps of the Carmelite church.

XI

DOÑA BEATRIZ was not only a fine organizer with a good head for business, but also a highly intelligent and level-headed woman. She had always discouraged visions, raptures and special graces among her nuns. She did not allow them to indulge in excessive austerity or in mortifications other than the Rule provided for; nothing escaped her notice, and when one of them showed signs of a religiosity that the Lady Prioress thought excessive she was promptly purged, forbidden to fast, and if that did not serve sent away to pass a few pleasant weeks with friends or relations. The strictness of Doña Beatriz in this respect was caused by her recollection of the trouble and scandal that had been caused at the Convent of the Incarnation at Avila by a nun who asserted that she had seen Jesus Christ, the Blessed Virgin and various saints and had received special graces from them. The Prioress did not reject the possibility of such occurrences since it was certain that some saints had been the recipients of similar favours, but she could not bring herself to believe that the nun of Avila, Teresa de Cepeda, with whom she had herself often spoken when she was a pupil at the convent, was anything but the hysterical and deluded victim of a disordered fancy.

It was highly improbable that there was anything in Catalina's queer story, but since the nuns were so excited about it that they could talk of nothing else, Doña Beatriz thought it advisable to send for the young woman and get it from her own lips. She called one of her nuns and told her to fetch the girl. In a little while the nun came back and informed her that Catalina was dutifully prepared to obey the Reverend Mother's order, but her confessor had forbidden her to repeat her story to anyone. Doña Beatriz, unused to being crossed, frowned; and when she frowned everyone in the convent trembled.

"Her mother is here, Your Reverence," said the nun, catching her breath.

"What should I want with her?"

"She had the story from the girl's own lips immediately after Our Lady appeared to her. The Father did not think to forbid her to speak of it."

A grim smile appeared on the Prioress's pallid lips.

"A worthy, but not a far-seeing man. You did well, my daughter. I will see the woman."

Maria Perez was ushered into the oratory. She had often seen the Prioress, but had never spoken to her, and she was flustered. Doña Beatriz sat in a high chair, with a leather seat and a leather back, the top of which was decorated with acanthus leaves in gilt wood. Maria Perez could not imagine that a queen could look more remote, dignified and proud. She knelt and kissed the thin white hand that was offered her. Then, bidden to tell what she had come to say, she repeated word for word what Catalina had told her. When she had finished the Prioress gave a slight inclination of her distinguished head.

"You may go."

For some time she pondered. Then she sat down at the table and wrote a letter in which she begged the Bishop of Segovia to do her the honour of coming to see her since she wished to speak to him on a matter that seemed to have some importance. She sent the letter and within an hour received a reply. The Bishop with equal formality said that he would be pleased to obey the command of the Reverend Mother and would visit the convent on the following day.

The nuns were in a turmoil when they learnt that this eminent and saintly person was expected, and they instantly jumped to the right conclusion that his visit had to do with the miraculous appearance of the Blessed Virgin on the steps of their own beautiful church. He came in the afternoon, after the siesta which the nuns took in the heat of summer, accompanied by the two friars who were his secretaries, and was received by the sub-prioress in the parlour. The nuns, much to their chagrin, had been told to keep to their cells. After the sub-prioress had kissed his ring she said that she would lead him to the Lady Prioress. The two friars started to go with him.

"The Reverend Mother desires to speak with your lordship in private," she said humbly.

The Bishop hesitated for an instant and then slightly inclined his head in assent. The friars fell back and the Bishop followed the nun through cool white passages and up a flight of stairs till he came to the oratory. She opened the door and fell back to allow him to enter. He went in. Doña Beatriz rose to meet him and falling to her knees kissed the episcopal ring; then she motioned him to a chair and sat down.

"I was hoping your lordship would see fit to visit this convent," she said, "but since you did not come I ventured to invite you."

"My teacher of theology at Salamanca told me to have as little to do with women as possible, to be polite to them, but to keep them at a distance."

She did not utter the tart reply that was at the tip of her tongue, but instead looked at him intently. He cast his eyes down and waited. She was in no hurry to speak. It was nearly thirty years since she had last seen him, and these were the first words they had ever exchanged. His habit was old and patched. His head was shaven except for the ring of black hair, only just touched with grey, that represented the Crown of Thorns. His temples were hollow, his cheeks sunken, his face, deeply lined, bore the mark of suffering; only the eyes, luminous with a strange light, darkly passionate, remained to remind her of the young seminarist she had known so long ago—known and loved so madly.

It had begun as a frolic. She had noticed him when first he served the Mass, as on occasion he did, at the church she attended with her duenna. He was thin even then, his hair was black and thick, for he wore only the tonsure of minor orders, his features were clean cut and there was a singular grace in his bearing. He looked like one of those saints who have received the call in their boyhood, so that they become an object of veneration to all, and die in youth and beauty. When he was not serving the Mass he knelt in the small chapel among the few who attended it at that early hour. He was attentive to his devotions and his eyes never left the altar. Beatriz in those days was light-hearted and full of fun. She knew the devastating power of her splendid eyes. She thought it would be a merry prank to make the serious young seminarist conscious of her, and she fixed him with her gaze, willing him with all her might to look at her. For days she gazed in vain and then a day came when she had an intuition that he was uneasy; she could not have told what gave her the impression, but she was certain of it; she waited, holding her breath; he looked up suddenly, as though he had heard an unexpected sound, and catching her eye turned quickly away. From then on she ceased to throw him even a glance, but a day or two later, though her head was bent as though she were praying, she was conscious that he was staring at her. She remained quite still, but she felt that he was looking at her, bewildered, with a look that he had never given anyone before. She knew a thrill of triumph and then, raising her head, deliberately met his eyes. He turned away as quickly as before and she saw his face suffused with a blush of shame.

Two or three times in the street with her duenna she saw him coming towards them, and though he passed them with his head averted she knew that he was shaken. Once indeed, catching sight of them, he turned on his heel and walked back the way he had come. Beatriz giggled so that the duenna asked what was amusing her and she had to tell the first lie she could think of. Then one morning it chanced that they entered the church just as the seminarist was dipping his fingers into the holy water to cross himself. Beatriz put out her hand to touch his fingers and thus receive the holy water on her own fingers. It was a common and a natural action and he could not refuse. He went very white and once more their eyes met. It was only for an instant, but in that instant Beatriz knew that he loved her with a human love, the love of a passionate boy for a beautiful girl, and at the same time she felt a sharp pain in her heart, as though it were pierced with a sword, and she knew that she loved him with the same human love,

57

the love of a passionate girl for a lovely youth. She was
filled with joy. She had never known a happiness so great.

He was serving Mass that day. Her eyes never left him.
Her heart beat so that she could hardly bear it, but the pain,
if pain it was, was greater than any pleasure she had ever
known. She had discovered before this that some errand
or occupation took him every day past the Duke's palace
at a certain hour and she found means to sit at a window
from which she could watch the street. She saw him come,
she saw his steps linger, as though unwillingly, as he passed,
and then she saw him hurry on as though flying temptation.
She hoped he would look up, but he never did, and once,
to tease him, she let a carnation fall just as he was approaching. Instinctively he glanced up then, but she drew back
so that she could see him without his seeing her. He stopped
and picked up the flower. He held it in both hands, as
though it were a precious jewel, and for a moment stood
looking at it like a man entranced. Then with a violent
gesture he flung it to the ground, stamped it in the dust
and ran, ran as fast as his legs would carry him. Beatriz
broke out laughing and then on a sudden burst into tears.

When he did not come to the early Mass for several days
running she could bear her anxiety no longer.

"What has happened to that seminarist who used to serve
Mass?" she asked her duenna. "I haven't seen him lately."

"How should I know? I suppose he's gone back to his
seminary."

She never saw him again. She knew by then that what
had started as a comedietta had turned into a tragedy, and
she bitterly regretted her folly. She loved him with all the
hot passion of her young body. She had never been crossed
in anything and it enraged her to think that now she could
not have her will. The marriage that had been arranged
for her was a marriage of convenience and she had accepted

it as the consequence of her station. As was her duty, she had been prepared to bear her husband children, but was decided to be no more troubled by him otherwise than if he were a flunkey; but now the thought of being united to the dwarfish, dull-witted creature filled her with loathing. She knew that her love for young Blasco de Valero could result in nothing. True, he was only in minor orders and could be released from them, but she did not even have to remember that her father would never consent to such a misalliance; her own pride would not have allowed her to bestow her hand in marriage on the gutter nobleman that he was. And Blasco? He loved her, she was certain of that, but he loved God more. When he had stamped with rage on the flower she had dropped at his feet it was to stamp out the unworthy passion that horrified him. She had terrible, frightening dreams, dreams of lying in his arms, her mouth against his, his breast pressing against hers, and she awoke with shame, anguish and despair. It was then she began to sicken. They could make nothing of her malady, but she knew what it was, she was dying of a broken heart. It was when she heard that he had entered a monastic order that she had her inspiration; she knew as if he had told her in so many words that in flying the world he was seeking to escape her, and it gave her a strange joy, a sense of triumphant power. She would do the same thing; to enter a convent would release her from a hateful marriage and in the love of God she might find peace. And at the back of her mind, hardly even hinted at in unspoken words, was the feeling that in that life, widely separated as they would be, each devoted to the service of the Highest, they would in some mystical way be united.

All this that has taken so long to tell passed through the mind of the grim, severe Prioress in a flash. She saw it as though it were one of those vast frescoes painted on the long wall of a cloister which yet you embrace in a comprehensive regard. All that passion, the passion that in her foolish youth she imagined would endure to the end, was long since dead. Time, the pious monotony of convent life, prayer and fasting, the multifarious duties of her position, had gradually dulled it till it was now no more than a bitter recollection. As she looked at the man now, so worn and haggard, with that look of suffering on his face, she wondered if he remembered that once he had loved against his will, yes, but with all his heart, a beautiful girl whom he had never even spoken to, but who tormented his dreams. The silence weighed upon the Bishop and he moved uneasily in his chair.

"Your Reverence said that she had a matter of importance on which she wished to consult me," he said.

"Yes, but first permit me to offer your lordship my felicitations on the dignity to which it has pleased His Majesty to advance you."

"I can only hope that I shall prove worthy to perform the duties of so great an office."

"There can be no doubt of that in the mind of anyone who knows with what zeal and discretion you acted during the ten years you spent at Valencia. Though this small city in the mountains is remote we manage to keep acquainted with what passes in the great world, and the fame of your lordship's austerity, virtue and unremitting diligence in defence of the purity of our faith has not escaped us."

The Bishop glanced at her for a moment from under beetling brows.

"Madam, I am obliged to you for your courtesy, but I must beg you to spare me your compliments. It has never been to my liking that people should talk of me to my face. I shall be grateful if you will tell me without further delay for what reason you requested me to visit you."

60

The Prioress was not at all abashed by this reproof. A bishop he might be, but as her duenna, now with God, had once said *Hidalgo de Gutierra*, a gutter nobleman; and she was the daughter of the Duke of Castel Rodriguez, a grandee of Spain and a Knight of the Golden Fleece. A word from her to her brother, confidant of King Philip the Third's favourite, would relegate this prelate to an obscure bishopric in the Canaries.

"I am sorry to offend your lordship's modesty," she answered coolly, "but it is your virtue and your austerity, your sanctity, if I may say so, which are the immediate occasion for my requesting the honour of a visit from you. Have you been informed of the strange experience of a girl called Catalina Perez?"

"I have. Her confessor, doubtless a worthy man, but neither learned nor intelligent, reported her story to me. I dismissed him. I have forbidden the friars in the convent to mention it to me or to talk about it among themselves. The girl is either an impostor, looking for notoriety, or a deluded fool."

"I do not know her, Señor, but from all accounts she is a good, sensible and pious girl. Persons of good judgment who know her are convinced that she is incapable of inventing such a story. She is truthful and, I am told, far from fanciful."

"If she had such a vision as she describes it can only be by a machination of Satan. It is well known that demons have the power of disguising themselves in celestial forms in order to tempt the unwary to perdition."

"The child suffers from an unmerited misfortune. We must not ascribe to the devil more cleverness than he has. How could he be so stupid as to think her soul would be endangered by having a saintly man lay his hand on her in the name of the Father, the Son and the Holy Ghost?"

CATALINA

During this conversation the Bishop had kept his eyes on the floor, but now he glanced at the Prioress, and there was anguish in them.

"Madam, Lucifer, son of the morning, fell through pride, and how could it be but through pride that I, a very wicked and a very sinful man, should take it upon myself to work miracles?"

"It may be fitting that in your humility you should regard yourself as a sinful and wicked man, my lord, but the rest of the world is well aware of your great virtue. Listen, Señor, this story has been bruited abroad and the whole city is talking about it. Everyone is excited and expectant. In some way satisfaction must be given to the people."

The Bishop sighed.

"I know the people are disturbed, groups stand outside the convent as though they were waiting for something, and when I am forced to go out they kneel as I pass to ask me for my blessing. Something must be done to let them see reason."

"Would your lordship allow me to give you advice?" the Prioress asked with great respect, but with a glint of ironical amusement in her eyes which somewhat modified it.

"I should be grateful."

"I have not seen the girl because her confessor ordered her not to repeat her story, but you have the power to overrule his order. Wouldn't it be well if you saw her? With your discernment, your knowledge of character and the skill you acquired in the Holy Office in the examination of suspects, you should be able to tell very quickly if she is an impostor, if she is deceived by the devil or if, finally, it was indeed the Blessed Virgin who condescended to appear to her."

The Bishop raised his eyes and looked at the image of the Redeemer nailed to the Cross in the shrine at which the

62

Prioress was wont to pray. His face was very sad. He was torn by indecision.

"I need not remind you, Señor, that this convent is under the special protection of Our Lady of Carmel. We poor nuns are doubtless unworthy of the honour, but it may be that she regards with peculiar favour this church which my father the Duke built for her in this city. It would be a great grace and a great glory to our house if by your lordship's intercession our heavenly patroness cured this poor child of her infirmity."

For a long time the Bishop was sunk in thought. At last he sighed again.

"Where can I see this girl?"

"Can there be a better place than in the chapel of our church dedicated to the worship of the Blessed Virgin?"

"What must be done had better be done quickly. Let her come tomorrow, madam, and I will be here." He rose from his seat and as he bowed to take his leave of the Prioress there was the shadow of a smile, but so rueful, on his lips. "A sorrowful night awaits me, Your Reverence." She knelt down once more and kissed his ring.

XII

NEXT day, at the appointed hour, the Bishop, accompanied by his two secretaries, entered the richly-decorated church. Catalina, with one of the nuns, was waiting in the Lady Chapel; with the help of her crutch she was standing, but when the Bishop appeared the nun touched her arm and she started to kneel. He prevented her.

"You may leave us," he said to the nun, and then when she had gone he turned to the two friars. "You may withdraw, but remain close at hand. I will speak to this girl alone."

They silently slid away. The Bishop watched them go. He knew they were curious and he did not wish them to hear what was said. Then he took a long look at the crippled girl. He had a tender heart and was always moved by distress, want or infirmity. She was trembling a little and she was very pale.

"Do not be frightened, child," he said gently. "You have nothing to fear if you tell the truth."

She looked very simple and very innocent. He saw that she had a singularly beautiful face, but he noticed it as indifferently as he might have noticed that a horse was roan or grey. He began by asking her about herself. She answered at first very shyly, but as he continued to press her with questions, after a little with greater confidence. Her voice was soft and melodious and she expressed herself with correctness. She told him the simple little story of her life. It was the story of any poor girl, a story of hard work, of harmless amusements, of church-going, of falling in love; but she told it so naturally, with such an ingenuous air that the Bishop was touched. He could not think this was a girl who had invented something to make herself important. Her every word suggested modesty and humility. Then she told him about her accident and how her leg had become paralysed and how Diego, the tailor's son, whom she was going to marry and whom she loved, had abandoned her.

"I don't blame him," she said. "Your lordship doesn't know, perhaps, that the life of the poor is hard, and a man doesn't want a wife who isn't able to work for him."

As tender a smile as the Bishop's haggard features permitted flitted briefly across his face.

"How is it you have learnt to speak so sensibly and so well, my daughter?" he asked.

64

"My uncle Domingo Perez taught me to read and write. He took great pains with me. He has been like a father to me."

"I knew him once."

Catalina was well aware of her uncle's bad reputation and she was afraid that her reference to him would do her little good in the eyes of that saintly man. There was a silence and for a moment she thought he was going to end the interview.

"Now tell me in your own words the story you told your mother," he said, fixing her with searching eyes.

She hesitated and he remembered that she had been ordered by her confessor not to speak of it. He gravely told her that he had authority to override the confessor's prohibition.

Then she repeated it exactly as she had told it to her mother. She told him she had been sitting on the steps weeping because everyone in the city was happy and she alone wretched, and how a lady had come out of the church and talked to her and how she had said that his lordship had the power to cure her of her infirmity, how she had vanished before her very eyes, and how then it had been borne in upon her that the lady was the Blessed Virgin herself.

She finished and there was a long silence. The Bishop was shaken, but at the same time distracted with indecision. The girl was no impostor, of that he was convinced, for her innocence, her sincerity were unmistakable; it could not have been a dream, for she had heard the bells ringing, the beating of drums and the blare of trumpets when he and his brother entered the city, and at that moment she was in speech with the lady who she had no reason then to suppose was more than she seemed; and how could Satan have the power to put on a false semblance when the girl

65

had been pouring out her poor little heart to the Mother of God and beseeching her to succour her in her distress? She was a pious creature and there was no presumption in her. Others had had their prayers answered, others had received spiritual grace, others had been cured of their ills. If he refused to do what it looked as if he had been bidden to do, because he was afraid, might he not be committing a grave sin of omission?

"A sign," he muttered to himself. "A sign."

He took a step or two forwards till he came to the altar above which in a great cloak of blue velvet, all stitched in gold, with a golden crown on her head, stood an image of the Mother of God. He knelt and prayed for guidance. He prayed passionately, but his heart was dry and he felt that the darkness of night shrouded his soul. At last, with a sad sigh, he rose to his feet and stood, his arms outstretched in supplication, with his despairing gaze fixed on the mild eyes of the Blessed Virgin. Suddenly Catalina gave a little startled cry. The two friars had withdrawn out of sight but, though they could not hear what was said, not out of earshot, and when they heard this they scuttled forth as quickly as rabbits into their burrow; but what they saw rooted them to the ground. They uttered no sound. They stood, their mouths open, as if like Lot's wife they had been turned to pillars of salt. Don Blasco de Valero, Bishop of Segovia, was slowly rising into the air, as slowly as oil slides down a plate ever so slightly inclined, rising with an even, almost imperceptible motion, as the water rises in a tidal river; the Bishop rose till he was face to face with the image over the altar and for a moment was suspended in the air for all the world like a falcon motionless on its outstretched wings. One of the friars, fearing he would fall, made as if to start forwards, but the other, Father Antonio, restrained him; and the

Bishop, slowly, slowly, so that you were barely conscious of movement, descended till his feet once more touched the marble floor in front of the altar. His arms fell to his sides and he turned round. The two friars ran up and falling on their knees kissed the hem of his habit. He seemed not to be aware of their presence. He walked down the three steps that led from the altar, and like a man in a daze groped his way out of the chapel. The two friars, in case he stumbled, kept close to him. Catalina was forgotten. They emerged from the church. The Bishop paused at the top of the steps, the steps on which Catalina had sat when Our Lady appeared to her, and looked at the little plaza dazzling in the light of the August sun. The unclouded sky was so blue, so bright after the incense-laden dimness of the church, that to look at it was blinding. The white houses, shuttered against the heat, seemed to sparkle with a gem-like brilliance of their own. The Bishop shuddered although the day had the heat of a furnace. He came to himself.

"Have the girl told that she shall hear from me."

He descended the steps and the friars followed him at a respectful distance. He walked through the plaza, his head bent, and they dared not speak to him. When they arrived at the Dominican convent he stopped and turned to them.

"Under pain of excommunication you will not utter a single word of what you have seen today."

"It was a miracle, Señor," said Father Antonio. "Is it fair that such a signal mark of divine favour should be kept secret from our brothers?"

"When you made your profession, my son, you took the vow of obedience."

Father Antonio had been the Bishop's pupil when he taught theology at Alcalá and it was through the Bishop's influence that he had entered the Dominican order. He was quick and intelligent, and when Friar Blasco was made Inquisitor at Valencia he took him with him as his secretary. He was grateful for the young friar's devotion, and though he often tried to reason him out of the inordinate admiration the youth had for him everything he said seemed only to increase it. Father Antonio, though as devout and careful to observe his religious duties as the Bishop could desire, blameless in his life and industrious in the service of the Church, suffered from a disease which Juvenal called *cacoëthes scribendi*: not content with acting as amanuensis for the Inquisitor's great correspondence and writing the multitudinous reports, documents, decisions and so forth that were necessary in the conduct of the affairs of the Holy Office, he spent all his spare moments scribbling; and the Inquisitor discovered, as he discovered everything that concerned him or his office, that Father Antonio was keeping a minute record of his actions, of every word he said and of the various events in his career. He was humbly conscious that the secretary held him in exaggerated esteem, and in his self-examination often asked himself whether he should not put a stop to this work, for he could not but know with what purpose the friar was writing. He had got it into his clever, foolish head that he, Friar Blasco de Valero, was the stuff of which saints were made, and that such a document as he was producing would be of value to the Curia when after his death proceedings for his beatification were instituted. Though so well aware of his unworthiness the Inquisitor was human enough to feel a little thrill of pious exultation when he thought there was a possibility, however remote, that one day he might be counted among the saints of the Church. He scourged himself till the blood flowed for his presumption, but could not bring himself to deprive the good and pious creature of an employment that was certainly harmless. And who could tell? It might be

that the writer's simple piety would enable him to produce a work which, of however little account was the subject, might prove edifying to the faithful.

And now, looking into the friar's heart, Bishop Blasco was positive that though no word of what had happened in the Carmelite church would cross his lips, a full account of it would be written in the book. The marvel, now known as levitation, of which he had been the instrument was familiar to him from his reading of the lives of various saints, and it was known throughout Spain that in recent years this sign of divine favour had been granted to Peter of Alcantara, Mother Teresa of Jesus and to more than one nun of the Discalced Carmelites. The Bishop could not expect Father Antonio to omit such a remarkable occurrence from his book, he did not even know if he had the right to do it, so without another word he entered the convent and went to his cell.

<h1 style="text-align:center">XIII</h1>

BUT it had not occurred to him to bind Catalina to secrecy, and no sooner had the three religious left the church than she hurried home as fast as her disabled state allowed. Domingo had gone on an errand to one of the outlying villages and so only her mother was there. Catalina in awestruck tones told her the wonder of which she had been a witness, and when she had finished told it all over again.

Maria Perez had something of the dramatic sense which was apparently denied to the playwright her brother, and so, restraining her impatience with an effort, she waited for the recreation hour at the convent when she knew that most of the nuns would be assembled talking with the lady boarders and visitors from the city and she thus could relate the amazing occurrence to the greatest possible effect. She had quite an audience when she told her story and the astonishment it caused highly gratified her. The sub-prioress was so much impressed with it that she felt not a moment should be lost in telling it to Doña Beatriz. In a little while Maria Perez was summoned to the presence. She repeated her narrative. The Prioress listened with a satisfaction she saw no reason to conceal.

"After this there can be no hesitation," she said. "It will be a great glory not only to this convent, but to the Order of Our Lady of Carmel."

She dismissed the two women and taking up her quill wrote a letter to the Bishop in which she told him that she had learnt of the grace that had been accorded him that morning. No further proof was needed that what the girl Catalina Perez had said was true, to be ascribed to no machination of the Evil One, but to the compassion of Our Blessed Lady. She conjured him to put aside his doubts and uncertainties, for nothing could be plainer than that it was his Christian duty to accept the charge laid upon him. It was a good letter, succinct but well argued, respectful but firm, and she requested, with great humility, that he would deign to perform the miracle in the church in which he had been granted this divine favour and for which it was evident the Blessed Virgin had conceived a particular affection. She sent the letter by messenger.

Two of the gentlemen who were in the parlour when Maria Perez told her story were so much struck with it that they went at once to the Dominican convent to inquire into its truth. The friars there of course knew nothing of it, but when it was repeated to them were far from surprised. They knew very well that the Bishop was a man of great sanctity, and nothing was more likely than that God should have accorded him the signal honour of levitation. Meanwhile one of the lady boarders went to see friends in the city and told them of the miraculous event. In a couple of hours the whole city knew of it. More gentlemen came to the Dominican convent in order to get information at first hand. The friars were in a tremor of religious enthusiasm. At last Father Antonio was obliged to go to the Bishop and tell him that though neither he nor his fellow friar had opened his mouth the occurrence was now common knowledge. The Prioress's letter was open on a table. The Bishop pointed to it.

"These wretched women, they cannot hold their tongues," he said. "It is a great humiliation to me that this thing should have become known."

"Our brothers of this convent hope that your lordship will now consent to cure the unhappy girl of her infirmity."

There was a knock at the door. Father Antonio opened it. A friar brought a message to ask if the Prior might see the Bishop.

"Let him come."

Father Antonio was present at the interview and he wrote an account of it at very tedious length. In the end the Bishop allowed himself to be convinced that it was the will of God that he should do what the Blessed Virgin required of him. He made conditions, however, which the Prior, much against his will, found himself obliged to accept. The Prior wanted a ceremony with all his friars assembled, in the presence of the notabilities of the city, both lay and clerical; but this the Bishop sternly refused to allow. He insisted on secrecy. He was prepared to go to the Carmelite church and say Mass there on the following morning. The doors must be closed so that no one should be admitted. He would himself be accompanied only by his secretaries. The Prior, not a little incensed at what he considered a slight on his dignity, left him. The Bishop then sent Father Antonio to inform Doña Beatriz of his decision. He gave her permission to bring her nuns, but forbade the lady boarders to come. He instructed her to make Catalina prepare herself to partake of Holy Communion after Mass and requested her and her nuns to pray for him that night.

Within an hour an excited nun came to Maria Perez and asked to see Catalina since she had something very private and important to tell her. When Catalina was called the nun put her finger to her lips to emphasize the silence that was required.

"It's a great secret," she said. "You mustn't tell anyone. His lordship is going to cure you and tomorrow you'll be running about on your two feet like any other Christian."

Catalina gasped and her heart began to beat like mad.

"Tomorrow?"

"You're to take Holy Communion, so you mustn't eat anything after midnight. You know that."

"Yes, I know that. But I never do eat anything after midnight."

"And you must put yourself in a state of grace. After you've received Communion he'll make you whole just as Our Blessed Lord did to the leper."

"Can Mamma and Uncle Domingo come?"

"Nothing was said about them. Surely they can come. It may well turn your poor uncle from his evil ways."

Domingo did not get back from the country till late that evening, but he was no sooner in the house than Catalina in a tremor of agitation told him her thrilling news. He stared at her with consternation.

"Aren't you glad, Uncle?" she cried.

72

He did not speak. He began pacing the room. Catalina could not understand his strange behaviour.

"What's the matter with you, Uncle? Aren't you pleased? I thought you'd be as happy as I am. Don't you want me to be cured?"

He shrugged his shoulders irritably and went on pacing the room. He had never been quite sure that the apparition was not a construction of his niece's distracted mind and he dreaded the consequences to her if the Bishop's intervention were vain. The Holy Office might well think then that the matter required investigation. That meant ruin. Suddenly he stopped and faced Catalina. He looked at her with a sternness she had never seen in him before.

"Tell me exactly what it was that the Blessed Virgin said to you."

She repeated the story.

"And then the lady said: The son of Don Juan de Valero who has best served God has it in his power to cure you."

Domingo interrupted her harshly.

"But that is not what you told your mother. You told her that Blasco de Valero had it in his power to cure you."

"It's the same thing. The Bishop is a saint; all the world knows that. Which of the sons of Don Juan has served God so well?"

"You fool!" he shouted. "You little fool!"

"It's you who are the fool," she answered hotly. "You never believed that the Blessed Virgin had appeared to me and spoken to me and then vanished from my sight. You thought it was a dream. Well, listen to this."

She told him then how she had seen the Bishop rise from the floor and stay suspended in the air and then sink down once more to the floor.

"That wasn't a dream. The two friars who were with him saw it with their own eyes."

73

"Stranger things have happened," he muttered.

"And yet you refuse to believe that Our Blessed Lady appeared to me."

He looked at her now with a twinkle in his eyes.

"I don't. I didn't believe it before, but I believe it now, not for what you saw this morning, but for the words the Blessed Virgin spoke to you. There is a meaning in them that convinces me."

Catalina was perplexed. She could not understand how the insignificant difference in the two versions could make any odds. He gently patted her cheek.

"I am a great sinner, my poor child, and what makes my situation desperate is that I have never yet succeeded in repenting of my sins. I have lived a hazardous and a worthless life, but I have read many books, ancient and modern, and I have learnt many things which perhaps it would be for my soul's good if I did not know. Be of good heart, my dear, perhaps all may yet be well."

He took up his hat.

"Where are you going, Uncle?"

"I have had a busy day and I am in want of relaxation. I am going to the tavern."

In this he departed from the truth, for instead of going to the tavern he went to the Dominican convent. Though it was still light, the hour was advanced and the porter would not admit him. Domingo insisted that he must see the Bishop on a matter of grave importance, but the porter, speaking through the judas, would not even open the door. Domingo told him that he was the uncle of Catalina Perez and begged him at least to fetch one of his lordship's secretaries. The porter was unwilling even to do this, but Domingo was so urgent that at last he consented. In a few minutes Father Antonio came to the door. Domingo besought him to let him see the Bishop, since he had a communication to impart to him that it was vital for him to hear. The friar had evidently been informed who he was and of what a bad reputation, for he answered coldly. He said it was impossible to disturb his lordship, for he was spending the night in prayer and had given orders that he was on no account to be disturbed.

"If you do not let me see him you will be responsible for a terrible mishap."

"Drunkard," said Father Antonio scornfully.

"A drunkard I am, but now I am not drunk. You will bitterly regret it if you will not let me in."

"What is this message that you wish me to deliver?"

Domingo hesitated. He was at his wits' end.

"Tell him that for the love he bears him Domingo Perez sends him this message: The stone which the builders rejected is become the head of the corner."

"*Hijo de puta*," cried Father Antonio, in a rage that this dissolute scamp should quote scripture.

He slammed-to the shutter of the judas. Domingo turned away. He was in a black mood. Habit bent his steps to the tavern and he went in. He was a sociable creature and had, if not many friends, at least a goodly number of drinking companions. He got drunk, and when he was drunk his tongue was loosened. He liked to hear himself talk and it was on this occasion as on many others no difficulty for him to find listeners.

XIV

NEXT morning, when, as Domingo would have put it in a poem, Aurora rubbed the sleep from her eyes with rosy fingers and Phoebus harnessed to his golden chariot the swift coursers of the sun, or in plain language

75

at break of day, three Dominican friars with their hoods drawn over their shaven heads, partly for concealment, partly to protect themselves from the noxious vapours of the lingering night, slipped out of the convent. But though it was so early the townspeople had gathered that there was something in the wind and there was already a group at the convent gate. In the tall cowled figure between the other two they at once recognized the saintly bishop. The three friars, followed at a respectful distance by the curious, walked swiftly to the Carmelite church. Here more persons were waiting. One of the friars knocked at the door. It was opened just enough to' let them pass through one after the other, and closed behind them. When the onlookers tried to enter they found it locked, and though they knocked, they knocked in vain.

Catalina was waiting in the Lady Chapel. Maria Perez and Domingo had accompanied her, but had been refused admittance. Doña Beatriz received the Bishop at the church door with her nuns, twenty in all, for that was the limit the Duke of Castel Rodriguez in his foundation had set to their number. The Bishop, with his two attendants, went into the sacristy and donned the sacred vestments. They walked slowly to the Lady Chapel. The nuns were on their knees. Catalina, supporting herself on her crutch, knelt at the foot of the altar steps. The Bishop said Mass. The nuns joined in the responses in awed undertones. He administered Holy Communion to Catalina. After the benediction and the reading of the last Gospel he knelt at the altar and prayed in silence. Then he rose to his feet and with his great tragic eyes upon Catalina walked down the steps. He placed his thin, brown hand on her head.

"I, the unworthy instrument of the Most High, in the name of the Father, the Son and the Holy Ghost bid you throw aside your crutch and walk."

He had begun tremulously, in so low a voice that the nuns could hardly hear, but he spoke the last words loud and clear in a tone of command. Catalina, her face pale with emotion, her eyes shining, raised herself to her feet, cast the crutch aside, took a step forward and with a cry of anguish crashed to the floor. The miracle had failed.

Immediately there arose a hubbub among the nuns. Some of them screamed, two of them fainted. The Prioress stepped forward. She gave Catalina a glance and then her eyes met the Bishop's. For a while they gazed intently at one another. Behind them the nuns were sobbing. Then the Bishop walked out of the chapel, the two friars at his heels, and returned to the sacristy. He did not utter a word. When they had discarded their vestments and wore once more their conventual habits they went back into the church. The portress was waiting to unlock the door. The Bishop, his cowl once more over his head, stepped out into the sunlight of the summer morning.

The news had spread that he was even then performing a miracle and the windows in the plaza were crowded with spectators. They were thick on the church steps and the square was filled with them. For a moment the Bishop was dismayed to see that great throng, but only for a moment; he pulled his habit close to him and drew himself up. He no sooner appeared than a shudder of consternation passed through the crowd, for in some strange way they knew at once, though they could not have said how, that the miracle had failed. Way was made and the Bishop, with the two friars following, walked down the steps. The people in the plaza pressed one another back, and as he passed along the path they thus made for him, his face hidden, his tall figure huddled in the black and white habit of his order, a dreadful silence fell upon them. You would have said that they were,

77

terrified as though some horrifying and unavoidable catastrophe impended.

XV

THE friars of the Dominican convent had been angered because the Bishop had refused to allow them to attend the ceremony, and when, with his two attendants, he returned to it they were loitering about to look at him. The news had already reached them. He passed as though he did not see them.

On hearing that they were to lodge such a distinguished guest they had furnished his cell with such luxury as they thought suitable to his grandeur. But he had immediately had everything removed that offended his austerity. He forced them to change the soft mattress on the bed for one of straw no thicker than a blanket, and he had the two arm-chairs they had put in the oratory replaced with three-legged stools. They had given him a handsome teak table to write at, but he asked that he should be given instead one of unpainted deal. He would have nothing that appealed to the senses and turned out the pictures they had hung on the walls. They were bare now but for a plain black Cross, without the figure of Our Lord either painted or carved, and this was so that he might more exactly picture himself nailed to it and so in his body feel the pain that the Redeemer for the sake of mankind had suffered.

When the Bishop entered his cell he sank on to the hard wooden stool and stared at the stone floor. Slow, painful tears trickled down his sunken cheeks. Father Antonio's heart was filled with compassion to see his master plunged in what looked very like despair. He whispered to his companion, who forthwith left the cell and in a few minutes returned with a bowl of soup. Father Antonio handed it to the Bishop.

"Señor, here is something for you to eat."

The Bishop turned his head away.

"I could eat nothing."

"Oh, my lord, no food has passed your lips since the morning of yesterday. I beseech you to take at least a few mouthfuls."

He knelt, filled a spoon with the steaming soup and held it to the Bishop's lips.

"You are very good to me, my son," he said. "I am not worthy of the care you take of me."

Not to appear ungracious he swallowed the contents of the spoon, and then the monk fed the broken man as though he were a sick child. The Bishop was well aware of his faithful attendant's deep attachment and had more than once warned him of its danger, for a religious should always be on his guard against conceiving affection for any one person, since it could not but hamper his whole-hearted devotion to God who was the only real object of love; and as for human beings, whether clerical or lay, he should regard them with good will, because they were God's creatures, but since they were perishable with an indifference that made it of no moment if they were present or absent. But the affections are difficult to control, and however hard he tried, Father Antonio could not destroy the love, the ecstatic devotion, with which his poor heart was filled.

When the Bishop had eaten, Father Antonio put aside the bowl and, still on his knees, ventured to take his hand.

"Do not take it so hard, Señor. The girl was deceived by demons."

"No, the fault was mine. I asked for a sign and the sign was given me. In my vainglory I thought myself not unfit to do what is vouchsafed to the saints whom God has chosen for His own. I am a sinner and I am justly punished for my presumption."

The Bishop was so broken that the friar dared to speak to him as otherwise he would never have done.

"We are all sinners, Señor, but I have been privileged to live close to you for many years and no one knows better than I your unfailing kindness to all men, your ceaseless charity and your loving kindness."

"It is your own goodness that speaks, my son. It is the affection you have for me which I have so often warned you against and which I so little deserve."

Father Antonio gazed with pity on the Bishop's agonized face. He still held his cold, emaciated hand.

"Would it not distract your mind if I read to you a little, my lord?" he said after a pause. "I have lately written something which I should value your opinion of."

The Bishop knew how bitterly grieved the poor friar was that the miracle, which he had anticipated with complete assurance, had not been performed, and he was touched when the dear, simple man mastered his own terrible disappointment to minister to him and to console him. He had never before consented to listen to a word of the book his secretary was so industriously writing, but now he had not the heart to refuse him a pleasure that he so ardently desired.

"Read, my son. I will listen gladly."

The Father, his cheeks flushed with delight, scrambled to his feet and took, from among the many papers his office required him to deal with, several sheets of manuscript. He sat down on a stool. The other friar, since there was no other place for him, sat on the floor. Father Antonio began to read.

He was an erudite and an elegant writer and none of

the artifices of rhetoric was unfamiliar to him. His style was rich in simile and metaphor, metonymy, synecdoche and catachresis. He never let a noun go by without an escort of two stalwart adjectives. Images sprang to his mind as profuse and fat as mushrooms after rain, and being well read in the Scriptures, the works of the Fathers and the Latin moralists, he was never at a loss for a recondite allusion. He was learned in sentence-structure, simple, complex, compound and compound-complex, and could not only compose a period, with clauses and sub-clauses, of the most choice elaboration, but bring it to a conclusion with a triumphant clang that had all the effect of a door slammed in your face. This manner of writing, to which an ingenious critic has given the name of Mandarin, is much admired by those who affect it, but it has the trifling disadvantage of taking a long time to say what can be said in brief; and in any case it would be discordant with the plain, blunt style in which this narrative is written; and so, instead of making a vain attempt to reproduce the good Father's grandiloquence, the author of these pages has thought it better to give the gist of the matter in his own simple way.

Father Antonio, not without tact, had chosen to read his account of the great *auto de fé*, which had been the crown of Friar Blasco's career in the Holy Office, and which, as before mentioned, had given so much pleasure to the Prince, now Philip III, and had in due course been at least the occasion for the saintly inquisitor's elevation to the important See of Segovia.

The impressive ceremony, devised to inspire awe for the authority of the Inquisition and edify the people, took place on a Sunday, so that none should have an excuse not to attend it, since to do so was a pious duty; and to secure as large an attendance as possible an indulgence of forty days

81

was granted to all who came. Three stagings had been erected in the great plaza of the city, one for the penitents with their spiritual attendants, one for the inquisitors, the officials of the Holy Office and the clergy, and a third for the civil authorities and the dignitaries of the city. The proceedings, however, began the night before with the procession of the Green Cross. First, with a standard of crimson damask embroidered with the royal arms, came a crowd of familiars and gentlemen; then the religious orders with the White Cross; the Cross of the parish church borne by the secular clergy; and finally the Green Cross carried by the Prior of the Dominicans, accompanied by his friars with torches. They sang the *Miserere* as they marched. The Green Cross was planted above the altar on the staging reserved for the inquisitors and it was guarded through the night by Dominicans. The White Cross was taken to the place of execution, where it was guarded by the soldiers of the Zarza, a body of men whose duty it was to keep watch over the *quemadero* or burning-place and provide wood for the bonfire.

One of the duties of the inquisitors was to visit during the night those condemned to death, inform them of their sentence, and assign two friars to each one to prepare him to meet his God. But on this occasion Father Baltasar, the junior inquisitor, was sick in bed of a colic, and so that he might be well enough to take part in the proceedings of the following day begged Friar Blasco to excuse him from accompanying him on this grim errand.

Dawn broke and Mass was celebrated in the audience chamber of the Holy Office and at the altar of the Green Cross. Breakfast was given to the prisoners and to the friars, doubtless glad of it by then, who had attended those about to die. They were then ranged in order according to the gravity of their offence against the Faith and dressed in *sambenitos*. The *sambenito* was a yellow tunic painted on one side with flames for those who were to be burnt, and on the other inscribed with their names, places of residence and crimes. Green crosses were given them to carry and yellow candles put in their hands.

Another procession was formed. The soldiers of the Zarza, who led it, were followed by a religious bearing a cross shrouded in black and an acolyte who from time to time tolled a bell. Then came the penitents one by one, with a familiar on either side; then the effigies and chests of bones of those whose flight or death had robbed the Holy Office of its rightful prey; then those who were to die, accompanied by the friars who had been with them throughout the night. Mounted officials followed, familiars in pairs, the magistrates of the city, and the ecclesiastical dignitaries, according to their official precedence. A noble of high rank bore a box of red velvet fringed with gold which contained the sentences of the condemned. Then came the standard of the Holy Office borne by the Prior of the Dominicans, followed by his friars and finally the inquisitors.

It was a fine, sunny day, the sort of day that elates the heart of young and old so that they feel it good to be alive.

The procession moved slowly through the tortuous streets till it reached the plaza. There was a vast concourse. People had streamed into the city from the fertile haciendas that surround it, from rice fields and olive groves; others had come from as far as Alicante with its vineyards and from Elche with its date trees. The windows of the surrounding houses were filled with nobility and gentry, and the Prince with his suite watched from a balcony in the town hall.

The culprits were seated on the staging created for them in the order in which they had marched, the least guilty on the lower benches and the most guilty on the highest. There were two pulpits on the staging that accommodated the tribunal, and from one of these a sermon was preached. Then a secretary in a voice so loud that he could be heard by all read the oath by which the officials and all present swore obedience to the Holy Office and pledged themselves to persecute heretics and heresy. Everyone said Amen. After this the two inquisitors went to the balcony in which sat the Prince, and on the Cross and Gospels administered to him an oath constraining him to obey the Catholic Faith and the Holy Office, to persecute heretics and apostates and help and assist the Inquisition to seize and punish, whatever their rank and station, the miscreants who rejected true religion.

"This I swear and promise on my faith and royal word," solemnly replied the Prince.

There was a bench between the two pulpits to which the penitents were brought one by one; their sentences were read to them from alternate pulpits. With the exception of those condemned to the flames this was the first announcement of their fate, and since some fainted when they heard it the Holy Office in its mercy provided a rail to the bench in case they fell and hurt themselves. On this occasion one man, broken by torture, died there and then of the shock. The last sentence was read and the culprits were delivered to the secular arm. The Holy Office rendered no judgment that involved the shedding of blood and indeed went so far as to urge the civil authorities to spare the life of the criminal. They were, however, required by the canon law promptly to punish the heretics consigned to them by the Inquisition, and an indulgence was accorded to the pious who contributed wood to the bonfire that was to burn them.

This ended the work of the inquisitors and they retired.

The soldiers of the Zarza marched into the plaza and discharged their muskets. They then surrounded the prisoners and marched with them to the place of execution to protect them from the fury of the populace who in their hatred of heresy would otherwise ill-treat and sometimes even kill them. The friars attended them and strove to the end to bring about their repentance and conversion. Among them were four Morisco women whose beauty excited the admiration of all, an impenitent Dutch merchant who had been caught smuggling into the country a Spanish translation of the New Testament, a Moor convicted of killing a chicken by cutting off its head, a bigamist, a merchant who had harboured a fugitive from the Holy Office, and a Greek found guilty of holding opinions condemned by the Church. An alguazil and a secretary went with the civil authorities to see that the sentences were duly executed. The secretary on this occasion was Father Antonio, so that he had an opportunity to make his account of the day's proceedings complete.

The *quemadero* was outside the city. Garrottes were attached to the stakes so that those who had professed a desire to die in the Christian faith, even those who did so at the last moment, might be spared death by fire and killed by the more merciful method of strangulation. The crowd had surged after the soldiers and the prisoners, and a great many, in order to get a better view of the proceedings, had hurried beforehand to the open space where the final scene was to take place. There was a vast multitude. This was natural, for it was a sight well worth seeing, a very proper entertainment for a royal guest; and the spectator had besides the satisfaction of knowing that he was performing an act of piety and a service to God. Those who were to be garrotted were garrotted and then the flames were kindled and the quick and the dead were burnt to ashes so that their memory might perish for ever. The people shouted

85

and clapped their hands as the flames soared, so that the shrieks of the victims were almost drowned, and here and there a woman broke into a shrill chant to the Blessed Virgin or to the crucified Christ. Night fell and the crowd streamed back into the city, tired with long standing and the excitement, but feeling that they had had a happy day. They flocked to the taverns. The brothels did a roaring trade and many a man that night put to the proof the efficacy of the fragment of Friar Blasco's habit that he wore round his neck.

Father Antonio was tired too, but it was his first duty to report the proceedings to the two inquisitors, and then, notwithstanding his fatigue which tempted him to go to bed, since he was a conscientious man he sat down and wrote a circumstantial account of all that had happened that day while every detail was fresh in his mind. He wrote rapidly, with an eloquence that seemed inspired by heaven, and when he read over what he had written he found that there was not a word that needed to be altered. Then at last, happy in the consciousness of having done his duty and besides contributed his small share to a pious work, he went to bed and slept the innocent sleep of a child.

All this then, giving dramatic emphasis to the most significant episodes, he read to the despondent Bishop in a loud, sonorous voice. He read with his eyes glued to the script. He felt strangely exalted. Thus was God served and thus was the purity of the Catholic faith maintained. He finished. He could not but feel that he had done the great ceremony justice. He had himself been struck by the vividness of his description and the artful way in which he had built up the narrative, he himself did not know how, to an impressive climax. He looked up. Like many another author who submits his work to a listener he would have been pleased to be rewarded with a word of praise. But this was merely a passing wish; his main object was to dispel the sombre fancies of his revered and beloved superior by reminding him of the most glorious incident of his career. Saint though he was, he could not but feel a thrill of pride when there appeared before his mind's eye that wonderful day when he had been the means of consigning to eternal torment so great a number of cursed heretics, thereby serving God, discharging his conscience and edifying the people. Father Antonio was surprised, more than surprised, aghast, to see that tears were coursing down the Bishop's withered cheeks and that his hands were clenched to control the sobbing that tore his breast.

He threw aside his manuscript, and jumping up from the stool on which he had been sitting flung himself at his master's feet.

"My lord, what is it?" he cried. "What have I done? I read only to distract your thoughts."

The Bishop thrust him aside and rising to his feet stretched out his arms in supplication to the black Cross on the wall.

"The Greek," he moaned. "The Greek."

And then able to contain himself no longer he broke into passionate weeping. The two friars gazed at him in consternation. They had never before seen that austere man exhibit emotion. The Bishop with the palm of his hand impatiently brushed the tears from his eyes.

"I am to blame," he moaned, "terribly to blame. I have committed a fearful sin and my only hope of forgiveness is in the infinite mercy of God."

"My lord, for God's sake explain. I am all confused. I am like a mariner in a storm when his bark is dismasted and he has lost his rudder." With his reading still ringing in his ears Father Antonio found it impossible not to speak like a book. "The Greek? Why does your lordship speak

87

of the Greek? He was a heretic and suffered the just punishment of his crime."

"You do not know of what you speak. You do not know that my crime is greater than his. I asked for a sign and the sign was given me. I thought it was a mark of God's grace; now I know it was a mark of His wrath. It is right that I should be humbled in the eyes of men, for I am a miserable sinner."

He did not turn to his companions. He did not speak to them, but to the Cross on which he had so often pictured himself with nails in his hands and nails through his feet.

"He was a good old man, in his poverty charitable to the poor, and in the many years I knew him I never heard him say an evil word. He looked upon all men with loving kindness. He had true nobility of soul."

"Many men, virtuous in their public and their private lives, have been justly condemned by the Holy Office, since moral rectitude weighs nothing in the balance against the mortal sin of heresy."

The Bishop turned and looked at Father Antonio. His eyes were tragic.

"And the wages of sin is death," he whispered.

The Greek of whom they spoke, Demetrios Christopoulos, was a native of Cyprus, a man of some property, which had enabled him to devote himself to learning. When the Turks, under Selim II, invaded the island, they took Nicosia, the capital, and put twenty thousand of its inhabitants to the sword. Famagusta, where Demetrios Christopoulos lived, was besieged and surrendered after a year of bitter resistance. This was in 1571. He fled from the doomed city and hid in the hills till he managed to escape in a fishing-boat and after many an adventure landed in Italy. He was penniless, but in due course found enough work as a teacher of Greek and an expounder of the ancient

88

philosophy to keep body and soul together. Then in an evil hour he attracted the attention of a Spanish nobleman attached to the embassy in Rome who during his sojourn in Italy had succumbed to the fashionable cult of Plato. The nobleman took him into his palace and they read together the immortal dialogues of the philosopher. After some years, however, he was recalled to Spain and he persuaded the Greek to go with him. He was appointed Viceroy for the Kingdom of Valencia and in the city of that name eventually died. The Greek, almost an old man by then, stranded, left the viceregal palace and found a modest dwelling in the house of a widow woman. He had acquired some reputation for his learning and eked out a meagre living by giving lessons in Greek to those who desired to acquire some knowledge of that noble tongue.

Friar Blasco de Valero had heard of him while he was still giving lectures in theology at Alcalá de Henares and soon after he took up his post as inquisitor at Valencia he made inquiries about the Greek, and hearing that he was a man of good repute and virtuous life sent for him. He was pleased with the old man's gentle approach and modest bearing and asked him if he would teach him the language in which the New Testament was written so that he might read the words with greater devotion. For nine years, whenever his manifold duties allowed him leisure, the Inquisitor and the Greek worked together. Friar Blasco was an industrious and an apt pupil, and after some months the Greek, who had a passion for the great and ancient literature of his country, persuaded him to embark on the works of the classical writers. He was himself a fervent platonist and it was not long before they were reading the dialogues. From them they went on to Aristotle. The friar refused to read the Iliad which he thought brutal or the Odyssey which he thought frivolous, but in the dramatists found much to admire. In the end, however, they always returned to the dialogues.

The Inquisitor was a man of sensibility and he was charmed by the grace, piety and profundity of Plato. There was much in his writings that a Christian could approve. They were the occasion for the pair of them to discuss many serious subjects. It was a new world Friar Blasco thus entered, and he felt a singular exultation in his perusal of these great works and a blissful repose after the labours of the day. In their long and fruitful intercourse he had conceived something very like affection for the unworldly Greek, and all he heard of him, of his simple decent life, his kindliness and charity, increased his admiration for his character.

It was a terrible shock to him when a Dutchman, a Lutheran, arrested by the familiars of the Inquisition for bringing into Spain translations of the New Testament, admitted under torture that he had given a copy to the Greek. Under questioning, emphasized by another turn of the rack, he stated that they had often conversed on religion and on many points were in full agreement. This was enough to oblige the Holy Office to make an investigation. This as always was thorough and secret. The Greek was not allowed to know that he was suspect. When Friar Blasco read the final reports he was horrified. It had never occurred to him that the Greek, so good, so humble, had not during his long years in Italy, his long years in Spain, abjured his schismatic opinions and embraced the Catholic faith of Rome. Witnesses were brought forward who swore that they had heard him utter damnable heresies. He denied the procession of the Holy Ghost from the Son, he rejected the supremacy of the Pope, and though he venerated the Virgin he refused to admit her immaculate conception. The woman of the house in which he lived had heard him say that indulgences were worthless and someone else testified that he did not accept the Roman doctrine of purgatory.

Friar Blasco's fellow inquisitor, Don Baltasar Carmona, was a doctor of laws and a rigid moralist. He was a dried-up little man, with a long sharp nose, tight lips and small restless eyes. He suffered from some malady of the intestines which soured his temper. His situation gave him immense power and he took a savage pleasure in exercising it. When these damning facts were laid before him he insisted on the arrest of the Greek. Friar Blasco did what he could to save him. He claimed that as a schismatic he was nò heretic, and therefore did not come under the jurisdiction of the Holy Office. but there was not only the evidence of the tortured Lutheran; a French Calvinist whom he had also incriminated stated that he had heard the Greek utter opinions that savoured of protestantism, and upon this Friar Blasco felt obliged to do his bounden duty at whatever cost to his feelings. Familiars went to the old man's lodging and took him to the prison of the Inquisition. He was examined and freely admitted the charges. He was given the opportunity to abjure his false beliefs and be converted to Catholicism, but to Friar Blasco's dismay he refused to do this. The offence was grave, but the evidence of protestantism was not decisive, and in order to give the Greek a chance of purging his offence Friar Blasco urged upon his fellow inquisitor who was all for condemning him out of hand that to induce his conversion and so save his soul he should be put to the torture.

When torture was applied both inquisitors were required by law to be present, with the episcopal representative and a notary to record the proceedings. It was an exhibition that always filled Friar Blasco with such horror that for nights afterwards he was harassed by fearful dreams.

91

The Greek was brought in, stripped and tied to the trestle. His feeble old body was emaciated. He was solemnly besought to tell the truth for the love of God, since the inquisitors did not wish to see him suffer. He remained silent. His ankles were tied to the sides of the rack, cords were passed round his arms, his thighs and his calves, and their ends were attached to a garrotte, a stick by which they could be twisted tight. The executioner gave a sharp turn of the garrotte and the Greek shrieked; another, and skin and muscle were cut through to the bone. On account of his great age Friar Blasco had insisted that not more than four turns should be given, since, though six or seven were the maximum, it was unusual even with strong men to exceed five. The Greek begged them to kill him at once and put him out of his agony. Though Friar Blasco was forced to be there, he was not forced to look, and he stared at the stone floor; but the shrieks of pain rang in his ears and tore his nerves to pieces. That was the voice with which his friend had recited those grave and noble passages of Sophocles; that was the voice in which with an emotion he could hardly control he had read the dying speech of Socrates. Before each turn of the garrotte, the Greek was ordered to tell the truth, but he clenched his teeth and would not speak. When he was released from the rack he could not stand and had to be carried back to the dungeon of the Holy Office.

Though he had admitted nothing he was condemned on the strength of what he had previously confessed. Friar Blasco sought to save his life, but Don Baltasar, the doctor of laws, contended that he was as guilty as the other Lutherans who had been sentenced to the stake. The episcopal representative and the other officials who were consulted agreed with him. Since the *auto de fé* was not to take place for several weeks Friar Blasco had time to write to the Inquisitor General and put the case before him. The Inquisitor General replied that he saw no reason to interfere with the decision of the tribunal. Friar Blasco could do nothing more, but still the shrieks of the old man rang in his ears and he suffered without respite. He sent spiritual advisers to see him and attempt his conversion, for though nothing now could save his life, repentance, allowing him to be garrotted, might still spare him the agony of death by burning. But the Greek was contumacious. Notwithstanding the torture and his long confinement in prison his mind remained clear and active. To the friars' arguments he answered with arguments so subtle that they were incensed.

At last came the eve of the *auto de fé*. Previous celebrations of the same kind had not affected Friar Blasco, for the relapsed Judaizers, the Moriscos who continued their devilish practices, the Protestants, were criminals before God and man, and for the safety of Church and State there was every reason that they should suffer. But no one knew better than he how good, how kind, how helpful to the needy was the Greek. Notwithstanding the authority of his fellow inquisitor, a cruel man with a dry, cold mind, he doubted the legality of the frightful punishment. Acrimonious words had passed and Don Baltasar had accused him of favouring the criminal because he was on friendly terms with him. In his heart Friar Blasco knew that there was at least a particle of truth in this; had he never known the Greek he would have accepted the verdict without protest. He could no longer save his life but he could still save his soul. Those friars he had sent to convince him of his error were not clever enough to deal with that man of learning. He decided to do an unprecedented thing. An hour before dawn he went to the prison of the Inquisition and had himself conducted to the Greek's cell.

93

Two friars were passing his last night on earth with him. Friar Blasco dismissed them.

"He has refused to listen to our exhortations," said one of them.

A smile hovered over the Greek's lips as they left the cell.

"Your friars are doubtless worthy men, Señor," he said. "But their intelligence is not remarkable."

He was calm and though so frail and old maintained an appearance of dignity.

"Your Reverence will forgive me if I remain on my bed. The torture left me very weak and I wish to preserve my strength for this day's ceremonies."

"Let us not waste time in idle speeches. In a few hours you must face a dreadful fate. God knows I would gladly give ten years of my life to save you from it. The evidence was damning and I should have been false to my oath if I had failed in my duty."

"I am the last man who would wish you to do that."

"Your life is forfeit and that I cannot save. But if you will recant and accept conversion I can at least spare you the agony of the flames. I have loved you, Demetrios, I can never repay the debt I owe you except by saving your immortal soul. Those friars are ignorant and narrow men. I have come here to make a last desperate attempt to persuade you of your error."

"You will only be wasting your time, Señor. We should employ it to better advantage if we talked as we have so often done before of the death of Socrates. They would not allow me to have books in this dungeon, but my memory is good and I have found solace in repeating to myself that speech in which he spoke so nobly of the soul."

"I do not command you now, Demetrios, I beseech you to listen to me."

"That last courtesy I am bound to grant you."

The Inquisitor in earnest tones, with learning and discretion, point by point, expounded the arguments which the Church had devised to substantiate her own claims and to refute the opinions of heretics and schismatics. He was well accustomed to discourse of this nature and he expressed himself ably and with impressive conviction.

"I should deserve little respect if for fear of a painful death I pretended to accept beliefs which I think erroneous," said the Greek when he had finished.

"I do not ask you to do that. I ask you to believe the truth with all your heart."

" 'What is truth?' asked Pontius Pilate. A man can as little constrain his belief as he can constrain the sea to calm when stormy winds assail it. I thank Your Reverence for your kindness and believe me I bear you no ill will for the misfortune that has befallen me. You have acted according to your conscience, and no man can do more. I am an old man and whether I die today or in a year or two is no great matter. I have only one request to make of you. Do not because I am gone relinquish your studies of the sublime literature of ancient Greece. It cannot fail to enlarge your spirit and ennoble your mind."

"Do you not fear the just vengeance of God for your contumacious obstinacy?"

"God has many names and infinite attributes. Men have called Him Jehovah, Zeus and Brahman. What does it signify what name you give Him? But among His infinite attributes the chief, as Socrates, pagan though he was, well saw, is justice. He must know that man does not believe what he would but what he can, and I cannot do Him so great a wrong as to suppose He will condemn His creatures for what is no fault of theirs. Your Reverence must not think I am wanting in respect if I beg you now to leave me to my own reflections."

"I cannot leave you thus. I must try to the end to save your immortal soul from the raging fires of hell. Say one word to give me hope that you may be saved. One word to show that you are not unrepentant so that I may at least mitigate your earthly punishment."

The Greek smiled and it may be that there was in his smile a touch of irony.

"You will do your part and I mine," he said. "It is yours to kill, mine to die without quailing."

The Inquisitor was blinded by his tears so that he could scarcely find his way out.

Much of this, in halting tones, the Bishop told the two friars and at this point he covered his face as though to continue were a shame greater than he could bear. They had listened to him with pain, but with rapt attention, and Father Antonio in his mind carefully noted every speech and every reply so that he could write it in his book.

"Then I did a dreadful thing. Don Baltasar was sick in bed and I knew he would stay there till the last moment, for he was mortally afraid of being too ill to attend the *auto de fé*. He is an ambitious man and wished to bring himself to the notice of the Prince. I was free to act on my own initiative. I could not bear the thought of that poor old man being burnt by those cruel flames. His screams when they tortured him still rang in my ears and I thought I should continue to hear them all my life. I told those it concerned that I had myself spoken with him and he had so far recanted as to accept the procession of the Holy Ghost from the Son. I gave orders that he should be garrotted before he was burnt and I sent money by a servant to the executioner to induce him to do his work with dispatch."

It should be explained that the executioner by tightening

96

and loosening the iron collar round the victim's neck could prolong the death-agony for hours and so had to be bribed to give the sufferer the quick release of death.

"I knew it was a sin. I was distraught with grief. I hardly knew what I was doing. It was a sin for which I can never cease to reproach myself. I told it to my confessor and performed the penance he imposed upon me. I received absolution, but I cannot absolve myself, and the events of this day are my punishment."

"But, my lord, it was an act of mercy," said Father Antonio. "Who that has worked with you as long as I have does not know the tenderness of your heart and who can blame you because for once you allowed it to override your sense of justice?"

"It was no act of mercy. Who knows but that the Greek was shaken by my reasoning and who knows but that when the fire licked his naked flesh the grace of God might have been vouchsafed to him and so moved his stubborn spirit to recant his errors? Many at that last dreadful moment when they are about to meet their Maker have thus saved their souls. I robbed him of the chance and so condemned him to eternal torment."

A hoarse sob broke from his throat, a sound like the strangled, mysterious cry of a bird of the night in the dark silence of the forest.

"Eternal torment! Who can picture to himself its pain? The damned writhe in a lake of fire from which rise noxious vapours which they breathe in agony. Their bodies are alive with worms. Raging thirst and ravenous hunger torment them. Their shrieks, wrung from them by the scorching flames, are a tumult and a confusion compared with which the crash of thunder, the howling of the storm-swept sea, are a deathly silence. Devils, frightful to look upon, mock and deride them, beat them with insatiable rage, but remorse tears them with a pain more cruel than the tortures of those hideous fiends. The worm of conscience gnaws their vitals. Fire crucifies their souls, and it is a fire compared with which the fire of this world is like the fire of a picture, for it is the wrath of God that lights it and maintains it as the terrible instrument of His just vengeance to all eternity.

"And eternity, how terrible is eternity! As many millions of years pass over the damned as drops of water have fallen upon the earth since the beginning of time; as many millions of years as there are drops of water in all the seas and all the rivers in the world; as many millions of years as there are leaves on all the trees that grow and as many millions of years as there are grains of sand on the shores of all the oceans; as many millions of years as all the tears that men have wept since God created our first parents. And after this incalculable number of years has passed, the anguish of those unhappy creatures shall continue as though it were but a beginning, as though it were the first day; and eternity will remain whole as though not one second had passed. And it is to that eternity of suffering that I have condemned that unhappy man. What punishment can make amends for such a frightful misdeed? Oh, I am afraid, afraid."

He was a man distraught. Great sobs rent his breast. He stared at the two friars with eyes dark with horror and when they looked into them there was a redness in their depths as though they saw in them, as if from a vast distance, the red flames of hell.

"Call the friars together and I will tell them I have sinned and for my soul's sake command them to inflict upon me the circular discipline."

This was the degrading punishment of scourging in which all present used the lash on the offender. Father Antonio, appalled, flung himself down on his knees and with his hands together as if in prayer implored his master not to insist on such a fearful ordeal.

"The brethren have no love for you, my lord, they are angry because you would not allow them to come to the church this morning. They will not spare you. They will use the lash with all their might. Friars have often died under their strokes."

"I do not wish them to spare me. If I die justice will have been administered. I command you under your vow of obedience to do as I tell you."

The friar raised himself to his feet.

"My lord, you have no right to expose yourself to such a mortal affront. You are the Bishop of Segovia. You will cast a slur on the whole episcopate of Spain. You will lessen the authority of all who have been appointed by God to your high station. Are you sure that there is not ostentation in the shame to which you would expose yourself?"

He had never dared to speak to his Father in God in such peremptory tones. The Bishop was taken aback. Was there some shadow of vainglory in his desire thus publicly to abase himself? He looked long at the friar.

"I do not know," he said at last miserably. "I am like a man stumbling across an unknown country in the darkness of the night. Perhaps you are right. I was thinking only of myself, I did not think how it would affect others."

Father Antonio gave a sigh of relief.

"You two shall give me the discipline here and in private."

"No, no, no, I will not. I could not bear to do violence to your sacred body."

"Must I remind you of your vows then?" asked the Bishop with all his old sternness. "Have you so little love for me that you can hesitate to inflict a trifling penance on me for my soul's good? There are scourges under the bed."

99

Silently, unhappily, the friar got them out. They were stained with blood. The Bishop slipped out of the upper part of his habit so that it fell to his waist. Then he removed his shirt; it was made of tin and pierced like a grater so that it should lacerate the flesh. Father Antonio knew that the Bishop was in the habit of wearing a hair shirt, not always, for then he would have grown used to it, but only so often as to make the torment of it ever fresh; he gasped when he saw that horrible shirt of tin, but at the same time was edified. This was indeed a saint. He would not fail to take notice of it in his book. The Bishop's back was scarred with the scourging he had at least once a week inflicted on himself and there were open and suppurating sores.

He threw his arms round the thin column that upheld the two arches by which his apartment was divided and exposed his back to the two friars. Each of them in silence took a scourge and one after the other brought it down on the bleeding flesh. At each blow the Bishop shuddered, but not even a groan escaped his lips. They had not given him more than a dozen strokes when he fell to the floor in a swoon. They picked him up and carried him on to the hard bed. They threw water over him, but he did not regain consciousness and they were frightened. Father Antonio sent his fellow to tell a lay brother to hurry for a doctor, since the Bishop was ill, and at the same time he bade him let the brethren know that on no consideration was he to be disturbed. He bathed the lacerated back; he anxiously felt the wavering pulse. For a while he thought the Bishop was dying. But at length he opened his eyes. It took him a moment to gather his senses together. Then he forced a smile to his lips.

"Poor creature that I am," he said. "I fainted."

"Do not speak, my lord. Lie still."

But the Bishop raised himself on an elbow.

100

"Give me my shirt."

Father Antonio looked with a shudder at that instrument of torture.

"Oh, my lord, you couldn't bear it now."

"Give it me."

"The doctor is coming. You would not want him to see you wear a garment of mortification."

The Bishop sank back on the hard pallet.

"Give me my Cross," he said.

At last the doctor came, ordered the patient to stay in bed and said he would send medicine. It was a soothing potion and after a while the Bishop fell asleep.

XVI

NEXT day he insisted on getting up. He said his Mass. Though weak and shaken, he was calm and went about his affairs as though nothing had happened.

Towards evening a lay brother came to tell him that his brother Don Manuel was in the parlour and desired to see him. Supposing that he had heard of his sickness he sent back word that he thanked him for coming, but pressing business prevented him from receiving him. The lay brother returned to say that Don Manuel refused to go till the Bishop saw him, since he had a communication to make to him that was of moment. With a sigh the Bishop told the lay brother to show him in. Since their arrival at Castel Rodriguez he had seen no more of him than courtesy required. Though he chid himself for his lack of charity he could not overcome the dislike he felt for that vain, brutal and callous man.

He came in, very grandly dressed, plethoric, rudely

healthy and full of an aggressive vitality. He carried himself with a swagger. His face bore a look of self-satisfaction, and if the Bishop did not deceive himself there was malice and cunning in his bold bright eyes. He smiled grimly when he looked round the bare and cheerless cell. The Bishop motioned him to a stool.

"Have you nothing more comfortable for me to sit on than this, brother?" he said.

"Nothing."

"I hear you were taken ill."

"It was a passing indisposition of no consequence. I am restored to my usual health."

"That is good."

There was silence between them. Don Manuel continued to look at him with a smile that was tinged with raillery.

"You said that you had a communication to make to me," said the Bishop at last.

"I have, brother. It appears that the ceremony of yesterday morning failed to realize your hopes."

"Be so good as to state your business, Manuel."

"What made you think that you were the chosen instrument to cure that girl of her disability?"

The Bishop hesitated. It was his inclination to refuse an answer, but, mortifying himself before the gross coarse man, he gave it.

"I received an assurance that what the girl said was true, and though I knew myself unworthy I felt bound to act upon it."

"You made a mistake, brother. You should have examined her more carefully. The Blessed Virgin told her that the son of Don Juan de Valero who had best served God had the power to cure her. Why did you jump to the conclusion that you were meant? Were you not a trifle wanting in Christian humility?"

The Bishop paled.

"What do you mean?" he cried. "She said to me that Our Lady had told her that it was I."

"She is an ignorant and foolish girl. She supposed that you must be designated because you are a bishop and, how I know not, the people of this city have heard much of your sanctity and mortifications."

The Bishop prayed a short mental prayer so that he could master the anger and shame with which his brother's words filled him.

"How do you know this? Who told you that those were the words of the Blessed Virgin?"

Don Manuel chortled at what seemed to him an excellent joke.

"It appears that the girl has an uncle called Domingo Perez. We used to know him when we were little. If I remember right you were at the seminary with him."

The Bishop inclined his head in token of assent.

"Domingo Perez is a toper. He goes to a tavern frequented by my servants, and he scraped acquaintance with them, doubtless in the hope of drinking wine at their expense. Last night he was in his cups. As was natural they were all talking of the events of the morning, for your fiasco, brother, is become the common talk of the city. Domingo told them he had expected nothing else and had sought to warn you, but was refused admission to the convent. He repeated then the exact words which Our Blessed Lady had spoken as his niece had reported them to him."

The Bishop was confounded. He did not know what to say. Don Manuel continued and now there was in his eyes a look of frank mockery. The Bishop asked himself miserably what sort of a man this was who could find so cruel a pleasure in thus humiliating his brother.

103

"Did it not occur to you, brother, that it was I that was meant?"

"You?" The Bishop could hardly believe his ears. If he had been capable of laughing, he would have laughed then.

"Does it surprise you, brother? For four and twenty years I have served my King. I have risked my life a hundred times, I have fought in glorious battles and my body bears the scars of my honourable wounds. I have suffered from hunger and thirst, from the bitter cold of those accursed Low Countries and from the torrid heat of summer. You have burnt a few dozen heretics at the stake, and I, to the glory of God, have killed the damned heretics by the thousand. To the glory of God I have laid waste their fields and burnt their crops. I have besieged thriving towns and when they surrendered put all their inhabitants, men, women and children, to the sword."

The Bishop shuddered.

"The Holy Office condemns the accused only by process of law. It gives them the opportunity to repent and purge their sin. It is careful to do justice, and if it punishes the guilty it absolves the innocent."

"I know those Dutchmen too well to think they are capable of repentance. Heresy is in their blood. They are traitors to their faith and their King and they deserve death. No one that knows me can deny that I have served God well."

The Bishop pondered. The brutality and boastfulness of his brother filled him with disgust. It seemed incredible that God could have chosen such an instrument for His work, yet it might be that He had done so just because he was the man he was, in order to put him, Blasco de Valero, to shame for his unforgiven sin. If so, it was his to kiss the rod.

"Heaven knows, I am conscious of my unworthiness,"

he said at last. "Should you attempt this thing and fail it will cause a scandal in the city and give a cruel opportunity to the wicked to mock. I beseech you to do nothing rashly; it is a matter that demands anxious consideration."

"That it has already received, brother," said Don Manuel coolly. "I have consulted my friends and they are the most important men in the city. I have asked the opinion of the archpriest and the prior of this convent. One and all, they consent."

Again the Bishop paused. He knew that there were many in the city who were envious of the positions he and his brother had achieved because, though gentlemen by birth, they were of small account. It might well be that they had agreed to his brother's preposterous demand only to throw discredit on them both.

"You must not forget that there is still the possibility that the girl Catalina Perez was deceived."

"The proof of the pudding is in the eating. If I fail it will be clear that the girl is a witch and should be handed over to the Inquisition for trial and punishment."

"If you have the consent of the authorities of the city and are determined to make the attempt I can do nothing to prevent you. But I beg you to do everything as secretly as may be so that greater scandal than has been caused already may be avoided."

"I am obliged to you for your advice, brother. I will give it the consideration it deserves."

Upon this Don Manuel withdrew. The Bishop sighed deeply. It seemed to him that his cup of bitterness was filled to the brim. He knelt down before the black Cross on the wall and silently prayed. Then he called a lay brother and bade him fetch the man Domingo Perez.

"If you cannot find him in his house, you will find him in the tavern near the palace in which my brother Don

Manuel is staying. You will ask him to do me the favour of coming to see me without delay."

XVII

AFTER a little the lay brother ushered Domingo into the Bishop's oratory. For a while the two men stared silently at one another. They had not met since they were young men, hardly more than boys, at the seminary of Alcalá de Henares. Both were now middle-aged, almost elderly, and both were emaciated and ravaged. But one was ravaged by austerity, long vigils, fasting and continuous labour; while the other was ravaged by drink and dissipation. Yet if there was a certain similarity in their appearance there was none in their expression: the Bishop's was harassed and anxious while the scrivener's was careless and good-humoured. As a clerk in minor orders he wore a cassock, and it was shabby, green with age and stained down the front with wine and food. But both wore an air of asceticism and of intellectual distinction.

"Your lordship desired to see me," said Domingo.

A slight, yet gentle smile was outlined on the Bishop's pale lips.

"It is a long time since we last met, Domingo."

"Our paths have gone very different ways. I should have thought your lordship had long forgotten the existence of so poor and worthless a creature as Domingo Perez."

"We have known one another all our lives. I am ashamed that you should address me with such ceremony. It is many years since I have heard a friend call me Blasco."

Domingo gave him his charming, disarming smile.

"The great have no friends, dear Blasco. It is the price they must pay for their greatness."

106

"Let us for an hour forget this poor greatness of mine and talk with one another like the old and intimate comrades we once were. You were wrong in thinking I had ever forgotten you; we were too close to one another for that. I have kept myself informed of your life."

"It has not been an edifying one."

The Bishop sat down on a stool and motioned to Domingo to take the other.

"But more than that I have kept in touch with you through your letters."

"How can you have done that? I have never written to you."

"Not as from yourself, but I read too many of the poems you wrote when we were boys together not to know your handwriting. Do you think I did not recognize it in the letters my father and my brother Martin sent me? I knew very well that they could never have expressed themselves with such elegance and propriety. And there were expressions, turns of phrase, reflections, in which I recognized your wayward spirit."

Domingo laughed lightly.

"The literary gifts of Don Juan and your brother Martin are not remarkable. When they had said they were in good health and hoped you were also, and that the harvest was poor, they had said all they had to say. For my own credit and theirs I felt bound to enliven their bald statements with the gossip of the town and such conceits and flippant jests as occurred to me."

"How sad it is that you should have let your great gifts run to waste, Domingo. What I had to learn by application and industry you acquired as it were by intuition. Often you used to terrify me by the audacity of your thought, by that flow of unexpected ideas that seemed to flow from your brain with as little effort as water gushes from a

107

spring, but I never doubted your brilliance. You were born to excel, and but for your restless temper you might by now be a shining ornament of our Holy Church."

"Instead of which," returned Domingo, "I am nothing but a poor scholar, a playwright who can find no actors to act his plays, a hack who writes sermons for priests too stupid to write their own, something of a drunkard and a ne'er-do-well. I lacked the vocation, my good Blasco. Life allured me. My place was neither the cloister nor the hearth, but the broad highway with its adventures and perils, its chance encounters and manifold variety. I have lived. I have suffered from hunger and thirst, I have been footsore, I have been beaten, I have suffered every mischance that can beset a man: I have lived. And even now when age is creeping upon me I have no regrets for the years I have wasted, for I too have slept on Parnassus; and when I walk to some distant village to write a paper for an illiterate clown, or when I sit in my little room surrounded by my books and rhyme the speeches in plays that will never be played, I am filled with such exultation that I would not change places with cardinal or pope."

"Do you not fear the wrath to come? The wages of sin is death."

"Is it the Bishop of Segovia who asks me that question or my old friend Blasco de Valero?"

"I have never yet betrayed a friend or an enemy. So long as you say nothing to offend the Faith say what you will."

"Then this must be my answer: We know that the attributes of God are infinite and it has always seemed strange to me that men have never given Him credit for common sense. It is hard to believe that He would have created so beautiful a world if He had not desired men to enjoy it. Would He have given the stars their glory, the

birds their sweet song and the flowers their fragrance if
He had not wished us to delight in them? I have sinned
before men and men have condemned me. God made me
a man with the passions of a man, and did He give them to
me only that I should suppress them? He gave me my
adventurous spirit and my love of life. I have a humble
hope that when I am face to face with my Maker He will
condone my imperfections and I shall find mercy in His
sight."

The Bishop looked sorely troubled. He could have told
the poor poet that we are placed on this earth to scorn its
delights, to resist temptation, to conquer ourselves and to
bear our cross; so that in the end, miserable sinners though
we be, we may be found worthy of communion with the
blessed. But would his words avail? He could only pray
that before death claimed him the Grace of God might
descend upon that wretched man so that he would repent
of his misdeeds. Silence fell between them.

"I did not send for you today in order to urge you to
mend your ways," said the Bishop at last. "It would not
be difficult for me to confute your wrongful opinions, but
I know of old how ingenious you are to make the worse
appear the better reason and I know too the pleasure you
take in uttering sophisms to tease. I am ready to believe
that much of what you said you said only to amuse yourself at my expense. You have a niece."

"I have."

"What do you make of this story that has brought unrest
upon the city?"

"She is a virtuous and truthful girl. She is a good
Catholic, but no more than properly religious."

"Since I understand that she owes her education to you
I can well credit that."

"Nor is she prone to idle fancies. She is indeed, as the

109

poor are bound to be, somewhat matter-of-fact. No one could accuse her of possessing the unfortunate faculty of imagination."

"Do you believe then that the Blessed Virgin did in fact appear to her?"

"I was in two minds until yesterday when she told me the exact words Our Lady had used. Then I was convinced. That is why I sought to see you. I knew at once what was meant and I wanted to spare you a useless intervention. They would not admit me."

The Bishop sighed.

"It is not the least of the crosses we are called upon to bear that the companions of our labours in their solicitude for our well-being prevent access to us of those whom it would be profitable for us to see."

"Time has not diminished the affection that bound me to you in my youth, for you see, I, a sinner, can afford to surrender to the blind impulses of my heart. I wished to save you from a humiliation which I knew would be very bitter to you. The moment the girl repeated to me the Blessed Virgin's exact words I knew who was designated to cure her of her infirmity."

"She told me that Our Lady had named me."

"That was a natural error for a girl to make who had heard of your mortifications, virtue and austerity. The Blessed Virgin told her that the power to cure her lay in the hands of that one of your father's sons who has best served God."

"I have but just heard that."

"Do you not know then who has done that? It is as plain as a pike-staff."

The Bishop paled. He gave Domingo an anxious glance.

"My brother Martin?"

"The baker."

Beads of sweat stood on the Bishop's brow. He shivered as though someone were walking over his grave.

"It is impossible. He is no doubt a worthy man, but of the earth, earthy."

"Why is it impossible? Because he has no learning? It is one of the mysteries of our Faith that God Who gave man reason and thereby raised him above the brutes has never so far as we are told laid great store on intelligence. Your brother is a good and simple man. He has been a faithful husband to his wife and a loving father to his children. He has honoured his father and mother. He has fed them when they were hungry and tended them when they were sick. He bore with submission his father's contempt and his mother's distress because, a gentleman by birth, he followed a calling that lowered him in the estimation of fools. He suffered with good humour the scorn of the gentry and the gibes of the vulgar. Like our father Adam he earned his bread by the sweat of his brow and he took a modest pride in the knowledge that the bread was good. He accepted the joys of life with gratitude and its sorrows with resignation. He succoured the needy. He was pleasant in his discourse and cheerful in his mien. He was a friend to all men. The ways of God are inscrutable and it may well be that in His eyes by his industrious, honest life, his loving-kindness, his innocent gaiety, Martin the baker has served Him better than you who have sought salvation by prayer and penance or your brother Manuel who glories in the women and children he has killed and the thriving towns he has left in desolate ruin."

The Bishop passed his hand wearily across his forehead. His face was anguished.

"You know me too well, Domingo," he said, his voice trembling, "to think that I undertook to do the thing I did without anxious searching of heart. I knew I was unworthy and my soul was dismayed, but I took the sign that was granted me as a command to do what I believed to be the will of God. I was wrong. And now my brother Manuel is determined to attempt what I failed to do."

"Even as a boy he was more remarkable for the strength of his body than for the force of his understanding."

"He is as obstinate as he is wrong-headed. The notabilities of the town are encouraging him so that they may deride him after the event. He has obtained the approval of the archpriest and of the prior of this convent."

"At all costs you must prevent him."

"I have no authority to do so."

"If your brother should persist in his folly he will seek to avenge himself for his discomfiture on that wretched girl. The people will side with him. They will have no mercy. In the name of our old friendship I beseech you to protect her from his enmity and from the blind violence of the mob."

"By the Cross on which Our Lord was crucified I swear to you that I will give my life if need be to save the child from harm."

Domingo rose to his feet.

"I thank you with all my heart. Farewell, my dear. Our paths are different and we shall not meet again. Farewell for ever."

"Farewell. Oh, Domingo, I am an unhappy man. Pray for me, pray for me in all your prayers that God may vouchsafe to release me from the cruel burden of this life."

He was so shattered, his mien so piteous, that the old toper was seized with compassion. On a sudden impulse he took the Bishop in his arms and kissed him on both cheeks. The sinner pressed the saint to his heart and was quickly gone.

THAT night a very strange thing happened. The full moon, pursuing its appointed course, shone with such a dazzling brilliance that the cloudless sky shone blue like the velvet cloak that covered the white garment of the Blessed Virgin. The people of Castel Rodriguez slept. Suddenly all the bells in the city began to ring with such a clamour as might rouse the dead. It woke the sleepers and some rushed to their windows, while others half-dressed, snatching up clothes as they passed, ran down into the streets. The ringing of the church bells at that unwonted hour meant that fire had broken out in some part of the town and timorous housewives set about getting their valuables together, for when a fire started none could tell how far it would spread, and it was well to save what one could before the flames caught the house. Some in their panic went so far as to throw their bedding out of the windows and some carried out pieces of furniture and deposited them outside their doors.

People poured out of their houses and the streets were thronged with them. By a common impulse they crowded into the great plaza which was the pride of the city. Each one asked his neighbour where the fire was. Men cursed and women wrung their hands. They rushed to and fro to find where houses were aflame; they looked up to heaven to watch for the tell-tale glow that would mark the spot. There was nothing to be seen. People surging into the plaza from the various quarters of the town said there was no fire where they came from. There was no fire anywhere. Then as though a wind had suddenly blown over them the idea seized them one and all that foolish youths were playing a prank and had mischievously set the bells ringing to get

113

the people out of their beds and frighten them out of their wits. Angry men, determined to beat them within an inch of their lives, rushed to the church towers. They were met with an amazing sight. The ropes were jerking up and down and not a soul was pulling them. They stared for a moment with astonishment at the strange sight and then, with torches and lanterns, ran up the steep steps of the towers. When they reached the platform where the bells hung they were deafened by their clanging. The bells tossed from side to side in a furious oscillation and the clappers thundered against their brazen sides. No men were there. No men could have moved those heavy bells to such a violent din. You might have thought the bells had suddenly gone mad. They were ringing of themselves.

With short gasps, with terror in their hearts, scuttling down the stairways as though the devil were after them, they ran into the streets and with frantic words and wild gestures told what they had seen.

It was a miracle. It was God that had set the bells ringing and none knew whether it betokened good or ill to the city. Many fell to their knees and prayed aloud. Sinners remembered their sins and thought of the wrath to come. The parish priests had the doors of their churches unlocked and the crowd flocked in and followed the priests in their prayers, which besought the Almighty to have mercy on His creatures. It was long before they quieted down and slunk, silent and sober, back to their homes.

XIX

NONE knew how it had started, whether the notion had occurred to one fanciful person or whether it had been independently conceived by many; it was like the cholera: you do not know if it has been brought into the city by a stranger from foreign parts or whether some ill wind has spread the disease; a man here falls sick, a woman there dies, and before you are aware of the danger pestilence sweeps through the streets and the grave-diggers can no longer dig graves fast enough to bury the dead. Before the day was well advanced the conviction had spread among all the people of Castel Rodriguez that the mysterious event of the night was bound up in some way with the appearance to Catalina Perez of the Blessed Virgin. They talked of nothing else. Magistrates discussed it in their council chambers, priests in their sacristies and nobles in their palaces. The common people in the streets, housewives in the market place, shopmen in their shops, spoke of it and wondered. Monks in their monasteries, nuns in their convents were distracted from their prayers.

And presently it was agreed that there could be no doubt who was designated by the Blessed Virgin's enigmatic words. There were not a few, especially among the secular clergy, who asked whether God was not displeased with the extravagance of the Bishop's austerity and whether a certain arrogance in his humility did not indeed merit a divine reproof. But on Don Manuel de Valero there was neither spot nor stain. He had given the best years of his life to the service of God and the King. His Majesty, vice-regent on earth of the Almighty, by conferring conspicuous honours upon him had set the seal of his approval on his valour and virtue. It was evident to all, cleric and lay, rich and poor, nobles and commoners, that Don Manuel was the man chosen to work the miracle ordained by the divine will. A deputation consisting of prominent ecclesiastics, members of the aristocracy and persons of authority in the city council, called upon him and announced their unanimous opinion. Don Manuel in his bluff, soldierly way told them

115

that he was prepared to put himself at their disposal. It was decided that the ceremony should take place on the following day in the Collegiate Church. Don Manuel asked the archpriest to receive his confession that afternoon, and since he proposed to take Holy Communion in the morning, which he must take fasting, he called off the supper party he had arranged to give to his friends that evening. He was a conscientious man and was determined to omit nothing that might render his intervention efficacious on such a solemn occasion. Thrice armed is he, shriven and free from guilt, who puts his trust in God.

The Prior of the Dominican convent himself informed the Bishop of what had been decided and at the same time invited him to head the friars who were going in procession to attend the ceremony. Don Blasco discerned the malice in the Prior's offer, but, thanking him for the honour, gravely accepted. He was helpless. He attached no importance to what Domingo had said about his brother Martin; he knew too well Domingo's love of teasing and the pleasure he took in paradoxical conceits; but for all that he had a firm conviction that Don Manuel was not the man to perform a miracle. He would willingly have escaped the obligation of seeing his brother confounded, but knew that if he refused to go it would be ascribed to pique. It did not become his high office to give evil minds opportunity to think ill of him. But putting that aside there was his promise to Domingo to fulfil. He was well acquainted with the folly and brutality of the rabble, rabble if they were nobly born or basely, and it was only too probable that if they were disappointed of the wonder they expected they would wreak their vengeance on the hapless girl. If he were there he might be able to save her from their savagery.

So next day, heavy at heart, with his two faithful secre-

taries, he walked at the head of the friars from the convent
to the church. It was thronged to the doors and still the
people, eager to see a miracle performed before their very
eyes, pressed in. Way was made and the Bishop, followed
by the friars, proceeded slowly up the nave. He took his
seat in a great chair beside, and a little in front of, the high
altar. The choir was filled with the notabilities of the city.
Presently Don Manuel came forward with a company of
gentlemen and seated himself in a chair that had been placed
for him on the other side of the altar. He was dressed in
a parade suit of armour, his breastplate damascened with
gold, and he wore the great cloak, with its green cross, of
the Order of Calatrava. The nobles in the choir were in
their best array. They were chatting and laughing. They
exchanged nods and smiles with one another. In the nave
the crowd were talking aloud and calling to one another as
though they were at a bull-fight. The Bishop surveyed them
with indignation. It was a mockery of religion, and he had it
in mind to rise and denounce them for their irreverent levity.

At the foot of the steps, supporting herself with a crutch,
knelt Catalina.

From the organ loft fell the first notes of a voluntary and
the florid sounds swept blithely over the heads of the
congregation. The church was in its architecture large and
plain, but successive heads of the great house of Henriquez
had enriched it with a plateresque ceiling of painted wood,
framed the pictures over the altars with frames massive and
gilt, and provided the images with gorgeous robes. The
choir stalls were elaborately carved. In the chapels were
the tombs, the early ones in stone, grim and austere, the
later ones of marble richly sculptured, in which lay the
mortal remains of the dead dukes and their consorts. A
dim light filtered through the windows of stained glass and
the air was heavy with incense.

117

The priests came in, clad in the costly vestments used on great occasions, which had been presented to the church by devout and noble ladies. The subdeacon held the chalice and the paten enveloped in the humeral veil. Mass was sung. A shiver of awe passed over the vast concourse as all fell to their knees at the thin tinkle of the bell that called attention to the elevation of the Host and Chalice. The archpriest, the celebrant, partook of Communion and administered it in turn to Don Manuel and to Catalina. At last the moment had arrived which the crowd had been impatiently awaiting. A strange sound came from them, not the sound of voices, not the sound exactly of restless movements, but a sound like the sighing of the wind in a wood of pine trees, as though their expectation itself was made audible.

Don Manuel rose to his feet and strode to the kneeling girl. In his armour, the great cloak of his order hanging from his shoulders, he made an imposing and even splendid figure. The scene, the moment had invested him with an unaccustomed dignity. He was confident in his power. He laid his hand on the girl's head and in a loud voice, as though he were giving his regiment the order to charge, so that he was plainly heard to the remotest corners of the great church, he repeated the words he had been given to say.

"In the name of God the Father, God the Son and God the Holy Ghost I command thee, Catalina Perez, to rise to thy feet, cast away thy useless crutch and walk."

The girl, spell-bound by the awfulness of the occasion, frightened, staggered to her feet and dropped the crutch. She took a step forward and with a cry of terror fell head-long. Once more the miracle had failed.

Then a great uproar arose and it was as though a sudden madness had seized the crowd. Men shouted and women screamed. They yelled with rage.

118

"A witch. A witch," they cried. "The stake. The stake. The stake. Burn her."

Then with a sudden impulse they surged towards the sacristy and would have torn the girl limb from limb. In their passion they pushed one another aside. Some fell and were brutally trampled on, and their shrieks were added to the din.

The Bishop sprang to his feet and with a swift sweeping movement strode down the sacristy till he came face to face with the frenzied mob. He raised his arms above his head and his great dark eyes blazed.

"Back, back," he cried in a voice of thunder. "Who are you to desecrate this holy place? Get back, I tell you. Get back."

His aspect was so terrifying that a gasp of horror was wrung from a thousand throats. As though a great abyss had suddenly opened before them the crowd on a sudden stopped dead. They shrank back. For a moment the Bishop eyed them, his eyes black with indignation.

"Vile, vile," he cried and then, clenching his fists, he flung out his arms as though he would fling at them the thunderbolt of his wrath. "Kneel, kneel and pray that you may be forgiven for the insult that you have offered to the house of God."

At his words, dominated by his authority, many fell sobbing to their knees. Others, as though too dazed to move, stood and stared vacantly at that fearful figure. Slowly the Bishop looked from side to side till his gaze had taken in the whole of that vast concourse and each one felt that those angry eyes were fixed upon him alone. Silence fell except for the hysterical sobbing of a woman here and there.

"Listen," said the Bishop at last. "Listen to what I say." And now his voice was no longer menacing, but grave,

119

stern and authoritative. "Listen. You know the words Our Lady vouchsafed to the girl Catalina Perez and you know the wonders that have occurred in this city and have given rise to confusion and unrest in your minds. The Blessed Virgin told this girl that the son of Don Juan de Valero who had best served God had the power by God's grace to cure her of her infirmity. In our sinful pride and vanity I who speak to you and Don Manuel my brother had the temerity to think that one or other of us was thus designated. We have been bitterly punished for our presumption. But Don Juan has still another son."

The crowd interrupted him with shouts and laughter.

"*El panadero*," they cried. "The baker."

Then they began to sing derisively in a sort of rude rhythm.

"*El panadero. El panadero.*"

"Silence," cried the Bishop.

People hushed one another.

"Laugh. As the crackling of thorns under a pot, so is the laughter of fools. What does the Lord require of you, but to do justly, to love mercy and to walk humbly with your God? Hypocrites and blasphemers. Fornicators. Vile. Vile. Vile."

He repeated the word each time with a more biting scorn so that they who heard him recoiled as a man would if a glass of icy water were thrown in his face. His wrath was terrible to see. He swept that multitude with a glance of withering contempt.

"Are the familiars of the Holy Office here?"

A strange sound, like a startled sigh, swept through the crowd as one and all caught their breath, for these instruments of the Inquisition were terrifying to the people. They did not know what the sinister words portended, and each one shook in his shoes. Behind the Bishop several men started up.

120

"Let them stand forth," he said.

Since the familiars of the Holy Office enjoyed power, influence and above all protection from its dread proceedings, theirs was a charge sought after by men of the highest rank. There were eight in Castel Rodriguez. There was a moment's pause while they left their seats and took up positions behind the Bishop. He waited till he knew from the quiet of their shuffling feet that they were behind him.

"Listen," he said again, and the index finger of his outstretched hand seemed to point in accusation at each one of those shivering creatures. "The Holy Office does nothing in anger nor in haste. It administers justice to the guilty, but is merciful to the repentant sinner."

He paused and the silence was awful.

"It is not for you, a generation of vipers, to lay hands on this wretched girl. If she is deceived or possessed of a devil it is for the Holy Office to take cognizance of it. If she fails in the test the familiars are here to deliver her to the tribunal. But the test is not complete. Where is Martin de Valero?"

"Here, here," cried several voices.

"Let him come forward."

"No, no, no."

It was the voice of Martin the baker.

"If he will not come of his own free will, constrain him," said the Bishop sternly.

There was a scuffle as Martin struggled with the men who pushed and pulled him, but after a little the crowd parted and he was urged forward to the sanctuary steps. The men fell back and left him standing alone. He had come in from his shop to see the wonder of which everyone was talking, and he was in his working clothes. His face was red from the heat of the ovens and from his vain effort to escape from the rude hands that hustled him. The day was hot and pearls of sweat stood on his forehead. His plump good-humoured countenance was heavy with consternation.

"Come," said the Bishop.

As though drawn by a force he could not withstand the baker ascended the sanctuary steps.

"Brother, brother, what is it that you are doing to me?" he cried. "How can I do what you could not? I am but a working man and no better a Christian than my neighbour."

"Be silent."

The Bishop had not even a remote notion that the baker could work a miracle, and he had only thought of him on the spur of the moment as the sole means by which he could save Catalina from the fury of the rabble. He wanted a brief respite which would allow him to calm their passion. He knew now that the girl was safe. The familiars were there to protect her, and since there was in the city no prison of the Inquisition they would take her on his order to a convent and when she was there it would be time to consider what further steps should be taken. The Bishop once more addressed himself to the awed people.

"Hath not the potter power over the clay, of the same lump to make one vessel with honour and another with dishonour? There is no respect of persons with God. He that humbleth himself shall be exalted and the haughty shall be abased. Bring forward the girl."

Catalina was lying where she had fallen, her face hidden in her arms, and sobs shook her thin little body. No one had paid more attention to her than if she were a dead dog by the roadside. Two familiars raised her to her feet and brought her face to face with the Bishop. As best she could, with the crutch under her armpit, she joined her hands together in supplication. Tears streamed down her face.

"Oh, my lord, my lord, have pity on me," she cried.

122

"Not again, I beseech you, it can come to nothing. Let me go home to my mother."

"Kneel," he ordered. "Kneel."

With a despairing sob the child sank to her knees.

"Lay your hand on her head," he bade his brother.

"I cannot. I will not. I am afraid."

"Under pain of excommunication I command you to do as I tell you," said the Bishop harshly.

A shudder shook the unfortunate man, for he knew that his brother would not hesitate to carry into effect his dreadful threat. He timidly laid a trembling hand on the girl's head. It was not even clean.

"Now say the words that you heard your brother Manuel say."

"I cannot remember them."

"Then I will say them and you shall say them after me. I, Martin de Valero, son of Juan de Valero."

Martin repeated the words.

"I, Martin de Valero, son of Juan de Valero."

The Bishop spoke the last fateful words in a loud strong voice, but Martin said them after him in a tone that was barely audible. Catalina, as she was bidden, scrambled to her feet and with a despairing gesture flung the crutch away from her. For an instant she wavered. She did not fall. She stood. Then, with a cry and a sob, forgetting the place and the occasion, she turned and ran down the sanctuary steps.

"Mother, mother."

Maria Perez, who was with Domingo, beside herself with joy, forced her way through the crowd and ran to meet her. Catalina threw herself into her arms and burst out crying.

The dense throng for a moment was too stunned to move. They gasped in amazement; then such a hullabaloo arose as never was heard.

"The miracle. The miracle."

123

They shouted. They clapped their hands. Women waved their handkerchiefs. The men cried *olè, olè,* as they would have done at a bull-fight when one of the toreros had made a dangerous pass; they flung their hats through the air as they flung them at the feet of the matador when with his *cuadrilla* behind him he walked round the ring to receive the plaudits of the public. Above the din rose the piercing tones of a woman here and there singing to a strange, half Moorish tune a hymn to the Blessed Virgin. It seemed as though the tumult would never cease. Strangers embraced one another. Men and women wept for joy. With their own eyes they had seen a miracle.

Suddenly a hush passed over that wild, madly-excited rout, and all eyes were turned upon the Bishop. Martin, in his shyness, hardly able to take in what had happened, had shrunk back, and the Dominican stood alone at the top of the sanctuary steps with his back to the High Altar. In his habit, patched and worn though it was, emaciated, but tall and erect, he made a figure that was awe-inspiring. But the marvellous thing was that he was bathed in light; it was not a halo that surrounded his head, but an aureole that seemed to clothe him from head to foot.

"A saint, a saint," cried the people and they stared with all their eyes at the strange and thrilling sight. "Blessed be the woman that bore you," they cried. "Now lettest thou thy servant depart in peace. Oh, happy, happy day!"

They did not know what they said. They were beside themselves with joy and love and fear. Only Domingo noticed that a pane of one of the stained-glass windows was broken and by a fortunate chance a ray of sun passed through the aperture to hit the Bishop and suffuse him with glory.

The Bishop raised his hand for silence and immediately that great noise was stilled. He stood for a moment surveying the sea of faces before him, his face sad and stern, and then, raising his head, his tragic eyes rapt as though with the eyes of the spirit he saw the heavenly host, he began in slow and solemn tones to recite the Nicene Creed. The words were familiar to all his listeners, for they heard them every Sunday at Mass and there was a low buzz, like the distant sound of shuffling feet, as they repeated the words after him. He came to an end. He turned and walked towards the High Altar. The light that had shone upon him was seen no more, and Domingo, looking at the window, saw that the sun in its relentless journey across the sky had passed on and no ray sent its light through the broken pane. The Bishop prostrated himself before the altar and gave thanks to God in silent prayer. A great weight was lifted from his tortured heart, for it was borne in upon him without a possibility of doubt that though it was the hand of Martin that had rested on the girl's head he was but an instrument, a tool as it were of which God had been pleased to make use, so that he, Blasco de Valero, might work a miracle to His glory. Moreover it was a sign, a sure and certain sign, that God forgave him for the grievous sin he had committed when in his weakness he had allowed the Greek to be garrotted before he was burnt. God Who knew all things, past, present and future, knew the hardness of the misbeliever's heart and so condemned him to everlasting death. It was well to pity the damned in their torments, but to repine was to impugn the justice of God.

The Bishop rose and slowly walked down the sanctuary. He walked like a man in a dream. The two religious, his friends and secretaries, saw his intention and followed him, whereupon the Prior, making a sign to his friars to come after him, walked behind them. When the Bishop came to the top of the sanctuary steps, he paused.

"The grace of the Lord Jesus Christ and the love of God and the communion of the Holy Ghost be with you all."

He descended. The crowd pushed back so as to leave a pathway for him and the religious who followed him. The friars broke into the *Te Deum Laudamus* and their strong deep voices rang through the church. The Bishop, as in a trance, passed through the kneeling multitude and gave the people his blessing as he went. He did not see Domingo's ironical glance.

At that moment the bells in the belfry started to peal and in a little while all the bells in the city were ringing. But this was owing to no supernatural intervention. Don Manuel, like the well-trained soldier he was, paid attention to the smallest detail, and he had seen to it that when the bells of the Collegiate Church were set ringing in celebration of the miracle he was confident of working, the bells of all the other churches should be rung too.

The great doors were swung open as the Bishop approached and he passed out into the blazing sunshine of the August day. The crowd surged out after him and followed the procession of friars till it reached the Dominican convent. The Bishop was about to enter when a great outcry arose in the throng. They wanted him to speak to them. Against the wall of the convent was a pulpit used when a preacher came to the city so celebrated for his eloquence that the convent church was too small to hold the vast congregation that desired to hear him. The Prior advanced and telling the Bishop what the people wanted begged him to accede to their wish. The Bishop looked about him as though he did not know where he was. One might have thought he had not till then been aware of all those devout and anxious creatures that had dogged his steps. He paused for an instant to collect himself and then without a word mounted the pulpit.

His voice was magnificent, rich in tone, and with an infinite variety of inflection. He began.

"Ye cannot find out the depth of the heart of man, neither

126

can ye perceive the things that he thinketh; then how can ye search out God, that hath made all these things, and know His mind, or comprehend His purpose?"

His gestures were powerful and significant. His voice reached to the farthest confines of the serried throng, and when he lowered it in compassion such was the beauty of his delivery that his every word was audible. When in passionate denunciation of the sins of men he raised it to its full splendour it was like thunder rolling in the bleak Sierras. He would pause on a sudden and the silence in that torrent of speech was like the crack of doom. The people winced when he reminded them of the shortness of life, the accidents that beset the sons of Adam from the cradle to the grave, the transitoriness of its pleasures, the anguish of its sorrows; they trembled when he painted the horrors of hell and the endless torture of the damned; and they wept when, his voice melting with tenderness, he described in ecstatic strains the communion of saints and the eternal joy of heaven. Many repented of their sins and from then on were changed men. He ended with a great peroration· in praise of the Blessed Virgin and to the glory of God. Never had he spoken with a more fiery eloquence nor with a more heartrending pathos.

When they conducted him to his cell he was so broken that he permitted his two faithful attendants to lay him on his hard bed. He was shattered with emotion and fatigue.

XX

THAT night there was great rejoicing in the city. In the taverns the tapsters could not fill cups and drinking-horns fast enough. Chattering crowds wandered round and round the plaza and talked of the wonderful event of the day. No one doubted but that it was the saintly Bishop who had performed the miracle and all were touched by his modesty in using his brother the baker as an instrument of his power. So he had taught them that in truth the humble would be exalted and the haughty abased. Many vowed that they had seen him rise in the air, two feet from the ground, said some, and four feet others, and remain there suspended in glory.

XXI

WHEN the multitude flocked out of the church in the Bishop's train, Martin, who had shrunk within himself in the hope that no one would pay attention to him, remained so that in the end there was no one there but he. He waited in order to escape unseen, but with some impatience, since he knew that all this excitement would bring a lot of custom and he had left his shop in the charge of his two apprentices and he was afraid they would not be able to cope with the stream of customers. For he not only baked bread, but also meat for people who brought joints or pies which they could not cook at home. A lot of them would think this was an occasion for a treat. When at last he thought it safe to slip out he noticed Catalina's crutch on the marble floor where she had thrown it, and since he was a tidy soul, who didn't like to see things lying about, he picked it up and carried it away with him.

But when the archpriest got back to his house, as he sat down to a meal which he richly deserved and badly wanted, it occurred to him that the crutch had been left in the church and that it was an object that should not be lost sight of.

michael
charlton

He immediately sent a servant to fetch it and was vexed when the servant told him that he could not find it. It was too valuable an article to lose, so he had no sooner finished his dinner than he sent people to find out what had become of it; but it was not till next day that he was informed that it was standing in a corner of the baker's shop. He dispatched someone to demand its return. The baker handed it over and the archpriest put it carefully away till he could decide how best to make use of it.

Now Doña Beatriz no sooner heard the great news than she sent two nuns to the house of Maria Perez to demand a circumstantial account of all that had occurred, see the girl for themselves, and if they found her cured as was reported, make her a present of a gold chain, delicately worked, which she put in their hands, and in return ask for the crutch which she had used in her infirmity so that it might be placed as a votive offering in the Lady Chapel of the convent church. She was far from pleased when the nuns came back to tell her that neither Catalina, her mother nor her uncle had any idea what had become of the crutch. The Prioress was determined to get it, but since it was not a matter that she could entrust to her nuns she sent for the steward of her estates and ordered him to find out who had got possession of the precious object and in her name demand its delivery. It was a couple of days before the steward came back with the information that the archpriest had the crutch and would not give it up.

Doña Beatriz gave way to a lively irritation and told the steward roundly that he was both a fool and a knave. But she was a woman of discretion. She sat down and wrote a polite and complimentary letter to the archpriest in which she asked him with honeyed words to let her have the crutch so that she might hang it in the church on whose steps the Blessed Virgin had appeared to Catalina. She pointed out to him that this was clearly the place where it should be preserved for the edification of future generations. The archpriest wrote back in terms as courteous as her own, but said that though for Christ's sake he was only too willing to grant her any favour within his power, since the miracle had taken place within the Collegiate Church he felt it his duty to keep for its greater glory this visible sign of God's grace. He pointed out further that the fact of its having been left in the sanctuary showed plainly that it was God's intention that there it should remain. Upon this an exchange of letters passed between the two from which by degrees all expressions of politeness and esteem for one another's virtue and piety were banished. The Prioress grew more and more peremptory, the archpriest more and more stubborn. Various persons took sides and what one said was repeated to the other. The Prioress described the archpriest as an insolent donkey, riddled with concupiscence, and the archpriest described the Prioress as an interfering old hag whose administration of her convent was a scandal to Christendom.

Doña Beatriz decided at last that she had kept her temper as long as Christian charity required and was now free to indulge in the righteous indignation which the archpriest's impertinent behaviour justified. She sent for her steward again. She instructed him to call upon the archpriest and taking care to treat him with the respect due to the cloth make it clear to him that if he did not hand over the crutch forthwith he need not expect the protection of her brother the Duke in the law case he was then engaged in nor such advancement in the Church as her favour at Court might enable her to obtain for him, and that she could no longer ignore the scandalous rumours that circulated about his relations with a certain woman and would be constrained to lay the facts before the bishop of the diocese. The

Prioress thus traded on his greed, his ambition and his incontinence. The archpriest through the influence of the reigning Duke of Castel Rodriguez had been appointed to a canonry in the Cathedral of Seville; and the chapter were bringing a suit against him to force his resignation owing to his non-residence. He did not wish to lose the handsome emoluments of the office, but since neither equity nor law was on his side he could only hope to win his case by the powerful intervention of his patron. He was besides not without a desire to serve the Church to greater advantage on the episcopal bench. For these reasons he could not afford to make an enemy of the Prioress; and, his bishop being of austere morals, he was uneasy at her threats to expose peccadilloes of which the weakness of his flesh had made him guilty. It did not take him long to see that he was beaten, and since he had to yield he was sensible enough to yield gracefully. He handed the crutch to her messenger and with it a letter in which with protestations of his deep regard for her virtue he said that on mature consideration he was obliged to agree with her that the proper place for the precious object was plainly the Church of Our Lady of Carmel.

The Prioress had it encased in silver and hung in the Lady Chapel for the edification of the faithful.

XXII

IN the confusion that ensued when the crowd streamed out of the church in pursuit of the Bishop, Domingo hustled his sister and his niece through a side door and taking unfrequented alleys brought them safely home. Maria Perez was all for putting her daughter to bed, giving her a purge and sending for a barber to bleed her, but Catalina, rejoicing in the free use of her limbs, would have none of it. Just for the fun of it she ran up and down stairs, and but that decency forbade would have turned cartwheels in the parlour. Neighbours came in to congratulate her and to marvel over the miracle that had been performed. She had to tell over and over again how the Blessed Virgin had looked when she appeared to her, what she wore and exactly what she had said. They in their turn told her of the wonderful sermon the Bishop had preached and how, such was his eloquence, they were unable to hold their water, so that their rapture was mingled with embarrassment. In the afternoon the great ladies of the city sent for Catalina and made her walk up and down, giving little cries of wonder as she did so, as if they had never seen anyone walk before. They gave her presents, handkerchiefs, silk scarves, stockings and even dresses which were only slightly worn; a gold pin, ear-rings of semi-precious stones and a bracelet. Catalina had never owned so many rich and beautiful things in her life. Finally, cautioning her not to become conceited because such a favour had been granted her, but to remember that she was a working girl and would do well not to forget her humble station, they sent her away.

Night fell. Maria Perez, Domingo and Catalina supped. They were tired after the adventures of the day, but restless too. Mother and daughter had talked till they had nothing more to say. Domingo urged them to go to bed, but Catalina said she was too excited to sleep, so to calm them both and at the same time by the magic of art to attune their minds to the contemplation of ideal beauty he started to read them a play he had lately finished. Catalina listened somewhat inattentively, with one ear as it were, but this, absorbed in the dramatic situation and enchanted with the mellifluous sound of his verse, its elegantly-varied pattern, Domingo did not notice. Suddenly she sprang to her feet.

"There he is," she cried.

Domingo stopped and there was a frown of exasperation on his good-natured face. They heard the twanging of a guitar in the street.

"Who is it?" asked her uncle crossly, for no author likes to be interrupted when he is giving a reading of one of his own compositions.

"Diego. Mother, I can go to the *reja*, can't I?"

"I should have thought you had more spirit."

The *reja* was the grille that secured the window from the intrusion not so much of thieves as of too enterprising swains. As a well-behaved girl, who knew that men were lascivious and a woman's virginity her crowning glory, it would never have occurred to Catalina to admit an admirer into the house, but it was the custom for a girl to sit at her window at night and with the grille between talk with the object of her affections of the mysterious things lovers are accustomed to entertain themselves with.

"He abandoned you when you were crippled," Maria Perez went on, "and now that you are a celebrity and the whole city is talking about you he comes running back with his tail between his legs."

"Oh, mother, you don't know men as well as I do," said Catalina. "They're weak and easily led. How could the world go on if we did not make allowances for their foolishness? Naturally he didn't want to marry me when I was a cripple. His mother and father had found a good match for him. He has told me a hundred times that he loves me better than his soul."

"You are a very silly girl. He is a shameless fellow and you should have more self-respect."

"Let her go," said Domingo. "She loves him and that

is the end of it. I dare say he is no more worthless than any other young man of this degenerate day."

With a shrug of her shoulders Maria Perez got up and taking the tallow candle by which Domingo had been reading, said:

"Come into the kitchen and read your play to me there."

"I will do no such thing," he answered. "The thread is broken and I am out of the mood. You are a good woman, Maria, but you do not know a pentameter from a cow's tail and I cannot do myself justice unless I have an appreciative audience."

Catalina was left alone. She went to the window and against the darkness of the night saw a figure which made her heart beat.

"Diego."

"Catalina."

Thus at this late stage is introduced into this story a hero.

His father was a tailor in a very good way of business who made clothes for the most notable persons in the city, and from his earliest years Diego had learnt to ply a needle, to cut out breeches and to fit a doublet. He had grown into a tall, strapping lad, with a fine pair of legs, a slim waist and broad shoulders. He had a handsome head of hair, which shone with the oil he plentifully applied to it, an olive skin, bold black eyes, a sensual mouth and a straight nose. He was in short a youth of a comely presence and Catalina thought him more beautiful than the day. He was of a gallant spirit and it irked him to sit cross-legged hour after hour stitching under his father's captious eyes cloth, silk, velvet and damask to be worn by the more fortunate than he. He felt himself born for greater things and in his wayward reveries played many a splendid role on the stage of life.

He fell in love. It was a shock to his parents when he

told them that unless they gave him permission to marry Catalina Perez he would go as a soldier to the Low Countries or work his way on a ship to seek adventure in the Americas. Catalina's only fortune was the house she would inherit on the death of her mother, and her only prospects the unlikely possibility that her father would one day return laden with gold from the unknown lands in the west. But Diego's parents were wily; he was but just eighteen and they thought his young man's fancy would in due course lightly turn to a more suitable object for his affections; they temporized; they said very sensibly that it was absurd to enter upon the married state before he was out of his apprenticeship, but that if he was then still of the same mind they would be prepared to discuss the matter. They raised no objection to his going night after night to Catalina's window and entertaining her with little tunes on his guitar and amorous conversation. But when a bull trampled on the girl and left her partly paralysed they could not but look upon it as a special interposition of Providence. Diego was distraught with horror at the accident, but he was obliged to agree with his fond parents that it was out of the question to marry a cripple, and when presently his mother told him that according to the reliable information she had received the only daughter of a well-to-do haberdasher had taken a fancy to him and would not be averse to receiving his addresses, he was sufficiently flattered to pay her a good deal of attention. The respective fathers of the young people came together and decided in principle that the match would be mutually advantageous. It only remained to settle the terms and since they were both shrewd business men this led to protracted negotiations.

Such then was the state of affairs when Diego presented himself once more at Catalina's window. Besides learning to measure, cut and sew he had learnt in the course of his short life that a man should never excuse himself, and she, young though she was, knew that it is vain to reproach a man. However heinous his offences, it only irritates him to have them thrown in his teeth. A sensible woman is content to let them weigh on his conscience if he has one, and if he hasn't, recrimination is wasted. So they lost no time in chiding on her side or apology on his, but went straight to the point.

"Heart of my soul," he said, "I adore you."

"My love, my precious love," she answered.

But it is unnecessary to repeat the sweet, foolish things they said to one another. They said what lovers say. Diego had a pretty gift of language, and phrases came unbidden to his lips that so enchanted Catalina that she felt it had been almost worth while to endure those long weeks of misery in order to enjoy at that moment such an ecstasy of bliss. The darkness of the room behind her hid her almost completely from his sight, but the sound of her voice, low and soft, and the ripple of her light laughter fired his blood.

"Cursed be this grille that separates us. Oh, why cannot I take you into my arms and cover your face with kisses and press my beating heart to yours?"

She knew very well what that would lead to, and the idea did not in the least displease her. She knew that man was a creature of licentious passion, and it gave her a thrill of pride and at the same time a sort of heartache that Diego should so vehemently desire her. She was a little breathless.

"Oh, my dear, what can you want of me that I do not want to give you? But if you love me you cannot ask me to do what would be a mortal sin and which in any case these iron bars make impracticable."

"Give me your hand then."

The window at which she sat was at some little height from the street, so that in order to do this she had to kneel on the floor. She slipped her hand through the grille and he pressed it to his greedy lips. Her hands were very small, with tapering fingers, hands of a lady of high degree; she was proud of them, and in order to keep them soft and white washed them every night in her urine. She gently stroked his face and she blushed and laughed when he put her little thumb in his mouth.

"Shameless one," she said. "What will you do next?" She withdrew her hand. "Behave yourself and let us talk sense."

"How can I talk sense when you rob me of my senses? Woman, you might as well ask a river to run uphill."

"Then you had better take yourself off. It is growing late and I am tired. The haberdasher's daughter must be waiting for you and you have no reason to offend her."

This she said with perfidious sweetness and it brought the answer she wanted.

"La Clara? What is she to me? She has a hump on her back, a squint in her eye and hair like a mangy dog's."

"Liar," she answered cheerfully. "It is true that she is somewhat marked with smallpox and her teeth are a little yellow and one is missing, but except for that she is not a bad-looking girl and she has a nice nature. I cannot blame your father for wishing you to marry her."

"My father can go and . . ."

What he said his father could go and do was so coarse that a decorous writer cannot but leave it to the reader's imagination. Catalina was not unused to the direct language of her day and she did not turn a hair. Indeed her lover's emphatic utterance gave her a certain satisfaction.

"I was in the church this morning," he went on, "and when I saw you stand there in all your beauty it was as if

a sword pierced my heart and I knew that all the fathers
in the world couldn't separate me from you."

"I was in a daze. I didn't know where I was nor what
had happened to me. I was giddy. And then it was as if
a million pins and needles were pricking my leg so that I
couldn't have borne the pain another minute, and I knew
nothing more till I found myself in mother's arms and she
was laughing and crying and I burst into tears."

"You ran and as you ran we all shouted with joy and
wonder. You ran like a doe that flees from the hunter, you
ran like a nymph of the woods because she has heard the
voices of men, you ran like . . ." Here his invention failed
him and he added rather tamely: "You ran like an angel
of heaven. You were more beautiful than the dawn."

Catalina listened to this with great content and was
willing to hear much more to the same effect, but her
mother's voice broke in.

"Come to bed, child," she said. "You don't want all the
neighbours talking and you should have a good night's rest."

"Good night, my beloved."

"Light of my eyes, good night."

Now it happened that Diego's father and the haberdasher
had been for some days at odds over a piece of land which
the tailor desired as part of the girl's dowry but which the
haberdasher could not bring himself to part with. The
matter would in all probability have been amicably settled
by compromise if the tailor had not on a sudden shown an
unreasonable and to the haberdasher's mind churlish
obstinacy. Angry words passed and in the end the marriage
was abandoned. It was not without motive that the tailor
refused to modify his demands: the miracle had given
Catalina a distinction which he realized would be useful in
his business; she was not only a good and honest girl, but a
clever sempstress; and there was some talk that various ladies

of the city, charmed with her modesty and good manners, were prepared to join with one another to give her an acceptable dowry. By consenting to the marriage of which he had formerly disapproved he decided that he could make his son happy and do a good stroke of business into the bargain. Thus the last impediment to the happiness of the fond lovers was removed.

XXIII

THEY little knew that while, with the iron grille between, they continued every night with little variety but to their mutual satisfaction to talk in the silly way above described, a great lady in her oratory, only a stone's throw away, was contriving a scheme that very much concerned them.

Doña Beatriz was a devout woman who scrupulously performed her duties. The convent she ruled was a model to the community and the inspectors who visited it had never had occasion to find fault with her. She maintained perfect discipline. The services of the church were conducted with exemplary decorum. In conduct and piety she was irreproachable. But she carried in her heart a deadly hatred for a certain nun of Avila, Teresa de Cepeda by name, which neither the precepts of religion nor the repeated censures of her confessor could mitigate. This nun, known in religion as Mother Teresa of Jesus, but by the Prioress never referred to but as La Cepeda, had entered the Convent of the Incarnation at Avila where Doña Beatriz had been first a pupil and then a novice. She had aroused a good deal of indignation by claiming to receive special graces, raptures and the vision of Our Lord, His face blazing with

139

glory; to say nothing of having driven away the devil who was sitting on her office book by throwing holy water at him; but the climax came when, dissatisfied with the laxity of the Carmelite rule, she had left the convent and established a new one where a stricter rule was followed. The nuns she had left looked upon this as a slur on themselves and an insult to the order and they did everything in their power to have the new foundation suppressed. But Teresa de Cepeda was a woman of energy, determination and courage, and surmounting ceaseless opposition she founded convent after convent of Discalced Carmelites as they were called, since instead of the stout shoes worn by the other members of the order they wore sandals with rope soles; and before her death, some years before the time with which this narrative deals, she had seen the triumph of the Reform.

No one had fought it with greater tenacity than Doña Beatriz. She had never had any patience with the excessive mortifications, the visions and raptures, which the nuns of La Cepeda professed to have. There was a natural antagonism between these two women of strong will. Who was this proud, meddlesome, presumptuous and wicked creature to set herself up above everybody else? At one time she had gone so far as to ask the Bishop to allow her to make a foundation at Castel Rodriguez; she had by then gained many powerful friends, both at Court and among the clergy, and Doña Beatriz, determined not to allow the woman to gain a foothold in the city which she looked upon as her own domain, had been obliged to use all her influence to combat the scheme. A desperate struggle ensued and the issue was still in doubt when Teresa de Jesus died.

Though she prayed for her misguided soul, Doña Beatriz could not but heave a sigh of relief. She was con-

vinced that now La Cepeda's restless and dominating spirit
was no longer active the Reform would soon be forgotten
and the nuns in due course return to the old rule. She little
knew how strong an impress she had left on her daughters
and on the priests who had come in contact with her. In
a little while stories began to be told of the miracles she
had performed in her lifetime and the marvels that attended
her death. As she expired so sweet a smell came from her
body that the windows of her cell had to be opened to
prevent those present from fainting, and when nine months
afterwards it was exhumed the body was found to be intact
and incorrupt, and the whole convent was filled with the
same sweet odour. Sick persons were cured by touching
her remains. Already many influential people were urging
her beatification and it was finally borne in upon Doña
Beatriz that sooner or later La Cepeda would be canonized.

The thought of this had for some time gravely disquieted
her. It would be, to put it profanely, a feather in the cap
of the Discalced Order. It was true that there had been
saints in the Carmelites of the mitigated rule; indeed both
its founders were canonized; but that was a long time ago,
and such was the frivolity of the people, they were more
inclined to pay their devotions to a saint who had recently
achieved that sublime rank than to one who had been for
centuries in possession of it. But if the Prioress could do
nothing to prevent the upstart order from receiving an
honour for which she could see no justification she could
do something to restore the balance by providing her own
order with a candidate for canonization. Providence had
shown her the way and it would be a sin if she did not
take it. Lazarus was a saint for no other reason that she
knew of than that he had been the occasion for one of Our
Lord's miracles. Catalina was a pious and a virtuous girl
and the miracle by which she had recovered her health had

been witnessed not by two or three emotional nuns or self-interested priests, but by a vast concourse. Having received so signal a mark of divine favour it seemed only proper that she should devote the rest of her life to the service of God. Doña Beatriz had heard that she fancied herself in love with a young man of the city, but she brushed this aside; she could not believe that a woman in her senses would think twice of marrying a tailor when she might enjoy the benefits, both spiritual and worldly, which she would have by entering the Convent of the Incarnation of which she was herself the Prioress. If the girl was what the nuns who knew her said she was, she could not fail to be a credit to the convent and the grace she had received would add a further distinction to the foundation. She was young enough to react to training and Doña Beatriz was confident that she could make her a worthy religious. There was no reason to suppose that the Blessed Virgin would cease to take an interest in her and it was far from impossible that she would be the recipient of further graces. Her fame would spread, and when in due course she was released from the martyrdom of life she would surely be as suitable a candidate for beatification as the turbulent nun of Avila.

Doña Beatriz brooded over her project for some days and the more she considered it the more it appealed to her; but, being a woman of discretion, she thought it prudent not to embark upon it without the approval of her spiritual director. She sent for him. He was a worthy, simple man whose piety she esteemed, but of whose intelligence she had no high opinion. He applauded her wish to give to Our Lord a bride to whom His Mother had condescended to show so great a favour and who thus would be a credit to the community; and this was natural since, though the Prioress had dwelt on the gratitude which the girl must

142

feel for her miraculous cure and the good disposition she surely had to spend the rest of her life in the service of God, she had thought it unnecessary to impart to the good man the hidden motives that were the mainspring of her desire. But he raised an objection.

"By the statutes laid down on the foundation of this convent admission to it is reserved to ladies of noble birth. Catalina Perez, though of untainted blood (*de sangre limpia*), is of modest extraction."

The Prioress was prepared for this.

"I regard the condescension Our Blessed Lady showed her as a patent of nobility. In my eyes it has made her the equal of the proudest in the land."

Such an answer in the mouth of so great a lady filled the friar with admiration and if possible increased the veneration in which he held her. This settled, it only remained to consider ways and means. Her plan was to have the girl brought to see her and then put before her the utility to her spiritual welfare of making a retreat of some duration at the convent so that she could give due thanks to the Creator for the blessings that had been bestowed upon her; and since she foresaw that Catalina, owing to the unfortunate attachment she had contracted, might raise objection to this, she begged the friar to disclose her plan to the girl's confessor and get him to urge her, or if necessary order her, to accept the proposition. This the Prioress's director very willingly consented to do.

On the following day, therefore, the Prioress had Catalina brought to her. She had seen her but once before and then had hardly noticed her. She was immediately struck by her beauty, and with a smile, in which there was little of her habitual grimness, amiably remarked on it. She did not like ill-favoured nuns. It had always seemed to her unbecoming to offer the celestial bridegroom brides who did not combine spiritual grace with a comely presence. She was charmed with Catalina's modest demeanour, her sweet voice and the distinction of her carriage. There was nothing vulgar in her manner, and her speech, owing to Domingo's teaching, was not only correct, but elegant. The Prioress could not but be surprised that so fair a flower had grown in such humble earth. Any doubt she might have had of the wisdom of her project was dispelled: the girl was evidently destined to honour, and what honour could be greater than to serve God?

Catalina was very much in awe of the great lady with whose reputation both for virtue and severity she was well acquainted, but Doña Beatriz set herself to put the girl at her ease. Her face wore an expression of benignity which the nuns but rarely saw and Catalina began to wonder why they were all so much afraid of her. She was a voluble young person and, graciously encouraged to talk, she was soon telling her kindly listener the whole story of her short life with its hardship of poverty, its tribulations and joys, and she never suspected with what skill the Prioress guided her recital to make her disclose her disposition, honest nature and charm of character. Without a tremor, but with an indulgent benevolence, the Prioress heard her describe the merit and beauty of Diego, his sweetness and goodness; and tell how his parents, so unkind to her before, had relented so that now no obstacle remained to their happiness. The Prioress desired to hear from her own lips how the Blessed Virgin had appeared to her, the very words she had spoken, and how in the twinkling of an eye she had vanished from her sight. It was then that she gravely but mildly suggested that in common gratitude for the grace she had received Catalina should make a retreat in the convent in order to collect herself and for a little while surrender her spirit to the contemplation of heavenly things.

144

Catalina was taken aback. But she was accustomed to say the first thing that came into her head and by now she had so much lost her fear of the Prioress that she did not hesitate to be frank.

"Oh, Reverend Mother," she cried, "I couldn't do that. We've been separated so long, it would break my Diego's heart to be parted from me now. He says that he only lives for the hour when we talk to one another at my window. I should pine away if I didn't see him then."

"I would not press you, child, to do anything that you do not wish. A retreat could only benefit you if you made it for the love of God and with a sincere desire to amend yourself. I confess I should be disappointed in you if you were so little grateful to the Blessed Virgin for her goodness to you that you grudged her a little time to give her thanks; and I cannot think that this young man, if he loves you as you say and is so good, could take it amiss if for a while, no more than two or three weeks perhaps, in return for the blessing that has reunited you, you devoted yourself to pray for his salvation as well as yours. But we will say no more about it; the only thing I would ask you is to consult your confessor on the matter. It may be that he will think my suggestion of no value and in that case your conscience will be at ease."

She then dismissed her with the present of a rosary of amber beads.

XXIV

IT was no surprise to the Prioress when two or three days later she was informed that Catalina was in the parlour and had come to beg permission to make a retreat. She sent for her, made her welcome, kissed her and put her in charge of the mistress of novices. Catalina was given a cell that looked over the nuns' well-tended garden. Though austerely furnished, it was roomy, clean and cool.

There was no need of Doña Beatriz's request—and her requests were orders—that Catalina should be treated with indulgence and kindness, for her beauty, modesty and charm immediately captivated all hearts. Nuns, novices, lay sisters and lady boarders, all joined in making much of her. They liked her gaiety; they spoilt her like a favourite child. Though the bed she slept in was such as the rule of the order directed, it was luxurious compared with that to which she was accustomed, and the food she ate, simple and unspiced as was proper, was such as in the poverty of her home she had never tasted. Fish, chickens, game were provided from the Prioress's estates, and the lady boarders invited her to their rooms to partake of sweetmeats and other delicacies.

Doña Beatriz kept her own counsel; she was content to let the girl see for herself the delight of conventual life, with its peace, its pleasant activity and its security from the turmoil and trouble of the world. Its monotony was relieved by the visits during the recreation hour of distinguished ladies of the city and of worthy gentlemen, for the most part relations of the Prioress or her nuns, whose conversation was not entirely restricted to religious topics. Catalina was not a little flattered by the attentions they paid her. She had entered upon her retreat somewhat rebelliously on the order of her confessor reinforced by the persuasion of her mother, but she found it far from unpleasant. It would have been strange if she had not compared to its advantage the happy, ordered life of the nuns with that she led at home, with its constant drudgery darkened always by the spectre of want. There had been periods when there was no call for the special work she and her mother did, and then they were saved from starvation only by the uncertain earnings of Domingo. She enjoyed the services which she attended with all the members of the community in the small but beautiful church attached to the convent. The Prioress had an ear for music and she had seen to it that the singing was good and the rites conducted not only with devoutness but with ceremony. Catalina, with her keen sensibilities, found in them not only a delight to her senses, but a spiritual enrichment. Very much to her surprise she found the life of the convent not an imprisonment as she had feared but a liberation. She liked to please, and she pleased; she wished to be loved, and loved she was. Although she missed Diego and thought of him constantly, she was obliged to admit to herself that she would look back later on her retreat as one of the most agreeable episodes of her life.

Every day, towards evening, Doña Beatriz sent for her and kept her for an hour. She never mentioned her wish that Catalina should enter the religious life; though soon she wished it not only for the motives that have been already related, but because with her insight into character she had quickly realized that besides being virtuous Catalina was intelligent and quick to learn, that she had personality and would be an ornament to the order. The Prioress talked to her, not as a great lady and the Mother Superior of a convent, but as a loving friend. She exerted herself to gain an influence over the girl, but she knew that she must tread warily. She told her stories of the saints to edify her and stories of the Court to show her that even a religious could play a part in matters of state. She talked to her of the affairs of the convent and the management of her properties not without a notion that it might favourably affect Catalina to see what a responsible and important position it was to be

the Prioress of the Carmelite convent at Castel Rodriguez.
The possibility of attaining it might well dazzle the daughter
of Maria Perez the sempstress.

But very little can be kept secret in a convent, and though
Doña Beatriz had never told anyone of her plan, it was not
long before it was generally known among the nuns and
the lady boarders to what end tended the privileges Catalina
enjoyed and the notice the awe-inspiring Mother Superior
took of her. An effusive nun one day told her how much
they all loved her and how much they wished that she would
remain with them for good. A lady boarder who was
staying at the convent because her husband was at the
wars told her that she only wished she were free to become
a religious.

"If I were in your place, child," she said, "I would ask
the Reverend Mother tomorrow to accept me as a novice."

"Oh, but I am going to be married."

"You will never cease to regret it. Men by their nature
are brutal, neglectful and faithless."

The lady was pasty-faced, lethargic and corpulent. Catalina could not but think that if her husband was as bad as
that there were excuses for him.

"How can you hesitate when the heavenly bridegroom
holds out his arms to receive you?" the lady went on as she
put a sweet into her mouth.

On another occasion during the recreation hour a lady
from the city pinched Catalina's cheek and archly said:

"Well, I hear that we are going to have a pretty little
saint in the convent very soon. You must promise to
remember me in your prayers, for I am a great sinner and
I shall count on you to get me into paradise."

Catalina was frightened. She had no wish to become a
nun and much less a saint. She remembered a number of
casual remarks to which at the time they were made she had

paid no attention. On a sudden it became clear to her that they all expected her to enter the religious life. That evening when as usual she entered the Prioress's oratory it was with a mind ill at ease. Doña Beatriz noticed that something was wrong. She was direct.

"What is the matter, child?" she asked, suddenly interrupting Catalina in what she was saying.

The girl started and flushed.

"Nothing, Reverend Mother."

"Are you afraid to tell me? Do you not know that I love you as if you were my own daughter? I was hoping you had at least a little affection for me."

Catalina burst into tears. The Prioress held out her arms in an affectionate gesture.

"Come and sit here, child, and tell me what is troubling you."

Catalina went and sat at the feet of the Prioress.

"I want to go home," she sobbed.

Doña Beatriz stiffened, but in an instant recovered herself.

"Are you not happy here, my dear? We have done all we could to make you so. You have gained the love of all."

"Their love imprisons me. I'm like a trapped hare. The nuns, the ladies, they seem to take it as a matter of course that I shall enter the convent. I don't want to."

The Prioress was seized with a sudden anger because those foolish women in their zeal had betrayed her, but she did not let a trace of it appear on her grave face. She answered gently.

"No one can wish to force you to do what should only be an act of free will under the inspiration of God. You must not blame the ladies because in the attachment they have formed for you they do not want to lose you. For my own part I will not deny that I have permitted myself to wish that Our Blessed Lady might arouse in your heart

149

the wish to become one of us in gratitude for the great mercy that has been shown you. You would be an honour and a glory to our convent. I know that not only are you humble and pious, but you have a clever head on your shoulders. Too many of our nuns, alas, fail to combine goodness with intelligence. I am an old woman, the burden of my office begins to be more than I can bear; perhaps it was a sin to indulge in idle dreams, but it would have been a great happiness to me if I could have had you by my side, with your tact, your natural kindliness and your good sense, to share my labours with me and to know that when in the fullness of time my Heavenly Father called me to Himself you would occupy my place."

She paused and waited for a reply. She gently stroked the girl's cheek.

"You are very good to me, Reverend Mother. I cannot thank you enough for your kindness. It would break my heart if you thought me ungrateful. I am unworthy of the great honour you have in mind for me."

Though in the words there was no blunt refusal of the dazzling offer, the Prioress was too clear-sighted not to see that this was what they implied. She had the sensation that along with the fear she felt in the girl there was stubbornness, and she had a notion that to try further persuasion would only increase her obstinacy. She was not beaten, but discretion suggested that for the moment retreat was wise.

"It is a matter for you to decide for yourself according to the dictates of your conscience and I am far from wishing to influence you."

"Then may I go home, Reverend Mother?"

"You are free to go whenever you like. I ask you as a favour out of respect to your confessor to stay for the period he appointed. I am sure you cannot be so unkind as to

deprive us of the charm and grace of your presence for the
few days that remain."

Catalina could do nothing but say that she would be happy
to stay. The Prioress dismissed her with a fond kiss. Once
more alone in her oratory she gave herself up to intensive
thought. She was not the woman to accept defeat. She had
a flash of impatience with Catalina, but since this was an
emotion of no profit she immediately suppressed it. Her
mind was strong and inventive and several plans suggested
themselves to her. She deliberately weighed their advantages and disadvantages. She felt herself justified in using
any means, so long as there was no sin in them, to secure
the girl's welfare in this world and salvation in the next and
at the same time to achieve an object which would bring
credit to the order. The first thing evidently was to try
whether by persuasion more efficacious than her own Catalina could not be brought to a proper state of mind. She
could think of no one more capable of doing this than Don
Blasco de Valero, Bishop of Segovia; he had performed the
miracle that had cured her, his high office was impressive,
his sanctity awe-inspiring. She sat down and wrote a letter
in which she begged him to come and see her on a matter
on which she needed his advice.

XXV

HE sent back a message to say that he would come next
day, and with a punctuality unusual in Spain presented
himself at the appointed hour. The Prioress went straight
to the point.

"I desired to see your lordship about the girl Catalina
Perez."

The Bishop took the seat Doña Beatriz offered him, but he sat on the edge of it as though unwilling to surrender to its scant comfort. He waited in silence and with downcast eyes for the Prioress to go on.

"On the advice of her confessor she has been making a retreat in our house. I have had occasion to talk with her. I have examined her character and disposition. She has a better education than many ladies of noble birth. Her manners are excellent and her behaviour exemplary. She has a very sincere devotion to Our Lady. She is in every way fitted to the religious life, and after the signal mercy which God at your hands was so gracious as to show her it seems only common gratitude on her part to devote her life to His service. She would be an ornament to our order and I should have no hesitation notwithstanding her modest extraction in admitting her to this house."

The Bishop made no reply. Without looking up he slightly inclined his head, but whether in approval or merely to indicate that he heard was not evident. The Prioress raised her eyebrows.

"The girl is young, she does not know her own mind and perhaps it is only natural that she should be attracted by the vain delights of the world. I am an ignorant and a sinful woman, I have not thought that I could speak to her with profit on the matter; it has occurred to me that it would be a worthy act on your lordship's part if you would see her and point out to her, as no one can do better than you, where her duty and at the same time her happiness lie."

Then he spoke.

"I do not choose to have commerce with women. I have made it a rule, which I have never broken, to refuse to receive their confessions."

"I am well aware of your lordship's disinclination to

have any dealings with my sex, but this is an exceptional case. You brought her back to life, you cannot leave her now to endanger her soul for want of a word of admonition. It is as though you had saved a man from drowning and then left him to perish of cold and hunger on the shore."

"If she has no vocation for a religious life it can be no duty of mine to urge her to enter upon it."

"Your lordship must know that many women have done so on account of a bereavement, because for one cause or another it has been impossible to marry them suitably, or even because of a disappointment in love. It has not prevented them from becoming excellent nuns."

"I have no doubt of it, and I am bound to believe that God on occasion dashes the cup from the lips of the worldly in order to call them to His service, but in the case of this girl there is no reason to suppose that any of the grounds you have mentioned exist. I venture to remind Your Reverence that it is no less possible to achieve salvation in the world than in a convent."

"But more difficult and less safe. Why should Our Blessed Lady have granted you the power to work this miracle to her glory unless with the design of causing this girl's light to shine before all men and lead them to repentance?"

"It is not for us, sinful creatures, to inquire into the motives of God Almighty."

"But at least we may be sure that they are good."

"We may."

Doña Beatriz was none too well pleased with the Bishop's laconic brevity. She was more accustomed to an effusive volubility in those with whom she troubled to converse. There was some sharpness in her tone when she went on.

"It is a very small return I ask for the favour and protection my family has always afforded your order. Will you

153

refuse my request to see this girl, examine her disposition, and if you form as high an opinion of it as I have, show her where her true happiness lies?"

The Bishop at last raised his eyes, not to meet those of the Prioress, but to gaze out of the window; it looked on to the garden, but in his preoccupation he saw neither the tall cypresses with which it was planted nor the oleanders in full flower.

He was puzzled by her insistence. He could not believe that this hard, proud woman had no more at heart than the welfare of a little sempstress. What was it that the Prior of the convent in which he was staying had told him about her? She had fought tooth and nail to prevent Mother Teresa of Jesus from founding a convent at Castel Rodriguez. The hatred the Carmelites of the old order bore for those of the new was common knowledge. A suspicion formed itself in his mind that it was for some reason connected with this that Doña Beatriz was trying to induce Catalina to enter the convent; and if she wished to enlist his aid it was because the girl was unwilling. He looked now for the first time at the Prioress and his dark, tragic eyes sought to pierce her innermost thoughts. She bore his gaze with a haughty composure.

"Supposing I saw this young person and came to the conclusion that it was my duty with God's help to persuade her to enter the life of a religious, I should be inclined to think that she would be more at her ease in a convent of the Discalced Carmelites than in this house of noble ladies."

The sudden flash of anger, immediately effaced, that he saw in the eyes of Doña Beatriz told him that he had hit upon something approaching the truth.

"It would be hard on the girl's mother to separate her entirely from her only child," answered the Prioress blandly. "The Discalced Carmelites have no house in this city."

"Only, if I am correctly informed, because Your Reverence persuaded the Bishop to refuse Mother Teresa of Jesus permission to make a foundation here."

"There are already too many convents in the city. La Cepeda would not accept an endowment, so that her community would have been a charge on the city which can ill afford it."

"Your Reverence speaks of a very holy woman with small respect."

"She was a woman of very humble origins."

"You are mistaken, Señora. She was of noble birth."

"Nonsense," said the Prioress sharply. "Her father received his patent of nobility early this century. You must forgive me if I have no more patience than our late revered King with these people who without any justification assume a rank to which they are not entitled. The country is swarming with this gutter nobility."

This was the order to which the Bishop himself belonged, and he smiled faintly.

"Whatever her extraction, it can hardly be denied that Mother Teresa was a pious woman, who received many graces from on high, and whose labours in the cause of religion are worthy of the highest praise."

Doña Beatriz was too angry to notice that the Bishop was watching every expression of her face, every impatient gesture of her delicate hands.

"Your lordship must permit me to disagree with you. I knew her and had occasion to talk with her. She was an unquiet and restless creature who went about amusing herself with crazy pranks under a pretext of religion. What business had she to leave her convent and to the scandal of her fellow citizens found a new one? There were good and holy nuns at the Incarnation and the Rule was severe."

This Rule, instituted by St. Albert and mitigated by Pope Eugenius IV, ordained fasting from the Feast of the Exaltation of the Holy Cross in September till Christmas on four days a week, and in Advent and Lent prohibited the eating of meat. Each nun had to take a scourging on Monday, Wednesday and Friday, and silence had to be observed from Compline until Prime. The habits were black and shoes were worn. The beds were without linen sheets.

"I must be a very stupid woman," continued the Prioress, "but I cannot see how it conduces to greater spirituality to wear rope sandals rather than leather shoes nor why it is to the glory of God to wear habits of sack-cloth rather than of serge. La Cepeda pretended she broke away from our ancient order so that she might have greater opportunity for mental prayer and contemplation, and yet she spent her whole life gadding about from place to place. She enjoined silence on her nuns and was the greatest chatterbox I ever met in my life."

"If Your Reverence would read the life she wrote of herself you would surely be moved to regard that saintly creature with greater indulgence," said the Bishop icily.

"I have read it. It was sent me by the Princess of Eboli. It is no business of women to write books; they should leave that to men who have more learning and a better understanding."

"Mother Teresa of Jesus wrote it in obedience to her confessor."

The Prioress smiled grimly.

"Is it not remarkable that her confessor never ordered her to do anything but what she had already made up her mind to do?"

"I regret that Your Reverence should think so harshly

156

of a woman who won the affection and esteem not only of her nuns but of everyone who was privileged to come into contact with her."

"She divided and threatened to destroy our ancient order with her innovations and it is impossible for me not to believe that she was actuated by ambition and spite."

"Your Reverence is undoubtedly aware that owing to the duly-attested miracles she performed during her life and the miracles that have been performed by her intercession since her death many influential and worthy persons are already urging His Holiness to declare her blessed."

"I am aware of it."

"And am I right in supposing that your reason for desiring the girl Catalina Perez to enter your order is that you have conceived the foolish notion that the notoriety which now surrounds her may in some way counterbalance the fame the Discalced Carmelites would acquire if their founder were beatified?"

If the Prioress was startled by the Bishop's discernment no sign of it appeared on her face.

"We have had enough saints in our order to maintain our equanimity if His Holiness should be so misguided by interested persons and superstitious nuns as to confer such an honour on a mischievous rebel."

"You have not answered my question, madam."

Doña Beatriz was too proud to lie.

"I should not look upon my life as misspent if in all humility I were enabled to help an aspiring soul to so great a perfection that she became worthy to join the company of saints. I could only look upon it as a good if she were thus enabled to undo the harm caused by Teresa de Cepeda. If you will not help me to do what I am assured is a meritorious service to a poor soul struggling with uncertainty I must help myself."

The Bishop looked at her long and sternly.

"It is my duty to remind Your Reverence that to compel anyone against his will to enter a religious institution is a crime which incurs a special censure and excommunication *latae sententiae*."

The Prioress went deathly white, not with fear at the dreadful threat, but with anger that he should venture to make it, and yet it sent a cold shiver down her spine. For the first time in her life she felt the domination of the male. She maintained an offended silence. The Bishop rose to his feet and with the customary expressions of courtesy took his leave. She bowed her head in haughty acknowledgment, but remained seated in her chair.

XXVI

SHE took part in the offices of the day with decorum, but it may be surmised with a distracted mind. She had no intention of abandoning her project and had already considered what to do if the Bishop refused to use his persuasion and authority to help her. Though she thought it would be to the advantage and glory of her order that Catalina should enter religion in the convent her father had founded, she was sincerely convinced that it would be also to the girl's welfare and to the edification of the faithful. The Prioress very well knew that the only real obstacle was the unfortunate attachment the foolish creature had contracted for the young tailor called Diego. It made her impatient to think that for such a trifling reason Catalina should be willing to forgo the great advantages, both here and hereafter, which the religious life offered her. But a wise person takes things as they are, and knowing the conditions proceeds to deal with them in such a manner as to achieve the desired result.

First, then, the Prioress sent for her mistress of novices. This nun, Doña Ana de San José, was discreet, intelligent and reliable, and she had the interests of the convent at heart. Her devotion to the Prioress was such, her obedience so perfect, that if she had ordered her to throw herself into a river she would have done so without a moment's hesitation. The Prioress began by asking her what opinion she had formed of Catalina. Doña Ana sang her praises. She was devout, obedient, kindly and helpful. She had fallen into the conventual life as though she were made for it.

"It is a pity that her modest extraction prevents her from joining our little community."

"God is no respecter of persons," said Doña Beatriz gravely. "In His sight there is no difference between the nobly and the basely born. If the girl has the proper disposition that is a difficulty that may be overcome. There is no reason why the rule my father made should not be changed by my brother if the circumstances are exceptional."

"Your daughters would welcome her as a companion."

"It would be a source of satisfaction to me to number her among the worthy women over whom by God's will I have the direction."

The Prioress paused for a while to consider her words. Then she suggested to Doña Ana that it would be a good thing to spread it among the nuns, the lady boarders, *damas de piso* they were called, and among the visitors that she was prepared to accept Catalina as a novice. After the wonderful occurrence that had brought her a fame that would in due course become known throughout Spain it was natural that she should wish to embrace the religious life, and it would be a glory to the city that she should dwell in their midst and by her prayers acquire for it the special favour of the

Deity. It would surely require more strength of will than a simple girl could be expected to have, to withstand the pressure of public opinion and to refuse the approbation, the admiration even, with which her decision to abandon the world, with its transitory pleasures, would be received. But Doña Beatriz was a practical woman and she was aware that practical advantages also have their weight. She instructed the obedient nun to see Maria Perez, tell her the good impression she, the Prioress, had formed of her daughter's virtue and aptitude, and what in consequence she was prepared to do for her. She knew that she could trust Doña Ana to make Maria Perez understand how great an honour was thus conferred on her daughter, an honour that would redound to her credit, and how much better a life, materially as well as spiritually, it would offer Catalina than if she married a poor man's son who might well turn out an idler, a drunkard and a gambler. Finally Doña Beatriz told the nun to say that she herself would pay the dowry which was necessary òn entering the religious life, and since Maria Perez was growing old and without her daughter's help might find herself in straitened circumstances she would be pleased to give her a pension large enough to keep her in comfort, without the necessity of working, for the rest of her life.

The offers were so handsome that Doña Ana was filled with admiration for her superior's charity and munificence. That wonderful woman forgot nothing. The Prioress dismissed her with the injunction to choose a suitable moment to deliver the message and to impress upon Maria Perez the need of absolute secrecy, for she had an inkling that if she talked about it to her brother, the dissolute Domingo, he might be wicked enough to persuade her to refuse her consent.

The mistress of novices executed the commission with

160

dispatch and dexterity and within twenty-four hours was able to tell Doña Beatriz that Maria Perez had received her generous offers with humility and gratitude. Being a Spanish woman, and the age devout, she had no doubt that to serve God in a religious house was the worthiest life anyone could adopt. To have a daughter who was a nun, a son who was a monk, was an honour to a family, and gave it, moreover, as it were a claim on the indulgence of God. But such a distinction as to have a daughter of hers an inmate of a house of noble ladies was something she had never dreamt of. She had a little flutter of pride when her visitor told her that already they looked upon Catalina as a little saint, and half jokingly, for she was a merry, good-natured creature, that if she went on as she had begun, if the Blessed Virgin continued to show her favour, there was no reason why Maria Perez should not one day be the mother of a virgin canonized by the Pope. Then they would paint pictures of Catalina which would be placed over altars and people would come from far and near to be healed of their maladies by touching her relics. It was a prospect dazzling enough to inflame any woman's ambition. Nor was Maria Perez insensible to the pension that was offered to her; the work by which she earned her living was laborious and cruel to the fingers, and it would be wonderful to have nothing to do from morning till night but to go to church and sit at her window watching the passers-by.

"Did she say anything about this young man who, I seem to have heard, has been paying Catalina some attention?" asked the Prioress, when she had listened with satisfaction to the nun's report.

"She doesn't like him. She says he behaved very badly when the poor child had her accident. She thinks he is selfish and has much too good an opinion of himself."

"It would be difficult to find a man who does not suffer from both of those defects," said the Prioress dryly. "It is their nature to be selfish and conceited."

"And she does not like his mother. It appears that when Maria's husband ran away to America the young man's mother told people that it served her right because she led him a dog's life."

"I dare say she did. That is the sort of life most women lead their husbands. Did you happen to suggest to her that she would be wise to let Catalina know, as though it came from herself, how much she would approve of her deciding to enter religion?"

"I thought there was no harm in it."

"On the contrary. You have done very well, Doña Ana, and I am pleased with your intelligent conduct of this matter."

The nun flushed with pleasure. Doña Beatriz was more apt to chide than to praise.

XXVII

THE Prioress allowed a few days to elapse so that the news might be spread that if Catalina was moved by the spirit of God to take the veil she would be received into the convent of the Carmelites. It was received with gratification. There was a general agreement that such a step would redound to the glory of the city and it was eminently fitting that the girl should take it. It was scarcely decent that the recipient of such a prodigious grace should become the wife of a tailor. The mistress of novices accomplished her particular mission with success. She saw Maria Perez again and warned her to deal tactfully with her daughter, not to press her, but when occasion arose to compare the peace and security of a religious life with the dangers, hardships and toils of the married state.

Doña Beatriz had the gift of gaining the devotion and loyalty of her dependants, and of these none was more loyal and devoted than the steward of the convent's properties and her own estates. He was a gentleman, Don Miguel de Becedas by name, and a distant connection of the Prioress's. He knew her bounty, for he administered her charities, and he admired her capacity. She was a good business woman and could drive as hard a bargain as any man. She was prepared to listen to reason, but having once made up her mind never changed it. When this happened there was nothing for it but to obey her, and this Don Miguel was prepared to do blindly. She sent for him and instructed him to make searching inquiries, both in the city and in Madrid, into the antecedents and present circumstances of Don Manuel de Valero, the soldier, and at the same time to find out all that was to be known about the young man Diego Martinez and his father.

By the time Don Miguel brought back the required information the Prioress had sent Catalina home with a handsome present and with the assurance of her unfailing affection. Catalina bade her farewell with tears in her eyes.

"Do not forget, child, that if ever you are in trouble or in any sort of difficulty you have only to come to see me and I will do everything in my power to help you."

Doña Beatriz listened attentively to everything the steward had to tell her and was well pleased with the results of his investigations. She then asked him to make an opportunity to see Don Manuel and in the course of a casual conversation tell him that she would be glad to receive a man of whom she had heard so much good.

After the fiasco in the Collegiate Church Don Manuel

had shut himself up in his apartments for three days and refused to see anyone. He was vain and thus sensitive to ridicule. He knew too well the mocking spirit of his compatriots and was fully aware that they were making merry at his expense. He did not think anyone would venture to make an allusion to his misadventure to his face, for he was a good swordsman and it would be a brave man who would risk being run through the body for the sake of a quip, but he could not prevent them from talking behind his back. When at last he ventured to show himself in company there was a truculence in his manner that served as ample warning to those present. He was angry, moreover, not only because he had made a fool of himself, but because he had jeopardized his prospects. His intention in coming to Castel Rodriguez, as perhaps the reader will remember, was to find in one of the noble but impoverished families of the place a girl to marry, and he had good reason to think that his handsome fortune would make him an acceptable suitor. But the public humiliation to which he had been exposed greatly reduced his chances. The nobility of the city were proud, pride in those hard times was all they had left them, and they would refuse the hand of one of their daughters to a man who was a common laughing-stock. It looked to Don Manuel as though the only thing left him was to go to Madrid, hoping the lamentable story had not reached it, and see whether he could not find there a suitable bride.

He was not a little surprised when Don Miguel brought him the Prioress's courteous message, and flattered, for it had never occurred to him that she would deign to receive him. She belonged to a world so much above his that she might have been an inhabitant of another planet. Don Manuel said he would look upon it as an honour to be allowed to pay his respects to the Prioress at whatever time was convenient to her. The steward replied that she saw few persons who were not members of her family, and mentioned an hour when her numerous duties left her free.

"I will come and fetch you tomorrow, Señor, if it suits you, and take you to the convent myself," he said.

It suited Don Manuel very well.

He was ushered into the oratory and left alone with the great lady. She was at her table writing and did not rise to receive him. He looked about for a chair to sit on, but as she did not invite him to take one remained somewhat awkwardly standing. Though a bold, impudent man, he was awed by her dignity. She addressed him with graciousness.

"I have heard much, sir, of the courage, devotion and capacity with which for so many years you have served His Majesty the King, and I was curious to see a fellow citizen who has by his own efforts raised himself to such distinction. I was hoping that you would find time to visit me so that I might congratulate you personally on your great exploits."

"I never dreamed that I might without offence intrude upon your privacy, madam," he stammered.

But he began to feel more at his ease. If the daughter of the great Duke of Castel Rodriguez paid him compliments his state could not be so desperate after all. But her next remark, though made with a smile, somewhat disconcerted him.

"You have gone a long way, Don Manuel, since you were a little barefoot boy running about the streets of your village and tending your father's swine."

He flushed, but not knowing what to answer, held his tongue. Doña Beatriz looked him up and down for all the world as though he were a lackey she was about to engage. If she noticed his embarrassment she was not concerned with it. She saw a well-set-up man, not unpleasing in appearance, with an erect carriage and an air of virility. She knew his age; it was forty-five, but he carried his years well. He was a little taller than his brother the Bishop, who was not a small man, and though his bones were well covered he was far from fat. His eyes were handsome, and though there was some brutality in his face, that was natural enough in a man who had been so long at the wars, and it did not particularly offend the Prioress who had no patience with a milksop. He was doubtless arrogant, boastful and licentious, but these were defects common to her own relations, and though as a religious she deplored them, as a woman she accepted them as masculine traits with the same resignation as she accepted the biting cold of the Castilian winter. Altogether the first impression Don Manuel made on her was not unfavourable.

She appeared for the first time to notice that he was still on his feet.

"Why do you stand, Senor?" she asked. "Will you not do me the favour of taking a seat?"

"You are very good, madam."

He sat down.

"I live a very retired life and my religious duties combined with the business of my office keep me fully occupied, but nevertheless from time to time a scrap of news reaches me from the world outside these walls. I have heard, for instance, that apart from performing a filial duty your object in visiting your native place was to choose a wife from among the noble families of this city."

"After serving my King and country for so many years it is true that I have the desire to make a home for myself and enjoy the delights of domesticity of which I have been hitherto deprived."

"Your desire is praiseworthy, Señor, and increases the

166

esteem in which owing to your reputation I already hold you."

"I am strong and active, and my fortune is considerable. I cannot but think that such talents as I am possessed of will be as useful at Court as they have proved to be in battle."

"And if I understand you, you are aware that a wife with intelligence and important connections can be of service to you there."

"I will not deny it, madam."

"I have a widowed niece, the Marquesa de Caranera, whose husband has unfortunately left her very ill provided for. She is at present living in this house. I had hoped that she would be moved to adopt the life of a religious so that when at last I lay down my arduous functions she might succeed me, as indeed, being the granddaughter of our founder, she would be entitled to. But she lacks the vocation, so I have come to the conclusion that a suitable marriage should be arranged for her."

Don Manuel was suddenly alert. But he was a shrewd man; the possibility of being allied with so great a family as that of the Duke of Castel Rodriguez was so far beyond his hopes that he could not but suspect some chicanery. He answered with prudence.

"I had not envisaged marrying a widow, but rather a young girl whom I could form to my liking."

"The Marquesa is twenty-four, which is a very suitable age for a man of your years," the Prioress replied somewhat sharply. "She is not lacking in beauty, and since she had a son by her husband, who died of the same distemper as carried off his father, she is certainly not barren. The fact that I intended her to be Prioress of this convent after my death proves that I have a high opinion of her ability. I need not point out to you that a Don Manuel de Valero could never have aspired to marry the niece of the Duke of Castel Rodriguez. I should in fact have to use all my powers of persuasion to induce my brother to consent to it."

Don Manuel had been thinking quickly. With the influence of that powerful family behind him there was no knowing to what heights he might rise. To make such a marriage would be to triumph over the fools who had held him up to ridicule.

"The Marquis of Caranera died without heirs to his title. I do not think it impossible that the King might be persuaded to grant it to you. It would be more suitable than this wretched Italian title which you now have."

That clinched it. Though the Marquesa was old, ten years older than the bride he had desired, and might be homely, the advantages of marrying her were too great for him to hesitate.

"I don't know how to show Your Reverence my gratitude for the honour you propose to confer on me."

"I will tell you," she said coolly, "and indeed it is only if you show your gratitude efficiently that I propose to enter into the matter further."

Don Manuel smothered a sigh of relief. He was far too astute not to know that this unexpected suggestion was made to him for a better reason than his wealth and his military reputation. Being a coarse man, the idea flashed across his mind that the Marquesa was pregnant and he had been chosen to father an illegitimate child. He would hardly know then whether to accept or decline the invitation, and he waited with some anxiety for Doña Beatriz to continue.

"I desire to enlist your influence on behalf of a young man of this city with the Archduke Albert. I should have no need to do this but for the unfortunate fact that my brother has had a violent quarrel with him and so cannot help me. I have been given to understand that you stand high in the Archduke's favour."

"He has been good enough to think well of my capacity."

The Archduke Albert, it should be explained, was at that time commander-in-chief of the Spanish forces in the Low Countries.

"It would be to this young man's advantage to enter the Archduke's service. He is strong and brave and would certainly make a good soldier."

Don Manuel was much relieved. The Archduke was in various ways indebted to him. He would surely be glad to oblige him by taking into his service anyone in whom he was interested.

"I think there would be no difficulty in effecting Your Reverence's desire. The young man is presumably of good family."

"He is an Old Christian of pure blood."

This of course only meant that there was no taint in him of Jew or Moor. Don Manuel noticed that the answer did not meet his question.

"And what, madam, is the young man's name?"

"Diego Martinez."

"The tailor's son? Then, madam, what you ask is impossible. The soldiers serving in the Archduke's army are gentlemen, and I could not put such an affront on His Highness as to make the request you wish."

"I have foreseen that difficulty. I have a small estate some miles from this city which I am prepared to settle on the young man, and through my brother I can get letters of nobility given to him. You would recommend to the Archduke not the tailor's son but the hidalgo Don Diego de Quintamilla."

"I cannot do it, Your Reverence."

"In that case there is nothing more to be said, and further

discussion is useless on the matter or on that I previously mentioned."

Don Manuel was a worried man. The marriage that the Prioress had proposed would give him the position that he hankered after to further his ambition and he had an inkling that if he refused to accede to her request he would make a dangerous enemy. On the other hand the consequences might be unfortunate to him if it were discovered that he had lent himself to a plan which the Archduke might very well regard as a personal insult. Doña Beatriz discerned his trouble.

"You are a fool, Don Manuel. Don Diego will be a man of property and, believe me, his estate will compare not unfavourably with the barren acres belonging to your father Don Juan."

Don Manuel was something of a bully. He cringed under the lash of the Prioress's tongue. She could ruin him and would not hesitate to do it.

"May I ask why Your Reverence takes an interest in this young man?" he asked hesitantly.

"My family have always looked upon it as a privilege as well as a duty to advance the fortunes of deserving persons in this city."

The guarded answer so far restored his confidence that he smiled, but his glance was shrewd.

"He is the lover of the girl Catalina Perez?"

Doña Beatriz was affronted by the question, his smile and the shrewdness of his glance. She had some difficulty in outwardly controlling her indignation.

"He has been pestering the unhappy girl with his attentions."

"And is that why you wish him sent to the Low Countries?"

The Prioress considered for a moment. It was probable that he knew the circumstances and it was evident that he

170

was a tactless fellow. There were many things that could be understood, but which it was better not to put into words. She answered him, however, with an impressive dignity.

"The girl is young and does not know her own mind. She has admirable dispositions for the life of a religious and there are many reasons which make it highly desirable that she should adopt it. I have no doubt that were it not for the presence of this young man she would soon see the advisability of taking a step which would give so much satisfaction to myself, to the most important personages in the city, and to her mother."

"But, madam, would it not be more expeditious and less costly to dispose of the young man on the spot? It would be very easy to have his throat cut one dark night."

"It would be a mortal sin, sir, and I am shocked that you should venture to propose it. It would make a scandal in the city, give rise to unpleasant gossip, and there is no certainty that it would achieve the desired result."

"Then what would you have me do, madam?"

She looked at him reflectively. For the present at least she felt it necessary to her plan that neither she nor anyone connected with her should be known to be concerned in it; she had to entrust its execution to someone else, and she was not sure that this man had the necessary intelligence or subtlety. She had to risk that, and she answered without further hesitation.

"Order a suit of clothes."

Don Manuel was so surprised that, thinking she must be jesting, he looked for a smile to hover on her decided lips. Her face was grim. She explained.

"Send for the tailor to take your measurements and to bring samples of materials. He will be flattered and impressed. You must make an opportunity to talk to him about his son and tell him that a person of consequence in the city has heard good reports of him and wishes to advance him. Then, binding him to secrecy, disclose to him the plan suggested for the boy's welfare. Let him send the young man to you on some pretext and put it before him. I am assured he looks upon himself as born for better things than to sit on a tailor's bench, and he will without doubt accept with alacrity."

"He will be a great fool if he doesn't."

"Let me see you again when you have something to tell me. I trust you to be discreet and tactful."

"Never fear, madam. In two days at the utmost I shall be able to inform you that the business is satisfactorily concluded."

"You may rest assured that in that case I shall perform my part to your satisfaction."

XXVIII

DON MANUEL sent for the tailor. He could be very affable when he chose, and when his measurements had been taken and various materials examined he set himself to be so. As natives of the same city they had certain common interests and Don Manuel talked to him good-humouredly of the changes that had taken place in it during his long absence. The tailor was a little dried-up man with a sharp nose and a querulous expression. But he was garrulous. Finding in Don Manuel a sympathetic listener he enlarged upon the hard times. The wars and the heavy taxation had impoverished everyone, and even gentlemen of the highest rank were content to wear their clothes till they were threadbare. It was not so easy to make a good living then as it had been thirty years before when the caravels were arriving regularly with their cargo of gold from America. A few well-directed questions brought out the fact that he was worried about his son. It was only right that he should follow in his father's footsteps, but the boy had silly ideas and it had required the exercise of parental authority to force him to go into the business.

"And now, if you please, though he's only eighteen, he wants to marry."

"That may settle him."

"That is the only reason I have consented."

"And I have no doubt the money of the girl's dowry will be useful," said Don Manuel archly.

"She has no money. There is some talk that certain ladies are prepared to give her a dowry, but how do I know that it will come to anything?"

The tailor then proceeded to tell Don Manuel who the girl was and how it had come about that he had at last yielded to his son's insistence, all of which of course Don Manuel knew already.

"I had another match in view for him, but the young person's father would not accept my very reasonable conditions, so I agreed to let the boy marry Catalina. After all that has happened and the notice that has been taken of her, I think it will bring me a nice lot of custom. My wife blames me. She asks what is the use of making clothes for gentlemen who can't afford to pay for them."

"A very sensible remark. But if business is so bad why don't you let your son go for a soldier?"

"The life is hard and ill paid. In the shop he can still earn enough to keep body and soul together."

"Listen, friend," replied Manuel with a frankness that charmed the poor tailor, "you know that when I left this city I was as poor as a church mouse. Now I am a Knight of Calatrava and a rich man."

"Ah, but Your Excellency was a gentleman and had friends to help you."

"A gentleman, yes, but the only friends I had to count on were my youth, my strength, my courage and my intelligence."

The tailor shrugged his shoulders despondently. Don Manuel from his greater height looked down upon him with benignity.

"I have heard nothing but good of your son, and if what they tell me is true I cannot but suppose he is fitted for better things than you think. I too have been poor; we are citizens of the same town; I should be glad to give the boy a helping hand if I were sure it met with your approval."

"I don't think I understand you, Señor."

"The Archduke Albert is my friend and will do anything for me. If I recommended a young man to him he would put him in his own regiment and would mark him out for advancement."

The tailor looked at him with gaping mouth.

"Of course we should have to provide him with certain advantages. There is a small estate not far from here of which I would give him the deeds, and with my influence in Madrid I can see that he gets letters of nobility. Your son will enter the service of the Archduke as Don Diego de Quintamilla."

Since the Prioress had told him that she did not wish her name to be mentioned Don Manuel saw no reason why he should not himself get what credit he could from a generous action. The tailor was so overwhelmed that his face twitched and he began to cry. Don Manuel kindly patted his shoulder.

"There, there, it's nothing to make a fuss about. Go home now, say nothing of this to anyone, and send your son to me. You can tell him that you forgot to bring me a pattern of some stuff you think I may like."

In a little while the boy came. Don Manuel noticed with relief that he was a youth of pleasing exterior. Suitably dressed he would certainly pass as a gentleman. He was neither pert nor shy. There was a confidence in his bearing which promised that he would be able to hold his own in any company. Already predisposed in his favour, after a few preliminary remarks Don Manuel broached the subject on account of which he had had Diego sent. They talked for an hour, after which they parted and Don Manuel went to see the Prioress.

"I have wasted no time in obeying your commands, madam," he said. "I have seen both the boy and his father."

"You have indeed been prompt, Señor."

"I am a soldier, madam. The father is in full accord with our plan. He is indeed overwhelmed by the opportunity that the kindness of a benefactor proposes to give his son."

"He would be a fool to be anything else."

Don Manuel moved uneasily from one foot to the other.

"I had better tell Your Reverence word for word what passed between me and the boy."

The Prioress gave him a quick look of inquiry and slightly frowned.

"Go on."

"He is a very presentable lad and my first impression was good."

"Your impressions do not interest me."

"I very soon discovered that he dislikes and despises the trade to which his father has put him. He has only adopted it because there was no help for it."

"That I already knew."

175

"I told him that I could not understand how a young man of spirit and intelligence, endowed with all the qualities necessary for success in the world, could think of wasting his life in a humble occupation. He answered that he had often thought of running away to seek adventure, but was held back by the fact that he hadn't a penny in his pocket. I then told him that the King wanted soldiers and that it was a career that might easily lead a man of courage and resource to position and wealth. After that I disclosed to him little by little exactly what was proposed to enable him to achieve his natural and laudable ambition."

"Very good."

"He took the prospect more calmly than I expected, but it was evident that it tempted him."

"Naturally. He accepted then?"

Don Manuel hesitated briefly, for he knew that what he had to say would not satisfy Doña Beatriz.

"Conditionally," he answered.

"What d'you mean by that?"

"He said he wanted to marry his sweetheart, but in a year, when she'd had a baby, he wouldn't be unwilling to go to the Low Countries."

The Prioress was enraged. What use could she make of a married woman with a squalling brat? Catalina's virginity, her perpetual virginity, was essential to her purpose.

"You've bungled the whole thing, you fool," she cried.

Don Manuel flushed angrily.

"Is it my fault if the young idiot is head over ears in love with this girl?"

"Hadn't you the sense to tell him that it was madness to refuse such an opportunity?"

"Yes, madam, I had. I told him that in this life when you get a chance to better yourself you must take it and take

it quickly, because if you let it slip it may never come again.
I told him that it was absurd at his age to hamper himself
with a wife and that as an officer and a gentleman he could
in due course do much better for himself than the penniless
daughter of a sewing-woman. And if he wanted a girl to
amuse himself with he would find plenty in the Low
Countries who would be delighted to oblige a good-looking
young man and not a few who would be prepared to show
their gratitude in a substantial manner."

"And what did he say to that?"

"He said he loved his sweetheart."

"No wonder the world is in a mess and the country is
going to the dogs when it's governed by men, and men
haven't the elements of common sense."

Don Manuel did not know what to say to this and so said
nothing. The Prioress gave him a look of cold disdain.

"You have failed, Don Manuel, and I can see no profit
in our further communication."

He was acute enough to see that with these words she
intimated to him that he need no longer entertain the hope
of marrying the widowed marchioness. He was not prepared to give up the chance of so advantageous an alliance
without a struggle.

"Your Reverence is easily discouraged. The boy's father
is on our side. He does not like the idea of Diego marrying
the girl Catalina and I have no doubt that I can get him to
withdraw his consent. You can be sure that he will use
every effort to persuade the boy to accept our proposition."

Doña Beatriz made an impatient gesture.

"You know little about human nature, Señor. Parental
opposition has never made lovers love one another less.
That is not the frame of mind in which I should be prepared
to accept the girl in this house. If the boy had fallen in with
my proposal she would have seen how worthless is a man's

love compared with the love of God. She would have been unhappy, but I should not have regretted it if it taught her where the only real happiness may be found."

"There are more ways than one of being rid of a troublesome fellow. I have men I can trust. The boy can be seized one night, taken to a sea port and put on a ship. Youth is fickle. Once in the Low Countries, with new sights to see, adventures to be encountered, with the standing of a gentleman and by the Archduke's favour brilliant prospects, he will forget his love and in a short while thank his stars that he has been saved from an unfortunate entanglement."

The Prioress did not answer for a while. She was a woman of robust conscience and the plan Don Manuel suggested did not outrage her. Unruly sons were often packed off to America just as daughters, unwilling to accede to their parents' matrimonial designs, were placed in a convent until they were prepared to listen to reason. She was fully convinced that to part Diego from Catālina was to the advantage of both of them.

"Your Reverence may be certain that the boy will tell Catalina of the offer that has been made him."

"Why?"

"To make himself more precious in her sight by showing her what advantages he is prepared to forgo for her sake."

"You are shrewder than I took you for, Señor."

"When he is missing one morning she will naturally suppose that he found himself unable to resist the temptation."

"That is probable enough. There is still his father to consider. It would not do if he made trouble with the authorities."

"So that he should not do that I propose to take him into my confidence. He is ambitious for his son. He will agree to the plan without hesitation. He will hold his tongue, and by the time the boy's absence is noticed he will be safely aboard a ship."

The Prioress sighed.

"I do not like the plan, but it is evident that the young are foolish and it is often better that their fate should be decided by older and wiser heads. I should require to be assured that no unnecessary violence would be used on the boy."

"I can promise Your Reverence that no harm shall come to him. I will have him accompanied by a man I can rely on to see that he is well treated."

"It will be to your interest," she said grimly.

"Of that I am fully aware, madam. You can safely leave everything in my hands."

"When do you propose to act?"

"As soon as I can make the necessary arrangements."

For a moment Doña Beatriz was silent. It was evident that Diego's disappearance would give rise to gossip and it was not unlikely that it would reach the Bishop's ears. She had experienced his perspicacity. He might very well put two and two together and come to the conclusion that she was concerned in the matter. She bitterly regretted that during their interview she had been led by anger to speak without discretion. She did not quite know what he could do, but he was a determined man, and a powerful; she was not frightened of him, but was wise enough to see that it was better to avoid an open breach which would not only cause scandal but might also frustrate her design.

"When does your brother leave the city, Don Manuel?" she asked.

The question surprised him.

"I do not know, Your Reverence, but if it interests you I can inquire."

"I do not wish anything to be done till after his departure."

"Why?"

"Because it is my pleasure. Let it be enough for you to know that such is my desire."

"It shall be as you will, madam. The boy shall be taken on the night of the day on which my brother leaves the city."

"That will do very well, Don Manuel," she said graciously.

She gave him her hand to kiss as he took his leave.

XXIX

BUT though her reason assured her that she was acting for the best and was fully justified, Doña Beatriz could not dispel the peculiar uneasiness that possessed her. It was so compelling that once or twice she was in mind to tell Don Manuel to abandon his scheme. But she chid herself for her weakness. Much was at stake. Yet she fretted and her nuns found her unaccountably irritable. Then one morning the sub-prioress informed her that the Bishop had gone. To avoid attention he had slipped away at crack of dawn with his secretaries and servants. An hour later Don Manuel conveyed a message to her that arrangements were complete and the plan would be carried into effect that night. That settled it. She examined her conscience and knew that her intention was blameless.

Towards evening she was told that Catalina was asking to be allowed to see her. She was shown into the oratory. The Prioress noticed with dismay that she was violently agitated. She guessed that something had gone wrong.

"What is it, my child?" she asked.

180

"Your Reverence told me that if ever I was in trouble
I could come to you."

She burst into tears. Doña Beatriz told her to calm herself and tell her what had happened. Sobbing, the girl told
her that a principal gentleman of the city had offered to
send Diego to the wars, with the promise of giving him
an estate and getting the title of Don for him. He had
refused for love of her and in consequence had had a violent
quarrel with his father. His father had said at last that if
he did not accept these magnificent offers as any sensible
man would, if he did not go peacefully he should go by
force, and added that he withdrew his consent to his
marriage with Catalina. The Prioress frowned when she
heard of the threat. The man was a fool to have made it.
Now if Diego disappeared the girl would know that it was
not of his own free will. The Prioress had counted on the
effect it would have on her if she thought that he had
succumbed to temptation and abandoned her.

"He could never have hoped for such good fortune,"
she said. "It is a chance no young man would hesitate to
seize. Men are vain and cowardly and though they act
badly they take pains to be thought well of. How do you
know that he is not deceiving you and talking of force
being applied in order to make you think he has abandoned
you through no fault of his own?"

"How do I know? I know because he loves me. Ah,
madam, you are a saintly woman, you don't know what
love is. If I don't have my Diego I shall die."

"No one ever died of love yet," said the Prioress with a
savage bitterness.

Catalina fell to her knees and put her hands together in
passionate supplication.

"Oh, Mother, Reverend Mother, have pity on us. Save
him. Don't let them take him away. I cannot live without

him. Oh, madam, if you knew the anguish I suffered when I thought I'd lost him for ever and how night after night I cried until I thought I should go blind! Why did the Blessed Virgin cause me to be freed from my infirmity if not that I should be fit once more to be my lover's wife? She had pity on me, and will you do nothing to help me?"

The Prioress clenched her hands on the arms of her chair, but said nothing.

"All that time I longed for him. My heart was breaking. I am only a poor and ignorant girl. I have nothing in the world but my love. I love him with all my heart."

"He's nobody. He's only a boy like another," said Dona Beatriz hoarsely, so that her voice sounded like the croak of a raven.

"Ah, madam, you say that because you have never known the pain and bliss of love. I want to feel his arms round me, I want to feel the warmth of his mouth on mine, the caress of his hands on my naked body. I want him to take me as a lover takes the woman he loves. I want his seed to flow into my womb and to create the child within it. I want to suckle his child at my breast."

She put a hand to each breast and sensuality poured from her in a flame so fierce that the Prioress shrank back. It was like the heat of a furnace and she put up her hands as though to shield herself from it. She looked at the girl's face and shuddered. It was strangely changed, pale, and one might have thought the features were swollen; it was a mask of desire. She was breathless with lust for the male. She was like one possessed. There was something not quite human about her, something even slightly horrible, but so powerful that it was terrifying. It was sex, nothing but sex, violent and irresistible, sex in its awful nakedness. Suddenly the Prioress's face was contorted in a grimace, a grimace of

unendurable agony, and tears poured down her cheeks.
Catalina gave a cry of dismay.

"Oh, Mother, what have I said? Forgive me. Forgive
me."

She clasped the knees of the Prioress. She was startled
by this exhibition of emotion in one whom she had never
seen but calm, grave and dignified. She was bewildered,
She didn't know what to do. She took the thin hands in
hers and kissed them.

"Madam, why do you cry? What have I done?"

Doña Beatriz withdrew her hands and clenched them in
the effort to regain her self-control.

"I am a wicked and unhappy woman," she moaned.

She leant back in her chair and covered her face with her
hands. Memories of long ago crowded upon her and she
gritted her teeth to choke back the sobs that tore her throat.
The little fool, the silly little fool had said she had never
known love. How cruel it was that after all these years that
old wound should be so green! She gave the ghost of a bitter
chuckle as the humour of it struck her that she had eaten
her heart out for a boy who was now a wasted, haggard
priest. She brushed away the tears that dimmed her eyes
and taking Catalina's face in her hands gazed at her as
though she had never seen her before. There was no trace
now of the carnality that for an instant had so hideously
changed the comely features. She was all tenderness,
solicitude and purity. The Prioress was entranced by
her loveliness. So young, so beautiful and so passionately in love. How could she break that poor little heart
as hers had been broken? She, who thought she had conquered every human weakness, felt weak, pitifully weak,
and yet there was in the feeling something strange and
uplifting, something that warmed her heart and at the same
time, oh, so comfortingly, crippled her will; it was as though

a knot had been loosened deep within her breast, and she rejoiced to be relieved of the aching pain. She bent down and kissed the girl's red mouth.

"Have no fear, my sweet," she said. "You shall marry your lover."

Catalina gave a cry of joy and broke into voluble expressions of gratitude, but the Prioress harshly told her to be quiet. The situation was delicate and she had to think. In a few hours they were to spirit Diego away; it was true that she could send for Don Manuel and tell him that she had changed her mind; she could cut his expostulations short; but that would not solve the difficulties she had got herself into. The seed she had sown had been sown well. There was a feeling widespread in the city that it behoved Catalina to become a religious. Doña Beatriz knew well the passionate devotion the people had for the Faith; they would not only be disappointed if she did not do what was expected of her, they would look upon it as an indecency, almost as an insult to religion if after receiving such a grace she married a tailor. The worldly would laugh and make bawdy jokes; the pious would be incensed. Catalina was regarded now with admiration, even with awe, but that could easily change into indignation and contempt. The Prioress knew the violent nature of her countrymen; they were capable of burning down the house in which she lived, they were capable of stoning her as an abandoned wanton and driving a dagger into Diego's back. There was but one thing to do and that must be done quickly.

"You must leave the city, you and this boy, and you must go tonight. Fetch Domingo, your uncle, and come back here with him."

The girl, inflamed with curiosity, wanted to know what the Prioress had in mind, but the Prioress very peremptorily told her not to ask questions, but do as she was told.

When Catalina in a few minutes came back with her uncle, the Prioress sent her down to wait in her own cell so that she could speak to him alone. She told him such of the facts of the situation as she thought it needful for him to know, gave him certain instructions and with them a short note which she had already written for her steward. She then told him to get hold of Diego, let him know what had been decided, and see that he followed the directions given him. Having dismissed him she called Catalina.

"You will spend the evening with me, my child. At midnight I will let you out by a door in the city wall and you will find Domingo with a horse which I have ordered my steward to let him have. He will ride with you to a spot which has been arranged, and there Diego will be waiting. He will change places with Domingo and you are to ride South till you come to Seville. I will give you a letter to friends I have there and they will find suitable work for you and him."

"Oh, madam," cried Catalina, wild with excitement, "how can I show my gratitude for what you are doing?"

"I will tell you," answered the Prioress with some severity. "Ride fast and on no account linger on the way. You have desperate men to deal with and it may be they will pursue you. Chastity is a woman's crown, and you must preserve it till the Church has blessed your union. Intercourse between unmarried persons is a mortal sin. You will seek out a priest at the first village you come to after day-break and ask him to join you to Diego in holy matrimony. Do you see what I have here?"

Catalina looked and saw a plain gold ring.

"It is the ring I had destined for your consecration on your profession. It will be your wedding ring."

She put it on the palm of Catalina's hand. It made her

185

heart beat nineteen to the dozen. The Prioress then proceeded to instruct her on the duties and responsibilities
of married life. She listened with becoming gravity, but
with some distraction, for she was in a flutter and her mind
was more occupied with its delights. They prayed together.
The hours passed slowly. At last the convent clock struck
midnight.

"It is time," said Doña Beatriz. She took a small bag
from a drawer in her writing-table. "Here are some gold
pieces. Put the bag in a place where you are sure you will
not lose it and do not let Diego get hold of it. Men do
not know the value of money and when they have any
spend it on foolishness."

Catalina modestly turning her back pulled up her skirt,
put the bag inside her stocking, and tied the strings round
her leg.

The Prioress lit a lantern and told the girl to follow her.
They walked softly through silent passages till they came
out into the garden. Then, in case some wakeful nun
happened to see a light and wondered what it meant, she
extinguished the lantern and taking Catalina's hand led her
along the pathways. They came to the small door that the
Prioress had caused to be cut in the city wall so that if need
be she could leave the city unobserved or receive persons
whose visits for some reason had to be secret. She alone
had the key. She unlocked the door. Domingo on horseback was waiting in the shadow of the wall, for the moon
was shining and the night was bright.

"Now go," said the Prioress. "God bless you, my child,
and remember me in your prayers, for I am a sinful woman
and I need them."

Catalina slipped out of the door and the Prioress closed
and locked it behind her. She listened till she heard the
horse's hoofs. They sounded very loud in the silence of

michael
charlton

the night. Doña Beatriz with lagging steps walked back
to the convent building. She could hardly see her way, for
she was almost blinded by her tears. She returned to her
oratory and spent the rest of the night in prayer.

XXX

DOMINGO gave Catalina his hand and helped her up
on to the horse so that she could sit on the pillion
behind him. It was still and warm, but high up in the
heavens there was wind, and little clouds sped across the
sky, black but edged with the silver of the shining moon.
The countryside was deserted and they might have been
riding in a world of which they were the only habitants.

"Uncle Domingo."

"Yes?"

"I'm going to be married."

"Make quite sure of it, child. It is a sacrament necessary
to salvation, but one which men in general hesitate to avail
themselves of."

They passed a sleeping hamlet and beyond it was a clump
of trees. As they came to it a figure detached itself from
their shadow. Catalina slipped off the horse and flung
herself into Diego's arms. Domingo dismounted.

"Come, come," he said. "You'll have plenty of time for
that sort of thing later. Get on the horse both of you and be
off. There's food and a bottle of wine in the saddlebags."

He kissed Catalina and Diego, saw them start, and then,
since the city gates were shut and he could not get in till
dawn, settled himself down as comfortably as he could
under a tree. He had taken the precaution to bring wine
and he put the bottle to his mouth. It was the very place to

compose poetry and he prepared to await daybreak in commerce with the Muse. But before he had made up his mind whether to indite a sonnet to the moon or an ode to love triumphant he fell sound asleep and did not wake till sunrise.

The lovers rode for an hour and Catalina talked her head off. It seemed that she had a thousand things to say, much to tell Diego, plans to divulge, and since she had a pretty way of putting things she made it all sound very delightful and amusing. Diego was so happy he was prepared to laugh at everything she said. And she was enraptured. She could not imagine anything more like heaven than to ride through the night in the open country with her arms clasped round her lover. They had to be, of course, for that was the only way to hold on, but it was very pleasant.

"I could ride like this to the end of the world," she said.

"I'm hungry," he answered. "Let us stop here and see what is in those saddlebags."

They were passing a wood and he reined in the horse. Catalina was well aware that his appetite just then was not for food and drink, and a tremor of desire tingled down her body; but it had needed the admonitions neither of the Prioress nor of Domingo to tell her that it was very imprudent to let a man have his will of you until the Church had sanctified the union. She knew that men have an instinctive disinclination to marry and she had known cases of girls who had yielded to their lovers only to have them refuse afterwards to fulfil their promises. Then nothing was left them but the brothel.

"Let us ride on, dear," she said. "The Prioress said we might be pursued."

"I'm not frightened," he said.

He passed his leg over the horse's head and slipping to the ground lifted Catalina off the horse's back. She was in his arms and he kissed her on the eyes and on the mouth. He took hold of the bridle and with his arm still about Catalina's waist made for the wood. But at that moment a sharp shower of rain fell upon them. They were both startled, for the night had seemed fair and they had not noticed the black cloud over their heads. Now Diego was as brave as a lion and would have faced armed men with intrepidity, but he was terrified of rain. Moreover he had put on his best clothes before starting and could not bear to get them wet.

"It's not raining over there," he said, pointing a little way down to the other side of the road. "Let's run."

But they had no sooner reached the spot he indicated than the rain suddenly began to fall there too and more heavily. Diego gave an exclamation of annoyance.

"It's only a local shower," he said. "If we ride quickly we shall get out of it."

He mounted, helped Catalina up, and clapping his spurs to the horse's flanks galloped down the road. But no sooner had they got away from the wood than the rain stopped as abruptly as it had begun. He looked up at the sky. There were dark clouds behind them, but ahead the sky was blue and serene. They rode in silence. After a little while, perhaps half an hour, they came to a little copse.

"This'll do," said Diego, reining in the horse.

The words were hardly out of his mouth when a heavy drop of rain fell on his nose.

"It's nothing," he said, and once more swung his leg over the horse's head; but he had no sooner done this, he had not even got to the ground, when the drops began to fall more and more frequently. "The devil's in it."

He put his foot back in the stirrup and rode on. The rain stopped. Catalina pondered.

"It's not the devil," she said.

189

"What is it then?"

"It's the Blessed Virgin."

"You're talking nonsense, woman, and in a little while I'll prove it."

He kept a sharp look-out. For some time they did not pass a tree to which he could tie up the horse.

"I ought to have brought a rope to hobble him," said Diego.

"One can't think of everything," she answered.

"The horse ought to have a rest. It wouldn't hurt us to have a bit of sleep by the roadside."

"I couldn't sleep a wink."

"I dare say you wouldn't want to," he grinned.

"Look," she said, "it's going to rain again." And in fact several drops began to fall. "We shall only get wet through."

"A few drops of rain won't do us any harm."

As he spoke, the rain on a sudden fell heavily. He uttered a curse and spurred his horse.

"This is the strangest thing I've ever seen in my life," he said.

"Almost a miracle," she murmured.

Diego gave it up as a bad job. Though the rain stopped they were both pretty wet by then and Diego's amorous ardour was sensibly mitigated by his concern for his clothes. In extenuation it should be stated that it was not only his best but his only suit that he wore, for Domingo had told him it would be unwise to leave his home with anything but what he stood up in. They went on through the night, passing no one, but occasionally in the moonlight catching a glimpse of a farmhouse or a few cottages. At last the sun rose. They were on the top of a little hill and looking down saw in the grey dimness of dawn a small village. There sould not but be an inn there where they could get something to eat and drink, for by this time they were both quite honestly hungry and thirsty. They rode on and now encountered peasants going to work in their fields. They entered the village and suddenly the horse stopped dead.

"What's the matter with you, you brute? Get on with you," cried Diego, digging in his spurs.

The horse did not move. Diego hit him over the head with the ends of the reins and again sharply kicked him. It made no impression on the horse. He stood stock still. He might have been turned to stone.

"You shall go, you brute."

Diego was angry now and he slapped the horse's neck as hard as he could. The horse reared up on his hind legs and Catalina gave a shriek. Diego hit him on the head with his closed fist and the horse got back on to his four legs, but still nothing Diego could do got him to move a step forwards. He stood as if rooted to the ground. Diego, red in the face, was sweating profusely.

"I can't make it out. Is the devil in the horse too?" Catalina began to laugh and he turned on her furiously. "What is there to laugh at?"

"Don't be cross with me, my love. Don't you see where we are? The church."

Diego, frowning, looked and noticed for the first time that the horse had stopped in front of the church, which was on the very edge of the village.

"What of it?"

"The Prioress made me promise that we'd get married in the first church we came to. That's it."

"There's plenty of time for that later," he said.

Once more he dug his spurs savagely into the poor brute's flanks and as he did so the horse humped his back, kicked up his hind legs, and before they knew what had happened the two riders were flying through the air. Fortunately they fell on a pile of hay and so were not hurt.

191

They lay for a moment somewhat shaken and very much startled. The horse, after this strange show of spirit, stood as still as before. Just as this happened the priest, who had been saying his Mass, came out of the church and seeing the accident hurried up to see if he could be of help. They got up, shook themselves, and finding that no harm had come to them brushed off their clothes the hay that stuck to them.

"You're lucky it was there," said the priest, a short, red-faced man on the plump side. "If you had come a little later it would have been in my barn."

"It's providential that this should have occurred at the church door," said Catalina, "for we were looking for a priest to marry us."

Diego gave her a glance of surprise, but did not say anything.

"To marry you?" cried the priest. "You are no parishioners of mine. I have never seen you before. I certainly will not marry you. I have had nothing to eat since my supper yesterday evening and I am going to my house now to get some food."

"Please wait, Father," said Catalina.

She turned her back on them, raised her skirt and quickly got a gold piece out of the bag the Prioress had given her. With her bewitching smile she showed it on the palm of her hand. The priest looked at it and grew redder in the face than ever.

"But who are you?" he asked doubtfully. "Why do you want to be married in a strange place and in such a hurry?" He did not take his eyes off the glistening coin.

"Have pity on two young lovers, Father. We have run away from Castel Rodriguez because my father wanted to force me to marry a rich old man for his money; and this youth, to whom I was betrothed, was being forced by his

192

avaricious parents to marry a woman without a tooth in her head and only one eye."

To make her story more convincing Catalina put the gold piece in the priest's hand and firmly closed it upon the coin.

"You have a very persuasive manner with you, young woman," said the priest, "and your story is touching enough to bring tears to my eyes."

"You will not only be doing a meritorious deed, Father," Catalina continued, "but you will be saving two virtuous young people from committing a mortal sin."

"Follow me," said the priest and re-entered the church. "Pepe," he called in a loud voice as he proceeded towards the high altar.

"What is it?" came back.

"Come here, you idle scoundrel."

A man, broom in hand, came out from a chapel beside the sanctuary.

"Why can't you let me get my sweeping done?" he asked gruffly. "Never was a sacristan paid such a miserable wage and then you never give me a moment's peace. How am I to get out to my field if you interfere with me in the middle of my work?"

"Hold your impudent tongue, you son of a bitch. I am going to marry these young people. Ah, but there must be two witnesses." He turned to Catalina with a smirk on his fat face. "You will have to wait while this drunken ruffian goes down to the village to find someone and that will give me a chance to get something to eat."

"I will be the second witness."

It was a woman who spoke. They all turned round and saw her walking towards them. She wore a blue cloak and her head was covered with a great white scarf the ends of which were thrown over her shoulders. The priest looked at her with surprise, for he had not noticed that there was anyone in the church when he said his Mass, but he gave his shoulders an impatient shrug.

"Very well. Let us get it over as quickly as possible. I want my breakfast."

Catalina gave a start when the stranger joined them and tremulously took Diego's hand. The stranger, a faint smile in her eyes, put her finger to her lips enjoining Catalina to silence. The ceremony was speedily performed and Catalina Perez was joined in the bonds of holy matrimony to Diego Martinez. They went into the vestry to sign the book. The priest wrote down the names of the newly-married couple, and the names of their parents. Then the sacristan laboriously wrote his.

"That's the only thing he can write," said the priest, "and it took me six months to drive that into his thick head. Now, madam, it's your turn."

He dipped the quill into the ink and handed it to the strange lady.

"I cannot write at all," she said.

"Then make a cross and I will write your name."

She took the quill and did as he directed. Catalina, her heart beating, watched her.

"Well, I cannot write your name unless you tell it me," said the priest sharply.

"Maria, daughter of the shepherd Joachim," she answered.

He wrote it.

"That's all," he said. "And now I am going to eat."

They followed him out of the church, all but the sacristan, who took up his broom and with mutters of irritation resumed his sweeping. But the Spanish have always been a courteous people and the priest, with the gold piece safely tucked away, was no exception.

"If, gentleman and ladies, you will do me the honour of

coming to my humble dwelling next door I shall be happy to offer you such refreshment as my poverty can provide."

Catalina, who was well brought up, knew that such an offer should be declined with grace, but Diego was ravenous and did not give her time to speak.

"Señor," he said, "neither I nor my wife have had anything to eat since yesterday, and however poor your fare, it will seem a feast to us."

The priest was a little taken aback at this, but was too polite to say anything but that they would confer a favour on him. They walked the few steps to his house and he showed them into a small bare room which served as refectory, parlour and study. He set before them bread and wine, goat cheese and a dish of black olives. He cut four hunks of bread and filled four horn tumblers with wine. He set about the food greedily and Diego and Catalina followed his example. He looked up to help himself to an olive and noticed that the strange lady had touched nothing.

"Pray eat, madam," he said. "It is simple fare, but good, and it is the best I can offer you."

She gave the bread and wine a smile in which there was a singular sadness and shook her head.

"I will eat an olive," she said.

She took one and delicately nibbled it with white teeth. Catalina gave her a glance, their eyes met, and in the lady's was a look of infinite kindness. At that moment the sacristan burst into the room.

"Señor, Señor," he shouted, beside himself with excitement, "they've stolen the Virgin."

"I'm not deaf, you old fool," cried the priest. "What in heaven's name do you mean?"

"I tell you they've stolen our Virgin. I went in there to sweep and the pedestal on which she stood was empty."

195

"You're mad or drunk, Pepe," the priest shouted back at him, jumping to his feet. "Who would do a thing like that?"

He flung out of the house and followed by the sacristan, Diego and Catalina, ran to the church.

"I didn't do it, I didn't do it," cried the sacristan, waving his hands distractedly. "They'll all say I did it and put me in prison."

They scrambled up the church steps, and ran to the Lady Chapel. The sacristan gave a great cry. The image of the Blessed Virgin stood in its accustomed place.

"What do you mean?" yelled the priest furiously.

"It wasn't there a minute ago. I swear by all the saints the pedestal was empty."

"You drunken swine. You old wineskin."

The priest seized him by the neck and kicked the wretched man's backside till he was exhausted and then for good measure slapped his face on both sides with all the strength he had left.

"If I only had a stick I'd break every bone of your body."

When the three of them got back to the priest's house to finish their frugal repast they were surprised to find that the strange lady was nowhere to be seen.

"Where can she have gone?" the priest exclaimed. Then he slapped his forehead. "Fool that I am! Now I see it all. Of course she's one of these Moriscos and when Pepe came in and said the Virgin had been stolen she thought she'd better make her escape. They're all thieves and she thought some of her cursed infidels had taken the image. Did you notice she wouldn't drink the wine? They've been baptised, but they keep to their pagan customs. I had my suspicions when she gave me her name; that isn't the name of a good Christian."

"We got rid of the Moriscos at Castel Rodriguez long ago," said Diego.

196

"And quite right too. I pray every night that our good King may be brought to see his duty to the Faith and expel every one of these odious heretics from the kingdom."

"It will be a great day for Spain when he does."

It is perhaps worthy of note to add that the worthy priest's prayers were answered, for in 1609 all the Moriscos were driven out of the country.

It was now time for Diego and his bride to resume their journey to Seville, and thanking the priest for his hospitality, they took leave of him. The horse meanwhile had been making a good meal off the hay on to which he had pitched his riders. Diego watered him and as soon as they were on his back the horse without urging set out at a comfortable amble. It was a beautiful day and there was not a cloud in the sky. The priest had told them that some fifteen miles along the road was an inn, patronized by carters and muleteers, where they could get lodging, and there they decided to stay the night. They rode in silence for three or four miles.

"Are you happy, dear?" asked Catalina at last.

"Of course."

"I will be a good wife to you. For love of you I will work my fingers to the bone."

"There will be no need for you to do that. There's plenty of money to be made in Seville by a clever man and no one has ever taken me for a fool."

"I should think not indeed."

They were silent again for a while and it was Catalina who spoke again.

"Listen, my lover, that was no Moorish woman who came to our wedding."

"What are you talking about? One only had to look at her to tell that she was no Old Christian."

"But I'd seen her before."

"You? Where?"

"On the steps of the church of the Carmelite nuns. It was she who told me how I could be cured of my infirmity."

He stopped the horse and looked around.

"My poor child, you're crazy. The sun has addled your brains."

"I'm as sane as you are, my sweet. I tell you it was the Blessed Virgin, and when she refused to eat of the bread and wine I knew why. I knew she remembered her bitter. bitter sorrow."

Diego stared at her with a puzzled frown.

"The Reverend Mother told me a hundred times it was quite certain I was under the special protection of our most Holy Lady. That is why she pressed me so constantly to enter the convent. Those sudden showers last night and the horse stopping at the church door and refusing to move and then throwing us both. You must see that all that was no accident."

He looked at her for a moment longer and Catalina to her distress thought there was some displeasure in his eyes. Without another word he turned round again and with a click of his tongue started the horse off. Somewhat timidly Catalina hazarded a casual remark now and then, but he either answered not at all or with a monosyllable.

"What is the matter with you, darling?" she said at last. trying not to cry.

"Nothing."

"Look at me, sweetheart. I'm hungry for a glance of your eyes."

"How can I look at you when the road is full of ruts and holes? If the horse stumbled we might break our necks."

"You're not angry with me because the Blessed Virgin saw fit to protect my virtue and was so gracious as to be a witness to our marriage?"

"It is an honour to which I would never have ventured to aspire," he said dryly.

"Then why are you vexed with me?"

He took some time to reply.

"It does not augur well for our future happiness if whenever we have a difference of opinion a miracle will occur to let you have your own way. A man should be master in his own home. It is a wife's duty to yield to her husband's wishes, and it should be her pleasure."

Catalina had her arms round him and he felt them shaking.

"You won't make it any better by crying," he said.

"I'm not crying."

"What are you doing then?"

"Laughing."

"Laughing? It's no laughing matter, woman. It's very serious and I have the right to be disturbed."

"You are very sweet, my darling, and I love you with all my heart, but sometimes you are not very sensible."

"Explain," he said coldly.

"The Prioress told me that I owed the favours I have received at the hands of Our Blessed Lady to my virginity. It appears that in heaven they set great store on that. It may be that when I have lost it I shall receive no more."

Upon this Diego turned as far round in the saddle as he could and there was a sly smile on his handsome face.

"Blessed be the mother that bore you," he cried. "We will put the matter to the test without delay."

"The sun is growing warm. It would be pleasant to rest for a while under the shade of trees till the heat of the day is past."

"That is the very thought that was passing through my head."

"And unless my eyes deceive me there is a wood not more than a mile away that will do very nicely."

"If your eyes deceive you my eyes are deceiving me too."

He gave the horse a touch of his spurs and galloped hell for leather till they came to the wood. He jumped off and lifted Catalina down. While he tied the horse to a tree she got out what the forethought either of the Prioress or Domingo had provided. Bread and cheese, sausage, a cold chicken and a bulging skin of wine. Who could want a better wedding breakfast? It was cool and dark under the trees and a trickle of water flowed down the bed of a tiny, limpid stream. The spot was propitious.

XXXI

WHEN they emerged from the wood, Diego leading the horse, the sunrays flamed less fiercely.

"It was just as well to make assurance doubly sure," he said.

"Trebly," she murmured, not without a certain smug self-satisfaction.

"That is nothing, child," he returned with a very pardonable complacency. "You do not know yet of what I am capable."

"You are as shameless as you are adorable," she said.

"I am as God made me," he answered modestly.

They rode on slowly, up hill and down dale, not talking very much, but chewing the cud as it were of their happiness; they rode for six or seven miles and then saw in the mellow light of the late afternoon a ramshackle building by the roadside. That was evidently the inn of which the priest had spoken.

"We snall be there very soon. Are you tired, sweetheart?"

"Tired?" she answered. "Why should I be tired? I'm as fresh as a lark."

They had ridden a good forty miles and since the day before she had not slept more than an hour. She was sixteen.

They were in the plain now and the country stretched widely on both sides of the road. The harvest had been gathered and the fields were brown and dry. Here and there grew a few gnarled oak trees; here and there a grove of age-old olives. They were less than a mile from the inn when they saw galloping towards them in a great cloud of dust a horseman of such a strange appearance that they were filled with amazement, for he was in full armour. He pulled up sharply as he came to them and posted himself in the middle of the road. Couching his lance he seated himself firmly in his saddle and in a haughty tone thus addressed Diego:

"Stand and whoever you be tell me who you are, whence you come, whither you go, and who is the fair princess you carry pillion behind you. For I have every reason to believe that you are bearing her to your castle against her will and it is requisite that I should be informed of the matter to punish you for the wrong you have done her and return her to her sorrowing parents."

For a moment Diego was so astonished that he had no answer to make. The horseman had a long cadaverous face, a short ragged beard and an immense moustache. His armour was rusty and old-fashioned and his helmet looked more like a barber's basin than a knight's helmet. His horse was a wretched jade fit for nothing but the knacker's yard and so thin that you could count his ribs. His head drooped so that it seemed as though at any moment he would tumble down from sheer weakness.

"Sir," said Diego, putting on a bold front to impress

Catalina with his valour, "we are on our way to the inn we see from here and I see no reason to answer your impertinent questions."

With this he clapped his spurs to his horse and moved forward, but the knight seized the bridle and stopped him.

"Mind your manners, proud, discourteous knight, and give me instantly an account of yourself or I defy you to mortal combat.

Just then a very fat little man, with an immense paunch, came scampering up on a dappled ass and significantly tapping his forehead sought to indicate to the travellers that the horseman so strangely accoutred was out of his senses. But on hearing those threatening words Diego had drawn his sword and seemed ready to defend himself. The little fat man pressed forward.

"Contain your anger, Señor," he said to the knight. "These are inoffensive travellers and that young man has every appearance of being able to give a good account of himself should it come to blows."

"Peace, varlet," cried the horseman. "If the adventure is perilous it will give me greater occasion to exercise my strength and prove my courage."

At this Catalina slipped off the horse and advanced to the stranger.

"Señor, I will answer your questions," she said. "This youth is no knight, but an honest citizen of Castel Rodriguez and a tailor by trade. He is not carrying me by force to his castle, for he hasn't got one, but of my own free will to Seville where we hope to find decent occupation. We have run away from our native city because enemies sought to prevent our marriage, and we were married this morning at a village some miles from here. We are making all the haste we can in case we are pursued, overtaken and obliged to return to our city."

The knight looked from Catalina to Diego, then handed his lance to the little man on the ass, who grumbled but took it.

"Put up your sword, young man," said the fantastic creature, with a grandiose gesture. "You have nothing to fear, though I am well aware from your appearance that fear is an unworthy emotion to which your noble heart is a stranger. It may suit you to assume the humble guise of a tailor, but your bearing and demeanour betray your illustrious lineage. It is fortunate for you that you have crossed my path. I am a Knight-errant and my employment is to visit all parts of the world in quest of adventure, to right the wrong, relieve injured innocence and punish oppression. I take you under my protection, and should your enemies come ten thousand strong and attempt to take you captive I, single-handed, will put them to flight. I will myself escort you to the inn where it so happens that I too am lodging. This my squire will ride with you. He is an ignorant, garrulous fellow, but well-meaning, and he will obey your commands as if they were my own. I will ride a little behind you so that if I see an army approaching I can attack it and you will be able to escape with this beauteous maiden to a place of safety."

Catalina jumped up behind her husband and with the squire accompanying them they set out once more. He told them that his master was as mad as a hatter, to which conclusion his remarks had already led them, but added that for all that he was a good and worthy man.

"And when the fit is not on him, poor gentleman, he can talk better sense in an hour than any sane man can talk in a month of Sundays."

They reached the inn. A group of people were sitting on benches at the door; they gave the two travellers a glance of curiosity, but otherwise took no notice of them. They

203

appeared sunk in a lethargy of gloom. The fat little man tumbled off his ass and called the landlord, but when he came and Diego asked for a room he told him in a surly tone that there wasn't an unoccupied bed in the place. A troupe of actors had arrived the day before to give a performance at a neighbouring castle where its lord, a grandee of Spain, was celebrating the marriage of his son and heir. The people on the benches, evidently the actors of whom he spoke, stared at the young couple with a somewhat hostile indifference.

"But you must find us something, mine host," said Diego. "We have ridden far and can ride no further."

"I tell you, I have no room, Señor. They are sleeping in the kitchen, they are sleeping in the stables."

The knight now rode up.

"What is this I hear?" he cried. "You refuse to harbour these gentlefolk? Churlish fellow. Under pain of incurring my displeasure I command you to provide them with a decent lodging."

"The inn is full," the landlord shouted.

"Then let them have my room."

"That they can have if it is your wish, Sir Knight, but where will you sleep?"

"I shall not sleep," he answered grandly. "I shall keep guard. This is their wedding-day and the most solemn occasion of a maiden's life. The apostle has taught that it is better to marry than burn. The end of marriage is not to satisfy the lusts of the flesh, but to effect the procreation of children, and for that purpose the blushing bride is called upon to abandon her natural modesty and in the arms of her lawful husband sacrifice the priceless pearl of her virginity. It is a duty of my calling not only to guard the privacy of the nuptial couch from the intrusion of the enemies who pursue these noble creatures with their malignity but also to prevent

michael charlton

the horseplay with which the vulgar are apt on these occasions to exercise their humour."

This speech covered Catalina with confusion, but whether from shame or modesty is uncertain.

In the Spain of that day innkeepers provided only lodging and the traveller had to bring his food with him. But on this occasion the great lord had sent the actors by his steward a kid and a hunk of pork; and the knight's squire by methods of his own had acquired two brace of partridges; so that the company could look forward to a more sumptuous repast than usual, for their evening meal ordinarily consisted of no more than bread and garlic with sometimes a piece of cheese. The innkeeper announced that it would be ready in half an hour and the knight with elaborate courtesy asked the newly-married couple to do him the honour of being his guests. He told his squire to remove his belongings and conduct the bride and bridegroom to the chamber where in due course they would solemnize the sacred rites. The bedrooms were up a flight of stairs and the doors opened on to a gallery round the courtyard. When they had repaired as best they could the disorder of their toilet Diego and Catalina went down again to get a breath of the cool evening air. The actors were sitting as they had left them. They seemed a sullen lot, on edge, and when they spoke to one another it was with bitterness. Presently the knight joined them. He had removed his armour and now wore a pair of breeches and a doublet of chamois leather, stained with the rust of his breastplate, leggings and shoes. His trusty sword hung by his side from a belt of wolf's skin.

The landlord called them in and they sat down to supper. The knight, putting Catalina on one side of him and Diego on the other, took the head of the table.

"And where, pray, is Master Alonso?" he asked, looking round. "Has he not been told that supper is ready?"

205

"He will not come," said a middle-aged woman who played duennas, wicked stepmothers and widowed queens and was also the wardrobe-mistress. "He says he has no heart to eat."

"An empty stomach only makes misfortune doubly hard to bear. Go and fetch him. Tell him that I shall look upon it as a grave discourtesy to my honoured guests if he deprives me of the pleasure of his company. We shall not eat till he comes."

"Go and fetch him, Mateo," said the wardrobe-mistress.

A skinny little man with a long nose and a big loose mouth got up and went out. The wardrobe-mistress sighed.

"It is a sad business," she said, "but as you wisely remark, Sir Knight, going without one's supper will not help it."

"If you will not think me impertinent," said Catalina, "I should like to ask you what the trouble is."

They were only too glad to tell her, for it was very much on their minds. The company belonged to Alonso Fuentes, who also wrote many of the plays they acted, and his wife Luisa was his leading woman. Early that morning she had run away with the leading man and taken with her all the cash she could lay hands on. It was a catastrophe. For Luisa Fuentes had been a great attraction and they were well aware that it was she that had brought the money into the box-office. Alonso was in despair. He had not only lost a wife, but an actress and a source of income. It was enough to upset any man. Now their tongues were loosened. The men reviled the perfidy of women and wondered how such a fine creature could throw herself away on the indifferent actor their leading man had been. The women on the other hand asked how any woman could be expected to stay with a bald fat man like Alonso when she had the chance of a handsome young fellow like Juanito Azuria. The conversation was interrupted by the appearance of the abandoned

206

husband. He was small and plump, no longer young, with the rubber face of the actor of many parts. He sat down morosely and a great dish of olla podrida was set on the table.

"I have come as a compliment to you, Sir Knight," he said. "This is my last meal on earth, for after supper I have every intention of hanging myself."

"I must insist on your waiting till tomorrow," answered the knight gravely. "This gentleman and his lady whom you see on either side of me were married this morning and I cannot allow their first night to be disturbed by such an unseemly incident as you suggest."

"I do not care a fig for this gentleman and his lady. I am going to hang myself."

The knight sprang to his feet and drew his sword.

"If you do not swear to me by all the saints that you will not hang yourself tonight I will cut you into a thousand pieces with my sword."

Fortunately the sturdy little squire was standing behind his master to wait on him.

"Have no fear, Señor," he said. "Alonso will not hang himself tonight because he has to give a performance tomorrow, and once an actor always an actor. He won't disappoint his public. If he will reflect for a moment he will remember that it's a long lane that has no turning, what can't be cured must be endured and every cloud has a silver lining."

"Stop prattling your pointless proverbs," said the knight angrily, but he sheathed his sword and sat down. "It is not becoming to make so much of a misadventure that has happened to many a better man than this Alonso. With a little thought I could give both from Holy Writ and from profane history the names of many great men whose wives have made cuckolds of their husbands; but at the moment the only ones that occur to me are King Arthur whose wife Guinevere betrayed him for Sir Lancelot and King Mark whose wife Iseult deceived him with Sir Tristram of Lyonesse."

"It is not the injury to my honour that has driven me to desperation, Sir Knight," said the actor and playwright, "but the loss both of the money and the two most important members of my company. We have to play tomorrow, and the sum that has been promised me would to some extent compensate me financially, but how can I give a performance without actors?"

"I could very well play the part of Don Ferdinand," said the skinny fellow who had gone to fetch Alonso.

"You?" cried the actor-manager scornfully. "How could you with your horse face and your shrill voice play the part of a gallant, audacious, headstrong and passionate prince? No, that is a part *I* could play, but who is going to take the part of the lovely Dorotea?"

"I know the lines," said the wardrobe-mistress. "It is true that I am not so young as I was. . . ."

"Very true," Alonso interrupted, "and I beg to remind you that Dorotea is an innocent virgin of unsurpassed beauty and your mature figure suggests that you may at any moment give birth to a litter of pigs."

"Is it possible that you are referring to *Truth with Zeal even Heaven can Move*?" asked Catalina, who had been following the conversation with attention.

"It is," said Alonso, not without surprise. "But how did you know?"

"It is one of my uncle's favourite plays. We used to read it together. He often said that Dorotea's speech when she indignantly rejects the dishonourable advances of Don Ferdinand is equal to anything that the great Lope de Vega has written."

"Do you know it?"

"By heart."

She began to recite, but then, noticing that the company were watching her with curiosity, was seized with shyness and, faltering, stopped.

"Go on, go on," cried the actor.

She blushed, smiled, and plucking up her courage started again and spoke the long tirade to its end with so much grace, pathos and sincerity that they were all amazed. Several indeed were moved to tears.

"Saved," cried Alonso. "You shall play Dorotea with me tomorrow and I will play Don Ferdinand."

"How could I?" she said in a fright. "I should die. I have never acted. It is impossible. I should be struck dumb."

"Your youth and beauty will make up for any deficiencies. I will help you. Listen, fair one, you alone can save us. If you refuse we cannot play and there is no money to pay for our lodging in this inn and for our food. We shall be reduced to begging our bread in the streets."

Then the knight put in his word.

"I can understand, gracious lady, that your modesty makes you hesitate to expose yourself on the stage to the gaze of a company of strangers and it would be unbecoming of you to do so without the permission of the lord your husband." For the knight had made up his mind that the young couple were of high degree and nothing they said could persuade him to the contrary. "But remember that it is the part of a noble nature to succour the distressed and relieve the necessities of the needy."

The rest of the company joined their entreaties to those of Alonso Fuentes and in the end Catalina agreed, with Diego's willing consent, to rehearse the play and if the rest thought she acquitted herself with credit to risk a performance; so after supper the table was pushed to one side and the rehearsal begun. She had a good memory and she had recited the scenes in which Dorotea appeared often enough with Domingo to be tolerably sure of her words. At first she was nervous, but the encouragement of the players helped her, and presently, losing herself in the part, she lost her self-consciousness. She profited then by the lessons she had received from her uncle and spoke her lines with point and sincerity. She did remarkably well and Alonso was confident that with another rehearsal next morning she would be competent to appear before an audience. She was flushed and happy and looked so beautiful that he felt certain her inexperience would pass unnoticed.

"Go to bed, children," he said to his company, "and sleep in comfort. Our troubles are at an end."

But now that they were relieved of their anxieties they were much too excited to do this and so, calling for wine, settled down to make a night of it. The knight, comfortably seated in a chair, had watched the rehearsal with a critical eye. Now, rising somewhat stiffly to his feet, he called the duenna aside.

"Lead the fair Catalina to the nuptial chamber," he said, "and since she has no mother to tell her what on this grave occasion it behoves her to know, it is your part to explain to her in terms that will not offend her modesty the ordeal to which as an obedient wife it will be her duty to submit. You must in short prepare her for the mysteries of love which as an innocent virgin she must be unacquainted with."

The duenna blinked, but promised to do her best.

"Meanwhile," the knight went on, "I will explain to the young lord, her husband, that he must restrain his natural impetuosity, for the aversion a virtuous female must feel for the intimacies of sexual congress can only be overcome by patience. The depravity of the times is such that I cannot suppose he has maintained his innocence to this day."

"Saving your presence, Sir Knight," said the duenna, "it is better that the man should not be entirely without experience in the act of love, for in this no less than in the arts and handicrafts practice makes perfect."

"That is a matter on which I will not venture an opinion, madam. Suffice it to say that after a decent interval I will myself conduct the bridegroom to the threshold of the nuptial chamber and then, after donning my armour, mount guard on the balcony so that the marriage may be consummated in a style fitting the distinction of the parties concerned."

He dismissed the duenna and called Diego.

"You are now entering upon a state," he began, "in which few conduct themselves in such a way as to attain happiness themselves or bring happiness to their partners in life; and the circumstances of your marriage are of a nature that makes it incumbent upon me to give you the advice which otherwise would have been given you by your noble father." The knight then proceeded to speak to the young man on the lines that he had indicated to the duenna and finished as follows: "I do not condemn the necessary pleasures of the body, which refresh it in its exhaustion and hinder it from being importunate; but food and drink, and still more, sexual congress are no more than assuagements provided for the body lest the work of the soul be impeded. Yet the love that is sanctioned by marriage has its touch of upward striving, and in so far as it has this leads the souls of the young towards the Good. In the chaste love that has drawn you to this maiden there cannot but be in you a desire for such immortality as lies within mortal reach and, when you clasp her to your heart, through your own kinship with the beautiful, you will sow in beauty and thus sow

211

towards eternity. For the eternal and the beautiful are one."

Diego listened to this harangue with the politeness natural to him, but with a wandering attention, for he was impatient to be with Catalina. The knight took him by the hand and led him to what he was pleased to call the nuptial chamber; then, summoning his squire, he resumed his martial equipment and spent the night, tramping up and down, occupied with thoughts of the unapproachable object of his own devotion.

XXXII

EARLY next morning they rehearsed the play again and then carriages arrived to take them to the Duke's castle. The knight and Diego mounted their horses and the squire his ass and set forth. But at the last moment Catalina's heart failed her, and crying that she could never face the ordeal of appearing before an audience, she begged Alonso to let her stay behind; he flew into a passion and telling her it was now too late to withdraw bundled her into a carriage and seated himself beside her. She was in a flood of tears, but with the duenna to help him, he managed presently to calm her and by the time they arrived she was sufficiently composed. The players were honourably received and by the Duke's instructions suitably entertained, but word had reached him of the knight's extravagances, and thinking his conversation would divert his guests, he begged him to favour the Duchess and himself with his company at dinner. A stage had been erected in the courtyard and when the gentry had eaten their fill the actors were summoned to give their performance. The distinguished audience were not a little amused by Alonso in the part of a gay seducer, for it was not one that his appearance made plausible; but they were charmed by Catalina's grace, the music of her voice and the elegance of her delivery, and when the play was over paid her many fine compliments. The knight had given them his own romantic version of the young couple's elopement and this naturally increased their interest. The Duchess sent for them and all were astounded by their beauty, the modesty of their demeanour and their gallant bearing. The Duchess gave Catalina a gold chain and the Duke, not to be outdone, took a ring off his finger and gave it to Diego. Alonso was richly rewarded and the company, tired but happy, returned to the inn. Shortly afterwards the knight and his squire rode up. He dismounted somewhat stiffly and taking Catalina by the hand added his compliments to those she had already received.

"You have come in the nick of time, Sir Knight," said Alonso, "to hear me make a proposition to these young people." He turned to Catalina. "I invite you to join my troupe."

"Me?" said Catalina astounded.

"Though you still have everything to learn, you have gifts that it would be a sin to waste. You do not know how to act. You say your lines as you would say them in real life. That is futile. The stage does not deal with truth, but with verisimilitude, and it is only by artifice that the actor can be natural. Your gestures want amplitude and you have yet to acquire authority. The good actor even by his silence dominates his audience. If you will place yourself in my hands I will make you the greatest actress in Spain."

"Your suggestion is such a surprise to me that I can hardly believe you mean it. I am a married woman and my husband and I are on our way to Seville where we have the assurance of honest occupation."

Alonso Fuentes had caught the look she gave Diego and now with a smile turned to him.

"You have good looks, young fellow, and a fine presence. There is no reason why with experience you should not be able to make yourself useful in suitable parts."

The applause that had rewarded her performance and the compliments she had received had excited Catalina and she was not a little fluttered by this unexpected offer; but she saw that her husband was displeased by the casual way in which Alonso proposed to include him in the arrangement and so hastened to say:

"He can sing like an angel.'

"All the better. There are few plays in which there is not a song or two to enliven the proceedings. Well, what do you say? The opportunity I offer you is surely more alluring than the occupation, honest perhaps, but certainly modest, that awaits you in Seville."

During this time the knight had sat silent, listening, but now he spoke.

"The proposition that Master Alonso has put before you is one that should not be hastily rejected, for consider: you are pursued by the rage of your outraged parents and they will stop at nothing to snatch you from one another's arms. But time assuages wrath and the day will come when your respective parents will lament your loss and regret that from ambition or greed they wished you to contract distasteful alliances. You will be restored not only to their love but to the rank and station to which your high birth entitles you. But till this happens you will be wise to remain in concealment, and how can you be better concealed than in a troupe of actors? Nor must you think that you demean yourself by treading the boards. They who write plays and they who act them deserve our love and esteem, for they serve the good of the commonwealth. They set before our

214

CATALINA

eyes a lively representation of human life and show us what
we are and what we ought to be. They ridicule the vices
and foibles of the times and give praise where praise is due,
to honour, virtue and beauty. The playwrights improve our
minds by their wit and wisdom and the actors refine our
manners by the grace of their demeanour and the dignity of
their carriage."

He went on for some time in this strain and all were
amazed that a man so crazy you couldn't account for his
actions should yet express himself with such good sense.

"And let us not forget," he ended, "that just such a
comedy as we see played on the stage of a theatre is played on
the stage of the world. We are all actors in a play. To some
it is allotted to play kings or prelates, to others merchants,
soldiers or husbandmen, and each should see that he acts
the part given to him; but to select it belongs to a greater
power."

"What do you think, beloved?" asked Catalina, with her
most charming smile. "As the knight so truly says, it is not
an offer to be lightly rejected."

She had in point of fact by now made up her mind to
accept it, but she well knew that men like to think they
decide matters for themselves.

"You will not only be helping me in my difficult situation," said Alonso, "but you will be benefiting yourselves,
for you will visit with me the most famous cities of
Spain."

Diego's eyes sparkled. He could not but see that this
would be vastly more amusing than to sit for twelve hours
a day on a tailor's bench.

"I've always wanted to see the world," he smiled.

"And you shall, my sweet," said Catalina. "Master
Alonso, we will gladly join your troupe."

"And you shall be a great actress."

215

"*Olé, olé!*" cried the other members of the company.

Alonso called for wine and they drank to the health of their new comrades.

XXXIII

NEXT day, having courteously taken leave of the knight, the strolling players started off for the neighbouring town of Manzanares, where a fair was being held and where consequently they were confident of finding a good audience. Alonso had hired mules for the actors to ride and to carry the chests that contained their clothes and costumes. Catalina and Diego went on the horse Doña Beatriz had given them. Including Master Alonso himself and Diego there were now seven men in the company, and besides the duenna and Catalina there was a boy to play second women's parts. He was also what is now called a barker, and when they reached a town where they wanted to play, while Alonso went to see the mayor to obtain permission, he walked the streets, beating a drum, and announced to all and sundry that the celebrated troupe of Alonso Fuentes would give a performance of the magnificent, witty and immortal play So and So.

Since at that time there were no theatres in Spain plays were given in courtyards where the windows and balconies of the surrounding houses could serve as boxes for the nobility and gentry. The ceiling was the blue heaven except in the height of summer, when awnings against the sun were drawn from roof to roof. In front of the stage were a few benches and round the courtyard others, arranged stepwise, for the respectable middle class. The common people stood on the bare ground, the men in front and the women, squeezed together in a boarded-off space, behind. Partly for fear of fire and partly for morality's sake the performance took place in the afternoon. The scenery consisted of a single backcloth, and change of scene was indicated by the players' words.

The elopement of Alonso's wife with the leading man had caused him to change his route, and when they had played at Manzanares he set forth with his company for Seville, where he knew he would be able to engage an actor for the parts which his own age and appearance prevented him from playing himself. They went first to Ciudad Real, a rich city, and from there to Valdepeñas; they made the ascent of the Sierra Morena and entered Andalusia by the rocky defile called the Puerto de Despeñaperros. They crossed the Guadalquivir and at last reached Cordova, where they played for a week; then, after following for a while the noble river, they came to Carmona, where they gave one performance, and finally reached Seville. Master Alonso engaged the actor he wanted and they settled down for a month. After that they took to the road again. It was a hard life. The inns they slept in were miserable and the beds so bad and filthy that, tired though they were and exhausted by the heat of summer or chilled to the bone by the cold of winter, they often preferred to sleep on the floor. They were bitten by fleas, stung by mosquitoes, tormented by bugs and vexed by lice. When they were playing they rose at dawn to study their parts. They rehearsed from nine till twelve, dined and went to the theatre; they left it at seven; and then, however weary, if they were wanted by persons of consequence, the mayor, a judge, a nobleman who was giving a party, off they had to go and give another performance.

Alonso Fuentes was a slave-driver and as soon as he discovered that Catalina was skilful with her needle and

Diego no mean tailor he set them, whenever they were not otherwise occupied, to making or altering the costumes needed for the repertory, which consisted of eighteen plays. It did not take him long to find out that Diego, notwithstanding his good looks and his self-assurance, would never be much of an actor, so he contented himself with letting him sing the songs with which the plays were interspersed, for his voice was pleasing, and giving him small parts. But on the other hand he took pains to make an actress of Catalina. He knew his business and had a lively sense for theatrical effect; she was an apt pupil and a quick study, so that under his tuition, which was intensive and sometimes brutal, she ceased in time to be a clever amateur and became a competent professional. Alonso was rewarded for his trouble, for she found favour with the public and brought prosperity to the company. He enlarged his troupe and extended his repertory. Among others he engaged a young actress called Rosalia Vazquez, partly to console himself for the loss of his wife and partly to play seconds, for the boy who had been used to play them had by then lost his treble voice and was starting to shave. Moreover Catalina had first one baby and then another, so that it was necessary to have a good enough actress to replace her when child-birth for a period kept her out of the bill.

Thus three happy, strenuous years passed. By then Catalina had learnt all that Alonso Fuentes could teach her, and with two young children to take care of she began to find it irksome to be constantly on the move. Her beauty and her talent had attracted the attention of influential persons and more than one had suggested that she and Diego should form their own company and establish themselves in Madrid. Some in their admiration for her gifts went so far as to offer financial assistance. Now Alonso Fuentes was not only manager, director and actor, but also author, and every year, mostly during Lent when play-acting was prohibited, he turned out two or three plays. It had not escaped Catalina's notice that in the plays he wrote presumably to show *her* off to best advantage the parts he wrote Rosalia Vazquez tended to become more and more substantial. In his last the parts had been of almost equal length and only Catalina's greater talent had enabled her to make it appear the more important. When she expressed her displeasure, which she did not hesitate to do, Alonso shrugged his shoulders and laughed.

"My dear," he said, "when you sleep with a woman you have to keep her in a good humour."

This, though obviously true, was unsatisfactory. Catalina was no prude, but it seemed to her only just that a respectably married woman should have better parts than one who was no more than a baggage.

"Things can't go on like this," she told Diego.

And he agreed they couldn't. The notion of having a company of her own was tempting, but she was well aware of the difficulties she and Diego would have to cope with. Catalina was greatly loved in the company and she was pretty sure that several of the members would be glad to go to Madrid with her. With sufficient funds she could engage other actors there, buy the necessary costumes and acquire a number of plays. But Madrid audiences were well known to be hard to please: she would need the influence of her friends as well as their money. Diego was all for making the venture, but she knew that, dissatisfied with the small parts allotted to him by Alonso, he would, as manager, look upon it as his right to cast himself for whatever roles took his fancy. Though she loved him as passionately as ever she was not convinced that he was competent to play the leading parts he hankered after, and she guessed that she would have to exercise a great deal of tact to persuade him to engage a well-known actor to play them. She hesitated. They talked and talked, and could not arrive at a decision; then, one day, Catalina conceived the bright idea of sending for Domingo Perez and asking for his advice. He had been an actor himself, he was a playwright, and if they finally decided to go into management for themselves they might put on one or two of his plays and he would certainly be able to put them in touch with authors. Diego approved, so she wrote to him. She had already written three or four times, first to tell him that she was married, well and happy, and then to announce the birth of her children; but knowing how bitterly it would grieve her mother, she had thought it better not to say that she and Diego were become strolling players. She asked him now, but without giving any particular reason, to visit them at Segovia. They were spending Lent there, partly because it happened to be Alonso's native city, but chiefly because his company had been engaged to play a religious drama in the Cathedral at Easter and it was now in rehearsal. It was Alonso's latest play and he had chosen the life of Mary Magdalen as his subject.

XXXIV

DOMINGO, always glad of a jaunt, no sooner received Catalina's letter than he hired him a horse, packed food and a couple of shirts in the saddlebags and set out. He was pleased on his arrival at Segovia to find Catalina with her husband and children installed in a decent lodging, and delighted to see that she was even more beautiful than before. She was then nineteen. Success, happiness and maternity had combined to give her self-confidence and a certain dignity, but also a tender voluptuousness that was vastly alluring. Her face had lost its appealing childishness, but had gained perfection of line. Her figure was as slender as ever and she moved with an enchanting grace. She was a woman now, a very young woman certainly, but a woman of character, sure of herself and conscious of her beauty.

"You look prosperous enough, my dear," he said. "What do you do for a living?"

"Oh, we'll come to that later," said Catalina. "First tell me how my mother is and how is everyone at Castel Rodriguez and what happened after we ran away and how is Doña Beatriz."

"One thing at a time, child," he smiled. "And remember I have come a long way and I am thirsty."

"Run to Rodrigo's and get a bottle of wine, dear," said Catalina, and Domingo smiled when he saw her dive into some recess of her petticoats and taking out a purse give Diego a few coins.

"I shan't be a minute," said Diego as he went out.

"I see that you are prudent, sweetheart," grinned Domingo.

"It didn't take me long to discover that men can't be trusted with money, and if a man has no money he can't get into mischief," she laughed. "But now answer my questions."

"Your mother is in good health, she sends you her love, her piety is exemplary and it is doubtless for that reason that the Prioress gives her a pension so that she is no longer obliged to work."

This he said with a twinkle in his eye and Catalina laughed again. Her laughter was so frank and at the same time so musical that Domingo in his poetic way likened it to the purling of water in a mountain stream.

"There was quite a commotion in Castel Rodriguez after you disappeared," he went on. "My poor child, no one had a good word to say for you any more and your wretched mother was in despair. It was not till the nun Doña Ana came and told her that the Prioress proposed to come to her assistance pecuniarily that she was able to console herself for your abandoned behaviour. For ten days people talked of nothing else. The nuns were horrified that after all the kindness Doña Beatriz had shown you, after the great favour she was prepared to confer on you, you should have put such an affront on her. The principal persons of the city went to the convent to offer her proper expressions of sympathy, but she was evidently so upset that she refused to receive them. She did, however, consent to see Don Manuel, but what passed between them is unknown; the lay sister who waits upon her heard their voices raised in anger, but though she did her best she could not hear a word they said, and shortly afterwards Don Manuel left the city. I would have written to tell you all this long ago if you had given me an address."

"It was impossible to do that. You see, we were moving from place to place and I never knew where we should be going next till we were starting to go."

"Why were you doing that?"

"Can't you guess? How often have you told me of the days when you wandered over Spain under the burning sun of summer, in the bitter cold of winter, barefoot, not to save your boots but because you had worn out your only pair, and with but one shirt to your back."

"God in heaven, you're not strolling players?"

"My poor uncle, I am leading woman in the celebrated company of Alonso Fuentes and Diego sings and dances and is a much better actor than Alonso will allow."

"Why didn't you tell me sooner?" cried Domingo. "I would have brought half a dozen plays with me."

At this moment Diego returned with the wine and while

222

Domingo drank Catalina told him how it had come about that she and Diego had become actors.

"And everyone agrees," she finished, "that I am now the greatest actress in Spain. Is it true, Diego of my soul, or is it not?"

"I would cut the throat of any man who ventured to deny it."

"There can be no doubt that I am wasting my talent in the provinces."

"I have been telling the girl that our place is Madrid," said Diego. "Alonso is jealous of me and will not give me the parts in which I can distinguish myself."

It will be seen that neither suffered from that false modesty which may well prove a bane to the artist. They proceeded then to tell Domingo what was on their minds. He was a prudent man and when they had finished said that he was not prepared to advise them one way or the other till he had seen them act.

"Come to rehearsal tomorrow," said Catalina. "I am playing Mary Magdalen in Alonso's new play."

"Are you pleased with your part?"

She shrugged her shoulders.

"Not altogether. It's well enough at the beginning, but it falls off in the last act. I don't appear in the last three scenes at all. I've told Alonso that as the play is about me I should be on at the end, but he says he must follow Holy Writ. The fact is, the poor man has no imagination."

Diego took Domingo to the tavern to which Alonso Fuentes and other members of his troupe were in the habit of going and introduced him not only as Catalina's uncle, but also as at one time an actor and now a playwright. Alonso received him with civility and the elderly scrivener quickly gained the good graces of the company by his wit, his good humour and his stories of the hardships in the old days of a strolling player's life. Alonso consented to his attending a rehearsal and he went next day.

He was amazed by the naturalness of Catalina's delivery, the eloquence of her gestures and the grace of her movements. Alonso had taught her well. She had an ear for verse and a lovely voice. She had gaiety and pathos. She had sincerity. She had power. It was astonishing that in three years she had learnt so completely the technique of her art. She seemed incapable of uttering a false note. And her native gifts, her acquired skill, the self-control she had learnt by experience, were all wonderfully enhanced by her great beauty.

When the rehearsal was over Domingo kissed her on both cheeks.

"Dearest one, you are very nearly as good an actress as you think you are."

She flung her arms round his neck.

"Oh, uncle, uncle, who would have thought when I was a child and we used to recite those scenes of Lope de Vega's that the day would come when people would fight to gain admission to see me play? And you have only seen me rehearse. Wait till you have seen me with an audience."

Diego was playing John, the Beloved Disciple, and the part was small. He was good to look at, but colourless. When there was an opportunity Domingo asked Alonso what he thought of him.

"He has a good appearance, but he'll never be an actor. I only let him play to please Lina. If only actors and actresses wouldn't marry one another! It is that that makes the life of a manager a burden."

This did not prevent Domingo from advising Catalina and Diego to have no fear, but to leave Alonso and set up for themselves in Madrid. During the twenty-four hours

224

he had been with them he had discovered that Catalina had good sense, and he was confident that she would not jeopardize her own success by letting Diego play parts that he could not do justice to. He felt sure that somehow or other she would arrange matters to their mutual satisfaction.

But it was not only his desire to see his niece and her husband that had led Domingo to undertake the somewhat arduous journey from Castel Rodriguez to Segovia; he hoped too to see his old friend Blasco de Valero. He was curious to know how he fared in his exalted station. So, for the next few days while Catalina and Diego were busy with their rehearsals, he wandered about the city and in one way and another, with his pleasant gift for social intercourse, managed to scrape acquaintance with a good many people. From them he learnt that the mass of the population looked upon their bishop with veneration. They were impressed by his piety and the austerity of his life. News of the miraculous events at Castel Rodriguez had reached them and filled them with wonder and awe. But Domingo learnt also that he had aroused the hostility of his chapter and of the city clergy. He had been shocked by the looseness of their lives and the negligence with which many of them performed their religious duties. With zeal but with little discretion he started upon a passionate campaign of reform. He had no mercy on those who would not mend their ways and as at Valencia was no respecter of persons. The clergy, with very few exceptions, bitterly resented his harsh intolerance and employed every method their subtlety could devise to hamper his activities. Those who dared were openly defiant, the rest contented themselves with passive resistance. The people approved his strictness, justified by his own virtue, and did what was in their power to support him. There had been in consequence unfortunate occurrences and the authorities had been obliged to intervene. He had brought not peace to the city, but a sword.

Domingo had arrived at Segovia at the beginning of Holy Week and he knew that during that period the duties of his office would prevent the Bishop from receiving him, so it was not till the following Tuesday that he presented himself at the episcopal palace. It was an imposing, but severe building with a granite façade. Domingo gave his name to a porter and after waiting some time was led up a flight of stone stairs, through cold, lofty rooms, sparsely furnished, and hung with pictures, dark and gloomy, of religious subjects; but the room into which he was at length shown was no larger than a cell. Its only furniture was a writing-table and two high-backed chairs. On the wall hung the black cross of the Dominicans. The Bishop rose and took Domingo in his arms and warmly embraced him.

"I thought we should never meet again, brother," he said with an affectionate cordiality that surprised Domingo. "What has brought you to this city?"

"I am a restless fellow. I love to wander."

The Bishop, dressed as ever in the habit of his order, had aged. He was emaciated, his lined face was haggard, and his eyes had lost their fire. But notwithstanding these signs of decrepitude there was in his aspect something luminous, a change in his expression that Domingo was conscious of, but failed to interpret; and, he could not tell why, it recalled to his mind the afterglow when the sun has set at last after the long hours of a summer day. The Bishop asked him to sit.

"How long have you been here, Domingo?"

"A week."

"And you have waited all this time to see me? That was not kind."

"I did not wish to intrude on you before, but I have seen you more than once. In the processions of Holy Week and in the Cathedral on Good Friday and again at Easter, and at the play."

"I have a horror of these performances they give in the House of God. In other cities of Spain they give them on the feasts of the Church in the plaza, and I do not disapprove them since they edify the people, but Aragon is tenacious of its old customs and notwithstanding my protests the chapter has insisted that they should be held in the Cathedral as has been done from time immemorial. I attended only because it was a duty of my office."

"The play was reverent, dear Blasco; there was nothing in it to offend you."

A frown darkened the Bishop's brow.

"When I came here I found a terrible laxity in those whose charge it is to fulfil their function and give a good example to the people. Some of the canons of the Cathedral had not been near the city for years, too many of the secular clergy were living in open immorality, in the convents the rule was not obeyed with proper rigour and the Inquisition had renounced its vigilance. I was determined to put a stop to these abuses, but I was met with hatred, malice and obstruction. I have succeeded in restoring a certain decency, but I wanted them to behave well for the love of God: if they behave less scandalously than they did it is only for fear of me."

"I have heard something of this in the city," said Domingo. "I have heard even that efforts have been made to remove you."

"If they only knew how happy I should have been had they succeeded!"

"But you have this consolation, dear friend; the people love you and reverence you."

"Poor creatures, they little know how unworthy I am of their reverence."

"They honour you for the asceticism of your life and your charity to the poor. They have heard of the miracle of Castel Rodriguez. They look upon you as a saint, brother, and who am I to blame them?"

"Do not mock me, Domingo."

"Ah, dear friend, I have too much affection for you ever to do that."

"It would not be the first time," the Bishop said with a smile in which there was something of pathos. "During these three years I have thought often of our last meeting and of what you said to me. At the time I paid little attention to it. It seemed to me no more than the paradoxical, cynical talk in which you have always indulged. But since I came here, in the loneliness of this palace, your words have haunted me. I have been tortured by doubt. I have asked myself if it is possible that my brother the baker, modestly doing his duty in his lowly station, has served God better than I who with prayer and mortification have given my life to His service. If so, whatever others think, whatever I myself thought for one rapt moment, it was not I that performed the miracle, but Martin."

The Bishop was silent. He looked at Domingo with searching eyes.

"Speak," he said. "Speak and by the love you once bore me tell me the truth."

"What is it you want me to tell you?"

"You were certain then that it was my brother who was chosen to effect the cure of that poor girl. Are you certain of it now?"

"As certain as I was then."

"Then why, why was I granted the sign that dispelled

my trembling hesitations? Why did the Blessed Virgin use words that might so easily give rise to a mistaken interpretation?"

His distress was so great that Domingo, as once before, was moved to pity. He wanted to console him, but scrupled to say what was in his mind. He knew Don Blasco's inflexible integrity, and it was far from improbable that his sense of duty would oblige him to report to the Holy Office things said, even by a friend, that seemed to require examination. The old seminarist had no wish to be a martyr to his opinions.

"You are a difficult man to speak freely to, my dear," he said. "I do not want to say anything that may be an offence to you."

"Say on, say on," cried the Bishop with something like impatience.

"Do you remember that on the occasion to which you just referred I told you how surprising it seemed to me that among the infinite attributes that men ascribe to God they have never thought of including common sense? But there is another that has even more completely escaped their attention, and yet, if a creature may venture to judge of these things, it is of even greater value. Omniscience would be incomplete without it and compassion repellent. A sense of humour."

The Bishop gave a slight start, seemed about to speak, but stopped himself.

"Do I shock you, brother?" Domingo asked seriously, but with a faint twinkle in his eyes. "Laughter is not the least precious of the gifts that God has granted us. It lightens our burdens in this hard world and enables us to bear many of our troubles with fortitude. Why should we deny a sense of humour to God? Is it irreverent to suppose that He laughs lightly within Himself when He speaks in

229

riddles so that men, deceived in their interpretation, may learn a salutary lesson?"

"You put things strangely, Domingo, and yet I do not know that there is anything in what you say that a good Christian need reject."

"You are changed, brother. Is it possible that in your old age you have learned tolerance?"

The Bishop gave Domingo a quick, inquiring glance, as though, surprised by his remark, he wondered what he meant; and then looked down at the bare stone floor. He seemed to be plunged in thought. After a while he raised his eyes and gazed at Domingo as though he wanted to speak, yet could not quite manage it.

"A very strange thing has happened to me," he said at last, "and I have dared to tell no one of it. Perhaps providence sent you here today so that I might tell you, for you, my poor Domingo, are the only man in the world that I can call my friend."

Once more he hesitated. Domingo, watching him intently, waited.

"As bishop of the diocese I was obliged to attend the play they gave in my Cathedral; someone told me it dealt with the life of St Mary Magdalen; but I was not obliged to listen or to look. I abstracted my mind. I prayed. But my soul was weary and disquieted. So it has been ever since I came to this city. I have suffered from distraction and dissipation of spirit. I have felt myself despoiled of everything, so that I could neither love nor hope. My understanding has been in darkness, my will dry, and I have found no comfort in the things of God. I prayed, as I had never prayed before, that He might see fit to succour me in my deep affliction. I was oblivious of my surroundings. I was alone with my sorrow. Suddenly I was startled by a cry and I remembered where I was. It was a cry, a cry so moving, so pregnant with significance that against my will I was compelled to listen. Then I remembered that they were acting a play. I do not know what had passed before, but, listening then, I understood that it had reached the point where Mary Magdalen and Mary the mother of James, bringing spices, came to the sepulchre where Joseph of Arimathæa had laid the body of Jesus and found the stone rolled away. And they entered in and found not the body of Jesus. And as they stood there perplexed a traveller, a follower of Jesus, came to them and Mary Magdalen told him what she and the other Mary had seen. And then, because he knew nothing of the terrible events that had taken place, she told him of the capture, the trial and the shameful death of the Son of God. The description was so vivid, the words so well chosen, the verse so mellifluous that even if I had not wanted I should have been forced to listen."

Domingo, holding his breath, leant forward eagerly.

"Ah, how right was our great emperor Charles when he said that Spanish was the only language in which to address God. The speech rolled on line after line. There was a fiery indignation in the voice of that woman who played the Magdalen when she told of the betrayal of Jesus, and a fierce anger seized the multitude in the Cathedral and they shouted curses on the traitor; her voice was broken with anguish when she told how they had scourged Our Lord, and the people gasped with horror; but when she told of the agony on the cross they beat their breasts and sobbed aloud. The pain in that golden voice, the heartrending pathos in it, were such that the tears ran down my cheeks. There was a tumult in my soul. My spirit quivered as the leaves of a tree quiver with a sudden flurry of wind. I felt something strange was about to happen to me and I was afraid. I raised my downcast eyes and gazed at the speaker

231

of those lovely, cruel words. She was of a beauty I have never seen on earth. It was no woman who stood there, wringing her hands, with streaming eyes, it was no actress, but an angel from heaven. And as I looked, spell-bound, on a sudden a ray of light transfixed the dark night in which I had so long languished; it entered my heart and I was rapt in ecstasy. It was a pain so great that I thought I should die, but at the same time it was a delight so sweet; and I felt myself released from the body and a stranger to the flesh. At that happy moment I tasted of the wonderful peace that passeth all understanding, I drank of the wisdom of God and I knew His secrets. I felt myself filled with all good and emptied of all evil. I cannot describe that bliss. I have no words to tell what I saw and felt and knew. I possessed God and in possessing Him possessed everything."

The Bishop sank back in his chair and his face shone with the recollection of his great experience.

"The desires of hope no longer afflict my soul. It is satisfied in its union with God, so far as in this life it is possible, and it has now nothing of this world to hope for and nothing spiritual to desire. I have written a letter in which I have begged His Majesty to allow me to resign my ecclesiastical offices and dignities so that I may retire to a convent of my order and spend the remainder of my life in prayer and contemplation."

Domingo could contain himself no longer.

"Blasco, Blasco, the girl who took the part of Mary Magdalen is my niece, Catalina Perez. When she ran away from Castel Rodriguez she joined the troupe of Alonso Fuentes."

The Bishop stared at him with amazement. He was dumbfounded. Then with a sweetness Domingo had never seen on his face before he smiled.

"Truly the ways of God are inscrutable; how strange are those He has chosen to lead me to my goal! Through her He wounded me and through her He healed me. Blessed be the mother that bore her, and all glory to God, for when she spoke those heavenly words she was inspired by Him. I shall remember her in my grateful prayers to my dying day."

At that moment Friar Antonio, still Don Blasco's secretary, came into the room. He gave Domingo a glance, but gave no indication that he recognized him; he went up to the Bishop and whispered in his ear. The Bishop sighed.

"Very well, I'll see him." Then to Domingo: "I'm afraid I must ask you to leave me, dear friend, but I shall see you again."

"I'm afraid not. I leave for Castel Rodriguez tomorrow."

"I am sorry."

Domingo knelt down to kiss the Bishop's ring, but he raised him to his feet and kissed him on the cheek.

XXXV

DOMINGO walked back to his lodging, a skinny, elderly man, with great pouches under his eyes, a reddish nose and not a dozen teeth in his head, an old reprobate in a patched cassock green with age and spotted with wine-stains and the droppings of food; but he walked on air. He would then, as he had once told the Bishop, have changed places neither with emperor nor pope. He talked to himself aloud and waved his arms, so that passers-by thought he was drunk: and drunk he was, though not with wine.

"The magic of art," he chuckled gaily. "Art also can work its miracles. *Et ego in Arcadia natus.*"

233

For it was he, the despised playwright, the dissolute scapegrace, who had written those lines that had so profoundly affected the Bishop. It had come about after this wise:

Catalina had not been dissatisfied with the first two acts of the play Alonso had written for her. He had made her the mistress of Pontius Pilate and in the first act she appeared gorgeously arrayed, proud in her sinful life, extravagant, wilful, luxurious and mercenary. Her conversion took place in the second act, and there was a good scene when, knowing that Jesus sat at meat at a Pharisee's house, she brought an alabaster box of ointment, washed His feet and anointed them with the ointment. The last act took place on the third day after the Crucifixion. There was a scene in which Pilate's wife reproached him for having allowed a blameless man to be put to death, another in which the disciples mourned the death of their master, and still another in which Judas Iscariot went to the Elders of the Temple and flung down the thirty pieces of silver they had given him to betray Jesus; but Mary of Magdala did not appear till she and Mary the mother of James went to the sepulchre and found it empty. The play ended with the two disciples walking to Emmaus, when they were joined by a stranger whom they later discovered to be the risen Christ.

Catalina had not been a leading lady for three years for nothing, and when she discovered that she had so little to do in the last act she was incensed. She reproached Alonso with acrimony.

"But what can I do?" he cried. "You are on the stage almost all the time during the first two acts. In the third there is no occasion for you to appear except in that one scene."

"But that is out of the question. Is the play about me or

is it not about me? The audience will want to see me and if they don't it will simply ruin your play."

"But, my dear child, this isn't a play in which I can give free rein to my imagination. I must stick to the facts."

"I don't deny it, but you are an author. If you know your business you ought to be able to think of something that will bring me in. Now, for instance, there is no reason why I shouldn't come on in the scene between Pontius Pilate and his wife. You have only to exercise a little ingenuity."

Alonso began to get angry.

"But, my poor Lina, you were Pilate's mistress. Is it likely that you would be in his palace and present when he is having an intimate conversation with his wife?"

"I don't see why not. I could have had a scene with Pilate's wife first and it is on account of what I have said to her that she reproaches Pilate."

"I never heard of anything so ridiculous. If you had attempted to approach Pilate's wife he would have had you whipped."

"Not when I threw myself on my knees, and begged her pardon for my past wickedness. I would be so moving that it would be impossible for her not to relent."

"No, no, no," he shouted.

"Then why shouldn't I be with the two disciples when they go to Emmaus? I, being a woman, would know who the stranger was, and he, knowing that I had recognized him, would put his finger to his lips to bid me be silent."

"I will tell you why you can't be with the two disciples when they go to Emmaus," Alonso bellowed. "Because you weren't, or it would have said so in the Gospel. And when I want you to write my plays for me I'll tell you."

They parted that day with some heat. Catalina was much inclined to refuse to play the part, but she knew that Alonso would then give it to Rosalia, and in the first two acts it was so fat that she might very well make a success in it.

"If he had been writing the part for Rosalia he would never have dared give her so little to do in the last act," she told Diego.

"There is no doubt about it," said he, "he is not treating you well. He doesn't appreciate you."

"I have felt that ever since Rosalia joined the company."

Catalina, full of her grievances, told her troubles to Domingo before he had even seen the play. He was properly sympathetic and asked to read it. The actors had only their parts and Alonso alone had a full manuscript which he kept jealously to himself in case one of them should copy it and sell it to another manager.

"Alonso is as vain as a peacock," said Catalina. "Go to him after rehearsal tomorrow and tell him his play is so wonderful you will never have a moment's peace till you read it. He won't be able to resist letting you have it."

This accordingly Domingo did and Alonso, flattered, but taking no risks, gave him the manuscript on his promising to return it in two hours. When Domingo had read it he went for a walk and on his return made a suggestion to Catalina. She threw herself in his arms and kissed him.

"Uncle of my soul, you are a genius."

"But like many another, unrecognized," he grinned. "Now listen, child, don't whisper to a living soul, not even to Diego, what I have in mind, and at rehearsal play with all the talent you have. Be as sweet and as friendly to Alonso as though you had never had a difference of opinion, and he will think you are willing to let bygones be bygones. You will rehearse so beautifully that he will be pleased with you."

They were to have two rehearsals on the Saturday and a final one early on the morning of Easter Day. On the

Saturday, after the first rehearsal, when the company were separating for dinner, Catalina detained Alonso. She addressed him in her most cajoling way.

"You have written a beautiful play, my Alonso. The more I know it, the more astonishing do I find your genius. Even the great Lope de Vega does not excel you. You are a great, a very great poet."

Alonso beamed.

"I will admit that I am not entirely dissatisfied with it," he said.

"There is only one little thing that I find amiss."

Alonso started and frowned, for authors are such that a pennyweight of reservation put in the balance will far, far outweigh a pound of praise. But Catalina, at her most endearing, paid no attention.

"The longer I rehearse the more convinced I am that you have made a mistake in not letting me appear to more advantage in the third act."

Alonso gave a gesture of irritation.

"We have gone into all that before. I have told you a dozen times that there is no place in the act where you can possibly be brought in."

"And you were right, you were a thousand times right, but listen to me. I am an actress and I feel it from the bottom of my heart that when I stand at the sepulchre of our risen Lord I should have more to say than you have given me."

"And what, pray?" he asked indignantly.

"Well, it has occurred to me that it would be wonderfully effective if I narrated the story of Our Lord's betrayal, trial, crucifixion and death. It would only need a hundred lines."

"And who do you suppose will listen to a speech of a hundred lines at that stage of the play?"

237

"Everyone if I say them," replied Catalina. "I shall have the audience beating their breasts, crying out and weeping. The dramatist that you are must see how striking such a scene would be just at that moment."

"It's out of the question," he cried impatiently. "We play tomorrow. How could I write a hundred lines and rehearse them in that time? How could you learn them?"

Catalina smiled sweetly.

"Well, it so happens that my uncle and I have talked it over and he was inspired by the beauty of your play to write the lines which he agreed with me the scene demanded. And I have learnt them by heart."

"You?" cried the manager to Domingo.

"The eloquence of your play excited me," said he, "and I was as one possessed, so that it was as if you were holding my pen."

Alonso looked from one to the other. Catalina saw that he was undecided and she took his hand.

"Won't you let me say the speech to you, and then if you don't like it, I promise to say no more about it. Oh, Alonso, do me this favour. I know how much I owe to you, but do not forget that I have never spared myself to please you."

"Say this cursed speech then," he cried angrily, "and let me get to my dinner."

He sat down and with a scowl on his face prepared to listen. Catalina began. In three years her voice had gained in richness and she had a wonderful command over its modulations. The emotions proper to the narrative chased one another across her mobile face and she expressed apprehension, dismay, fear, indignation, horror, pain, anguish, grief without exaggeration; but with a telling truth. Angry though he was Alonso was too competent a dramatist not to realize very soon that the lines were well written and

238

that as she spoke them, with the eloquence of her gestures, with the touching quality of her voice, an audience would be held. He leant forward and clasped his hands. Presently he listened spell-bound. Then, such was her pathos, so moving her sincerity, he could no longer control himself, he began to sob and great heavy tears coursed down his cheeks. She finished and he wiped his eyes with his sleeve. He saw that Domingo was crying too.

"Well?" said Catalina with a smile of triumph.

With the last line she had stepped out of her part and was as cool as if she had been reciting the alphabet. Alonso shrugged his shoulders. He tried to make his tone gruff and business-like.

"The lines are tolerable for an amateur. We will rehearse the scene this afternoon and if I am satisfied with it you shall play it tomorrow."

"Soul of my heart, I adore you," said Catalina.

"I shall have trouble with Rosalia," he muttered gloomily.

The scene was rehearsed and played, with the effect on the Bishop of which the reader has been apprised. But this was not its only effect. Rosalia violently upbraided Alonso for his partiality to Catalina and he was obliged to make a great many promises to pacify her, some of which he knew he would have to keep; this irked him, but for another reason he was none too pleased with what had happened, since many persons, naturally thinking he had written them, singled out Domingo's hundred lines for special praise and told him that for language and versification they excelled anything else in the play. When Diego very indiscreetly let it be known by whom in fact they had been written Alonso was deeply mortified. In retaliation he told friends that Catalina was nothing like the actress she thought she was and without him to coach her would prove to have had very little talent. This was no sooner repeated to Catalina than she decided finally to take the step she had been contemplating. As she said to Diego, a woman has her self-respect to think of. She severed her connection with the ungrateful manager and with her husband and her children set out for Madrid.

XXXVI

Don Blasco, his resignation having been accepted, retired to a remote convent of his order with the intention of devoting the last of his years to the contemplation which Aristotle declared was the end of life and which the mystics have thought precious in the eyes of God. He refused to accept favours or privileges which, owing to the exalted positions he had held, were offered him, and insisted on having a cell similar to those occupied by the other friars and being in every way treated as they were. After some years his strength failed, and though he appeared to suffer from no definite disease it was plain to those about him that it would be no long time before he was released from the burden of the flesh. Friar Antonio, who had accompanied him to the convent, and the Prior begged him to relinquish the more severe of his austerities, but he refused; he persisted in observing the rule of the order in its utmost rigour and only consented to abstain from attending matins in the sharp cold of night when the Prior, exercising his authority, owing to Friar Blasco's increasing frailty forbad him to do so. Gradually he became so weak that he was obliged to spend much of his day in bed, but he seemed to be in no imminent danger of death. His life was like a flickering candle that any breath of wind may extinguish, but, protected from it, still continues wanly to give light. The end was sudden.

One morning Friar Antonio, after he had performed his religious duties, went to his old master's cell to see how he was. It was winter and snow was on the ground. The cell was bitterly cold. He was surprised to find him flushed, with bright eyes, and he rejoiced because he looked more like himself than for many weeks. The hope arose in his heart that the sick man had taken a turn for the better and might even then be restored to health. He uttered a short mental prayer of thanksgiving.

"You have a good colour this morning, Señor," he said, for Friar Blasco had long since desired him never again to address him as though he were still a bishop. "I haven't seen you look so well for days."

"I am very well. I have just seen the Greek Demetrios."

Friar Antonio repressed a start, for of course he knew that Demetrios had years before, as was only fitting, perished at the stake.

"In a dream, Señor?"

"No, no. He came through that door and stood by the side of my bed and spoke to me. He was exactly as he had always been, in that same threadbare robe he wore, and with the same benignity in his expression. I recognized him at once."

"It was a devil, my lord," cried Friar Antonio, forgetting the injunction his master had laid upon him. "You drove him from you?"

Friar Blasco smiled.

"That would have been discourteous, my son. I do not think it was a devil. It was Demetrios himself."

"But he is in hell suffering the just punishment of his damnable heresy."

"That is what I thought, but it is not so."

Friar Antonio listened with increasing dismay. It was likely enough that Don Blasco had had an infernal vision.

241

Pedro of Alcantara and Mother Teresa of Jesus had often had encounters with devils and Mother Teresa kept Holy Water by her for the express purpose of driving them away by throwing it at them. But his old master's attitude was so horrifying that he could only hope he was not in his right mind.

"I asked him how he fared and he said well. When I told him what cruel pain I had suffered because he was in hell he laughed lightly and told me that before ever the flames had consumed his body his soul flew to the meadow at the parting of the ways and thence, because he had lived in holiness and truth, Rhadamanthus sent him to the Islands of the Blest. And there he found Socrates, surrounded as always by young men of a comely aspect, asking and answering questions; and he saw Plato and Aristotle walking together in amicable converse as though there were no longer any difference of opinion between them; but Æschylus and Sophocles were gently chiding Euripides for having ruined the drama by his innovations. And many more, too numerous to mention."

Friar Antonio listened with consternation. It was evident that his old and revered friend was delirious. That was the meaning of those flushed cheeks and shining eyes. He did not know what he was saying, but the poor honest creature was thankful that there was no one but himself to hear. He trembled when he considered what the other friars would think if they heard him whom they regarded as saint utter words that were almost blasphemous. He racked his brains for something to say, but in his agitation could think of nothing.

"And when he had talked for some time in the friendly way in which we used to talk long ago in Valencia the cock crew and he said that he must leave me."

Friar Antonio thought it better to humour the invalid.

242

"And did he say why he had come to see you?" he faltered.

"I asked him. He said he had come to bid me farewell since after this we should never meet again. 'For tomorrow,' he said, 'when it is no longer night and not yet day, when you can just see the shape of your hand, your soul will be released from your body.'"

"That proves that it was an evil spirit that visited you, my lord," cried Friar Antonio. "The doctor says that you have no mortal illness and this morning you are better than you have been for many days. Let me give you the medicine he has sent and the barber shall bleed you."

"I will take no more medicine and I will not be bled. Why are you so eager to detain me when my soul yearns to escape from the prison in which it has dwelt for so long? Go, tell the dear Prior that I wish to make my confession and receive the Blessed Sacrament. For tomorrow, I tell you, when I can just see the shape of my hand I shall depart this life."

"It was a dream, Señor," cried the poor friar distraught. "I beseech you to believe it was a dream."

Don Blasco made a sound which in anyone else you would have called a titter.

"Don't talk nonsense, son," he said. "It was no more a dream than it is a dream that I am talking to you now. It was no more a dream than that this life, with its sin and sorrow, its anguished questions and mysterious secrets, is a dream, a dream from which we shall awake to life eternal which alone is real. Now go and do what I tell you."

Friar Antonio, with a sigh, turned and went. Don Blasco made his confession and received the Blessed Sacrament. After the last rites of the Church had been celebrated he bade farewell to the friars with whom he had lived for several years and gave them his blessing. By this time the day was far advanced. He desired then to be left alone, but Friar Antonio besought him so earnestly to be allowed to stay with him that with a gentle smile he consented on the condition that he should remain silent. Don Blasco lay on his back on the hard pallet with its thin mattress which the rule of the order required, covered, notwithstanding the piercing cold, by no more than one light blanket. Now and then he dozed. Friar Antonio was deeply distressed. The certainty that possessed Don Blasco had shaken him and he was by then more than half assured that death would come as his saintly master had said. The hours passed. The cell was dimly lit by a single taper and every now and then Friar Antonio snuffed it. The bell rang for matins. He was startled to hear Don Blasco break the long silence.

"Go, my son. You may not neglect your religious duties on my account."

"I cannot leave you now, my lord," the friar answered.

"Go. I shall still be here when you come back."

The long habit of obedience was effectual and he did as he was told. When he returned Don Blasco had fallen asleep and for a moment Friar Antonio thought that he was dead. But he was breathing peacefully and a faint hope arose in the friar's breast that he might thus be strengthened and perhaps even recover. He knelt down by the bed and prayed. The taper spluttered and went out. It was black night. The hours passed. At last Don Blasco made a slight movement. Friar Antonio in the heavy darkness could not see, but he had the intuition that his dear friend was feeling for the crucifix which hung by a cord round his neck. He placed it in the old man's hands, but when he wanted to withdraw his own he felt it lightly held. A sob broke from his throat. In all those years this was the first time that Don Blasco had given him a sign of affection. He tried to look into the eyes that once had shone with so intense a light, and though he could not see, he knew that they were open. He looked down at the hand that gently clasped his over the crucifix and as he looked he was aware that the blackness of night was not so impenetrable; he looked, and was on a sudden terrifyingly aware of the shape of an emaciated hand. A faint sigh escaped Don Blasco's lips and something, he did not know what, told the friar that his beloved master was dead. He burst into passionate weeping.

Don Manuel had by this time been for some years living in Madrid. Doña Beatriz had refused to go on with the plan she had been the first to propose that he should marry her niece, the Marquesa de Caranera; and since it had not been found possible to find her a suitable husband this widowed lady entered religion and was now sub-prioress of the Carmelite convent at Castel Rodriguez. Don Manuel felt that Doña Beatriz had treated him very badly, for the plot they had hatched between them had miscarried through no fault of his, but he was not one to cry over spilt milk; he went to Madrid and when he allowed his matrimonial designs and the extent of his fortune to be known it was not long before he was able to make a very satisfactory match. He attached himself to the Duke of Lerma, the favourite of King Philip III, and by the exercise of sub-servience, flattery, duplicity, unscrupulousness and venality finally succeeded in becoming highly respected. But his ambition was great. Don Blasco left behind him a saintly reputation, and Don Manuel was shrewd enough to see that it would increase his consequence if his brother were beatified, and the repute of his family (for heaven had blessed his union with two fine sons) if he were eventually canonized. He set about collecting the necessary evidence. No one could deny that the one-time Bishop of Segovia had been a man of exemplary piety; there were many witnesses who were prepared to declare that fragments of his habit worn round the neck had prevented them from catching the pox (great and small), and the various miraculous happenings at Castel Rodriguez were well authenticated; but the examining body at Rome demanded proof of two major miracles performed by the candidate's remains after death and this could in no manner be provided. The lawyers Don Manuel had engaged were honest men, for though a rogue himself he was too astute to employ rogues, and they told him that though it might be possible to get his brother beatified the chance of having his name included in the roll of saints was small. He flew into a passion when they told him this and accused them of incompetence, but on consideration came to the conclusion that they were in all probability right. He had already spent a good deal on the preliminary inquiry and saw no object in throwing good money after bad. After thinking it over in cold blood therefore, he decided that the beatification of his brother would not be worth the expense, and so contented himself with having the Bishop's remains transferred to the Collegiate Church at Castel Rodriguez, where he built a sumptuous monument, if not to perpetuate his memory of his father's eldest son, at least to manifest his own munificence.

In passing it may possibly be of interest to mention that Martin de Valero, the third of Don Juan's sons, sank back into the obscurity from which the exciting visit of his two distinguished brothers had momentarily raised him. He continued to bake bread, and that is all that can be said of him. It never even occurred to him, as indeed it never occurred to his fellow citizens, that on one occasion the Blessed Virgin had vouchsafed him the power to work a miracle.

Doña Beatriz lived to a great age in full possession of her

faculties and might have lived longer but for an untoward accident. On hearing of the beatification of her old enemy Mother Teresa of Jesus she had taken to her bed for three days, but when in 1622 she received news of her canonization she was seized with such rage that she had a stroke. She recovered consciousness, but on one side was completely paralysed, and it was evident that her end was near. Fear was an emotion unknown to her and she remained calm and collected. She sent for her favourite friar to hear her confession, after which she gathered her nuns around her and gave them suitable counsel for their future conduct. A few hours later she asked for the Blessed Sacrament. The priest was again sent for. She asked pardon for her sins and begged the weeping nuns to pray for her. For some time she lay in silence. Suddenly in a loud voice she said:

"A woman of very humble origins."

The nuns who heard her thought she referred to herself; and knowing that there flowed in her veins the royal blood of Castile and that her mother was of the illustrious house of Braganza, were deeply moved by this mark of humility. But her niece, the sub-prioress, knew better. She knew that the words referred to the rebellious nun who was become Saint Teresa of Avila. They were the last uttered by Doña Beatriz Henriquez y Braganza, in religion Beatriz de Santo Domingo. The Holy Oils were administered and shortly afterwards she died.

XXXVII

WHEN Catalina arrived in Madrid she still had the gold Doña Beatriz had given her and during the three years on the road, being a thrifty young woman, she had saved money, so that, notwithstanding Diego's somewhat extravagant tastes, she could look forward to the immediate future without anxiety. They called upon the patrons who had promised their influence and money to help them to get started, and finding them prepared to fulfil their promises were able to form a company. They were successful even beyond their hopes and Catalina became the rage of the town. Many fine gentlemen sought to obtain her favours, but though she accepted their presents with gratitude they received in return no more than a smile of her beautiful eyes and a pretty speech. She became then as greatly admired for her virtue as for her beauty and genius. She sent for Domingo and he came with a dozen plays in his wallet. She produced two of them. They were hissed off the stage, and, as was the way then, the audience showed its displeasure by shrill whistles, cat-calls and scurrilous abuse. Domingo, angry and humiliated, went home and shortly afterwards died, but whether of drink or disappointment has never been definitely settled. Some years later Catalina, by then acknowledged to be the greatest actress in Spain, sure of her hold on the public, determined, out of piety to his memory, to put on yet another of Domingo's plays; but, so that it should not suffer from the ill success of the first two, anonymously. It pleased; and indeed was so good that it was ascribed to the great Lope de Vega, and though he denied its authorship no one believed him, and in fact it has been printed among his works to this day; so poor Domingo was robbed even of that will-o'-the-wisp which has consoled many an author for the neglect of his contemporaries, posthumous fame.

Diego, notwithstanding his comely presence and his assurance, never succeeded in being anything but an indifferent actor. Fortunately, however, he proved himself a good business man and an efficient manager, so that with the years they became rich. They had long before agreed that it would be indiscreet to speak of the supernatural occurrences of which Catalina had been the occasion, and so, neither when they were with the strolling players, nor later, did anyone discover that she was in any way connected with events that for a time had been much talked about. Though, as she suspected, no more miracles took place to disturb the course of their married life, Diego was never, as he thought right and proper, master in his own house; but since Catalina was clever enough to let him think he was, he remained satisfied and happy. He was somewhat unfaithful to her, but, knowing that this is what you must expect of men, and so long as his amours were transitory and did not cost too much money, she accepted his infidelities with composure. Indeed it was a very happy marriage. She had six children by him, and being an actress with a conscience, rather than disappoint her public, would keep on playing persecuted virgins and austerely chaste princesses to the last possible moment of her successive pregnancies. She continued to play such parts to an advanced age, and a Dutch traveller who went to Spain in the latter part of the reign of Philip IV has left it on record that though she had grown corpulent and was several times a grandmother, such was her grace, the melody of her lovely voice and the magic of her personality, that before she had been on the stage five minutes you forgot her age and figure and accepted her without question as the passionate girl of sixteen she was representing.

So, with Catalina as it began, ends this strange, almost incredible, but edifying narrative.

25th January, 1947

THEN AND NOW

I

Plus ca change, plus c'est la même chose.

II

BIAGIO BUONACCORSI had had a busy day. He was tired,
but, being a man of methodical habit, before going to
bed made a note in his diary. It was brief: "The City
sent a man to Imola to the Duke." Perhaps because he
thought it of no importance he did not mention the
man's name: it was Machiavelli. The Duke was Cæsar
Borgia.

It had been not only a busy day, but a long one, for
Biagio had set forth from his house at dawn. With him
on a stout pony went his nephew, Piero Giacomini,
whom Machiavelli had consented to take with him.
It happened to be Piero's eighteenth birthday, October
6th, 1502, and so was a fitting day for him to go out
into the world for the first time. He was a well set-up
youth, tall for his age and of an agreeable aspect. Under
his uncle's guidance, for his mother was a widow, he
had received a good education; he could write a good
hand and turn a comely phrase, not only in Italian,
but in Latin. On the advice of Machiavelli, who
passionately admired the ancient Romans, he had
acquired more than a cursory knowledge of their
history. Machiavelli cherished the conviction that men
are always the same and have the same passions, so
that when circumstances are similar the same causes

253

must lead to the same effects; and thus, by bearing in mind how the Romans coped with a given situation, men of a later day might conduct themselves with prudence and efficiency. It was the wish of both Biagio and his sister that Piero should enter the government service, in which Biagio held a modest post under his friend Machiavelli. The mission on which Machiavelli was now going seemed a good opportunity for the boy to learn something of affairs, and Biagio knew that he could not have a better mentor. The matter had been settled on the spur of the moment, for it was only the day before that Machiavelli had been given his letter of credence to the Duke and his safe conduct. Machiavelli was of an amiable disposition, a friend to his friends, and when Biagio asked him to take Piero with him immediately agreed. But the lad's mother, though she saw that it was a chance that could not be missed, was uneasy. He had never been parted from her before and he was young to go out into a hostile world; he was besides a good boy and she was afraid that Machiavelli would corrupt him, for it was notorious that Machiavelli was a gay fellow and a dissolute. He was, moreover, not in the least ashamed of it, and would tell improper stories about his adventures with women of the town and with maid-servants at wayside inns which must bring a blush to a virtuous woman's cheek. And what made it worse was that he told them so amusingly that though outraged you could not keep a straight face. Biagio reasoned with her.

"Dear Francesca, now that Niccolo is married he will abandon his loose habits. Marietta, his wife, is a good woman and she loves him. Why should you think him so foolish as to spend money outside for what he can get at home for nothing?"

"A man who likes women as much as Niccolo will never be content with one," said she, "and if she is his wife, less than ever."

Biagio thought there was something in what she said, but he was not prepared to admit it. He shrugged his shoulders.

"Piero is eighteen. If he has not lost his innocence already it is quite time he did. Are you a virgin, nephew?"

"Yes," answered Piero, with so much candour that anyone might have been forgiven for believing him.

"There is nothing that I do not know about my son. He is incapable of doing anything of which I should disapprove."

"In that case," said Biagio, "there is no reason why you should hesitate to entrust him to a man who can be useful in his career and from whom, if he has sense, he can learn much that will be valuable to him all his life."

Monna Francesca gave her brother a sour look.

"You are infatuated with the man. You're like putty in his hands. And how does he treat you? He makes use of you; he makes fun of you. Why should he be your superior in the Chancery? Why are you satisfied to be his subordinate?"

Biagio was of about the same age as Machiavelli, who was thirty-three, but because he had married the daughter of Marsilio Ficino, a celebrated scholar patronised by the Medici, who then ruled the city, he had entered the government before him. For in those days influence got a man a job as often as merit.

Biagio was of the middle size, plump, with a round face, a high colour and an expression of great good nature. He was honest and hard-working, a man without envy who knew his own limitations and was satisfied with his modest position. He liked good living and good company, and since he asked for no more than he could have, might be counted a happy man. He was not brilliant, but neither was he stupid. Had he been so Machiavelli would not have endured his companionship.

"Niccolo has the most brilliant mind of anyone at present in the service of the Signory," he said now.

"Nonsense," snapped Monna Francesca.

(The Signory was the City Council of Florence and, since the expulsion of the Medici eight years before, the chief executive body of the State.)

"He has a knowledge of men and of affairs that men twice his age might envy. Take my word for it, sister, he will go far, and take my word for this too: he is not one to abandon his friends."

"I wouldn't trust him an inch. He'll cast you aside like an old shoe when he has no further use for you."

Biagio laughed.

"Are you so bitter because he never made advances to you, sister? Even with a son of eighteen you must be still attractive to men."

"He knows better than to try his tricks with a decent woman. I know his habits. It's a disgrace that the Signory allows harlots to flaunt themselves in the city to the scandal of respectable people. You like him because he makes you laugh and tells you dirty stories. You're as bad as he is."

"You must remember that no one tells a dirty story

better."

"And is it that that makes you think him so wonderfully intelligent?"

Biagio laughed again.

"No, not only. He made a great success of his mission to France and his dispatches were masterly; even the members of the Signory who don't like him personally were obliged to admit it."

Madonna Francesca shrugged her shoulders crossly. Meanwhile Piero, like the prudent young man he was, held his peace. He looked forward without enthusiasm to the job in the Chancery to which his uncle and his mother had destined him, and the idea of going on a journey was very much to his liking. As he had foreseen, his uncle's worldly wisdom triumphed over his mother's anxious scruples, and so it came to pass that on the following morning Biagio called for him and, Biagio on foot, Piero on his pony, they went the short distance to Machiavelli's house.

III

THE HORSES were already at the door, one for Machiavelli and two for the servants he was taking with him. Piero, giving his pony to one of the servants to hold, followed his uncle into the house. Machiavelli was waiting for them with impatience. He greeted them curtly.

"Now let us start," he said.

Marietta was in tears. She was a young woman of no great beauty, but it was not for her beauty that Machiavelli had married her; he had married her, that very year, because it was proper that he should marry, and she was of a reputable family and brought him as good a dowry as a man of his means and position could expect.

"Don't weep, dearest," he said, "you know I shall be gone only a little while."

"But you ought not to go," she sobbed, and then, turning to Biagio: "He's not fit to ride so far. He's not well."

"What is the matter with you, Niccolo?" asked Biagio.

"The old trouble. My stomach is out of order once more. It can't be helped."

He took Marietta in his arms.

"Good-bye, my sweet."

"You will write to me often."

"Often," he smiled.

When he smiled his face lost the sardonic look it generally wore, and there was something engaging in him so that you could understand that Marietta loved him. He kissed her and patted her cheek.

"Don't fret, my dear. Biagio will look after you."

Piero, on entering the room, had stood just within the door. No one paid him attention. Though his uncle was Machiavelli's most intimate friend, he had seen little of him and had not exchanged more than a few words with him in all his life. Piero took the opportunity to have a good look at the man who would be thenceforth his master. Machiavelli was of the middle height, but because he was so thin looked somewhat taller than he was. He had a small head, with very black hair cut short which fitted his skull like a velvet cap. His dark eyes were small and restless, and his nose long; his lips were thin, and when

258

he was not speaking so tightly closed that his mouth was little more than a sarcastic line. In repose his sallow face wore an expression that was wary, thoughtful, severe and cold. This was evidently not a man you could play pranks with.

Perhaps Machiavelli felt Piero's uneasy stare, for he gave him a quick, questioning glance.

"This is Piero?" he asked Biagio.

"His mother hopes you will look after him and see that he doesn't get into mischief."

Machiavelli gave a thin smile.

"By observing the unfortunate consequences of my errors he will doubtless learn that virtue and industry are the highways to success in this world and happiness in the next."

They set forth. They walked the horses over the cobblestones till they came to the city gate, and when they got on to the open road broke into a jog-trot. They had a long way to go and it was prudent to spare the horses. Machiavelli and Piero rode together and the two servants behind. All four were armed, for, though Florence was at peace with her neighbours, the country was unsettled and you could never be sure that you might not run across marauding soldiers. The safe conduct the travellers carried would have been of small help to them then. Machiavelli did not speak, and Piero, though not by nature shy, was somewhat intimidated by that sharp, set face, a slight frown between the brows, and thought it wise to wait till he was spoken to. The morning, notwithstanding an autumnal chill, was fine, and Piero's spirits were high. It was grand to be setting out on such an adventure and it was hard to keep silent when he was bubbling over with excitement. There were a hundred questions he wanted to ask. But they rode on and on. Soon the sun was bright in the heavens and the warmth of it was pleasant. Machiavelli never said a word. Now and then he raised one hand to indicate that they should walk the horses.

IV

MACHIAVELLI WAS BUSY with his thoughts. It was much against his will that he went on this mission and he had done his best to get someone else sent in his place. For one thing, he was far from well and even now as he rode he had an ache in his stomach; and then, having recently married, he did not wish to pain his wife by leaving her. He had promised her that his absence would be short, but in his heart he knew that the days might run into weeks and the weeks into months before he got permission to return. His mission to France had taught him how protracted diplomatic negotiations might be.

But these were the least of his troubles. The state of Italy was desperate. Louis XII, King of France, was the paramount power. He held a large part of the kingdom of Naples, though insecurely, since the Spaniards who held Sicily and Calabria continually harassed him, but he was in firm possession of Milan and its territories; he was on good terms with Venice and for a consideration had taken the city states of Florence, Siena and Bologna under his protection. He had an alliance with the Pope, who had granted him a dispensation to put away his barren and scrupulous wife so that he might marry Anne of

Brittany, the widow of Charles VIII, and in return
the King had created the Pope's son, Cæsar Borgia,
Duke of Valentinois, given him Charlotte d'Albret,
sister to the King of Navarre, in marriage, and promised to supply troops to enable him to recover the
lands, lordships and dominions of the Church, possession of which she had lost.

Cæsar Borgia, known now throughout Italy as Il
Valentino from the Duchy that Louis XII had bestowed upon him, was still well under thirty. His
mercenary captains, of whom the most important
were Pagolo Orsini, head of the great Roman house,
Gian Paolo Baglioni, Lord of Perugia, and Vitellozzo
Vitelli, Lord of Città di Castello, were the best in
Italy. He proved himself a bold and astute commander. By force of arms, treachery and the terror he
inspired, he made himself prince of a considerable
state, and Italy rang with his exploits. Taking advantage of a favourable opportunity he blackmailed the
Florentines into hiring him at a large salary with his
men-at-arms for a period of three years; but then,
having assured themselves of the protection of King
Louis by a further payment in hard cash, they revoked
Cæsar's commission and stopped his salary. This
enraged him, and presently he took his revenge.

In June of the year with which this narrative is
concerned Arezzo, a city subject to Florence, revolted
and declared itself independent. Vitellozzo Vitelli, the
ablest of Il Valentino's commanders and bitter enemy
of the Florentines because they had executed his
brother Paolo, and Baglioni, Lord of Perugia, went
to the support of the rebellious citizens and defeated
the forces of the Republic. Only the citadel held out.

261

The Signory in a panic sent Piero Soderini to Milan to hasten the expedition of the four hundred lancers King Louis had promised them. Piero Soderini was an influential citizen and as Gonfalonier occupied the position of president of the Republic. They ordered their own troops, encamped before Pisa, which they had long been trying to subdue, to advance to the rescue, but before they arrived the citadel fell. At this juncture Il Valentino, who was at Urbino, which he had recently conquered, sent the Signory a peremptory demand for the dispatch of an ambassador to confer with him. They sent the Bishop of Volterra, Piero Soderini's brother, and Machiavelli accompanied him as his secretary. The crisis was resolved, for the French King sent a strong force to fulfil his obligation towards Florence, and Cæsar Borgia, yielding to the threat, recalled his captains.

But his captains were themselves lords of petty states, and they could not but fear that when they had served his purpose he would crush them as ruthlessly as he had crushed other lords of other states. They received information that he had made a secret arrangement with Louis XII by the terms of which the King was to provide a contingent to assist him first in the capture of Bologna and then in the destruction of the captains, whose territories it would be convenient for him to incorporate in his own dominions. After some preliminary discussion they met at a place called La Magione, near Perugia, to consider how best to protect themselves. Vitellozzo, who was ill, was carried to the meeting on a litter. Pagolo Orsini came accompanied by his brother the Cardinal and his nephew the Duke of Gravina.

Among others who attended were Ermek Bentivoglio, the son of the Lord of Bologna, two Baglionis from Perugia, the young Oliverotto da Fermo, and Antonio da Venafro, the right-hand man of Pandolfo Petrucci, Lord of Siena. Their danger was great and they agreed that for their own safety they must act, but the Duke was a dangerous man and they knew that they must act with prudence. They decided for the present not to break with him openly, but to make preparations in secret and attack only when they were ready. They had in their pay a considerable body of troops, horse and foot, and Vitellozzo's artillery was powerful; they sent emissaries to hire several thousand of the mercenaries that then swarmed in Italy, and at the same time agents to Florence to ask for aid, for the Borgia's ambition was as great a threat to the Republic as to them.

It was not long before Cæsar heard of the conspiracy, and on his side he summoned the Signory to provide him with the troops which he declared they had engaged to let him have in case of need and requested them to send him an envoy empowered to treat with him. This was how it came about that Machiavelli was on his way to Imola. He went with misgiving. The Signory had dispatched him because he was a man of no official consequence, with no authority to make an agreement, who could only refer back to Florence and at every step must await his government's instructions. It was invidious to send such an emissary to one who, though a bastard of the Pope, in official documents styled himself Duke of Romagna, Valencia and Urbino, Prince of Andria, Lord of Piombino, Gonfalonier and Captain-General of the Church. Machiavelli's instructions were to inform him that the Signory had refused the conspirators' request for help, but that if he wanted either men or money he must apprise the Signory and await their reply. His business was to temporise, for such was the consistent policy of the Republic. The Signory could always find excellent reasons for doing nothing. If they got into too tight a corner they would untie the strings of their money-bags and disburse as small a sum as was acceptable. His business was to allay the impatience of a man unused to procrastination, to make no promises that had substance, to cajole a suspicious man with specious words, to use craft against craft, to counter deceit with deceit, and to discover the secrets of one who was notorious for his dissimulation.

Although he had but briefly seen him at Urbino, Machiavelli had been deeply impressed by him. He had heard there how the Duke Guidobaldo di Montefeltro, confiding in Cæsar Borgia's friendship, had lost his state and barely escaped with his life; and though he recognised that Il Valentino had acted with shocking perfidy he could not but admire the energy and adroit planning with which he had conducted the enterprise. This was a man of parts, fearless, unscrupulous, ruthless and intelligent, not only a brilliant general but a capable organiser and an astute politician. A sarcastic smile played upon Machiavelli's thin lips and his eyes gleamed, for the prospect of matching his wits with such an antagonist excited him. He began in consequence to feel much better and was no longer conscious of his queasy stomach; he was able indeed to look forward without displeasure to eating a snack at Scarperia, which was about half-way between Florence and Imola, and where he had decided to hire post horses. They had ridden as fast as was reasonable, for he wanted to get to Imola that day, and the horses, carrying not only their riders, but a good deal of baggage as well, could hardly be expected without hurt to themselves to go so far without more rest than he could afford to give them. He proposed to go on with Piero, leaving the two servants to follow next day with his own horse and Piero's pony.

They stopped at the Albergo della Posta and Machiavelli, dismounting, was glad to stretch his legs. He enquired what food could be prepared without delay and was not dissatisfied when he learnt that he could have macaroni, a dish of small birds, sausage from Bologna and a pork chop. He was a good trencherman and he devoured the meal that was set before him with enjoyment. He drank the strong red wine of the country and felt all the better for it. Piero ate as copiously as his master, and when they got into the saddle again and set out, he felt good and happy, so happy indeed that he began to hum one of the popular songs that ran about the streets of Florence. Machiavelli pricked up his ears.

"Why, Piero, your uncle never told me you had a voice."

Piero let it out with complacency and sang an ascending scale.

"A pretty tenor," Machiavelli said with a warm and friendly smile.

He reined in his horse to a walk, and Piero, accepting this as an invitation, broke into a well-known air, but the words were some that Machiavelli had written himself. He was pleased, but did not fail to reflect that the boy sang them to ingratiate himself with him. It was a neat device and he did not disapprove of it.

"How did you learn those words?"

"Uncle Biagio wrote them out for me and they fitted the tune."

Machiavelli made no reply and broke again into a canter. It occurred to him that it would be worth while to find out what he could about this boy whom he had taken, certainly, to oblige his friend Biagio, but whom also he had the intention of making good use of; so during the rest of the journey, when hilly country obliged them to walk the horses, he set out to do this. No one could be more affable, interesting and amusing than he when he chose, nor so subtle, and Piero would have had to be more worldly-wise than at his age he could be to discover that the friendly, careless questions put to him were designed to make him discover himself naked as when he was born. Piero was neither shy nor self-conscious, he had indeed the assurance of youth, and he answered frankly and ingenuously. To talk about himself seemed a very pleasant way of passing time that was beginning to grow tedious. Marsilio Ficino, the famous old scholar, had died only three years before; he was Biagio's father-in-law and had directed the young boy's studies. It was on his advice that Piero had acquired a sound knowledge of Latin and, though against his will, a smattering of Greek.

"It is one of the misfortunes of my life that I never learnt it," said Machiavelli. "I envy you for having read the Greek authors in the original."

"What good will that do me?"

"It will teach you that happiness is the good at which all men aim, and that in order to attain it you need nothing but good birth, good friends, good luck, health, wealth, beauty, strength, fame, honour and virtue."

Piero burst out laughing.

"It will also teach you that life is uncertain and full of tribulation, from which you may conclude that it is only reasonable to snatch what pleasure you can while you are of an age to enjoy it."

"I didn't need to learn the tenses of Greek verbs to know that," said Piero.

"Perhaps not, but it is reassuring to have good authority for following one's natural inclinations."

By well-directed questions Machiavelli learnt who the boy's friends were in Florence and what life he had led there, and by flattering attention to the opinions on one subject and another that he inveigled him into pronouncing he gained presently a fair impression of Piero's capacity and character. He was inexperienced, of course, but quick-witted, more so than his Uncle Biagio, who, though good and honest, was of mediocre intelligence; he had the high spirits of his youth, a natural wish to enjoy himself, and an adventurous temper; though ingenuous and in a way simple, he was not over-scrupulous, a trait to Machiavelli's mind of no disadvantage, for it meant that he would not be hindered by a too delicate conscience if he were wanted to do something that was a trifle less than honourable; he was strong and active and there was no reason to suppose that he lacked courage; his open face, his air of frankness, his engaging manner might all turn out to be valuable assets; it remained to discover whether he knew how to keep his own counsel and whether he could be trusted. It required only a little time to find out the first, and as to the second, Machiavelli had no intention of trusting him or anyone else more than need be. In any case the boy was clever enough to know that it could only be to his benefit to gain the good opinion of his master. A good word from Machiavelli could assure his future; a bad report would entail his dismissal from the service of the Republic.

V

THEY WERE NEARING IMOLA. It was situated on a river in a fertile plain, and the surrounding country showed none of the ravages of war, since it had capitulated on the approach of Cæsar's forces. When they were about two miles away they met seven or eight horsemen and Machiavelli recognised among them Agapito da Amalia, the Duke's First Secretary, whose acquaintance he had made at Urbino. He greeted Machiavelli warmly, and, on learning the errand on which he was bound, turned back and accompanied him to the city. The Signory had sent a courier a day before to inform their agent at the Duke's court of their envoy's arrival and the courier was waiting for him at the city gate. It had been a long ride and Agapito asked Machiavelli whether he would not like to refresh himself and rest before presenting his credentials to the Duke. Though the army was encamped outside the walls, the small city, now Il Valentino's capital, was crowded with his personal

268

staff, the members of his court, agents of other Italian
states, merchants with necessities or luxuries to sell,
solicitors of favours, sycophants, spies, actors, poets,
loose women, and all the rag-tag and bobtail that
followed a victorious condottiere in the hope of
making money by fair means or foul. The result was
that lodging was hard to get. The city's two or three
inns were chock-a-block and men were sleeping three,
four and five in a bed. But the Florentine agent had
made arrangements for Machiavelli and his servants
to be put up in the Dominican monastery and it was
thither that the courier now suggested conducting
him. Machiavelli turned to Agapito.

"If His Excellency can receive me I should prefer
to see him at once," he said.

"I will ride on and find out if he is at liberty. This
officer will lead you to the Palace."

Leaving the man he had indicated behind, Agapito
trotted off with the rest of his party. The others
walked their horses through the narrow streets till
they came to the main square. On the way Machiavelli asked the officer which was the city's best inn.

"I don't fancy the fare those good monks of the
monastery will provide and I have no wish to go
supperless to bed."

"The Golden Lion."

Machiavelli addressed himself to the courier.

"When you have deposited me at the Palace go to
the Golden Lion and see that an ample meal is prepared for me." Then to Piero: "Attend to the stabling
of the horses. The courier will show you the way to
the monastery and you will leave the saddle-bags in
charge of Antonio." This was one of his two servants.

"Then you and the courier will come to the Palace and wait for me."

The Palace, a large but unpretentious building, for Caterina Sforza, who had built it, was a thrifty woman, took up one end of the square, and here Machiavelli and the officer, dismounting, were admitted by the guard. The officer sent a soldier to tell the First Secretary they were there. In a few minutes he came into the room in which Machiavelli was waiting. Agapito da Amalia was a swarthy man, with long black hair and a small black beard, with a pale skin and sombre, clever eyes. He was a gentleman, with good manners, suave of speech and with a candid air which deceived many into thinking less of his abilities than was wise. He was devoted both to the person and the interests of the Duke, for Il Valentino had the gift of attaching to himself those whose loyalty was necessary to him. He told Machiavelli that the Duke would receive him at once. They ascended a fine flight of stairs and Machiavelli was ushered into a handsome apartment, the walls painted in fresco, with a large stone fireplace, on the hood of which were carved the arms of the intrepid, but unfortunate Caterina Sforza, whom Cæsar Borgia now held prisoner in Rome. A bright fire of logs blazed on the hearth, and the Duke stood with his back to it. The only other person in the room was Juan Borgia, Cardinal of Monreale, the portly, shrewd nephew of Pope Alexander. He was seated in a carved, high-backed chair, toasting his toes at the fire.

Machiavelli bowed to the Duke and the Cardinal, and the Duke, coming towards him graciously, took his hand and led him to a chair.

"You must be cold and tired after your long journey, Secretary," he said. "Have you eaten?"

"Yes, your Excellency, I ate on the way. I offer you my apologies for presenting myself as I am, in my riding clothes, but I did not wish to delay telling you what I have to say on behalf of the Republic."

He then presented his letter of audience. The Duke gave it a brief glance and handed it to the secretary. Cæsar Borgia was a man of striking beauty, of more than common height, with broad shoulders, a powerful chest and a slim waist. He was dressed in black, which emphasised his vivid colouring, and besides a ring on the index finger of his right hand his only ornament was the collar of St. Michael, the order which King Louis had conferred upon him. His hair, of a rich auburn and carefully dressed, was worn long and reached his shoulders; he had a moustache and a short beard trimmed to a point. His nose was straight and delicate and his eyes, under well-marked brows, were fine and bold; his well-shaped mouth was sensual; his skin clear and glowing. His gait was stately, yet graceful, and in his bearing was something of majesty. Machiavelli asked himself how it came about that this young man, the offspring of a Roman woman of the people and a fat, hook-nosed Spanish priest who had bought the papacy by shameless simony, had acquired the demeanour of a great prince.

"I requested your government to send me an envoy because I wish to know exactly how I stand with the Republic," he said with deliberation.

Machiavelli delivered the discourse he had prepared, but, though the Duke listened, Machiavelli could not but see that he looked upon the assurances of good will to which on the Signory's instructions he gave utterance as no more than fine phrases. There was a moment's silence. The Duke leant back in his chair and with his left hand fingered the order on his breast. When he spoke, it was with a certain coolness.

"My dominions border upon yours along an extended frontier. I am bound to take every means in my power to safeguard them. I know only too well that your city is ill-disposed to me. You have tried to embroil me with the Pope and the King of France. You couldn't have treated me worse if I were a murderer. Now you must choose whether you will have me as a friend or as an enemy."

His voice was musical, light rather than deep, and it had a quality, not acid, but cutting, which gave his words an insolence which was not easy to bear. He might have been speaking to a scullion. But Machiavelli was a practised diplomatist and knew how to keep his temper.

"I can assure Your Excellency that there is nothing my government wants more than your friendship," he answered blandly, "but they have not forgotten that you allowed Vitellozzo to invade our territories and they are doubtful of its value."

"I had nothing to do with that. Vitellozzo acted on his own account."

"He was in your pay and under your command."

"The expedition was begun without my knowledge and continued without my aid. I will not pretend I regretted it. I didn't. The Florentines had broken faith with me and it was right that they should suffer for it. But when I thought they had been

272

sufficiently punished I ordered my captains to withdraw. It has won me their enmity and they are now
conspiring my overthrow."

Machiavelli did not think it the moment to remind
the Duke that he had recalled his commanders only
on the peremptory command of the King of France.

"You are to blame for that, just as you are to blame
for Vitellozzo's invasion of your territory."

"We?" cried Machiavelli in frank astonishment.

"Nothing of this would have happened if you
hadn't been such fools as to torture and execute Paolo
Vitelli. You can hardly be surprised that his brother
Vitellozzo should seek his revenge, and because I
prevented him from pursuing it to the end he has
turned against me."

It is necessary to explain what the Duke meant by
this.

The Florentines had long been engaged on the siege
of Pisa, but things had gone badly and the army of
the Republic suffered a severe defeat which the
Signory ascribed to the incompetence of their
Captain-General; so they engaged two condottieri
then in the service of King Louis, Paolo and Vitellozzo
Vitelli, and gave the chief command to Paolo, a
captain of renown. A battle was fought, a breach was
effected in the walls and the army was on the point
of storming the city when suddenly Paolo Vitelli gave
the order to retreat. Though he said he had done this
to save further loss of life since he was sure of the
city's surrender on conditions, the Signory was convinced that he was playing them false, and sent two
commissioners ostensibly to furnish funds but in fact
to seize the persons of the two generals. Paolo Vitelli

273

was quartered about a mile beyond Cascina, and the commissioners requested him to meet them there so that they might discuss with him the conduct of the war. They gave him dinner and then, leading him into a secret chamber, arrested him. He was taken to Florence and beheaded, though under torture he would not admit his guilt.

"Paolo Vitelli was a traitor," said Machiavelli. "He had a fair trial and was found guilty. He suffered the just punishment of his crime."

"Whether he was innocent or guilty is no matter. To execute him was a blunder."

"It was necessary for our honour to act with energy against enemies of the Republic. It was necessary to show that Florence has the courage to provide for her safety."

"Why then did you leave his brother alive?"

Machiavelli irritably shrugged his shoulders. It was a sore point.

"Men were sent to fetch Vitellozzo and bring him to Cascina. He suspected a trap. He was ill in bed. He asked for time to dress and somehow managed to escape. The affair was bungled. How can you provide always against the stupidity of the people you have to act through?"

The Duke's laugh was light and gay. His eyes sparkled with good humour.

"It is an error to keep to a plan when circumstances have arisen that make its execution inadvisable. When Vitellozzo slipped through your fingers you should have taken Paolo to Florence, and instead of throwing him into a dungeon housed him in the best apartment of the Palazzo Vecchio. You should have tried him and, whatever the evidence, declared him innocent. Then you should have restored his command to him, increased his pay, and bestowed on him the highest honours at the disposal of the Republic. You should have convinced him that you had entire confidence in him."

"With the result that he would have betrayed us to our enemies."

"That might have been his intention, but for a while he would have had so to act as to prove that the trust you placed in him was justified. These mercenary captains are avaricious and will do anything for money. You might have made offers to Vitellozzo so handsome that he could not have brought himself to refuse; he would have rejoined his brother, and when you had lulled them into security, with a little ingenuity you could have found a suitable occasion to kill them both swiftly and without trial."

Machiavelli went red in the face.

"Such treachery would have been an eternal blot on the fair name of Florence," he cried.

"Traitors must be dealt with treacherously. A state is not governed by the exercise of Christian virtues, it is governed by prudence, boldness, determination and ruthlessness."

At this moment an officer came into the room and in a whisper spoke to Agapito da Amalia. Il Valentino, frowning at the interruption, with impatient fingers drummed on the table at which he sat.

"His Excellency is occupied," said Agapito. "They must wait."

"What is it?" asked the Duke sharply.

275

"Two Gascon soldiers have been caught looting, Excellency. They have been brought here under guard with the objects they seized."

"It would be a pity to make the subjects of the King of France wait," said the Duke, smiling faintly. "Let them be brought in."

The officer went out and the Duke amiably addressed himself to Machiavelli.

"You will excuse me if I attend to a little matter of business."

"My time is at Your Excellency's disposal."

"I trust you had no adventures on the road, Secretary."

Machiavelli took his cue from the Duke's tone.

"None. I was fortunate to find an inn at Scarperia where I was given a tolerable meal."

"It is my desire that men should travel in my dominions as safely as it is said they travelled in the Roman Empire of the Antonines. While you are here you will have opportunity to see for yourself that now that I have dispossessed those petty tyrants who were the curse of Italy I have by wise administration done much to render the lives of my people secure and prosperous."

There was a noise without of shuffling feet, voices were raised, and then, the great doors of the spacious chamber being flung open, a crowd surged in. First came the officer who had come in before, and he was followed by two men who from their respectable dress Machiavelli guessed must be dignitaries of the city. On their heels came two women, one old, the other middle-aged, and with them an elderly man of decent appearance. Then came a soldier carrying a

276

pair of silver candlesticks, and another with an ornamental goblet of silver gilt and two silver platters. They wore the red and yellow uniform of the Duke's own troops. Then, half pushed, half dragged by soldiers, entered two men with their hands tied behind their backs. They were shabby in non-descript garments and, standing among the Duke's uniformed men, looked a ruffianly pair. One was a scowling fellow of forty, of powerful physique, with a thick black beard and a livid scar on his forehead, and the other a smooth-faced boy with a sallow skin and shifty, frightened eyes.

"Stand forward," said the Duke.

The two men were given a shove.

"What is the charge?"

It appeared that the house of the two women had been broken into when they were at mass and the silverware stolen.

"How can you prove these articles were your property?"

"Monna Brigida is my cousin, Excellency," said one of the two respectable men. "I know the articles well. They were part of her dowry."

The other confirmed this. The Duke turned to the elderly man who seemed to be with the two women.

"Who are you?"

"Giacomo Fabronio, Excellency, silversmith. These two men sold me the pieces. They said they had got them at the sack of Forlì."

"You have no doubt that these are the men?"

"None, Excellency."

"We took Giacomo to the Gascon camp," said the

officer, "and he picked them out without hesitation."

The Duke fixed the silversmith with harsh eyes.

"Well?"

"When I heard that Monna Brigida's house had been broken into and her candlesticks and platters stolen, I became suspicious," the fellow answered, his face pale and his voice tremulous. "I went at once to Messer Bernardo and told him that two Gascon soldiers had sold me some silverware."

"Was it from fear or sense of duty?"

The silversmith for a moment could not find his voice. He was shaking with terror.

"Messer Bernardo is a magistrate, I have done much work for him. If the goods were stolen I didn't want them to be in my possession."

"What he says is true, Your Excellency," said the magistrate. "I went to see the articles and immediately recognised them."

"They are mine, Excellency," vehemently cried the younger of the two women. "Everyone will tell you they are mine."

"Be quiet." The Duke turned his gaze on the two Gascons. "Do you confess that you stole these things?"

"No, no, no!" screamed the boy. "It is a mistake. I swear on the soul of my mother that I didn't. The silversmith is mistaken. I have never seen him before."

"Take him away. A few turns on the rack will bring out the truth."

The boy gave a piercing shriek.

"No, not that. I couldn't bear that."

"Take him."

"I confess," gasped the boy.

The Duke gave a short laugh and turned to the other.

"And you?"

The older man threw back his head defiantly.

"I didn't steal them. I took them. It was our right; we had captured the city."

"A lie. You did not capture the city. It capitulated."

By the rules of Italian warfare at the time, if a city was taken by storm the soldiers were allowed to loot and keep everything they could lay hands on; but if it had capitulated, though the citizens were called upon to pay a large sum to defray the expenses to which the condittieri had been put to gain possession of their city, they saved their lives and their property. The rule was useful, for it made the citizens willing enough to surrender; it was not often that devotion to their prince induced them to fight to the death.

The Duke pronounced sentence.

"My orders were that the troops were to remain without the walls and that any harm done to the persons or property of the citizens should be punished by death." He turned to the officer. "Hang them in the square at dawn. Let it be published in the camp what their crime and its punishment were. Have two soldiers stand guard over the bodies till noon and let the town crier inform the population at proper intervals that they can rely on the justice of their prince."

"What does he say?" asked the terrified boy of his companion, for the Duke had spoken to the two Gascons in French and to the officer in Italian.

279

The man did not answer, but looked at the Duke with sullen hatred. The Duke, having heard, repeated the sentence in French.

"You will be hanged at dawn as a warning to others."

The boy gave a great cry of anguish and fell to his knees.

"Mercy, mercy!" he screamed. "I am too young to die. I don't want to die. I'm afraid!"

"Take them away," said the Duke.

The boy was dragged to his feet, screaming incoherently, tears running from his eyes; but the other, his face distorted with rage, gathered the spittle in his mouth and spat in his face. The pair were hustled from the room. The Duke turned to Agapito da Amalia.

"See that they are provided with the consolations of religion. It would weigh on my conscience if they faced their Maker without having had the opportunity to repent of their sins."

A faint smile on his lips, the secretary slid out of the room. The Duke, apparently in high good humour, addressed himself to the Cardinal his cousin and together to Machiavelli.

"They were fools as well as knaves. It was an unpardonable stupidity to sell the articles they had stolen in the very town they had been stolen in. They should have hidden them till they came to a much larger city, Bologna or Florence for instance, where they could have disposed of them in safety."

But he noticed that the silversmith was lingering by the door and seemed to wish to say something.

"What are you doing there?"

"Who is to going to give me back my money, Excellency? I am a poor man."

"Did you pay a fair price for the articles?" Il Valentino asked suavely.

"I paid what they were worth. The sum the scoundrels asked was ridiculous. I had to make my profit."

"Let it be a lesson to you. Another time don't buy anything unless you are sure it has been honestly come by."

"I can't afford to lose so much money, Excellency."

"Go," cried the Duke in a tone so savage that the man, with a cry, scuttled out of the room like a frightened rabbit.

Il Valentino threw himself back in his chair and roared with laughter. Then he turned courteously to Machiavelli.

"I must ask you to pardon the interruption; I think it important that justice should be administered promptly, and I wish the people of the territories under my rule to know that they can come to me if they have been ill-used and be sure to find in me an impartial judge."

"It is the wisest policy for a prince who wishes to assure his hold on dominions that he has recently acquired," said the Cardinal.

"Men will always forgive the loss of their political liberty if their private liberty is left undisturbed," said the Duke casually. "So long as their women are not molested and their property is safe, they will be reasonably contented with their lot."

Machiavelli had watched the incident with calm, even with amusement, which he took care not to show,

for he was convinced that the whole affair was a piece
of play-acting. He knew very well that Il Valentino
would never dare to hang two subjects of the King of
France. In all probability they had already been
released, with a gift of money for the trouble they
had been put to, and on the following day would be
found again in the ranks of the Gascon contingent.
Machiavelli guessed that the scene had been arranged
so that he could tell the Signory how efficiently the
Duke was ruling his new conquests, but more particularly for his reference at the end to Florence and
Bologna. The suggestion that the troops might find
themselves there was a threat too plain to be missed
by anyone with so shrewd a brain as Machiavelli.

Silence fell. The Duke, gently stroking his neat
beard, stared at Machiavelli reflectively. Machiavelli
had the feeling that he was making up his mind what
sort of a man this was that the Signory had sent to
negotiate with him, and not wishing to meet the
searching eyes fixed on him he looked down at his
hands, as though wondering if the nails wanted cutting. He was perplexed, and being perplexed was
uneasy. For it was he that had conducted the business
that led to the execution of Paolo Vitelli. Assured of
his guilt, he had exercised all his powers of persuasion
to convince his nervous and temporising superiors
that action must be taken without delay. It was he
that had given the commissioners orders to proceed
with energy. It was he that had urged the death sentence notwithstanding the fact that Vitellozzo had
escaped. But his activities had been behind the scenes
and he could not imagine how Il Valentino was aware
of them. The thought crossed his mind that the Duke

had dwelt upon the unsatisfactory outcome of the affair only to show that he knew what part Machiavelli had played in it and was maliciously pleased to be able to point out to him that he had handled it incompetently. But that man did nothing without a reason. It was unlikely that he wished to let the Florentine envoy know that he was well-informed of what happened in the Chancery of the Republic; it was more probable that his object was to shake Machiavelli's confidence in himself and so render him more amenable. The idea caused the suspicion of a smile to appear on his lips, and he glanced at the Duke. It looked as though the Duke had been waiting to meet his eyes before speaking.

"Secretary, I desire to confide to you a secret I have told to no living man."

"Do you wish me to leave you, Cousin?" asked the Cardinal.

"No, I trust in your discretion as much as I trust in the Secretary's."

Machiavelli, his jaw set, his gaze fixed on the handsome Duke, waited.

"The Orsini have begged me almost on their bended knees to attack Florence. I bear your city no ill will and I have refused. But if the gentlemen of your government want to come to terms with me they must do it before I patch things up with the Orsini. We're both friends of the King of France; surely it's advisable that we should be friends of one another. With our territories adjoining each of us can make things easy for the other; each of us can make things difficult. You depend upon mercenary troops under unreliable captains; I have my own army, well-trained, well-armed, and my captains are the best in Europe."

"But no more reliable than ours, Your Excellency," said Machiavelli dryly.

"I have others who are reliable. Who are they, the fools who are conspiring against me? Pagolo Orsini, a fool; Bentivoglio, who thinks I have designs on Bologna; the Baglioni, who fear for Perugia; Oliverotto da Fermo; and Vitellozzo, who is laid aside by the French sickness."

"They are powerful, and in revolt."

"All their movements are known to me and when things are ripe I shall act. Believe me, the ground is burning under their feet and it needs more water to put out the fire than such men as they can throw. Be sensible, Secretary. With Urbino in my hands I command Central Italy. Guidobaldo di Montefeltro was my friend, and the Pope intended to give his niece Angela Borgia in marriage to Guidobaldo's nephew and heir. I would never have attacked him unless I had seen the strategic importance of his state. I had to have it in order to carry out my plans, and I could not allow sentiment to interfere with policy. I can offer you security from your enemies. If we were to act together, I with my armies, you with your rich lands and your wealth, and with the spiritual authority of the Pope to support us, we should be the strongest power in Italy. Instead of having to pay hard cash for the favours of the French, they would have to treat with us as equals. The moment has come for you to conclude an alliance with me."

Machiavelli was startled, but he answered with easy amiability.

THEN AND NOW

"I see the force of Your Excellency's arguments. No
one could have put them more clearly or more con-
vincingly. It is rare to find a man of action, and a
great general such as Your Excellency has shown himself, who possesses so logical a mind and such a gift of
expression."

The Duke with a slight smile made a modest
gesture of protest. Machiavelli, his heart in his mouth,
for he knew that what he had to say was not what the
Duke wanted, went on blandly.

"I will write to the Signory and tell the gentlemen
what you have said."

"What do you mean?" cried Il Valentino. "The
matter is urgent and must be settled at once."

"I have no power to make an agreement."

The Duke sprang to his feet.

"Then what have you come here for?"

At that instant the door was opened; it was only
Agapito da Amalia coming in after attending to the
Duke's order, but it had a startling effect. Machiavelli
was not a nervous man, but it shook him strangely.

"I have come because Your Excellency requested
my government to send an envoy to treat with him."

"But an envoy with full powers to treat."

Until now the Duke had treated Machiavelli with
tolerable courtesy, but now, his eyes blazing, he
strode up to him. Machiavelli rose and the two men
faced one another.

"The Signory is fooling me. They sent you precisely
because you have no power to decide anything. Their
eternal shilly-shallying exasperates me beyond endurance. How long do they think they can continue to
try my patience?"

285

The Cardinal, who had sat in silence, put in a word to calm the storm, but the Duke harshly told him to hold his tongue. He began to pace up and down the room, storming; he was bitter, brutal and sarcastic; he seemed to have lost all control over himself. Machiavelli, unmoved and far from frightened, watched him with curiosity. At last the Duke flung himself back into his chair.

"Tell your government that I am deeply affronted."

"The last thing my government would wish is to affront Your Excellency. They instructed me to inform you that the rebels had requested their aid and they had refused."

"Waiting as usual, I suppose, to see which way the cat would jump."

There was more truth in this than was pleasant for Machiavelli to hear. His face remained impassive.

"They have no love for the Orsini or for Vitellozzo. They are anxious to be on friendly terms with Your Excellency, and I must press you to be more definite. It is at least necessary that I should be able to tell the Signory precisely what sort of an agreement it is that you desire."

"The discussion is ended. You force me to come to terms with the rebels. I can reduce them to submission tomorrow by agreeing to the proposal of the Orsini to attack Florence."

"Florence is under the protection of the King of France," answered Machiavelli sharply. "He has promised us four hundred lancers and an ample force of infantry whenever we need them."

"The French promise much in return for the money they continually demand, but when they have received it seldom keep their promises."

Machiavelli knew that was true. The Florentines had suffered much from the rapacity and double-dealing of King Louis. He had more than once undertaken at a price to send troops to assist them in their difficulties and then, having received the money, had delayed and delayed, and in the end sent only half the number paid for. The Duke could not have made himself more plain. The Florentines must either accept the alliance he offered them (and everyone in Italy knew what a faithless friend he was), or else he would compose his differences with his discontented captains and together with them attack the Republic. Blackmail! The situation was alarming, and Machiavelli in distress sought for something to say that would at least leave the way open for further negotiations; but the Duke prevented him from speaking.

"What are you waiting for, Secretary? You may withdraw."

He did not trouble to acknowledge Machiavelli's low bow. Agapito da Amalia accompanied the envoy down the stairs.

"His Excellency is a quick-tempered man and is unused to being crossed," he said.

"That is a fact which has not escaped my observation," replied Machiavelli acidly.

VI

PIERO AND THE COURIER were waiting in the guard-room, and when the doors were duly unbarred and unlocked the three of them went out into the square. His attendants conducted Machiavelli to the Golden

Lion. They had made much of the fact that the repast
they had ordered was for the Florentine envoy, and
he ate well and amply. The wine of the country,
though not to be compared with the Tuscan wine,
was strong, and he drank freely. On reflection he came
to the conclusion that his conversation with the Duke
was after all not unsatisfactory. Il Valentino's anger
seemed to indicate that he was nervous, and his insistence on an immediate alliance with the Republic
that he knew his position was perilous. Machiavelli
was indifferent to the scant courtesy with which he
had been treated. He knew when he started on his
mission that he need not expect to be used with consideration. Having done eating and belched his full,
he bade the courier show the way to the monastery
where he was to lodge. In view of his importance a
cell had been vacated for him, but Piero and the
courier were to share a straw mattress in a corridor
along with a number of transients only too glad to
have a roof over their heads. But before going to bed
Machiavelli wrote a letter to the Signory in which he
described the events of the evening. The courier was
to take it back to Florence at the crack of dawn.

"You had better write to Biagio, so that he can tell
your mother you have arrived here without mishap,"
he said to Piero. "And ask him to send me a Plutarch."

Machiavelli had brought his Dante with him, and
besides that only Livy's *Annals*. Plutarch offered
entertainment as well as instruction. When Piero had
finished, Machiavelli without ceremony took the
letter and read it. He smiled faintly when he read:
*"Messer Niccolo was silent throughout the morning,
and thinking he was occupied with weighty matters I*

did not disturb him; but after he had dined he talked with so much wit, clearness and good sense that it seemed to me we had hardly left Scarperia when we were arrived at Imola. He thinks I have a good voice. I wish it had been possible to bring my lute."

"A very good letter," said Machiavelli. "The message you have asked Biagio to deliver to your mother is very fit and proper. And now after this long day let us take a well-earned rest."

VII

MACHIAVELLI NEEDED LITTLE SLEEP and awoke soon after sunrise. He called Piero to help him dress. His riding clothes were packed in the saddle-bags and he put on the sober black raiment which was his usual wear. He had no intention of remaining at the monastery, for he needed quarters where he could if necessary receive persons in secret, and he knew very well that at the monastery his visitors and his movements would be conspicuous. The courier was already on his way to Florence. With Piero to accompany him, Machiavelli set out for the Golden Lion. Imola was a bright little town and there was no sign that it had not long since changed masters. As they walked through the narrow, tortuous streets they passed a good many people going about their various business, and they looked contented. You received the impression that the tenor of their lives remained unaltered. Now and then pedestrians had to make way for a man on horseback or for a string of donkeys with a load of firewood. A man sauntered by with she-asses, whose milk was good for pregnant women, and announced

289

his presence with the habitual cry; an old crone popped her head out of a window and called him; he stopped, and in a minute she appeared at her door with a beaker. A pedlar of pins and needles, thread and ribands passed along, raucously calling his wares. There were shops in the street in which was the Golden Lion; there was a customer at the saddler's, a man was having his hair cut at the barber's, and a woman was trying on a pair of shoes at the shoe-maker's. There was about all an air, not of opulence, but of a comfortable prosperity. No beggars pestered.

They entered the Golden Lion and Machiavelli ordered for himself and Piero bread and wine. Dipping the bread in the wine they made it palatable and then drank what remained of the wine. Thus fortified they went to the barber's and Machiavelli had himself shaved; the barber sprinkled strongly-scented water on his short black hair, and combed it. Meanwhile Piero had been meditatively stroking his smooth chin.

"I think I need a shave, Messer Niccolo," he said.

"It can wait a few weeks yet," said Machiavelli, smiling thinly; then to the barber: "Put some of your scent on his head and run a comb through his hair."

They were both ready. Machiavelli enquired of the barber where was the house of a certain Messer Bartolomeo Martelli, whom he desired to visit. The barber gave them directions, but they were so complicated that Machiavelli asked if he could not get someone to show them the way. The barber went to the door of his shop, and calling an urchin who was playing in the street, told him to conduct the strangers. Their way led through the principal square, the square in which was the palace occupied by the Duke, and since it was market day it was crowded with the stalls of the farmers who had brought into the city for sale fruits and vegetables, chickens, meat and cheese, and with the stalls of chapmen with brass, ironmongery, cloth goods, old clothes and what not. A great throng of people were bargaining, buying, or merely looking, and there was a din of voices. It was a gay and busy scene under the bright October sun. As Machiavelli and Piero entered the square they heard the wail of a brass horn and some of the noise was stilled.

"It's the crier," yelled the little boy excitedly, and seizing Machiavelli's hand he began to run. "I have not heard him yet."

A number of people surged forward, and, looking in the direction they took, Machiavelli saw that there was a gallows at the other end of the square and two men were hanging there. It was not a sight he cared to see, and he snatched his hand away. Forgetting his errand the boy raced towards the centre of interest. The crier in a loud voice began to speak, but he was too far away for Machiavelli to hear what he said. He turned impatiently to a stout woman who was standing guard over her stall.

"What has happened?" he asked her. "What is the crier saying?"

She shrugged her shoulders.

"It's only two thieves who've been hanged. By the Duke's orders the crier comes every half hour till noon and says they've been hanged because they stole the property of citizens. They're French soldiers, they say."

Machiavelli repressed a start. It could not be what he suspected, but he had to see for himself. He strode forward, squeezing his way through the crowd, jostling and jostled, his eyes fixed on the the two hanging bodies. The crier had said his say and, stepping down from the platform on which the gallows had been erected, sauntered nonchalantly away. The crowd thinned and Machiavelli was able to get close: there was no doubt about it; though their faces were horribly distorted by the strangling rope, they were the two Gascon soldiers, the man with the scowl and the scar, the boy with the shifty eyes, who had been brought in the night before to be judged and sentenced by the Duke. It hadn't been a comedy, then. Machiavelli stood stock still and stared with dismay. His small guide touched his arm.

"I wish I'd been here when they hanged them," he said regretfully. "No one knew anything about it till it was all over."

"It's nothing for little boys to see," said Machiavelli, hardly knowing that he spoke, for his thoughts were busy.

"It wouldn't be the first time," the child grinned. "It's fun to see them dancing in the air."

"Piero."

"I'm here, Messere."

"Come, boy, take us to Messer Bartolomeo."

For the rest of the way Machiavelli, frowning, his lips closed so tightly that his mouth was no more than a bitter line, walked in silence. He tried to think what had been in Il Valentino's mind. Why should he have hanged two useful soldiers because they had stolen a few bits and pieces of silverware when a

292

flogging would have adequately punished the crime?
It was true that human life meant nothing to him,
but it was unbelievable that he should be so eager
to win the confidence of the people of Imola as to
risk the anger not only of the commander of the
Gascon troops, but of the troops themselves. Machiavelli was puzzled. He was convinced that his presence
at that moment was in some way necessary to the
Duke's purpose; otherwise, even if he had troubled
to deal with the affair in person, he would have
waited till he had finished his important conversation with the Florentine envoy. Did he want to show
the Signory that he was independent of the French
and, notwithstanding the revolt of his captains,
strong enough to risk their displeasure; or was the
whole point of the scene the scarcely veiled threat he
had made when he told Machiavelli that the soldiers
could have safely sold their loot when they were in
Florence? But who could tell the workings of that
ruthless, crafty brain?

"This is the house, Messere," said the boy suddenly.

Machiavelli gave him a coin and the urchin with
a hop, skip and a jump ran off. Piero raised the
bronze knocker and let it fall. There was a delay and
Piero knocked again. Machiavelli noticed that the
house was of handsome proportions, evidently the
abode of a man of substance; and the windows on the
second floor, the *piano principale,* were not, as might
have been expected, of oiled paper, but of glass,
which showed that he had ample means.

VIII

MACHIAVELLI DID NOT KNOW Bartolomeo Martelli, but he had been instructed to get in touch with him. He was a person of consequence in the small city, an alderman, and a man of property. He owned land in the immediate neighbourhood of Imola and several houses in the town itself; his father had made money by trade in the Levant and he had himself spent some years of his youth in Smyrna. It was on this account that he had connection with Florence, since the Florentines had always traded with the Near East and many of the citizens were settled in its various cities. Bartolomeo's father had been in partnership with a Florentine merchant of good family and had eventually married his daughter. He was distantly related to Biagio Buonaccorsi, for their maternal grandmothers, long since dead, were sisters; this indeed was one of the inducements Biagio had held out to Machiavelli to persuade him to take young Piero with him. The connection would make it easier for Machiavelli to get on intimate terms with the useful man.

And Bartolomeo might be very useful. He was not only a considerable man in Imola, but it was he who had led the party that brought about the capitulation of the city without a struggle. The Duke, who was always generous with other people's property, had rewarded him with the gift of an estate which carried with it the title of count, a fact Machiavelli had learnt from the loquacious barber, and he had learnt also that Bartolomeo, though he pretended

294

otherwise, was inordinately pleased with his rank. The Duke trusted him, knowing it was to his advantage to be trustworthy, and had employed him on various commercial missions in which he had conducted himself with credit. The Duke was secret, but it was likely that Bartolomeo knew as much about his plans as anybody, and Machiavelli was confident that he would in due course succeed in extracting from him anything he knew. The Signory had a hold on him. He had inherited from his mother two houses in Florence, and if he did not behave an accidental fire might easily destroy one of them; and if this were not a sufficient deterrent, means might possibly be found to damage the business in the Levant in which he still had a large interest.

"It is good to have friends," Machiavelli reflected, "but it is as well that they should know you can retaliate if they should be led to act otherwise than as friends should."

The door was opened by a serving-man. When Machiavelli, first giving his name, asked for his master, he said:

"The Count is expecting you."

He led them into a court-yard, up an outside staircase, and into a room of moderate size which a glance showed was used by the master of the house as his office. They waited a minute or two and Bartolomeo blustered in. He greeted his visitors with noisy heartiness.

"I heard of your arrival Messer Niccolo, and I have been awaiting you with eagerness."

He was a big, corpulent man of about forty, with long hair, receding from his forehead, and a full

295

black beard; he had a red face, shining with sweat, a double chin, and a somewhat imposing paunch. Machiavelli, himself as lean as a rail, did not like fat men; he was used to say that no man could grow fat in Italy without robbing the widow and the orphan and grinding the faces of the poor.

"Biagio Buonaccorsi wrote and told me you were coming. A courier brought the letter yesterday."

"Yes, a courier was coming and Biagio made use of him. This is Piero Canestrini, son of our good Biagio's sister."

Bartolomeo gave a ringing laugh, and taking the boy in his arms, pressed him to his paunch and kissed him on both cheeks.

"Then we are cousins," he cried in a loud, booming voice.

"Cousins?" murmured Machiavelli.

"Did you not know? Biagio's grandmother and my grandmother were sisters. They were both daughters of Carlo Peruzzi."

"Strange he should never have told me. Did you know this, Piero?"

"My mother never told me."

Machiavelli only disclaimed knowledge of this fact, with which of course he was perfectly acquainted, because it was one of his principles never to let anyone know how much you know except with good reason. He was pleased to see that Piero had taken the cue without a moment's hesitation. A good boy.

Bartolomeo asked them to sit down. There was no fireplace in the room, but a brazier of live charcoal took the chill off the air. He asked after his friends in Florence, which he frequently visited on business, and Machiavelli gave him news of such as he knew. They chatted about one thing and another, and presently the conversation turned upon Piero Soderini, who had just been elected Gonfalonier for life.

"He is a good friend of mine, a very worthy and honest man," said Machiavelli. "It is at his express desire that I have come to Imola now."

He thought it well to let Bartolomeo know that he had the confidence of the head of the Republic.

"I am very glad to see you and you may be assured that you can count on my services. I asked Biagio to send me a bolt of fine linen, but in the circumstances I suppose you had no opportunity to bring it."

Biagio, since he was ever ready to do a service, was constantly asked to do commissions for all and sundry, and no one used him more unconscionably than Machiavelli.

"On the contrary," he answered. "Biagio made a point of my bringing it, but my servants have it and they will not get to Imola till later in the day."

"My wife is making me some shirts. She was taught embroidery by the nuns and I have no hesitation in saying that there isn't a woman in Imola to equal her. She is an artist."

Machiavelli's mind was busy. He was trying to size the man up. Bluff and hearty, plethoric, which suggested that he liked to eat well and drink deep, with a fat laugh and a booming loquacity. It remained to be seen whether the jovial manner and frank cordiality masked an astute and scheming brain. He had the reputation of being a good business man who drove a hard bargain. Machiavelli turned the con-

versation to Imola and its condition. Bartolomeo was
eloquent in praise of the Duke. He had adhered
scrupulously to the terms of the capitulation; the
sum he had exacted on occupying the city was not
unreasonable, and he was proposing to spend much
on making it a finer and grander place. For Imola
was the capital of his newly-acquired state. He was
having plans drawn out for building a new palace
for himself, a new house for the merchants to meet
at, a hospital for the poor; order reigned in the city,
crime had diminished and justice was prompt and
cheap. Poor and rich were equal before the law.
Commerce was flourishing; bribery and corruption
had ceased. The Duke interested himself in the agri-
cultural resources of the country and had given
instructions that everything possible should be done
to foster them. The troops were stationed outside the
city, which was spared the cost of their maintenance.
In short the city was entering upon an era of prosperity and everyone was well satisfied.

"Long may it last," said Machiavelli pleasantly;
"and what will happen to you if the Duke's captains
overthrow him and march into your city with their
troops?"

Bartolomeo burst into a bellow of laughter and
slapped his thigh.

"They amount to nothing. They know they're
powerless without the Duke and they'll come to
terms with him. Believe me, it will all blow over."

Machiavelli could not make up his mind whether
Bartolomeo believed what he said, wanted to believe
what he said, or was just saying what he wanted
Machiavelli to believe. He had still not made up his

mind whether the man was stupid or clever. That frankness, that enthusiasm, that guileless air and those smiling, friendly eyes might conceal anything. He changed the conversation.

"You were good enough to say that you would be pleased to be of service to me. Can you tell me where I can find a place to live with Piero and my servants?"

"I wish you had asked me anything but that." Bartolomeo laughed boisterously. "What with the Duke's court and all the hangers-on, poets, painters, architects, engineers, to say nothing of the people from his other possessions who are here on business, and the merchants, the vendors of this and that, who've been attracted by the opportunities to make money, there isn't a hole or corner in the city that isn't occupied."

"I wish to stay here no longer that I need, but I am at the orders of the Signory. I cannot conduct my business in a monastery cell. I must find accommodation for Piero and my servants."

"I will ask my mother-in-law. She knows more about a matter like this than I do. I will call her."

He left the room, and on his return after an interval invited his guests to follow him. He led them into a much larger apartment, with handsomely-painted walls and a fireplace. The ladies were seated at work by the fire. They rose when the strangers entered and curtsied in response to their low bows. One of them was a middle-aged woman of a comely presence.

"This is my mother-in-law, Monna Caterina Cappello," said Bartolomeo. "And this is my wife."

She was young enough to be his daughter. Following the fashion of the day her hair, naturally dark, was dyed very fair; and since the swarthy skin of Italian women did not go with this, her face, neck and bosom were heavily coated with a white cosmetic. The contrast of the golden hair with her handsome black eyes was very effective. Her eyebrows were plucked to a thin line. She had a small straight nose and a lovely mouth. She was dressed in pale grey, with a full skirt, billowing sleeves, and a bodice fitting her slim figure tightly and cut low in a square to show her snowy bosom and the outline of her young full breasts. There was a virginal quality in her beauty and at the same time a ripeness that made a highly attractive combination. Machiavelli, though his face gave no indication of it, felt a queer sensation in what he was pleased to call his heart.

"A very pretty young woman," he said to himself. "I should like to go to bed with her."

While the two ladies brought up chairs for the visitors to sit on, Bartolomeo explained to Monna Caterina Machiavelli's difficulty and then, as an afterthought, added that in Piero he had found a cousin whom he had never seen. Both women gave the boy a smile when the relationship was explained to them, and Machiavelli noticed with pleasure that Bartolomeo's wife had good teeth, small, even and white.

"Would these gentlemen not like some refreshment?" asked Monna Caterina.

She was dressed very like her daughter, but in a darker colour, and since it was not thought proper for a respectable elderly woman to dye her hair or to paint her cheeks she was as nature made her; but she

300

had her daughter's fine black eyes and in youth must have been as beautiful. Machiavelli said they had already breakfasted, but his host insisted that they should at least drink a glass of wine.

"Aurelia, go and tell Nina," he said to his wife.

The young woman went out. He repeated to his mother-in-law what Machiavelli had told him about his requirements.

"It's impossible. There's not a room to be let in the whole city. But wait. Since Messere is a person of consequence and this young man your cousin, it may be that Serafina would take them. She has always refused to take lodgers; only the other day I told her it was a shame to keep that room empty when people were willing to pay anything to have a roof over their heads."

Bartolomeo explained that Monna Serafina was the widow of one of his factors in the Levant and the house she lived in belonged to him. Her eldest son was in his office at Smyrna, and she had two children living with her, a boy who was to be a priest and a girl of fourteen. It was on their account, so that they might not be exposed to the danger of bad company, that she had refused to have strangers in her house.

"She could hardly refuse you, my son, if you made a point of it."

It was odd to hear Monna Caterina address the fat man as her son, for she could not have been more than two or three years older than he.

"I will take you round myself," said Bartolomeo. "I'm sure it can be arranged."

Aurelia came back and was immediately followed by a maid who brought in a salver on which were glasses, a bottle of wine and a dish of sweetmeats. Aurelia sat down and resumed her work.

"Messer Niccolo has brought you the linen, dear," Bartolomeo said, "so you can get to work on my shirts."

"God knows you needed some new ones," said Monna Caterina.

Aurelia smiled, but did not speak.

"Let me show you how beautifully my wife embroiders."

Bartolomeo went over to Aurelia and took the material on which she was busy.

"No, Bartolomeo, these are women's things."

"If Messer Niccolo has never seen a woman's shift it is high time he did."

"I am a married man, Monna Aurelia," said Machiavelli with a smile that made his thin face not unattractive.

"Look at the beauty of her needlework and the elegance of her design."

"Is it possible that she draws it herself?"

"Of course. She is an artist."

Machiavelli made a suitable compliment and the garment was returned to her. She thanked him with a smile of her bright eyes. When they had eaten of the sweetmeats and drunk a glass of wine Bartolomeo proposed that he should take them round to the widow Serafina.

"Her house is just behind this one," he said.

Machiavelli and Piero accompanied him downstairs, and through a small yard in which was a well with a carved well-head and a chestnut-tree, its leaves now scattered after the first frost of autumn, to a small door that led into a narrow alley.

"Here we are," said Bartolomeo.

The deserted alley suggested to Machiavelli that visitors could in all likelihood come to see him without being observed. Bartolomeo knocked, and in a minute the door was opened by a thin, tallish woman with a lined face, darkly pale, sullen eyes and grey hair. The look of suspicion she wore changed, when she saw who it was that had knocked, into one of effusive welcome. She begged them to enter.

"This is Messer Niccolo Machiavelli, First Secretary of the Second Chancery, and envoy to the Duke from the Florentine Republic, and this youth is my cousin Piero, nephew of my good friend and relative, Biagio Buonaccorsi."

Monna Serafina led them into a parlour and Bartolomeo set forth the purpose of their visit. Monna Serafina's face went glum.

"Oh, Messer Bartolomeo, you know I've refused everybody. You see, with two young children in the house. And people one knows nothing about."

"I know, I know, Serafina, but here are people I vouch for. Piero is my cousin; he will be a good friend to your Luigi."

The discussion proceeded. Bartolomeo, in his bluff, hearty way, managed to convey to the unwilling woman that the house was his and if he wanted to he could turn her out, and that her elder son was in his employment; but it was done in such a friendly, advancement; but it was done in such a friendly, bantering manner as to excite Machiavelli's admiration. The man, simple though he looked, was no fool. Serafina was poor and she could not afford to offend

Bartolomeo. With a grim smile she said that she would be happy to do him and his friends a service. It was arranged that Machiavelli should have a room and the use of the parlour, Piero would double up with her son Luigi, and she would put down mattresses for the two servants in the attic. The sum she asked for rent was high, and Bartolomeo remarked on it, but Machiavelli thought it beneath his official dignity to haggle and said that he would be glad to pay it. He knew that nothing more predisposes someone in your favour than to let him rob you a little. There was of course no glass in the windows, but there were shutters to them and oiled paper screens which could be opened entirely or in part to let in air and light. There was a fireplace in the kitchen and the parlour could be warmed by a brazier. Serafina consented to give her own room to Machiavelli and move in with her daughter to a smaller room on the ground floor.

IX

THIS HAVING BEEN SETTLED, Bartolomeo left them, and Machiavelli and Piero went back to the Golden Lion to have dinner. They were just finishing when the two servants arrived from Scarperia with the horses and the baggage. Machiavelli told Piero to show them the way to the monastery and fetch the saddle-bags which had been left there.

"Take the bolt of linen to Messer Bartolomeo's and bid the maid take it up to the ladies. She wasn't a bad-looking wench; it might be worth your while to get into conversation with her. Then go back to Serafina's and wait till I come."

He paused for a moment.

"She's a talkative woman and certainly a gossip. Go and sit with her in the kitchen. She'll be glad of company. Let her talk to you about her children, and talk to her about your mother. Then find out all you can about Bartolomeo, his wife and his mother-in-law. Serafina's under too great an obligation to him not to bear him a grudge; you have a frank, honest face, you're only a boy, if you can gain her confidence she'll pour out her soul to you. It will be good practice for you to learn how with kind words and pretty speeches you can get someone to betray the hatred that is in his heart."

"But, Messer Niccolo, why are you so certain that she hates him?"

"I'm not certain at all. It may be that she's only a foolish, garrulous woman. The fact remains that she is poor and he is rich, and that she depends on his bounty; the burden of gratitude is very hard to bear. Believe me, it is easier to forgive the offences your enemy does you than the benefits your friend confers upon you."

He smiled acidly and went his way. He had an appointment with the Florentine agent to meet a fellow-citizen, Giacomo Farinelli by name, who had been exiled with the Medici, and who, being a clever accountant, had been engaged by the Duke; but he was anxious to get back to Florence and have his confiscated property restored to him, and so could be counted on to make himself useful. He confirmed what Bartolomeo had told Machiavelli in the morning. The Duke's new subjects were contented with his rule. The administration was severe, but competent.

The people who had groaned under the tyranny of their petty princes enjoyed a freedom from oppression they had not known for a century. By conscription, taking one man from every house in his dominions, the Duke had created an army which was much more reliable than the hirelings of which, in general, armies consisted. The French men-at-arms and the Gascons might at any time be recalled by their King, the Swiss were always prepared to desert if another power made it worth their while, and the Germans ravaged every district they went through and were a terror to the population. The Duke's soldiers were proud of the red and yellow uniform into which he had put them; they were well paid, well drilled and well armed; and he had succeeded in inspiring them with loyalty.

"And what of the captains, Vitellozzo and the Orsini?" asked Machiavelli.

There was no news of them. No one knew what they were doing.

"What is the feeling at the Palace?"

"You would say that nothing was the matter," said Farinelli. "The Duke is secret and keeps to his apartments. The secretaries give no sign that there is cause for anxiety. I have never seen Messer Agapito in a better humour."

Machiavelli frowned. He was puzzled. It was evident enough that something was brewing, but though the accountant was very willing to tell all he knew, at the end Machiavelli was obliged to admit that he was no wiser than before. He returned to his lodging, where Piero was waiting for him.

"Did you deliver the linen?" he asked.

"Yes. Messer Bartolomeo was at the Palace. The maid told me to wait while she took it up to the ladies, and when she came down said they wanted to thank me in person for bringing it. So I went up."

"Then you didn't make friends with the maid as I told you to."

"There was no opportunity."

"You might have pinched her or at least told her she was pretty. There was opportunity for that."

"The ladies were very nice to me. They gave me fruit and cake and wine. They asked me a lot of questions about you."

"What did they ask?"

"They wanted to know how long you'd been married and whom you'd married and what Monna Marietta was like."

"And have you talked to Serafina?"

"You were right about her, Messere. If you hadn't come in she'd be talking still. I thought she'd never stop."

"Tell me."

When Piero had finished Machiavelli gave him a genial smile.

"You have done very well. I knew I was right, I knew that your youth would appeal to the ageing woman and your simple and innocent look make it easy for her to confide in you."

Piero had found out a great deal. Bartolomeo was in high favour with the Duke. He was one of the first men in the city. He was honest, kindly, generous and devout. This was his third marriage. His first had been arranged by his parents, and his wife after eight years died of cholera. After a decent interval he married again, but eleven years later his second wife also died. Both had brought him handsome dowries, and both were childless. He had remained a widower for three years and then suddenly married Aurelia. She was a native of Sinigaglia, a port on the Adriatic, and her father was owner and master of a coasting vessel that carried merchandise to the Dalmatian cities. He was lost with his ship in a storm, and his widow was reduced to poverty so that she had to earn her living as a sempstress. She had three daughters, a son having been drowned with his father, but two of them were married. Aurelia was sixteen when accident brought her to the notice of Bartolomeo. He was struck by her virginal beauty, but neither by birth nor fortune was she a proper match for a man of his consequence; but, young though she was, there was in her a ripeness that gave promise of fecundity, and that was a matter of moment to Bartolomeo, for there was nothing in the world he wanted more than a son. During the lifetime of his two wives he had kept likely young women of humble station, but none of these irregular amours had resulted in issue. The fact that Monna Caterina had had six children (two had died in infancy) showed that the stock was fruitful, and by discreet enquiries he discovered that Aurelia's older sisters had already had three or four babies each. They had in fact given birth once a year with the regularity which was proper to a healthy young person of the female sex. But Bartolomeo was cautious. He had married two barren women and did not want to marry a third. Through an intermediary he proposed to Monna Caterina that he should install her and her daughter on a handsome allowance in one of his villas outside Imola, with a promise that he would recognise any child that might be born. He went so far as to permit the intermediary to hint at the possibility of marriage if the child were male. But Monna Caterina, whether owing to religious scruples or wordly wisdom, refused the offer with indignation. Her dead husband, though no more than the master of a small coasting vessel, had been an honourable man, and her two daughters were respectably, if not richly, married. Sooner than see her beloved child the kept woman of a merchant she would put her in a nunnery. Bartolomeo reviewed the marriageable young women in Imola and could think of none who attracted him so much as Aurelia or who seemed more likely to give him the son he yearned for. He was a business man and a sensible one. He knew that if you wanted something enough and could not get it at your own price there was only one thing to do and that was to give the price asked for it. With a good grace he made an offer of marriage. It was promptly accepted.

Bartolomeo was not only a business man, but a shrewd one. Aurelia was twenty years younger than he, and he thought it advisable that she should have someone to keep an eye on her. He invited Monna Caterina to live with him and his bride.

Serafina sniggered.

"The old fool trusts her. But look at her; that isn't a woman who was faithful to her husband. You can tell at once. When her husband was at sea she wasn't so virtuous as all that."

"She evidently doesn't like Monna Caterina," said Machiavelli. "I wonder why. Perhaps she wanted to marry Bartolomeo herself and have him adopt her children. Perhaps merely envy. It may be of no importance, but it is just as well to know."

The marriage had been happy and Bartolomeo was delighted with his young wife. He gave her fine clothes and fine jewels. She was dutiful, respectful, submissive, in fact all that a wife should be, but though they had been married three years she had not had a baby and showed no sign of having one. It was the great cross of Bartolomeo's life, and now that he had a title to transmit he wanted a son more than ever.

"Did Monna Serafina hint that the beautiful Aurelia might be unfaithful to her old husband?" Machiavelli asked with a smile.

"No. She seldom goes out except to go to mass, and then only with her mother or the maid to accompany her. According to Monna Serafina she is very pious. She would look upon it as a mortal sin to deceive her husband."

Machiavelli pondered.

"When you were talking with the ladies about me did you happen to mention that Monna Marietta was pregnant?"

The boy flushed.

"I thought there was no harm."

"None at all. I'm not sorry they know."

Machiavelli smiled significantly, but the significance of his smile escaped Piero. It has been said that Machiavelli had not married Marietta for love. He respected her, he appreciated her good qualities, and he approved of her devotion to him. She was a thrifty housekeeper, an important matter to one of his small means, and she never wasted a penny; she would be

310

the mother of his children, and a good mother; there was every reason why he should regard her with indulgence and affection, but it had never entered his mind that he should be faithful to her. Aurelia's beauty had taken his breath away, but it was not only her beauty that had moved him, he could not remember any woman who had so immediately and so violently excited his senses. His very stomach ached with the vehemence of his desire.

"I'm going to have that woman if I die for it," he said to himself.

He knew a great deal about women and it was not often that he had failed to satisfy his lust. He had no illusions about his appearance; he knew that other men were handsomer than he and that many had the advantage of him in wealth and station. But he was confident in his powers of attraction. He could amuse them, he knew just how to flatter them, he had a way with him that put them at their ease with him, but above all he desired them; they were very conscious of that and it excited them.

"When a woman feels with every nerve in her body that you want her she can resist only if she's passionately in love with another," he had once told Biagio.

It was impossible to suppose that Aurelia loved her fat husband, a man so many years older than herself, to whom she had been married by her mother because it was a good business proposition. But Bartolomeo must know that there were young men in the city, dissolute fellows attached to the Duke's court, who had noticed that she was beautiful, and he must be on his guard. The serving-man had suspicious eyes. He was beetle-browed, a sullen fellow with a great bony nose and a cruel mouth; he might well have been put there to spy on his young mistress. And then there was the mother. Serafina said she had been gay in her youth and it might be true; she had the bold, roving eye of the woman who has had adventures, and though it might be that it would be no outrage to her virtue if her daughter took a lover, it was a risk to run. Machiavelli had come to the conclusion that Bartolomeo was a vain man, and he knew that no one can be so vindictive as the vain man who discovers that he has been fooled. It was no easy matter that Machiavelli was undertaking, but that did not disturb him, he had confidence in himself, and the difficulty made the affair more interesting. It was evident that he must cultivate Bartolomeo and lull him into security, and it would be well to get on good terms with Monna Caterina. It had been a sound idea to get Piero to question Serafina and it had given him some notion of the situation. But he had to know more, and then some plan might suggest itself to his fertile mind. He knew it was no use to rack his brain. He must wait for an inspiration.

"Let us go and have supper," he said to Piero.

They walked to the Golden Lion and having eaten returned to their lodging. Serafina had put her children to bed and was in the kitchen darning a pair of stockings. Machiavelli sent Piero up to the room he shared with her son, and, politely asking if he might warm himself for a little by her fire, sat down. He had an inkling that Monna Caterina would be over very soon to ask Serafina about him and he wanted her to give a good report of him. He could be very charming when he chose, and now he did. He told her of his

312

mission to the court of France, partly because he knew
it would interest her, but more to impress upon her
his own importance; he talked of the King and of his
minister the Cardinal as though he were hail-fellow-
well-met with them, and told her scandalous and
amusing stories of the gallantries of great ladies. Then
he took another line: he told her of Marietta, and how
hard it was to leave her when she was pregnant, and
how much he wanted to go back to Florence and his
happy home. Serafina would have had to be a very
clever woman to doubt that he was the good and
devoted husband, the plain, honest man he made
himself out to be. He listened with sympathetic
interest while she told him of her husband's illness
and death, the better days she had seen, and the
responsibility it was to have two young children to
launch into the world. Of course she thought him a
delightful, distinguished and kindly man. When he
told her that he was delicate, with a digestion that was
the torment of his life, and that the food at the Golden
Lion didn't agree with him, for he was used to Monna
Marietta's simple fare, it was natural enough for
Serafina to say that if he wasn't too proud to eat with
her and her children she would gladly provide meals
for him and Piero. This suited him very well, for it
would save money and in other ways be more convenient. He left her with just the impression of himself that
he wanted, went up to his room, and by the light of a
candle read his Livy till he felt inclined to sleep.

X

MACHIAVELLI LAY IN BED LATE next morning. He read
one of the cantos of the *Inferno*. Though he knew

the noble poem almost by heart it filled him as usual with exaltation; he could never read it without being ravished by the beauty of its language; but at the back of his mind hovered the picture of Aurelia primly at work on her embroidery, and now and then he was obliged to put the book down and indulge in thoughts of some indecency. He wondered how on earth he could arrange to see her again. Of course it might be that on a second meeting she would seem less desirable, and in a way it would be a blessing, for he had enough to do without engaging in a love affair. On the other hand it would be a pleasant distraction from his political labours. His reflections were interrupted by his servant Antonio, who told him that Messer Bartolomeo was below and desired to see him. Sending down a message that he would join him immediately, Machiavelli threw on his clothes and went downstairs.

"Forgive me for keeping you waiting, Count, but I was just finishing a letter to the Signory," he lied easily.

Bartolomeo, with a slight gesture of deprecation at Machiavelli's use of his title, as though to say that it was a trifle of no account, was obviously flattered. He brought news. The strongest fortress in the Urbinate was San Leo; it was perched on a steep, isolated rock and was reputed to be impregnable. It happened that it was undergoing repair, and taking advantage of this a number of armed peasants had rushed the gate and massacred Il Valentino's garrison. The news spread quickly and other villages at once rose in revolt. Il Valentino had flown into a temper when intelligence of this was brought him; it was evident that the rising had been instigated by the conspirators at La Magione, and that could only mean that they had decided to attack him. The Palace was in a turmoil of activity.

"What are the troops the Duke can at present dispose of?" Machiavelli interrupted.

"You'd better come and see for yourself."

"I doubt whether His Excellency would give me permission."

"Come with me. I'm going to the camp now. I'll take you."

It flashed across Machiavelli's mind that Bartolomeo had not come in a friendly way to give him information which in any case could not have been for long kept secret, but had been sent by the Duke expressly to tender this invitation. Like a hunter in the forest who hears a rustling in the undergrowth, Machiavelli was on a sudden alert, but he smiled amiably.

"You must be a powerful man, friend, if you can come and go about the camp at your own free will."

"No, it isn't that," Bartolomeo replied, with a semblance of modesty. "The Duke has put me at the head of the citizens commissioned to see to the provisioning of the troops."

"You must be making a pretty penny out of it," said Machiavelli slyly.

Bartolomeo burst into a fat laugh.

"A bare profit, if that. The Duke isn't a man to trifle with. At Urbino the men almost mutinied over the quality of their food, and when the matter was brought to his attention and he discovered that their complaints were justified, he hanged the three commissioners."

315

"I can well understand that it makes you careful."
They rode out to the camp. It was three miles from
the city. There were three companies of fifty lancers
under Spanish captains, and a hundred lancers,
Roman gentlemen who had joined the Duke's army
for adventure and to win renown. Each lancer was
mounted, and had a page on a pony and an infantry-
man as attendants. There were twenty-five hundred
mercenaries; and the Duke's conscripted soldiers, six
thousand of them, were expected to arrive in two days.
He had sent an agent to Milan to collect five hundred
of the Gascon adventurers who were scattered in
Lombardy and another to hire fifteen hundred Swiss.
His artillery was formidable and in good condition.
Machiavelli was interested in military affairs, of which
he had gained some experience in the unsuccessful
siege of Pisa, and he flattered himself on his knowledge. He kept his eyes open. He asked a lot of
questions, both of officers and men, and sorting the
answers, accepting what looked like truth and reject-
ing what was improbable, formed the opinion that the
Duke's force was far from negligible.

On getting back to the city he found a message from
Agapito da Amalia to say that the Duke desired to see
him at eight o'clock that evening. After dinner he
sent Piero over to Bartolomeo's house to tell him that
he was to have an audience with the Duke that night,
and if Bartolomeo would meet him later at the Golden
Lion they might drink a cup of wine together; it was
possible that he could only get into communication
with Aurelia through her husband and therefore must
make friends with him. Bartolomeo was a trusting
soul, who liked good cheer and good company, and

such a proof of confidence as the envoy of the Republic was now offering could not fail to flatter his conceit.

Machiavelli went to his room and had a siesta, then decided that it would be worth his while to have another talk with Serafina. He had a notion that he could get more out of her than Piero had. She had spoken well of Bartolomeo to him, but that might have been from discretion; if he knew anything about human nature she must be less grateful for the benefits the fat man had conferred on her than resentful on account of those he had omitted. Machiavelli thought himself clever enough to induce her to divulge her real feelings.

When he awoke he strolled downstairs as though to go to the parlour and on his way sang, a little more loudly than was necessary, the catch of a Florentine song.

"Are you there, Monna Serafina?" he said as he passed the kitchen door. "I thought you were out."

"You have a fine voice, Messere," she said.

"A thousand thanks. May I come in for a minute?"

"My eldest son has a beautiful voice; Messer Bartolomeo used often to have him over and they would sing together. Messer Bartolomeo is a bass. It is strange that a man so big and strong should have a voice of so little power."

Machiavelli pricked up his ears.

"My friend Biagio Buonaccorsi, Messer Bartolomeo's cousin, and I are fond of singing together. What a pity I couldn't bring my lute with me! It would have been a pleasure to me to sing some of my songs to you."

"But my son left his lute here. He wanted to take

317

it with him, but it's a valuable instrument which was given to his father, my poor husband, by a gentleman to whom he had done a service, and I wouldn't let him take it."

"Will you let me see it?"

"It hasn't been touched for three years now. I dare say some of the strings are broken."

But she fetched it and put it in Machiavelli's hands. It was a lovely thing of cedar with ivory inlay. He tuned it and proceeded in a low voice to sing. He was not only very fond of music, but had a technical knowledge of it, and he had written the words and himself composed the melody of several songs. As he finished he noticed that tears were in Serafina's eyes. He put down the instrument and looked at her kindly.

"I didn't wish to make you cry."

"It reminds me of my boy, so far away and exposed to so many dangers among those heathen people."

"It'll be good experience for him, and under the protection of Messer Bartolomeo his future is assured."

She gave him a pinched glance.

"Lazarus must be thankful for the crumbs that fall from the rich man's table."

Her acid remark assured him that he had not been far wrong in his conjecture.

"The Holy Scriptures assure us that in heaven the position will be reversed," he answered.

She gave a laugh that was more like a snort.

"He would give half his wealth to have my children."

"It is strange that none of his three wives should have produced a child."

"You men, you always think it's the woman's fault.

318

Monna Caterina has her head screwed on her
shoulders all right; she knows that if Aurelia doesn't
have a baby soon it'll go badly with both of them. No
more fine dresses then. No more rings and bracelets.
I've known Bartolomeo all his life. He doesn't give
much away for nothing. Monna Caterina is wise to
worry. She's giving Fra Timoteo money to pray that
Aurelia should conceive."

"Who, pray, is Fra Timoteo?" asked Machiavelli.

"Their confessor. Bartolomeo has promised to give
a Virgin and Child when Aurelia has a son. Fra
Timoteo is making a pretty penny out of them. He
twists them round his little finger, and he knows as
well as I do that poor Bartolomeo is impotent."

Machiavelli had learnt more than he had hoped; a
scheme beautiful and simple flashed through his mind
and he thought it wise to drop the conversation. He
idly plucked the strings of the lute.

"You're right, it's a beautiful instrument. It's a
pleasure to play on it. I don't wonder that you were
unwilling to let your son take it overseas."

"You are very sympathetic, Messere," she said. "If
it gives you pleasure to play, I will lend it you while
you're here. I know you'll be careful with it."

Machiavelli had been wondering how he could
induce her to make such an offer: she saved him all
further trouble. There was no doubt about it, he had
a way with women: it was a pity she was old, haggard
and sallow; otherwise he might have permitted himself a little nonsense with her. He thanked her
warmly.

"It will be a comfort to me to sing the little songs
my wife is fond of. I haven't been married to her long

and she is pregnant; it was hard to leave her. But how could I help it? I am a servant of the Republic and I must put my duty before my inclination."

When, a little later, Machiavelli left her he had persuaded Serafina that he was not only a person of distinction, but a good husband, a sincere friend, and an honest, charming and reliable man.

XI

AT THE APPOINTED TIME one of the Duke's secretaries, accompanied by men with torches, came to fetch him, and Machiavelli, calling one of his servants to follow, started out for the Palace. The Duke received him with a show of affection that was the more surprising since, two nights before, he had dismissed him in a passion. He appeared to be in high spirits. He mentioned the fall of the fortress of San Leo in an off-hand way and seemed to have no doubt that he would easily settle the trouble in Urbino. Then in an intimately confidential manner that would have flattered Machiavelli had he been sensible to flattery he told him that he had sent for him to impart some news that would interest the gentlemen of the Signory. He produced a letter he had just received from the Bishop of Arles, the Pope's legate in France, in which the Bishop told him that the King and the Cardinal, his minister, were anxious to please him and knowing that he needed men for his attack on Bologna had given orders to Monsieur de Chaumont at Milan to send him three hundred lancers under Monsieur de Lancres, and on the Duke's demand to march in person on Parma with another three hundred lancers. The Duke showed the letter to Machiavelli so that he could vouch for its authenticity.

The cause of the Duke's good humour was obvious. If he had not marched on Florence after his capture of Urbino it was only because the French had sent a force to protect it, and the only conclusion to be drawn from this was that he could no longer count on their aid. It was the assurance of this that had encouraged the captains to revolt. But if the French, for reasons which could only be surmised, were once more prepared to support him his situation was much improved.

"Now listen to me, Secretary," he said. "This letter was written in answer to the request I made for help to attack Bologna. You can see for yourself that I shan't lack strength to cope with these rascals. They couldn't have discovered themselves at a more convenient time. I know now against whom I have to protect myself and who are my friends. I am telling you this so that you may write to your masters and show them that I'm not bowing before the storm. I have good friends, and among them I should like to count the Signory—if they're disposed to come to terms quickly; but if they're not I'm finished with them for good and all, and even if I were up to my neck in water I wouldn't talk of friendship again."

Though his words were menacing, he spoke in such a gay and debonair fashion that they hardly seemed offensive. Machiavelli said he would write at once to the Signory to inform them of what the Duke had told him. The Duke bade him good night with cordiality.

When Machiavelli arrived at the inn he found

Bartolomeo waiting for him. They ordered mulled wine. Machiavelli, pledging him to secrecy to make what he had to say appear more important, though he guessed that if Bartolomeo did not know it already he soon would, told him what he had learnt from the Duke. It suited him then to invent a little; he told Bartolomeo that the Duke had spoken obligingly of him, and when the fat man wanted to know in exactly what terms, Machiavelli had no difficulty in specifying them. Bartolomeo beamed.

"You are already the first man in Imola, Messer Bartolomeo; if the Pope lives and things prosper with the Duke you may well be one of the first men in Italy."

"I am nothing but a merchant. I do not aim so high."

"Cosimo de' Medici was nothing but a merchant, and yet he became the master of Florence, and his son, Lorenzo the Magnificent, treated on equal terms with kings and princes."

The expression on Bartolomeo's face showed him that the dart had hit its mark.

"It it true that your wife is pregnant, Messere?"

"It is a great joy to me. She expects her confinement some time next year."

"You are more fortunate than I," sighed Bartolomeo. "I have had three wives and not one of them has borne me a child."

"Monna Aurelia is a strong and healthy young woman. It is impossible to believe that she is barren."

"What other explanation can there be? We have been married three years."

"Perhaps if you took her to the baths. . . ."

322

"I took her to the baths, and when that failed, we went on a pilgrimage to Santa Maria de la Misericordia at Alvanio, where there is a miraculous image of the Madonna which causes barren women to conceive. It had no effect. You can imagine what a mortification it is to me. My enemies say that I am impotent. That is absurd. Few men are more virile than I am. Why, I have bastards in every village within ten miles of Imola."

Machiavelli knew that was a lie.

"Would you imagine that anyone could have such bad luck as to marry three barren women?"

"You mustn't despair, my friend. A miracle is always possible and you have surely deserved well of our Holy Church."

"That is what Fra Timoteo says. He prays for me daily."

"Fra Timoteo?" asked Machiavelli as though the name meant nothing to him.

"Our confessor. He tells me to have faith."

Machiavelli called for more wine. By the exercise of judicious flattery, namely by asking Bartolomeo's advice on how he should conduct himself in his difficult negotiations with the Duke, he soon brought him to a more cheerful state of mind. Then he told him a number of highly indecent stories, of which he had a great store and which he told with effect. Bartolomeo laughed with great guffaws and by the time they parted he had decided that he had never known a more entertaining fellow. On his side Machiavelli thought that he had spent his evening to advantage. He was a temperate man, but he had a strong head, and the wine that had made Bartolomeo a trifle tipsy had not affected him at all. When he got back to his room he proceeded to write a long letter to the Signory telling them of his interview with the Duke and what forces he had at his disposal or within easy call. He wrote fluently and without erasures. Then he read what he had written. It was a good letter.

XII

IL VALENTINO was in the habit of working far into the night, and so did not get up early in the morning. His secretaries, kept busy till all hours, took advantage of this to sleep late, and so next morning Machiavelli, with nothing much to do till after dinner, his letter to the Signory dispatched, thought he would take things easily. He read his Livy and made a few notes of the reflections his reading had occasioned, and then to pass the time took his borrowed lute. It had a good tone, resonant but sweet, and he had noticed when first he tried it that it suited his light baritone. It was a sunny day and he sat by the open window enjoying the grateful warmth. Somewhere in the not far distance they were burning wood and the smell of it was pleasant in his nostrils. The lane that separated Serafina's house from Messer Bartolomeo's was so narrow that a donkey with panniers could hardly have scraped its way through, and from his window Machiavelli looked down into the tiny court-yard with its well-head and its chestnut-tree. He began to sing. He was in good voice that morning and liking the sound of it went on. Then he noticed that the window in a room opposite was being opened, he could not see by whom, he did not even see the hand that fixed the

324

paper panel, but he had a sudden thrill of exultation, for he was convinced that the unseen person could be none other than Aurelia. He sang two of his favourite songs, love songs both of them, and was in the middle of a third when the window was suddenly closed as though someone had come into the room. This somewhat disconcerted him and a suspicion passed through his mind that it might have been the maid interrupted by her mistress who did not want to be found neglecting her work to listen to a stranger singing in the next house. But at dinner-time his well-directed conversation discovered to him that the window that had been opened was that of the nuptial chamber of Bartolomeo and his young wife.

Later on in the day he went to the Palace, but succeeded in seeing neither the Duke nor any of the secretaries. He entered into conversation with various persons who were lounging about apparently with nothing to do and asked them what the news was. They knew nothing, but he received the impression that they knew at least that something had happened. Whatever it was, a secret was being made of it. Presently he ran across Bartolomeo, who told him he had an appointment with the Duke, but he was too busy to see him.

"We're both wasting our time here," said Machiavelli with his pleasant friendliness. "Let us go to the inn and drink a cup of wine. We might have a game of cards, or if you can play chess, a game of chess."

"I'm fond of chess."

On their way to the Golden Lion, Machiavelli asked him what everyone at the Palace was so busy about that day.

"I haven't a notion. I can't get anyone to tell me anything."

By the slight peevishness of Bartolomeo's tone Machiavelli guessed that he was telling the truth. He had a great idea of his own importance and it humiliated him to find that he was not in the Duke's entire confidence.

"I have heard that when the Duke wishes to keep something secret not even those closest to him know about it," said Machiavelli.

"He's been occupied with his secretaries all day. Messengers have been dispatched one after the other."

"It's evident that something has happened."

"I know that a courier arrived from Perugia this morning."

"A courier, or someone disguised as a courier?"

Bartolomeo looked at him quickly.

"I don't know. What do you suspect?"

"Nothing. I was only asking."

It was but a short walk to the inn. They ordered a flagon of wine and asked for chessmen. Machiavelli was a good player and it did not take him long to discover that Bartolomeo was no match for him, but he amused himself by giving him a hard game and letting himself be beaten in the end. Bartolomeo was puffed up with pride and while they drank their wine pointed out to Machiavelli exactly what mistakes he had made and what his move should have been to counter his opponent's strategy. Machiavelli blamed himself for his want of foresight. On their way back to their respective domiciles Bartolomeo remarked:

"My mother-in-law says she heard someone singing in your house this morning. A very pretty voice. Was that you or my young cousin Piero?"

"Piero's voice is better than mine, but it was I who was singing. I'm flattered that Monna Caterina should not have thought too badly of my efforts. Biagio and I and one or two more used often to while away the time by singing."

"I sing a very good bass myself."

"Piero sings tenor. It would be an excellent combination. If you don't object to my humble quarters it would be a great pleasure to me if you would come in when you have nothing better to do, and we'll give our good friend Serafina a little concert."

Would the fish swallow the fly that was so skilfully cast? There was no sign of it.

"We will certainly do that. It will bring me back my youth. When I was a young fellow in Smyrna we Italians would sing all the time."

"Patience," Machiavelli muttered to himself. "Patience."

When he got in, taking a greasy pack of cards, he began to play patience, but as he played he turned over in his mind what Bartolomeo had told him and what he had learnt from Serafina. He had a plan, and it was a good one, but to carry it out called for ingenuity. The more he thought of Aurelia the more she inflamed his fancy, and it tickled him to death to think that he could provide Bartolomeo with the child, preferably male, that he so much wanted.

"It is not often," he reflected, "that you can do a good action with so much pleasure to yourself."

It was evident that he must ingratiate himself with Monna Caterina, for without her he could do nothing, but the difficulty was to get on terms with her sufficiently intimate to enable him to enlist her help. She was a woman of voluptuous appearance, and it occurred to him that he might persuade Piero to go to bed with her. Piero was young. At her age she could not fail to be grateful. But he dismissed the notion; it would serve his purpose better if Piero became the maid's lover. But they said that in her time Monna Caterina had been gay. If there was one thing of which Machiavelli was convinced it was that when a woman ceases to be desirable a procuress is born. He thought there was a natural instinct in the sex that led them to enjoy vicariously pleasures that were no longer befitting to their age. And what should she care about Bartolomeo's honour? It was to her interest that Aurelia should have offspring.

And what about this Fra Timoteo? He was their confessor; he was a friend of the house. It might be worth while to see him and find out what sort of a man he was. It might be that he could be put to good use. Machiavelli's meditation was on a sudden disturbed by a tap on the shutter. He looked up but did not move; the tap, low and discreet, was repeated. He went to the window and slightly opened the shutter. A name was muttered.

"Farinelli."

"Wait."

"Are you alone?"

"I am alone."

He went into the passage and opened the door. In the darkness he could see nothing but that someone was standing there. Farinelli, it may be remembered, was the Florentine accountant with whom Machiavelli had made contact the day after his arrival. Huddled

in a cape, with a scarf to conceal his face, he slipped in
and followed Machiavelli into the parlour. It was lit
by a single candle. He sat at the table close to Machiavelli so that he need hardly raise his voice above a
whisper.

"I have something important to tell you."

"Speak."

"Can I count on the generosity of the Signory if
what I say is useful to them?"

"Without doubt."

"A messenger, riding post, arrived at the Palace
today. The rebels have at last signed articles of agreement. They are pledged to stand by Bentivoglio in
defence of the Bologna, to reinstate the dispossessed
lords in their dominions, and not to undertake any
separate negotiations with the Duke. They have
decided to collect seven hundred men-at-arms, a
hundred light horses and nine thousand foot. Bentivoglio is to attack Imola and Vitellozzo and the Orsini
are to march on Urbino."

"That is news indeed," said Machiavelli.

He was pleasantly excited. Stirring events exhilarated him and he looked forward with the anticipation
of a spectator at a play to seeing how the Duke would
cope with the danger that confronted him.

"There is one more thing. Vitellozzo has given the
Duke to understand that if he can have reliable
assurances that no attempt will be made to deprive
him of his own state of Castello he will rejoin him."

"How do you know this?"

"It is enough that I know it."

Machiavelli was perplexed. He knew Vitellozzo, a
sullen, suspicious, moody man, subject to wild rages

and to attacks of profound depression. The syphilis from which he suffered had so affected him that sometimes he was hardly sane. Who could tell what wicked plans that tortured brain was contriving? Machiavelli dismissed the accountant.

"I can count on your discretion, Messer Niccolo? My life would be short if it were discovered that I have told you what I have."

"I know. But I am not one to kill the goose that lays the golden eggs."

XIII

FROM THEN ON, things moved quickly. On hearing of the uprising in Urbino the Duke had sent two of his captains, Spaniards both, Don Ugo da Moncada and Don Michele da Corella, to put it down. Making Pergola and Fossombrone their headquarters they ravaged the surrounding territories, sacked the towns and killed most of the inhabitants. At Fossombrone women threw themselves and their children into the river to escape the savagery of the soldiery. The Duke, sending for Machiavelli, told him of these exploits with a great deal of good humour.

"It looks as though the season were not too healthy for rebels," he said with a grim smile.

He had just received news from an envoy of the Pope at Perugia that on his arrival the Orsini had come to assure him of their loyalty to the Holy Father and to excuse their acts. Machiavelli remembered what Farinelli had told him about Vitellozzo.

"It is difficult to understand why they have done that," he said.

"Use your brain, Secretary. It can only mean that they're not yet ready and want to gain time by behaving as though an accommodation were still possible."

A few days later Vitellozzo carried the city of Urbino by assault and the Duke again sent for Machiavelli. Machiavelli expected to find him disconcerted by the bad news, but he did not even mention it.

"I want to confer with you as usual on the matters that concern your government and our common interests," he said. "I have received this letter from someone I sent to Siena."

He read it aloud. It was from the Chevalier Orsini, a bastard of that noble and powerful house, who was in the Duke's service. He had spoken with the leaders of the conspiracy, and they had declared their desire to be on good terms with the Duke and professed their willingness to re-enter his service if he would abandon his attack on Bologna and instead combine with them to invade the Florentine territories.

"You see what confidence I place in you," he added, when he had finished, "and what trust I have in the good faith of your government. In return they should place more reliance on me than they have in the past and they can be sure that I shall not fail them."

Machiavelli did not know how much of this to believe. The Orsini were the bitter enemies of Florence and would welcome the opportunity to restore the exiled Medici to power. It was not unlikely that they had made some such offer. He could only suppose that the Duke had not accepted it for fear of angering the French and was divulging it in order to put the Republic under such an obligation that the Signory would be willing to give him again the profit-

331

able *condotta* he had not long before forced upon them at the sword's point, but which, the danger passed, they had to his vexation withdrawn from him. A *condotta* was the term used for the engagement of a mercenary captain, hence called a condottiere, for a period of time. On his salary, settled after a lot of haggling on both sides, he paid his men and made a pretty penny for himself.

Two days later the rebel forces attacked the Duke's army under the joint command of the two Spaniards and defeated it. Don Ugo da Moncada was taken prisoner and Don Michele da Corella, wounded, fled to the stronghold of Fossombrone. It was more than a set-back, it was a disaster. The news was kept secret in Imola, for, as Machiavelli wrote to the Signory, in the Duke's court things which were not to be bruited about were not spoken of; but he had his ways of finding out what was important for him to know, and as soon as the event reached his ears he went to the Palace and requested an audience.

Machiavelli entered the presence with a lively sense of curiosity. He was desirous to see in what state he would find the Duke, hitherto self-confident and imperturbable, now that ruin stared him in the face. He could not but know that he could expect no mercy from his enemies. He was calm and even gay. He spoke of the rebels with disdain.

"I don't want to boast," he said, "but I expect the outcome, whatever it is, will show what stuff they're made of and what stuff I'm made of. I know them well, the whole gang of them, and I think nothing of them. Vitellozzo has a great reputation, but all I can tell you is that I've never seen him do a thing that needed courage. His excuse is the French sickness. The fact is, he's good for nothing but to ravage undefended territories and rob those who haven't the guts to stand up to him. A false friend and a treacherous enemy."

Machiavelli could not withold his admiration for this man who faced destruction with such an indomitable spirit. His situation was desperate. The Bentivogli, Lords of Bologna, were on his northern frontiers; Vitellozzo and the Orsini, flushed with victory, must be advancing from the south. Attacked simultaneously on two fronts by superior forces he could not escape annihilation. Il Valentino was no friend of Florence and his downfall and death would be a relief to the Republic, but Machiavelli, against his will, had an inclination—it was no more than that —to wish that he might succeed in extricating himself from the strait he was in.

"I have received letters from France," said the Duke after a pause, "from which I learn that the King has instructed your government to give me every possible assistance."

"I have heard nothing of it," said Machiavelli.

"Well, it is true. You will write to your masters and tell them to send me ten squadrons of cavalry, and you may add that I am ready to make a firm and indis-soluble alliance with them from which they will gain all the advantages that may be expected from my help and my good fortune."

"I will naturally carry out Your Excellency's instructions."

The Duke was not alone. With him were Agapito da Amalia, the Bishop of Elna, his cousin, and another

secretary. There was an ominous silence. The Duke
stared at the Florentine envoy reflectively. The silence
and those staring eyes would have incommoded a more
nervous man than Machiavelli, and even he had to
exercise some self-control to maintain an air of composure.

"I've heard from various sources," said the Duke at
last, "that your government is urging the Lords of
Bologna to declare war on me, and that they're doing
this either because they wish to ruin me or to make a
pact with me on more favourable terms."

Machiavelli contrived to smile with as much
geniality as his cold and somewhat austere cast of
countenance allowed.

"I don't believe it for a moment, Excellency," he
replied. "The letters I receive from the Signory never
fail to contain protestations of friendship for the Holy
Father and yourself."

"I don't believe it either, but protestations of friendship are more convincing when acts conform with
them."

"I am sure my government will do everything in
it's power to show the sincerity of its intentions."

"If it is as wise as it is dilatory I am sure it will."

Within himself Machiavelli shivered. He had never
in his life heard such cold ferocity in a man's voice.

XIV

FOR SOME DAYS after this Machiavelli busied himself
in gathering information from his agents, from Bartolomeo, from Farinelli and from those about the Duke.
He could trust no one completely and he knew that

Il Valentino's intimates told him only what they wanted him to know. But the most puzzling fact of all was the inactivity of the revolting captains. The Duke's troops, which he had been enlisting wherever men were for sale, had not yet arrived, and though he still held some fortresses in the states that had rebelled, it was impossible to believe that he could withstand a determined assault. Now was the time to attack. Now. Yet they did nothing. Machiavelli was at his wit's end; he could not for the life of him understand what caused them to delay. Then an event occurred that increased his bewilderment: the Orsini sent an emissary to the Duke's court, who arrived one evening and left next day; Machiavelli for all his efforts could not find out the purpose of his visit.

He had by now received the Signory's reply to the Duke's demand for armed help, and in the hope of getting some inkling of what was happening, he applied for an audience. It was not without trepidation that he went to the Palace, for what he had to tell the Duke was that the Florentines had no troops to send and all they were prepared to offer was an assurance of their benevolence. Machiavelli had seen Il Valentino in a rage and he knew that it was terrible; he braced himself to bear the storm with fortitude. No one could have been more astonished than he when the Duke received the intelligence he brought with indifference.

"I've told you several times and tonight I tell you again that I'm not devoid of resources. The French lancers will be here soon and so will the Swiss infantry. You can see for yourself that I'm engaging troops every day. The Pope has no lack of money, nor the King, of men. It may well be that my enemies will regret their treachery."

He smiled, and his smile was cruel and cunning.

"Would it surprise you to know that they've already made offers of peace?"

Machiavelli repressed a start.

"Messer Antonio da Venafro came on their behalf."

This was evidently the mysterious visitor of whom Machiavelli had heard. He was the confidant and trusted adviser of Pandolfo Petrucci, Lord of Siena, who by common report was the brains of the conspiracy.

"He made the proposal that we should overthrow the government of Florence, but I answered that your state had never offended me and that I was on the point of signing a treaty with you. 'Don't sign on any account,' he said. 'Let me go back and return and we'll do something worth while.' To which I answered: 'We've gone so far it's impossible to withdraw.' And I tell you once more that though I'm prepared to listen to these people and throw dust in their eyes I'll do nothing against your state unless it forces me to."

As Machiavelli was taking his leave the Duke in a very casual fashion dropped a remark which astounded the envoy of the Republic, as in all probability he expected it to do.

"I'm expecting Pagolo Orsini at any moment."

Piero had accompanied Machiavelli to the Palace and was waiting for him in the guard-room with a lantern to light him back to their lodging. Piero had learnt to read his master's face and he saw at a glance that he was in no mood for conversation. They walked

336

in silence. When Machiavelli had taken off his cloak and his headgear he told Piero to bring him ink, quills and paper, and sat down to write to the Signory.

"I shall go to bed," said Piero.

"No, wait," said Machiavelli, throwing himself back in his chair. "I want to talk to you."

He did not know how much to believe of what the Duke had told him and he thought it might help him with his letter if before writing he put into words what he had in mind.

"I'm confused by this guile, these lies, and the deceit of everyone I have to deal with."

In no more words than were necessary he repeated to Piero what the Duke had said to him.

"How is it possible for Il Valentino, with his spirit, his good fortune and his great ambition, to condone the acts of men who've not only prevented him from acquiring a state he has cast his eyes on, but have caused him to lose a state had had already acquired? The captains revolted because they wanted to destroy him before he could destroy them. Why have they delayed to attack when they had him at their mercy?"

Machiavelli looked at Piero with frowning eyes, but Piero, very sensibly surmising that the question was rhetorical, made no attempt to answer.

"Now he's strengthened his fortress and garrisoned important places. Every day more troops are arriving. He's getting money from the Pope and men from the French. And he has the great advantage that he need consult no one but himself. The captains are united only by their hatred and fear of the Duke. Alliances are fragile because the respective parties are more concerned with their particular interests than with their common advantage. Allies cannot act swiftly because every step must be discussed, and the folly, unpreparedness or incompetence of one may cause the disaster of all. They're necessarily jealous of one another, for no one of them wishes any one of the rest to gain so much power that he will be later a danger. The captains must know that emissaries are passing to and fro—you can be sure that Il Valentino has seen to that—and each at the back of his mind must be haunted by the suspicion that he is to be thrown to the wolves."

Machiavelli nervously gnawed his thumbnail.

"The more I think of it the more I believe that the rebels can no longer do much harm to the Duke, they've missed their opportunity, and in that case they may think it better worth their while to seek a reconciliation."

Machiavelli gave the boy an angry look, for which there was no justification, since he had not opened his mouth.

"D'you know what that means?"

"No."

"It means that with their forces joined to his the Duke will have under his orders a formidable army, and it's inevitable that it will be put to use. No one can afford to pay troops to sit about in idleness. How will it be used? Against whom? That will be decided, I suspect, when Il Valentino and Pagolo Orsini come face to face."

XV

SINCE NO ONE IN ITALY was such a fool as to trust any-one else farther than he could see, and a safe conduct was worth no more than the paper it was written on, Cardinal Borgia, the Pope's nephew, put himself in the hands of the Orsini as a hostage, and two days later Pagolo, the head of the house, arrived at Imola disguised as a courier. He was a vain, loquacious, effeminate and silly man, middle-aged, plump and baldish, with a round, smooth face, and a fussy, familiar manner. Il Valentino treated him with great distinction and in his honour gave a great banquet followed by a performance of the *Menaechmi* of Plautus. The two leaders held long conferences, but what they discussed Machiavelli could discover neither for love nor money. Such of the Duke's secretaries as had seemed friendly disposed deliberately avoided him. He had nothing to go on but a smiling remark of Agapito da Amalia's that the negotiations were devised only to keep the enemy from taking action. Neither army in fact moved, and indeed the Bolognese troops withdrew from the places in the Duke's dominions that they had occupied. The suspense soon grew too great for Machiavelli to bear and, taking advantage of a letter he had just received from Florence, he asked the Duke to see him. Il Valentino received him in bed. He listened with his usual good humour to the Signory's protestations of friendship and then entered upon the topic which so much concerned Machiavelli.

"I think we shall come to an agreement," he said. "They want no more from me than that the possession of their states shall be secured to them and now we've only got to decide how that can be arranged. Cardinal Orsini is drawing up articles and we must wait and see what they are. So far as you're concerned you can rest assured that nothing will be done contrary to the interests of your masters. I would never allow the slightest harm to be done them."

He paused, and when he spoke again it was with the smiling indulgence with which you might speak of the whims of a spoilt woman.

"Poor Pagolo is very much incensed with Ramiro de Lorqua. He accuses him of oppressing the people, of peculation, and of maltreating various persons who are under the protection of the Orsini."

Ramiro de Lorqua was the most trusted of the Duke's commanders. It was he who had conducted the retreat of the routed forces after the battle of Fossombrone and so saved them to fight another day. Il Valentino chuckled.

"It appears that on one occasion a page was bringing him some wine and spilt it, and Ramiro flew into a temper and had him thrown into the fire and burnt alive. For some reason Pagolo took an interest in the boy. I've promised to look into the charges and if they're proved give him satisfaction."

But then a piece of news arrived which suggested that the revolting captains were far from agreement among themselves: though the more prudent were ready to make peace, the more adventurous were still determined to wage war. Vitellozzo seized the Duke's fortress of Fossombrone and two days later Oliverotto da Fermo took Camerino by storm. This completed the loss of all the territories Il Valentino had won during his last campaign. It looked as though the ruffians were deliberately set upon frustrating the negotiations, and Pagolo Orsini was enraged. But the Duke maintained his equanimity. Bentivoglio and the

340

Orsini were the most powerful of his enemies and he knew that if he came to terms with them the others would have to toe the line. Pagolo went to Bologna. On his return Agapito da Amalia told Machiavelli that an agreement had been reached and only awaited the consent of Pagolo's brother the Cardinal.

Machiavelli was filled with apprehension. If this was a fact, if Il Valentino was prepared to forgive the injury the rebels had done him, if they were prepared to forget the fear that had driven them to take up arms, it could only be for one reason, which was that they had agreed to make a joint attack on a third party; and this third party could only be Florence or Venice. Venice was strong and Florence was weak. Her only safeguard was the power of France, but she had bought the protection of France with gold and the coffers of the Republic were empty. What would France do if she were confronted with the brute fact that Cæsar Borgia with his reconciled commanders had invaded the territories of Florence and captured her defenceless cities?

Machiavelli had a poor opinion of the French. Experience had taught him that they were more concerned with present loss and present gain than with future good and future ill. When asked to render a service their first thought was how it could be useful to them, and they kept faith only so long as it served their purpose. The Pope's jubilee had brought enormous amounts of money into the Vatican treasury, and his somewhat high-handed procedure of seizing a cardinal's property on his decease was continually adding to the sums at his disposal; for the mortality of these princes of the Church was high; and the malicious

indeed whispered that His Holiness found it convenient on occasion discreetly to come to the aid of
a dilatory Providence. Thus he had ample funds to
appease the anger of King Louis should he take it
amiss that his orders had been disobeyed. Il Valentino
had a well equipped and well trained army; the King
might hesitate to pit his strength against one who after
all was a vassal and a friend. The more Machiavelli
considered, the more likely it seemed to him that the
crafty Louis would accept a situation in which the
profit was immediate and the danger, that Cæsar
Borgia would grow too powerful, remote. There was
every reason for Machiavelli to fear that the Florence
he loved with all his heart was doomed.

XVI

But Machiavelli was not only the diligent and conscientious servant of the Republic, he was also a man
consumed with the lusts of the flesh; and while he
studied with attention the letters he received from the
Signory and wrote almost every day careful and exact
reports; while he received in Serafina's house, sometimes openly, sometimes in secret, messengers, spies,
agents; while he betook himself here and there, to
the Palace, to the market-place, to houses where he
had acquaintance to discuss and consult with: while
he gathered every scrap of news, every rumour, every
piece of gossip so that he could come to conclusions
that were at least plausible; he found time to pursue
the plan he had devised to seduce Aurelia. But his
plan involved spending money, and money was just
what he hadn't got. The Florentine government was

stingy, his salary was miserable, and he had already spent much of the sum he had been given on leaving Florence. He was extravagant and liked to live well. He had often to pay in advance the messengers who took his dispatches and he had besides to satisfy the various persons about the Duke's court who were prepared for a consideration to give him useful information. There were fortunately Florentine merchants in the city who would advance him money, and he wrote to Biagio urging him to send whatever he could raise by hook or by crook. Then a strange thing happened. Jacopo Farinelli, the accountant, who before had only come to see him at night, muffled-up so that no one should recognise him, appeared at the door in broad daylight and asked to see him. His manner, which hitherto had been furtive and frightened, was now open and cordial. He did not delay to come to the object of his visit.

"I am commissioned by someone who is your friend and who highly esteems your abilities to ask you to accept this small token of his appreciation."

From the folds of his dress he drew a bag and placed it on the table. Machiavelli heard the clink of coin.

"What is that?" he asked, his lips tightening and his eyes cold.

"Fifty ducats," smiled Farinelli.

It was a handsome amount. At the moment nothing could have been more useful to Machiavelli.

"Why should the Duke wish to give me fifty ducats?"

"I have no reason to suppose that the Duke is concerned. I was ordered to bring the money to you on behalf of a well-wisher who desired to remain unknown, and you may rest assured that no one but your well-wisher and I will ever know anything of the gift."

"It appears that both my well-wisher and you take me for a fool as well as a knave. Take your money, return it to him who gave it to you and tell him that the envoy of the Rupublic does not accept bribes."

"But it is not a bribe. It is a spontaneous gift offered by a friend in appreciation of your high talents and literary attainments."

"I do not know how this generous friend can have formed an appreciation of my literary attainments," said Machiavelli acidly.

"He had an opportunity to read the letters you wrote to the Signory during your legation to France and greatly admired your acuteness of observation, your good sense, your tact and, above all, the excellence of your style."

"It is impossible that the person of whom you speak could have had access to the files of the Chancery."

"I wonder. It is certainly not impossible that someone in the Chancery found your letters interesting enough to copy, and that by some hazard the person of whom I speak gained possession of them. No one knows better than you with what parsimony the Republic pays its officials."

Machiavelli frowned. He was silent while he asked himself which of the clerks it could be that had sold the letters to the Duke. It was true that they were all ill paid and some were doubtless secret adherents of the Medici. But perhaps there was no truth in what Farinelli said. It was easy enough to invent such a story, Farinelli went on:

"The Duke would be the last man to wish you to do anything against your conscience or to the injury of Florence. What he wants is to your mutual benefit, the Republic's and his. The Signory has confidence in your judgment and all he would have you do is to put his case in such a way as to appeal to the common sense of intelligent men."

"You need say no more," said Machiavelli, his thin lips curling into a sarcastic smile. "I have no use for the Duke's money. I shall continue to advise the Signory according to the best interests of the Republic."

Farinelli stood up and replaced the bag of gold from where he had taken it.

"The Duke of Ferrara's agent was not too proud to accept a present from His Excellency when it was a question of deciding his master to send a detachment to His Excellency's help. If Monsieur de Chaumont hastened the departure of the French troops from Milan it was because the King's orders were supplemented by a handsome present from the Duke."

"I am well aware of it."

When Machiavelli was once more alone he laughed out loud. Of course the possibility of accepting the money had never for an instant occurred to him, but he could not help being amused when he thought how devilish useful it would have been to him. But as he laughed, an idea on a sudden occurred to him and he laughed again. He was sure he could borrow the money he needed from Bartolomeo, who would be only too glad to oblige him; and it would be a priceless jest to seduce his wife by means of money he had himself provided. Nothing could be prettier. And what a good story it would make to tell when he got back to Florence! He could hear his friends chuckle as he gathered them round him one evening in a tavern and narrated it with all the effect he could contrive.

"Ah, Niccolo, Niccolo, what a good companion! No one can tell a story as he can. What humour, what wit! It's as good as a play to listen to him."

He had not seen Bartolomeo for two days when he ran across him just before dinner at the Palace, to which he had gone for news. After exchanging a few friendly words he said:

"Why don't you come this evening and we'll have a little music?"

Bartolomeo was pleased to say he could think of nothing he would enjoy more. Machiavelli proceeded:

"It's true the room is small and the vaulted ceiling echoes, but we'll have a brazier against the chill and with wine to keep the cold out we shall do very well."

He had not long finished eating when Bartolomeo's servant brought a letter. He wrote that the ladies of his house didn't see why they should be deprived of a treat, the big room in his house was much better suited for music than Serafina's cold small parlour, it had a fireplace so that they could warm themselves at its cheerful blaze, and if he and cousin Piero would do him the honour to come to supper his happiness would be complete. Machiavelli accepted with alacrity.

"It's as easy as falling off a log," he said to himself.

Machiavelli had himself shaved and his hair trimmed and he put on his best clothes, a long black damask sleeveless tunic and a tight-fitting jacket with billowing velvet sleeves. Piero had dressed himself up also for the occasion, but his pale blue tunic reached only half-way down his thighs and he wore a purple belt round his waist; his handsome legs were encased in dark blue hose, and his jacket with sleeves less ample than Machiavelli's was dark blue also; a purple cap was perched jauntily on his curly locks. Machiavelli looked at him with approval.

"You should make quite an impression on the little maid, Piero," he smiled. "What did you say her name was? Nina?"

"Why do you wish me to go to bed with her?" asked Piero, smiling.

"I like to think that you will not have entirely wasted your time on this trip. And besides, it may be useful to me."

"How?"

"Because I wish to go to bed with her mistress."

"You?"

There was so much surprise in Piero's tone that Machiavelli flushed angrily.

"And why not, if you please?"

Piero saw that his master was put out, and hesitated.

"You're married and—well, as old as my uncle."

"You speak like a fool. A woman of sense will always prefer a man in the flower of his age to an inexperienced boy."

"It never entered my head that she meant anything to you. Do you love her?"

"Love? I loved my mother, I esteem my wife and I shall love my children; but I want to go to bed with Aurelia. There is much you still have to learn, my poor boy. Take the lute and let us go."

But though Machiavelli was quick-tempered he

347

could not be angry long. He patted Piero's smooth cheek.

"It is very hard to keep secrets from a maid," he smiled. "You would be doing me a service if you shut her mouth with kisses."

They had only to step across the narrow lane, and on knocking were let in by the serving-man. Monna Caterina was handsomely gowned in black, but Aurelia wore a rich dress of Venetian brocade; its opulent colours enhanced the whiteness of her breast and the brilliant fairness of her hair. It was with a little sigh of relief that Machiavelli decided she was more beautiful even than he had imagined. She was very, very desirable and it was absurd that she should have for a husband that gross, self-satisfied man who would certainly never see forty again.

After the usual compliments they sat down to wait for supper. The ladies had been working when Machiavelli and Piero came in.

"You see, they've already got busy on the linen you brought me from Florence," said Bartolomeo.

"You are pleased with it, Monna Aurelia?" asked Machiavelli.

"It's impossible to get material of this quality in Imola," she said.

She looked at him as she spoke and her great dark eyes resting on him for a moment made his heart beat.

"I'm going to have that woman if I die for it," he said to himself; but of course he didn't quite mean that; what he meant was that he had never met a harlot with whom he more urgently wanted to go to bed.

"We do the rough work, Nina and I," said Monna Caterina. "We measure and cut and sew and my daughter does the embroidery. When it comes to that my fingers are all thumbs and poor Nina's no better than I am."

"Monna Aurelia never makes two alike," said Bartolomeo proudly. "Show Messer Niccolo the design for the shirt you're working on now."

"Oh, I should be ashamed," she said prettily.

"Nonsense. I'll show him myself."

He brought over a sheet of paper.

"Do you see how cleverly she's introduced my initials?"

"It is a masterpiece of elegance and ingenuity," said Machiavelli with a very good imitation of enthusiasm, for he was in truth entirely indifferent to such things. "I wish my Marietta had such a charming gift and the industry to make such good use of it."

"This woman of mine is as industrious as she is good," Bartolomeo said fondly.

Machiavelli could not but reflect that he was interested neither in her goodness nor her industry. He reflected further that husbands are often mistaken in the virtues they ascribe to their wives.

Supper was served and he exerted himself to be at his best. He knew that he told a story well and his sojourn in France had provided him with a number of spicy tales about the ladies and gentlemen at the King's court. Aurelia assumed a modest confusion when his indecencies grew too obvious, but Bartolomeo guffawed and Monna Caterina, enjoying herself hugely, egged him on. He could not but think that he was proving himself a most agreeable guest. They did full justice to a copious repast, and after a decent interval, during which he drew Bartolomeo out to talk about himself, his affairs and his properties, which he did with complacency, Machiavelli suggested that they should try their voices. He tuned his lute and by way of prelude played a gay little tune. Then they settled on a song they all knew. Part singing was a common accomplishment of the day, and with Bartolomeo's bass, Machiavelli's light baritone and Piero's agreeable tenor they acquitted themselves to their mutual satisfaction. Then Machiavelli sang one of Lorenzo de' Medici's songs and the other two joined in the chorus. As he sang he looked at Aurelia in the hope that she would guess he was singing only to her, and when their eyes met, and she looked down, he flattered himself that she was at least aware of his feelings. That was the first step. So the evening passed. It was a dull life the two ladies led and such a diversion was a rare treat to them. Aurelia's delight was plain in the shining of her splendid eyes. The more Machiavelli looked at them the more sure he was that here was a woman, unawakened still, who was capable of passion. He was prepared to awaken her. But before they separated he had something to say that he had been holding back for the proper moment. He did not think he was a vain man; but he could not help finding the idea ingenious. So when the occasion arose he said:

"You were good enough to say that you would be willing to do me a service, Messer Bartolomeo, and now I am going to take you at your word."

"I would do a great deal for the envoy of the Republic," answered Bartolomeo, who had drunk a great deal of wine and was, if not drunk, at least mellow. "But for my good friend Niccolo I would do anything."

"Well, the matter is this: the Signory are looking for a preacher to deliver the Lenten sermons in the Cathedral next year and they asked me to enquire whether there was anyone in Imola who could be entrusted with this important duty."

"Fra Timoteo," cried Monna Caterina.

"Be quiet, mother-in-law," said Bartolomeo. "This is a matter of consequence for men to settle after due deliberation. It may bring glory or discredit to our city and we must be sure to recommend only one who is worthy of the honour."

But Monna Caterina would not be so easily silenced.

"He delivered the Lenten sermons in our own church this very year and the whole city thronged to hear him. When he described the tortures of the damned strong men burst into tears, women swooned, and one poor creature who was near her time suddenly felt the pangs of childbirth and was carried shrieking from the church."

"I do not deny it. I am a hard-headed man of business and I sobbed like a child. It is true, Fra Timoteo has eloquence and a fine choice of words."

"Who is this Fra Timoteo?" asked Machiavelli. "What you tell me is interesting. The Florentines dearly love to be called to repentance at the proper season; it enables them to cheat their neighbours for the rest of the year with a good conscience."

"Fra Timoteo is our confessor," said Bartolomeo, a fact of which Machiavelli was well aware. "And for my own part I never do a thing without his advice. He is not only a worthy man, but a wise one. Why, only

351

a few months ago I was about to buy a cargo of spices
in the Levant and he told me that he had seen St. Paul
in a vision, who told him that the ship would be
wrecked on the coast of Crete, so I did not buy."

"And was the ship wrecked?" asked Machiavelli.

"No, but three caravels arrived in Lisbon laden
with spices, with the result that the bottom fell out of
the market and I should have lost money on the trans-
action, so it came to the same thing."

"The more you tell me of this friar the more curious
I am to see him."

"You are very likely to find him in the church in
the morning, and if not you can ask the brother
sacristan to fetch him."

"May I tell him that I come to him with your recommendation?" Machiavelli asked politely.

"The envoy of the Republic needs no recommendation from a poor merchant in a town which is of
small account compared with the magnificent city of
Florence."

"And what do you think of this Fra Timoteo?"
Machiavelli went on, addressing himself to Aurelia.
"It is important that I should have the opinion not
only of a man of position and discernment like Messer
Bartolomeo and of a woman of discretion and
experience like Monna Caterina, but also of one who
has the enthusiasm, the innocence and the sensitive-
ness of youth, one to whom the world and its perils are
still unknown; for the preacher I would recommend
to the Signory must not only call sinners to repentance,
but confirm the virtuous in their integrity."

It was a pretty speech.

"Fra Timoteo can do no wrong in my eyes. I am

prepared to be guided by him in everything."

"And I," added Bartolomeo, "am prepared that you should be guided by him. He will never advise anything that is not to your best advantage."

It had all gone very well and exactly as Machiavelli wished. He went to bed satisfied with himself.

XVII

EARLY NEXT MORNING, being market day, Machiavelli took Piero with him to the market-place and bought two brace of plump partridges. At another stall he bought a basket of the luscious figs which were the speciality of Rimini and were so much prized that they were sent all over Italy. These comestibles he told Piero to take to Messer Bartolomeo and deliver with his compliments. With Imola crowded with strangers food was scare and high in price, so that he knew his present would be welcome. Then he made his way to the Franciscan church attached to the monastery in which Fra Timoteo was a monk. It was not far from Bartolomeo's house. It was a building of some size, but of no architectural merit. It was empty but for two or three women praying, a lay brother, obviously the sacristan, who was sweeping the floor, and a friar who was pottering about the altar of a chapel. Machiavelli with a passing glance saw that he was only pretending to be busy and guessed that this must be Fra Timoteo, who had been warned by Monna Caterina to expect him.

"Pardon me, father," said he, with a polite inclination of his backbone, "I have been told that you are so fortunate as to have a miraculous Virgin in this church and I have a great desire to light a candle before her altar so that she may assist my dear wife, now pregnant, in the pains of childbirth."

"This is she, Messere," said the monk. "I was about to change her veil. I can't get the brothers to keep her clean and tidy, and then they're surprised because the pious neglect to pay their devotions to her. I remember when there were dozens of votive offerings in this chapel for graces received, and now there aren't twenty. And it's our own fault; they have no sense, my brothers."

Machiavelli chose a candle of imposing dimensions, paid for it extravagantly with a florin, and watched the monk while he fixed it on an iron candlestick and lit it. When this was done Machiavelli said:

"I have a favour to ask of you, father. I have reason to speak privately to Fra Timoteo and I should be grateful if you would tell me how I can find him."

"I am Fra Timoteo," said the monk.

"Impossible! It looks as though Providence had a hand in this. It is a miracle that I should come here and in the first person I see find the very person I am looking for."

"The designs of Providence are inscrutable," said Fra Timoteo.

The monk was a man of medium stature, of a comfortable but not disgusting corpulence, which suggested to Machiavelli's cool mind that he was given to fasting no more than the rules of his order demanded but not to the gross vice of gluttony. He had a fine head. It reminded one of a Roman emperor's whose fine features, not yet debased by luxury and

354

unlimited power, bore notwithstanding a suggestion of the cruel sensuality that would lead to his assassination. It was a type not unfamiliar to Machiavelli. In those full red lips, in that bold hook nose, in those fine black eyes he read ambition, cunning and covetousness, but these qualities were masked by a semblance of good nature and simple piety. Machiavelli could well understand how he had gained so great an influence over Bartolomeo and the women of his family. He felt instinctively that this was a man he could deal with; he hated monks; to him they were either fools or knaves, and this one was probably a knave, but he must step warily.

"I should tell you, father, that I have heard a great deal to your credit from my friend Messer Bartolomeo Martelli. He has the highest opinion both of your virtue and your ability."

"Messer Bartolomeo is a faithful son of the Church. Our monastery is very poor and we owe much to his generosity. But may I know whom I have the honour of addressing, Messere?"

Machiavelli knew that the friar was well aware of this, but answered gravely.

"I should have introduced myself. Niccolo Machiavelli, citizen of Florence and Secretary to the Second Chancery."

The monk bowed low.

"It is a great privilege to speak with the envoy of that illustrious state."

"You fill me with confusion, father, I am but a man with all the failings of humanity; but where can we speak in private and at length?"

"Why not here, Messere? The brother sacristan is

355

as deaf as a post and as stupid as a mule and the three or four old women you see are too busy with their prayers to listen to what we are saying and too ignorant to understand it if they did."

They sat down on two of the praying-stools which were in the chapel and Machiavelli told Fra Timoteo how he had been commissioned by the Signory to find a preacher to deliver the Lenten sermons in the Cathedral. The friar's Roman face remained impassive, but Machiavelli felt in him an alertness of attention which confirmed his assurance that he had been informed of the previous night's conversation. Machiavelli apprised him of the Signory's requirements.

"They are naturally nervous," he said. "They don't want to make again the mistake they made with Fra Girolamo Savonarola. It is very well that the people should be persuaded to repentance, but the prosperity of Florence depends on its commerce and the Signory cannot allow repentance to disturb the peace or interfere with trade. Excess of virtue can be as harmful to the State as excess of vice."

"Such, I seem to remember, was the opinion of Aristotle."

"Ah, I see that you, unlike friars in general, are a man of education. That is all to the good. The people of Florence have agile and critical minds and have no patience with a preacher, however eloquent, who is without learning."

"It is true that many of my brethren are of a shocking ignorance," Fra Timoteo replied complacently. "If I understand you aright you want to know if there is anyone in Imola who is in my opinion worthy of the honour you speak of. It is a matter that needs consideration. I shall have to think. I must make discreet enquiries."

"You will be doing me a great favour. I know from Messer Bartolomeo and his ladies that you are a man of singular perspicacity and of the highest rectitude. I am confident that you will give me a disinterested opinion."

"Messer Bartolomeo's ladies are saints. That is the only reason why they think so favourably of me."

"I live in the house of Monna Serafina just behind Messer Bartolomeo's. If I could persuade you to join us in our modest meal tomorrow evening we could discuss the matter further, and it would give my good Serafina infinite pleasure to have you at her table."

Fra Timoteo accepted the invitation. Machiavelli went home, but on the way called on Bartolomeo and asked him for a loan. He explained that he was put to great expense at Imola in connection with his mission, and the funds he was expecting from the Signory had not yet arrived. He pulled a long story about the parsimoniousness of the Florence government and complained that in order to maintain the dignity of his position and to meet the cost of information he had to pay money out of his own pocket. But Bartolomeo cut him short.

"Dear Niccolo," he said in his jovial way, "you do not have to tell me that in this court one can get nothing without paying for it. For your own sake as well as for that of the Signory I shall be happy to lend you whatever you require. How much do you want?"

Machiavelli was surprised and pleased.

"Twenty-five ducats."

"Is that all? Wait and I will give it you at once."

He left the room and in a minute or two came back with the money. Machiavelli regretted that he had asked for so little.

"And when you want more don't hesitate to ask me," said Bartolomeo, beaming. "You must look upon me as your banker."

"A fool and his money are soon parted," Machiavelli said to himself as he returned to his lodging.

XVIII

BROTHER TIMOTEO came to supper. Machiavelli had bidden Serafina to buy the best the city could provide and the friar needed little pressing to eat heartily. Machiavelli saw that his cup was well-filled and when, supper finished, he led him into the parlour so that they might talk undisturbed, he told one of his servants to bring a flagon of wine.

"Now let us get down to business," he said.

Fra Timoteo told him that he had been giving the subject of their conversation careful thought, and mentioned three monks who had some reputation in the city as preachers. He described their respective merits with candour, but with an ingenuity that Machiavelli could not but admire introduced into his eulogy of each a note of disparagement that effectively overrode his recommendation. Machiavelli smiled blandly.

"You have spoken of these excellent monks with a sincerity and a disinterestedness which are what I should have expected of you, father, but you have left out the name of one whose talents and piety according

358

to all accounts are infinitely superior to theirs."

"And who may that be, Messere?"

"Fra Timoteo."

The monk gave a start of well-simulated surprise.

"A good actor," Machiavelli said to himself. "A preacher must have histrionic gifts, and if the Signory had really given me the commission to find one I should be half inclined to propose this rascally friar."

"You are joking, Messere."

"What makes you think that I should joke on a subject of such importance, father? I have not been idle on my side. I have learnt that in the whole history of Imola no preacher has made such a profound impression as you did in the sermons you delivered this Lent. I am told that you have a remarkable eloquence and I can tell for myself that you have a melodious and a beautiful voice. Your presence is imposing and even in the short while that we have talked together I have discovered that you are intelligent, tactful and cultivated. I am assured that your knowledge of the Fathers is only equalled by your classical erudition."

"You cover me with confusion, Messere. The Signory want a monk of reputation, and I am but a poor friar in a poverty-stricken monastery of a provincial city. I have neither great birth to recommend me nor powerful friends. I thank you from the bottom of my heart for the good opinion you so generously have of me, but I am unworthy of the honour you propose."

"That is something that those can better judge who know you better than you know yourself."

Machiavelli was enjoying himself hugely. He

appreciated the monk's affectation of modesty, and with his sharp eyes delving into his innermost heart discerned the greediness of his ambition. With such a bait to dangle he was certain he could get him to do anything he wanted.

"I think I should be less than honest if I did not tell you that I am a person of no great consequence in the state of Florence. I can only advise; the last word is with the gentlemen of the Signory."

"I cannot think that they would lightly disregard the advice of their envoy to His Excellency the Duke of Romagna and Valentinois," said Fra Timoteo with an ingratiating smile.

"It is true that our new Gonfalonier for life, Piero Soderini, is my friend, and I think I may say without vanity that his brother the Bishop of Volterra has some faith in my honesty and good sense."

This remark led Machiavelli very naturally to tell the monk of the mission to Cæsar Borgia when he had accompanied the Cardinal, then a bishop, to Urbino to protest against the attack Vitellozzo had made on Arezzo; and this as naturally led him to describe his own activities in the war with Pisa and his legation to France. He was careful to minimise his role in these proceedings, and yet managed to suggest to the friar that it was he who had pulled the strings. He talked lightly, amusingly, in a familiar way, of kings and cardinals, princes and generals, and thus delicately led his listener to believe that he had the ear of the great both in Italy and France. Secrets of state were no secrets to him. Only a fool could doubt that he knew much more than he told. Fra Timoteo was dazzled.

"Ah, Messere, you cannot know what it means to me to talk with a man of your intelligence and experience. It is like a glimpse of the promised land. We live in this dull little town and know nothing of the world. There is not a man in Imola of culture or distinction. Our wits, if we have any, grow rusty because there is no occasion to use them. One needs the patience of Job to support the stupidity of the people among whom one is compelled to pass one's life."

"Father, I will admit that from what I know of you and from what I have heard I think it a thousand pities that a man of your capacity should be wasted on this place. It is not for me to remind one of your calling of the Parable of the Talents."

"I have often thought of it. I buried my talent in the ground, and when the Master asks me to what use I have put it I shall have no answer."

"Father, no one can do more for another man than give him an opportunity; he must know for himself how to make use of it."

"Who is going to give an unknown monk an opportunity?"

"I am your friend, father, and such little influence as I have is at your service. And you will not be entirely unknown when I have mentioned your name to the Bishop of Volterra. It would be unbecoming for a man of your habit to put himself forward; but there is no reason why I should not speak of the matter with our good friend Bartolomeo, and I have little doubt that I can persuade him that it is an idea of his own to write to certain powerful connections of his in Florence."

361

Fra Timoteo smiled.

"Our dear Bartolomeo! He is goodness itself, but it cannot be denied that he is a little simple. He does not combine the craftiness of the serpent with the innocence of the dove."

Thus Machiavelli conducted their colloquy to the point at which he had been aiming. He refilled the empty cups. The brazier gave out a pleasant warmth.

"Bartolomeo is a very worthy creature. It has often struck me as remarkable that business men should be able to conduct commercial transactions with success and yet remain so unversed in the affairs of the world. But I do not esteem him less on that account and I would do a great deal to promote his welfare. You have a strong influence over him, father."

"He is good enough to attach some small value to my counsels."

"There at all events he shows a natural good sense. How sad it is that such an excellent and deserving creature should not have been granted the dearest wish of his heart!"

Fra Timoteo looked at him enquiringly.

"You must know as well as I do that he would give half his possessions to have a son."

"It is an obsession with him; he can talk of nothing else. We have interceded for him with our miraculous Virgin, but to no purpose, and he is angry with us because our prayers have not achieved the desired result; be he is unreasonable. The poor man is sterile."

"Father, I have a small property not far from Florence called San Casciano, and to augment the poor salary I receive from the Signory I make what money I can by selling timber from my woods and farming my land. I have cows, and it sometimes happens that you get a bull, to all appearance strong and healthy, who for some reason suffers from the same unfortunate disability as our good friend Bartolomeo. Then you kill the bull for butcher's meat and on the proceeds buy another."

Fra Timoteo smiled.

"It is not practicable to go to such lengths with human beings."

"Nor necessary. But the theory is sound."

It took the friar a moment to grasp exactly what Machiavelli meant, and when he did he smiled again.

"Monna Aurelia is a virtuous wife, and she is well guarded, though for different reasons, by her mother and her husband. Bartolomeo is not so stupid as not to know that a young and beautiful wife must be a temptation to the dissolute youth of the city, and Monna Caterina lived in poverty long enough to make her take good care that she shall not lose a comfortable home through the indiscretion of her daughter."

"And yet it might well be that an indiscretion would turn out to be the height of discretion. Monna Caterina's position would be more secure if she had a little grandson to dandle on her knee."

"I don't deny it. Now that the Duke has bestowed this property on him, with the title that accompanies it, Bartolomeo is more than ever anxious to have an heir. The ladies of his family have discovered that he is thinking of adopting his two nephews. He has a widowed sister in Forlì, and she is willing enough that he should thus provide for her boys; but she will not be separated from them and makes it a condition that he should take her into his house along with them."

"It is natural that a mother should not wish to be parted from her children."

"Very. But the prospect distresses both Monna Caterina and Monna Aurelia. They see that their position would be difficult. Monna Aurelia had no dowry. Bartolomeo is a weak and foolish man; Monna Costanza, the mother of his adopted sons, would undermine the influence of a wife whom his vanity insists on thinking a barren woman, and his sister would in no long time be mistress of the house. Monna Caterina has besought me to dissuade him from a course in which there is so much danger to her daughter and herself."

"He has consulted you?"

"Naturally."

"And what advice have you given him?"

"I have temporised. His sister's confessor at Forlì is a Dominican, and if she came here it is likely enough that she would take a confessor from the same order. The Dominicans are no friends of ours. We owe much to the generosity of Bartolomeo, and it would be unfortunate if Monna Costanza took advantage of his disappointment with our efforts to get him to bestow his favours in another quarter."

"No one could see more clearly than I how difficult your situation is, dear father. The only possible solution is the one I suggest."

"Has it escaped you that it smacks somewhat of sin, Messere?" said the friar with an indulgent smile.

"A small sin, father, from which a great good may

come. You can bring happiness to a worthy man, security to two women whose piety merits your help, and last but not least you preserve for the brethren of your habit the munificence of a generous donor. It would be presumption on my part to recall the Holy Scripture to your memory, but I will venture to suggest to you that if the woman of Samaria had not committed adultery the Founder of our religion would never have had occasion to utter those precepts of tolerance and forgiveness which have been of such inestimable value to the miserable sinners that we are."

"It is a pretty point, Messere."

"I am human, father. I will not try to conceal from you that the beauty of Monna Aurelia has excited so violent a passion in me that I must satisfy it or die."

"I did not imagine that your desire for Bartolomeo's welfare and the peace of mind of his two ladies was prompted only by the goodness of your heart," said Fra Timoteo dryly.

"Your monastery is poor and you doubtless have many calls upon your charity. I would give twenty-five ducats to be assured of your good will, father."

Machiavelli saw the glint of greed in the monk's dark eyes.

"When?"

"Now."

He took the bag of money out of an inner pocket and flung it carelessly on the table. The coins made a pleasant clink against the wooden surface.

"You have acquired my good will by the charm of your conversation and the graciousness of your manner, Messere," said the monk. "But I do not see how I can be of service to you."

"I will ask you to do nothing that can weigh on your conscience. I should like you to arrange it so that I may have a conversation with Monna Caterina in private."

"I can see no harm in that. But it will get you no farther. Bartolomeo is a fool, but he is too good a business man to take unnecessary risks. When his affairs force him to absent himself his servant is there to protect Monna Aurelia from the importunities of unscrupulous and lascivious men."

"I am well aware of it. Our good Bartolomeo, however, has a confidence in you which is as implicit as it is well-deserved. He has taken Monna Aurelia to the baths and he has taken her on pilgrimages to the shrines of saints who are accredited with the blessed gift of ridding women of the curse of barrenness. I suggest to you that if our good Bartolomeo, accompanied by his servant, went to Ravenna and spent a night in prayer and meditation before the sarcophagus which contains the mortal remains of San Vitale, you could guarantee that Monna Aurelia would conceive."

"San Vitale was evidently a great saint, or a church would not have been built in his honour; but what makes you suppose that his bones have the power to cure men of sterility?"

"The name is eminently suggestive, and Bartolomeo knows no more of the miraculous powers of the saint than you or I. A drowning man will catch at a straw and Ravenna is but twenty miles from Imola. Can you believe that our friend would hesitate to make so short a journey to achieve a result he so much desires?"

"Let me ask you a question in return, Messere. Have you any reason to suppose that Monna Aurelia, a virtuous and timid wife, would respond to your advances? Have you made your desires known to her?"

"I have not exchanged more than a few words with her, but unless she is different from the rest of her sex she is well aware of them. Women are subject to two defects, curiosity and vanity."

"Venial sins," said the monk.

"And yet they lead these fair creatures to abandon the narrow path of virtue more often than passion."

"There is much of which my habit has kept me in happy ignorance."

"When your eminent merit has raised you to the position it deserves, you will learn that you can gain influence over men less by fostering their virtues or encouraging their vices than by humouring their foibles."

"Your scheme is ingenious. I have little doubt that you could persuade Monna Caterina to help you; she will stop at nothing to prevent Bartolomeo from adopting his nephews; but I know Monna Aurelia too well to believe that she would let herself be persuaded to commit a mortal sin either by her mother or by you."

"That is possible. There are many things which from a distance seem strange and terrifying, but when you come closer to them appear natural, easy and reasonable. I have no reason to suppose that Monna Aurelia is more intelligent than the majority of her

367

sex. It would be well if you explained to her that when there is in prospect a good that is certain and an evil that is uncertain, it is wrong not to do the good for fear of the evil. The certain good is that she will conceive and so create an immortal soul; the evil is that she may be found out, but with proper precautions the possibility of that is eliminated. And so far as sin is concerned—well, there is nothing in that, since it is the will that sins and not the body. It would be a sin to displease her husband, but in this she can only please him. In all things the end must be considered, and the end here is to fill a seat in Paradise and give a husband his heart's desire."

Fra Timoteo looked at Machiavelli without replying. It seemed to the Florentine that he was preventing himself from laughing only by an effort of will. The monk looked away and his eyes fell on the bag of gold that was lying on the table.

"I am sure that the Signory was well advised when they sent you on a mission to the Duke, Messere," he said at last. "I may condemn your intentions, but I can only admire your subtlety."

"I am very sensible to flattery," Machiavelli answered.

"You must give me time to think the matter over."

"It is always best to trust the impulse of the moment, father. But if you will excuse me I will go into the yard, for I wish to relieve nature. Your local wine is something of a diuretic, I fancy."

When Machiavelli returned, the monk was sitting as he had left him, but the bag of gold was no longer on the table.

"Monna Caterina will bring her daughter on

Friday for confession," he said, looking at his well-kept hands. "You will have an opportunity of talking to her while Monna Aurelia is in the confessional."

XIX

A HAPPY CHANCE gave Machiavelli an opportunity to pursue his suit which he was quick to seize. Unless obliged to, he did not get up early, and the sun had risen some time when, on the morning after his conversation with Fra Timoteo, he rolled out of bed and got into his clothes. He went into the kitchen, where Serafina gave him his frugal breakfast, and then out into the yard, where he drew water from the well and shudderingly washed his hands and face. Then he went up to his room to fetch such of his papers as he wanted. He raised the window to look at the weather and suddenly saw Nina, the maid, bring a chair and a footstool out on to the roof of Bartolomeo's house. The weather had been cloudy for some time, with occasional showers of rain, but that morning the sun shone brightly from an unclouded sky. He guessed what Nina's actions betokened. Presently Aurelia came on to the roof, swathed in a quilted wrapper, carrying a great straw hat in her hand. He was right. Aurelia had taken advantage of the fine day to dry her hair. She sat in the chair and the maid took the long fair hair in her hands and passed it through the hat, which had no crown but only an immense brim; then, placing the hat on Aurelia's head, she spread the hair all around the brim, so that the sun should shine on it and the dye colour it more brightly.

Machiavelli changed his plans. He left his letters

to a more suitable season and, taking his lute, ascended the stairs to a loggia on the upper storey of Serafina's house. By the time he got there the maid had gone about her business and Aurelia was alone. The wide brim of her hat prevented her from seeing him, and indeed she was certainly too much intent on the process of getting her hair a perfect shade to have thoughts of anything else; but when he began to sing, startled, she raised the brim and looked across the narrow space that divided the two houses. Before Machiavelli could catch her eye she lowered it. As though to himself he sang a little love song. Following the fashion of the time, his theme was Cupid and his darts, the cruel wounds his loved one's eyes inflicted, and the happiness that would be his if he could pass one moment without thinking of her. He had Aurelia at his mercy; from coyness she might have wished to withdraw, but the sun was essential to make the dye hold, and he felt it was not in a woman's nature to sacrifice her appearance to her modesty. If there had been any doubt in her mind of his feelings towards her there could surely be none now, but such an occasion might not soon recur, so he thought it just as well to make them unmistakable. He had composed a serenade to a woman called Fenice, which began, *Hail, Lady, from all women set apart,* and which went on to address her as a rare example of earthly beauty, a perfect soul imbued with every loveliness; and it was easy, without interfering with the scansion, to change *O only Fenice* into *O only Aurelia.* Plucking the strings of the lute he spoke the words in a recitative which was not wanting in a certain melodiousness. Aurelia sat still, her face

370

hidden by the wide brim of her hat and the over-
hanging hair, but Machiavelli had a notion that she
was listening intently. That was all he wanted. But
he had sung no more than two stanzas when she rang
a little bell she had evidently brought to call her
maid. Machiavelli paused. Nina appeared; Aurelia
said something to her and rose from her chair, which
the maid took to another part of the roof; Aurelia
moved over and the maid sat down on the footstool.
The two women began to talk and Machiavelli
guessed she was going to keep her there till he withdrew. He was not dissatisfied. He went down to his
room, got his papers out of the box in which he kept
them locked, and was soon immersed in a letter he
was writing to the Signory.

So far so good.

XX

HE WAS NOT IN THE HABIT of attending the services
of the Church, and on Friday waited till vespers were
over and the small congregation coming out before
entering the sacred edifice. He was just in time to see
Fra Timoteo go into the confessional. In a moment
Aurelia followed him. Monna Caterina was sitting by
herself in one of the chapels. Machiavelli joined her.
She did not seem surprised to see him, and he thought
it not unlikely that the monk had spoken to her and
she was expecting him. Anyhow he could see no
object in beating about the bush. He told her that
he had fallen passionately in love with her daughter
and asked her to plead his cause with her. Monna
Caterina seemed amused rather than indignant. She
informed him that he was not the first who had

371

attempted her daughter's virtue, but none had succeeded.

"I brought her up very strictly, Messer Niccolo, and since the night I put her to bed, an innocent virgin, with Messer Bartolomeo, she has been a faithful and dutiful wife to him."

"If I am rightly informed she has never had the opportunity to be anything else."

Monna Caterina gave a low, somewhat bawdy laugh.

"Messer Niccolo, you have lived long enough to know that when a wife wishes to deceive her husband no precautions he may take can stop her."

"All history bears you out, Monna Caterina, and I perceive from what you say that you are a woman with whom one can speak frankly."

She turned her head a little and looked at him earnestly.

"Messer Niccolo, I have had great misfortunes in my life. I have been tossed on stormy seas and now that I am safe in harbour I have no wish to expose myself again to the fury of the elements."

"I can well understand it, but are you so sure that your anchor is firm and your mooring taut?"

Monna Caterina did not answer and Machiavelli was conscious of the uneasiness of her silence. He went on.

"Am I not right in thinking that if Monna Aurelia does not soon produce the heir Bartolomeo craves he has it in mind to adopt the two sons of Monna Costanza?"

Once again Monna Caterina made no reply.

"You have too great an experience of the world,

Madonna, to make it necessary for me to tell you what your position and that of your daughter would be in such a case."

Two tears trickled down Monna Caterina's cheeks. Machiavelli patted her hand in kindness.

"Desperate situations demand desperate remedies."

She shrugged her shoulders despondently.

"Even though I should be able to overcome Aurelia's fears, the opportunity would be lacking."

"Am I displeasing to your daughter?"

"You make her laugh," smiled Monna Caterina, "and a jest will as often gain a woman's favours as a handsome face."

"You are a woman after my own heart, Madonna. Should the opportunity present itself so that what we both wish could be effected without danger, may I count on your help?"

"It is not only my daughter's fears that must be overcome, but also her scruples."

"Such of them as you will not have been able to dispel by the exercise of your common sense we can safely leave to be dealt with by the excellent Fra Timoteo. He does not like the Dominicans."

Monna Caterina gave a low laugh.

"You are a charming man, Messer Niccolo. If I were still desirable and you desired me, I would refuse you nothing."

"The old cow," Machiavelli said to himself, but he pressed her hand and aloud answered: "If I were not so passionately in love with your daughter I should not hesitate to take you at your word."

"There is Aurelia."

"I will leave you."

Slipping out of the church, he went to the silver-smith, and there bought a chain, only of silver gilt, certainly, for he had not the money for a gold one, but of very pretty workmanship. Next morning he sent Piero to buy a basket of the luscious figs which Monna Caterina had told him she liked so much, and putting the chain at the bottom of the basket told Piero to take it to her. He was to say that the figs were a gift from Machiavelli and to add that under-neath them she would find something that he begged her to accept as a mark of his esteem. He felt that he and Monna Caterina understood one another per-fectly, but he knew that nothing confirms an under-standing like a little present.

XXI

SOME DAYS LATER Bartolomeo suggested that they should repeat the evening of good cheer and singing which had been so enjoyable. They did so. Things went off as before, with pleasant conversation and some good music; Aurelia, never very chatty, was more silent than usual, but Machiavelli was conscious that when he was talking in his sprightly way to the others she looked at him appraisingly. He was pretty sure that she and her mother had discussed him and his desires, and these enquiring glances of hers meant that she was wondering what he would be like in the capacity of a lover. He knew that it was not his good looks that made his success with women, but his agreeable discourse, his wit and his easy manner. He put his best foot forward. He knew that women appreciated neither irony nor sarcasm, but simple jokes and funny stories. He was amply provided with both. The laughter with which his sallies were greeted excited him and he flattered himself that he had never been more amusing. He took care, however, to show that he was not only a jester, but a good-natured man, kindly and easy to get on with, one in whom you could have confidence and whom it would not be hard to love. Was it only his fancy that when from time to time he caught Aurelia's eyes he saw in them a smiling tenderness that suggested she was not indifferent to him? He had seen that look before in women's eyes. They were strange creatures: they had to bring sentiment in and thus tiresomely complicate a pleasure which a merciful Providence had provided for human beings in compensation for the expulsion of their first parents from the Garden of Eden. But sometimes it was convenient that they should have this foible. He gave a passing thought to Marietta, who had married him by arrangement with her parents and now so doted on him that she could hardly bear him out of her sight. She was a good woman and he had a real affection for her, but she couldn't expect him to be tied to her apron strings.

The affairs of his mission kept Machiavelli so busy that for several days after this he was obliged to devote his whole time to them; but through Piero he sent Aurelia a flask of attar of roses which he had bought at a cost he could ill afford from a merchant who had recently come from the Levant. It was a good sign that she did not refuse it. He congratulated Piero on the tact and skill with which he had managed to convey it to her without anyone's knowing, and gave him a scudo so that he could prosecute his suit with Nina.

"How are you getting on, my boy?" he asked.

"I don't think she dislikes me," said Piero. "She's frightened of that servant of theirs. He's her lover."

"I suspected that, but don't be discouraged; if she wants you she'll find ways and means to arrange things."

Then came a rainy afternoon. Bartolomeo sent round to ask Machiavelli if he could spare the time to come to his house and play chess. Machiavelli decided that what work he had to do could be done later, and went. Bartolomeo received him in his study. Though there was no fireplace a brazier warmed it not inadequately.

"I thought we could play more conveniently here than in company with a pair of chattering women," said Bartolomeo.

Machiavelli had gone in the hope of seeing Aurelia and was somewhat put out, but he answered civilly enough.

"Women will talk, and chess is a game that demands concentration."

They played, and perhaps because Machiavelli's attention was divided, Bartolomeo to his delight beat him without difficulty. He called for wine, and when it had been brought and Machiavelli was setting up the pieces for another game, he leant back in his chair and said:

"It was not only for the pleasure of playing chess with you that I asked you to be good enough to come here, dear Niccolo. I want to ask your advice."

"It is at your service."

"Have you ever heard of San Vitale?"

A faint sigh of satisfaction escaped Machiavelli's lips. Fra Timoteo had not failed him.

"Strange that you should ask that! You're speaking of the church at Ravenna? The saint's bones are buried there. Everyone in Florence was talking about him not so very long ago."

"In what connection?"

"There is no limit to the folly of mankind, and our good Florentines, who pride themselves on their lively intelligence, are of a credulity beyond belief."

He saw that Bartolomeo was all agog and he thought, "I will keep him on tenterhooks."

"What is it that you refer to?"

"The story is so absurd that I am really ashamed to tell it. Within the limits set by our Holy Church my fellow-citizens have a healthy scepticism, and are disinclined to believe in anything that they cannot see, smell or touch for themselves."

"That is what makes them the good business men they are."

"Maybe. But how surprising that now and then they fall prey to the most absurd superstition! To tell you the truth, I can't bring myself to tell you a story that shows them in such a ridiculous light."

"I am almost a Florentine myself and now I shall never rest till I hear it. It is always a pleasure to listen to you and on such a cheerless day it is well to laugh."

"Well, the facts are these: Giuliano degli Albertelli, a citizen of Florence, is a man of property, a man in the flower of his age, with a fine house in the city and a beautiful wife to whom he is greatly attached. He should have been a happy man, but he had no child, and this was a bitter grief to him because he had quarrelled desperately with his brother and could not endure to think that this man and his brood of squalling brats should one day inherit all he possessed. He took his wife to the baths, he took her on pilgrimages to various holy places, he consulted doctors and the old women who pretend to have secret herbs to make women conceive, but nothing served."

Bartolomeo, breathing heavily, listened as though his life depended on it.

"Then it happened that a monk who had been on a pilgrimage to the Holy Land told him that on his way home he had stopped at Ravenna, where there was the church of San Vitale, and the saint had the miraculous power of making sterile men fertile. Though his friends sought to dissuade him, Giuliano insisted on visiting the shrine, and you can imagine how everyone laughed when he set out on the journey. Lampoons were written and passed from hand to hand. When he came back men had to turn away to prevent themselves from bursting into laughter before his face. Nine months to a day from the date of his return his wife was delivered of a nine-pound son. It was Giuliano who laughed then. All Florence was confounded and the pious cried out that it was a miracle."

The sweat glistened on Bartolomeo's brow.

"If it wasn't a miracle, what was it?"

"Within these four walls, dear friend, I will tell you that I think the time of miracles has passed, doubtless because owing to our sins we are no longer worthy of them, but I must confess that this occurrence has greatly shaken me. I can only repeat after you, if it wasn't a miracle, what was it? I have given you the facts and it is for you to make what you can of them."

Bartolomeo took a long draught of wine. Machiavelli decided to offer another candle at the shrine of Fra Timoteo's wonder-working Madonna: his invention had served him well.

"I know I can trust you, dear Niccolo," said Bartolomeo after a pause. "I am a judge of human nature and I am sure that you are a man of discretion. It was not for nothing that I asked you if you had ever heard of San Vitale, but I never expected you to confirm so promptly the information I have received."

"You talk in riddles, friend."

"You are well aware that I too have a great desire for a son to whom I can leave my fortune, my lands and houses, and who will inherit the property and the title which the Duke has granted me. I have a widowed sister who has two sons and, having no child of my own, I have had it in mind to adopt them. Though it is to their advantage, she will not consent to be parted from them; she insists on our all living here together. But she shares with me the masterful character which has made me the man I am, and I can see little peace for me in a house inhabited by three jarring women. It would be the scene of incessant quarrels."

"That I can well believe."

"I shouldn't have a moment's peace."

"Your life would be a torment. They would tear you limb from limb."

Bartolomeo gave a deep sigh.

379

"And it is on this question that you want my advice?" asked Machiavelli.

"No. I was discussing my difficulties with Fra Timoteo only yesterday and strangely enough he spoke to me of San Vitale. I do not for a moment believe that I am at fault in this matter, but if the saint's relics have the miraculous property reported, it might be worth while to go to Ravenna. I have some business to transact there, so that even if my main object were not achieved my journey would not be wasted."

"In that case I don't see why you hesitate. You have everything to gain and nothing to lose."

"Fra Timoteo is a good and saintly man, but he knows nothing of the world. It seems strange to me that if the saint has the power he is reputed to have his celebrity should not have been bruited abroad."

For a moment Machiavelli was floored, but only for a moment.

"You forget that men are unwilling to admit that they suffer from a deficiency which they prefer to ascribe to their wives. You may be sure that the men who have availed themselves of the saint's intercession go in secret and take care never to divulge by what means their wives have been able to conceive."

"I hadn't thought of that. But don't forget this, if it were ever known that I had gone and my pilgrimage were not blessed with a happy event I should be a laughing-stock in this city. It would be an admission of impotence."

"But how could it be known? Has Fra Timoteo not told you what you must do? According to Giuliano you must spend the night in prayer and

380

meditation before the relics of the saint."

"But how is that possible?"

"For a gratuity the sacristan will let you remain when he locks up the church for the night. You will attend the first mass in the morning and then break your fast. Having done that, in your case, you will attend to your business and after that ride home to your expectant wife."

Bartolomeo gave his friend a smile.

"Then you would not think me too great a fool if I made the experiment?"

"My dear, the ways of Providence are inscrutable. I can only tell you what happened to Giuliano degli Albertelli. Whether it was a miracle or not, who am I to say?"

"It is my last hope," said Bartolomeo. "I will try it. It succeeded with Messer Giuliano; there is no reason why it should not succeed with me."

"None," said Machiavelli.

XXII

DURING THE FOLLOWING WEEK Machiavelli's emotions were as various as the colours of a crazy quilt. At one moment he was hopeful, at another despondent; he passed from happy anticipation to angry disappointment; now he was in a fever of excitement, then in the depths of despair. For Bartolomeo could not make up his mind. He was at once eager and loath to go. He was like a man who is tempted to risk his money on an off chance and is torn between his fear of losing it and his greed for gain. One day he would decide to make the journey and the next decide not to. Machiavelli's digestion was always delicate and this uncertainty gravely affected it. It would be too cruel if, everything being arranged, he were so indisposed that he could not take advantage of the opportunity he had taken such pains and spent so much money to create. He had himself bled, he took a purge, he ate nothing but slops. And, to make things worse, he had more work to do than ever; negotiations between the Duke and his rebellious commanders were coming to a head, and Machiavelli had to write constant letters to the Signory, see agents, spend hours at the Palace to pick up news, and visit influential persons who were come to Imola on behalf of their respective states. But at the last moment fortune smiled upon him. A letter reached Bartolomeo from his factor in Ravenna to say that if he did not immediately clinch the deal which he had been for some time negotiating, another offer would be accepted. This decided him.

Machiavelli's pains vanished. On the day after his conversation with Bartolomeo he had seen Fra Timoteo and the monk had agreed to give Bartolomeo the instructions which Machiavelli suggested. To ingratiate himself with Aurelia he went to one of the merchants whom the chance of easy money had attracted to Imola and bought a pair of scented gloves stitched with gold thread. They cost a great deal of money, but this was not an occasion on which he could stint. He sent them by Piero, telling the boy to ask for Monna Caterina, so that the servants might think no more than that he had a message to give her from his master; and at the same time he bade him tell her that he wished to talk with her and would

382

meet her in the church at whatever hour suited her. He was elated when Piero came back and told him that Monna Caterina had called her daughter in and she had been delighted with the costly present. Gloves of that kind were greatly prized, and the Marchioness of Mantua had thought such a gift not unworthy of the acceptance of the Queen of France.

"How did she look?" asked Machiavelli.

"Monna Aurelia? She looked pleased."

"Don't be stupid, boy. Did she look beautiful?"

"She looked as she always looks."

"Fool! When will Monna Caterina be at the church?"

"She is going to vespers this afternoon."

Machiavelli was well pleased when he returned from his interview with her.

"What a noble animal is man," he reflected, as he walked home. "With audacity, cunning and money there is practically nothing he cannot do."

At first Aurelia had been frightened and firmly refused to listen to the proposal, but little by little she had allowed herself to be convinced by Monna Caterina's arguments. They were indeed unanswerable, Machiavelli thought, and that was natural since he had himself suggested them. They were strengthened by the gentle yet firm admonitions of Fra Timoteo. Aurelia was a sensible girl and she could not but admit that it was unreasonable to jib at a small evil when a great good might come of it. The long and short of it was that if Bartolomeo were safely out of the way she was prepared to accede to Machiavelli's wishes.

Having made up his mind Bartolomeo saw no

reason to delay, and so, accompanied by his servant and a groom, he set out for Ravenna at noon on the following day. Machiavelli with his usual politeness went to bid him good-bye and wish him success on the expedition. Nina, the maid, was sent home to spend the night with her parents, and when she had gone Machiavelli dispatched Piero to Bartolomeo's house with a basket in which were fish fresh from the river, a pair of fat capons, sweetmeats from the confectioner's, fruit, and a demi-john of the best wine the city could produce. The plan was that Machiavelli should wait till three hours after sunset, nine o'clock, by which time Serafina would be in bed and asleep, and then present himself at the little door of the yard. Monna Caterina would let him in and they would have supper. At a convenient moment she would retire to her own bed-chamber and Machiavelli would be left with the object of his affections; but she made him promise that he would leave the house well before dawn. When Piero returned, having delivered the basket, he brought a last message from Monna Caterina. She would be waiting at the door as the church clock struck the hour. To make sure it was he, he was to knock twice quickly, wait a moment, knock once, and then after another brief pause again knock twice. The door would be opened and he was to step in without a word.

"What it is to have to do with a woman of experience!" said Machiavelli. "She leaves nothing to chance."

He told one of his servants to bring a pail of hot water to his bedroom and he washed himself all over. It was a thing he hadn't done since the night before

his marriage to Marietta. He remembered that he had
caught cold as the result and as was only natural had
given his cold to Marietta. Then he scented himself
with perfume he had bought at the same time as he
bought the attar of roses for Aurelia. He put on his
best clothes. Since he did not want to spoil his appetite
for the excellent supper he looked forward to, he
refused to partake of the modest meal Serafina had
prepared on the excuse that he was going to sup at
the inn with the agent of the Duke of Ferrara. He
tried to read, but was too excited to read with attention. He strummed a little on the lute, but his fingers
served him ill. He thought for a while of that
dialogue of Plato's in which he proves to his own
satisfaction that pleasure, being mingled with pain,
is an imperfect good. There was something in it, but
there were moments when meditation on eternal
things was but an insipid resource. He laughed in
his heart when he passed in review the difficulties of
his undertaking and the ingenuity of his devices to
overcome them. It would have been a false modesty
unworthy of him not to acknowledge that he had been
wonderfully clever. He didn't know anyone who
could so skilfully have worked on the passions, foibles
and interest of the parties concerned as to bend them
to his will. The church clock struck eight. He called
Piero, thinking to pass the long hour ahead by playing
draughts; ordinarily he could beat him easily, but
tonight he was careless and Piero won game after
game. It seemed as though the hour would never end,
and then on a sudden the clock began to strike.
Machiavelli sprang to his feet, flung his cloak round
him and opened the house door on to the darkness of

the night. He was about to step out into the alley when he heard the tread of feet on the cobbles. He closed the door partly and stood just within to wait till the men, whoever they were, had passed. But they didn't pass, they stopped at his door and one of them knocked; since it was not latched the knock pushed it back and the flare of the torches two of the men carried discovered Machiavelli in the passage.

"Ah, Messer Niccolo," said a man whom Machiavelli immediately recognised as one of the Duke's secretaries. "We were coming to fetch you. And you, you were just coming to the Palace? His Excellency desires to see you. He has important news for you."

For once Machiavelli lost his presence of mind. He could not think of any excuse to make. Had he not been caught thus, ready to go out, he could have sent a message to say that he was sick in bed and could not come, but how could he say that now? The Duke was not a man to whom you could say that you had other things to do, and besides, if he had important news to tell, it was essential that he should hear them. It might very well be that they concerned the safety of Florence. His heart sank.

"Wait a moment and I will tell my boy that he need not accompany me."

"It is quite unnecessary. Men will be sent to bring you safely back."

Machiavelli went into the parlour and closed the door behind him.

"Listen, Piero. The Duke has sent for me. I will make the interview short by telling the Duke I have the colic. Monna Caterina must be waiting. Go to the door and knock in the way she told you. Tell her what has happened and say I will come as soon as possible. Ask her to let you wait in the yard so that you can open for me when I knock."

"Very well."

"And say that I am distressed, mortified, miserable, woe-begone and exasperated. I shall be back in half an hour."

With that he joined the men who had come for him and went to the Palace. He was taken into an anteroom and the secretary left him, saying he would inform the Duke of his arrival. Machiavelli waited. Minutes went by. Five, ten, fifteen. Then the secretary returned to say that the Duke sent his excuses, but a courier had just arrived from the Pope with letters and he was closeted with the Bishop of Elna and Agapito da Amalia to consider them. He would send for Machiavelli as soon as he was ready. Once more Machiavelli was left alone. His patience was sorely tried. He fidgeted, he tossed from side to side in his chair, he bit his fingers, he walked up and down. He fretted, he chafed, he fumed, he raged. At last, in desperation, he flung out of the room and sought out the secretary who had come for him and in icy tones asked him if the Duke had forgotten that he was there.

"I have the colic," he said. "If the Duke cannot see me I will go home and return tomorrow."

"It is an unfortunate accident. Surely His Excellency wouldn't keep you waiting except for matters of the greatest urgency. I believe he has something to say to you that is of vital interest to the Signory. Please have patience."

Mastering his vexation as best he could, Machiavelli

threw himself into a handy chair. The secretary engaged him in conversation, and though Machiavelli answered in monosyllables and was evidently not paying attention to what he said, would not be discouraged. It was only by a great effort that Machiavelli prevented himself from telling the chatter-box to hold his silly tongue. He kept on saying to himself: "If they'd only come one minute later they wouldn't have found me." At last Agapito da Amalia himself came and said the Duke was ready to receive him. Machiavelli had been kept waiting an hour. He gave a sardonic smile as he thought of Piero standing inside the door shivering in the yard. It was some small consolation that he was not the only one to suffer.

The Duke was with his cousin the Bishop of Elna. He was gracious, but wasted no time on compliments.

"I have always been frank with you, Secretary, and I wish now to put my position quite plainly. I am not satisfied with the declaration of good will which at the Signory's direction you convey to me. The Pope may die any day, and if I want to keep my states I must take measures to secure myself. The King of France is my ally and I have an armed force; but that may not be enough and so I wish to make friends of my neighbours. These are Bologna, Mantua, Ferrara and Florence."

Machiavelli thought this was no time to repeat his assurances of the Republic's good will, so wisely he held his tongue.

"So far as Ferrara is concerned, I have acquired the Duke's friendship by his alliance with Monna Lucrezia, my beloved sister, the enormous dowry the

Pope gave her, and the benefits we have conferred on his brother the Cardinal. So far as Mantua is concerned, we are arranging two things: one is to give the Cardinal's hat to the Marquis's brother, for which the Marquis and his brother will deposit forty thousand ducats; and the other is to give my daughter in marriage to the Marquis's son, whereupon the forty thousand ducats will be returned as her dowry. I need not point out to you, Secretary, that mutual advantage is the most solid basis of enduring friendship."

"I would not dispute it, Excellency," smiled Machiavelli. "And Bologna?"

The Lord of Bologna, Giovanni Bentivoglio, had joined the rebellious captains, and though his army had withdrawn from the Duke's frontiers it remained on a war footing. Il Valentino stroked his well-kept, pointed beard and smiled maliciously.

"I have no wish to seize Bologna, but only to assure myself of that state's co-operation. I would sooner have Messer Giovanni my friend than drive him out of a state which I might not be able to hold and which might prove my ruin. Besides which, the Duke of Ferrara refuses to give me aid unless I come to an agreement with Bologna."

"Messer Giovanni has signed the articles of association with the rebels."

"For once your information is at fault, Secretary," the Duke answered good-naturedly. "Messer Giovanni is of the opinion that the articles do not safeguard his interests and has refused to agree to them. I am in communication with his brother the Protonotary and things are proceeding to our mutual satisfaction.

When we come to an agreement the Protonotary will receive a Cardinal's hat or, if he prefers to relinquish Holy Orders, the hand of my cousin, the sister of the Cardinal Borgia. The forces of our four states, supported further by the King of France, will be formidable, and then your masters will have more need of me than I have of them. I don't say that I bear them ill will, but circumstances alter cases, and if I am not bound to them by a definite pact I shall feel myself at liberty to act as appears best to me."

The velvet glove was off and the mailed fist was bared. Machiavelli allowed himself a moment's reflection. He was aware that Agapito and the Bishop of Elna were watching him intently.

"What exactly would Your Excellency have us do?" he asked as nonchalantly as he could. "I understand that you have already come to terms with Vitellozzo and the Orsini."

"Nothing has been signed yet and, as far as I'm concerned, I'd just as soon nothing were signed. It is not my policy to crush the Orsini; if the Pope dies I must have friends in Rome. When Pagolo Orsini came to see me one of his complaints was the behaviour of Ramiro de Lorqua; I promised to give him satisfaction and I shall be as good as my word. Vitellozzo is another matter. He is a snake and he has done everything he could to prevent my settling my differences with the Orsini."

"Perhaps it would be better if Your Excellency were more explicit."

"Very well. I desire you to write to your masters that it may very well be that the King of France will order them to restore to me the *condotta* which they withdrew without rhyme or reason and they will be obliged to obey. It is surely better for them to do this willingly than by compulsion."

Machiavelli paused to collect himself. He knew that every word he said was fraught with danger. When he spoke, it was in as ingratiating a manner as he could assume.

"Your Excellency acts with prudence in assembling his forces and making friends; but so far as the *condotta* is concerned, Your Excellency can't be classed with hireling captains who have nothing but themselves and a few troops to sell. Your Excellency is one of the powers of Italy, and it would be more suitable to make an alliance with you than to engage you as a mercenary."

"I should look upon such an engagement as an honour," the Duke answered suavely. "Come now, Secretary, surely we can arrange something that will be to our common advantage. I am a professional soldier, bound to your state by ties of friendship; it is a slight your masters put upon me in refusing my request. I don't believe that I'm mistaken in thinking that I could serve them as well as anyone else."

"I venture to point out that there would be no great safety for my government when three-quarters of its troops were in the hands of Your Excellency."

"Does that mean that you doubt my good faith?"

"Not at all," said Machiavelli with a fervour he was far from feeling. "But my masters are prudent and they must be circumspect. They cannot afford to take a step which they might have reason to regret. Their chief desire is to be at peace with all men."

"You are too intelligent not to know, Secretary,

that the only way to assure peace is to be prepared for war."

"I have no doubt that my government will take such steps as they deem necessary."

"By taking other captains into their service?" the Duke asked sharply.

This was the opportunity Machiavelli had been looking for. He knew that Il Valentino was subject to sudden attacks of rage, and having vented it would scornfully dismiss the object of his wrath. Machiavelli was too eager to get away to care if he angered him.

"I have every reason to believe that such are its intentions."

To his astonishment, the Duke laughed. He rose from his chair and stood with his back to the fire. He answered with complete good humour.

"Are they under the impression that it is possible to remain neutral in the unsettled conditions that now prevail? Surely they have more sense. When two neighbouring states go to war, the one that has counted on your help because of its intimate relations with you will consider you under an obligation to share his fortunes, and when you fail to do so will bear you a grudge: the other will despise you for your timidity and lack of spirit. To one side you are a useless friend and to the other an enemy little to be feared.

"The neutral is in such a position that he can help one party or the other; and in the end he is forced into such a situation that he is obliged against his will to join in the fray which he was unwilling at the beginning to enter boldly and with a good grace. Believe me, it is always wiser to take one side or the other without hesitation, for one or the other of them will be victorious and then you will fall prey to the winner. For who will come to your rescue? You can give no reason why anyone should protect you and will find no one to do it. The victor has no use for friends he can't trust, and the vanquished will do nothing for you, even if he could, because you wouldn't come to his help when your forces might have saved him."

Machiavelli had no wish at the moment to listen to a disquisition on neutrality and he only hoped that by then the Duke had said his say. But he hadn't.

"Whatever the risks of war, the risks of neutrality are greater. It renders you an object of hatred and contempt, and sooner or later you will fall victim to the first person who thinks it worth his while to destroy you. If on the other hand you come out vigorously on one side and that side wins, even though its power is so great that you may have cause to fear it, you have put it under an obligation and attached it to yourself by bonds of friendship."

"And it is Your Excellency's experience that men's gratitude for past benefits is so considerable that they will hesitate to exercise their power at your expense?"

"Victories are never so decisive that the victor can afford to alienate his friends. It is to his best interest to treat them with justice."

"And supposing the side you have taken loses?"

"Then you are all the more valuable to your ally. He helps you to the best of his ability and you are the companion of fortunes that may rise again. So, whichever way you look at it, neutrality is folly. That is all I have to say to you. You will be wise to repeat to your masters the little lesson in statesmanship that I have thought well to give you."

With these words the Duke sank into a chair and held out his hands to the blazing fire. Machiavelli, bowing, was about to withdraw, when the Duke turned to Agapito da Amalia.

"Have you told the Secretary that his friend Buonarotti is delayed in Florence and will not be arriving for some time?"

Agapito shook his head.

"I know no such person, Excellency," said Machiavelli.

"Surely. The sculptor."

The Duke was looking at him with smiling eyes and Machiavelli on a sudden guessed of whom he was speaking. He had written to his friend Biagio for money and had received an answer from him to say that he was sending it by Michelangelo, a sculptor. The name meant nothing to him. But the Duke's remark suggested that his effects had been searched, evidently with the connivance of Serafina, and he congratulated himself on having put his important correspondence in a safe place; he had kept in his lodging only papers of little consequence, but among them was Biagio's letter.

"There are many stone-cutters in Florence, Excellency," he said coolly. "I cannot be expected to know them all."

"This Michelangelo is not without talent. He made a Cupid in marble and buried it in the ground so that when it was dug up it was taken for an antique. Cardinal di San Giorgio bought it, but when he discovered the fraud returned it to the dealer and in the end it came into my hands. I have sent it as a present to the Marchioness of Mantua."

Il Valentino spoke in a jesting way and Machiavelli for a reason obscure to him received the impression that he was being made a fool of. He had the irascibility of the highly sensitive man he was, and his impatience overcame him. He was quite willing to affront the Duke if only he could secure his freedom to keep his appointment.

"And does Your Excellency propose to order from him a statue to rival the one Leonardo made for the Duke of Milan?"

The shaft quivered through the air, and the secretaries, startled, glanced at the Duke to see how he would take it. The great equestrian statue of Francesco Sforza, thought by many to be Leonardo's masterpiece, had been destroyed by the soldiery when Marshal Trevulzio captured the city; and Francesco's son, Lodovico il Moro, who had commissioned it, a usurper like Cæsar Borgia himself, driven from his city, was now a prisoner in the castle of Loches. Machiavelli's remark was well designed to remind Il Valentino how dangerous his position was and to what depths he might fall if his good fortune deserted him. The Duke laughed.

"No, I have more important work for this fellow Michelangelo to do than to make statues. The defences of this city are useless and I'm going to let him draw plans for its fortification. But you were speaking of Leonardo; I should like to show you some drawings he has made of me."

He made a sign to one of his secretaries, who left the room and soon returned with a portfolio, which he handed to the Duke. He showed the drawings to Machiavelli one after the other.

"Unless you had told me they were portraits of Your Excellency I should never have known it," said he.

"Poor Leonardo, he has no great gift for catching a likeness. But as drawings I am assured they are not without merit."

"That may be, but I think it a pity that with his gifts he should waste his time painting pictures and making statues."

"I can assure you that he will not do so while he is in my service. I sent him to Piombino to drain the marshes and lately he has been at Cesena and Cesenatico to cut a canal and make a harbour."

He handed the drawings back to the secretary and, with a graciousness which Machiavelli noted acidly was no less regal than that of the King of France, dismissed him. Agapito da Amalia accompanied him out of the Duke's study. During the month he had been at Imola, Machiavelli had taken pains to gain the Chief Secretary's confidence. He was related to the great Roman family of the Colonna, the bitter rivals of the Orsini, and so might be supposed to have a certain friendliness for the Florentines, whose enemies they were. From time to time he had given Machiavelli information which he accepted as true or false according to his judgment of its likelihood. As now they passed through the presence chamber which was used on ceremonial occasions he took Machiavelli's arm and said:

"Come into my room. I have something to show you that will interest you."

396

"It is late and I am sick. I will come tomorrow."

"As you will. I wanted to show you the articles of agreement between the Duke and the rebels."

Machiavelli's heart stood still. He knew that the document had arrived at Imola and he had in vain used every method he could think of to get a sight of it. It was of extreme importance to the Signory to know what the terms of the pact were, and they had written to complain of his negligence. It was useless for him to tell them that he sent them all the facts as he discovered them, but that in the Duke's court secrets were well kept and none knew what the Duke meant to do until he did it. At that moment a clock struck: he had kept Aurelia waiting for two hours. The fish fry would be ruined and the fat capons roasted to a cinder, and he was hungry, for he had eaten nothing since before noon. It was said that love and hunger were the two most deep-rooted instincts of man, and who could be blamed for yielding to them? Machiavelli sighed: the safety of Florence was at stake; her liberty in danger.

"Come, then," he said.

He thought bitterly that never had a man been called upon to sacrifice so much for the good of his country.

Agapito led him up a flight of stairs, unlocked a door, and ushered him into a small room, with a bed along one wall, which was dimly lit by the flame of an oil lamp. From it he lit a tallow candle and offered Machiavelli a chair, then he sat down himself, at a table littered with papers, and, leaning back, crossed his legs comfortably. He had the appearance of a man to whom time was no object.

"I could not give you a copy of the articles before for a reason I will tell you, and for the same reason I did not give one to the agent of the Duke of Ferrara or to anyone else. The Duke and Pagolo Orsini drew up a draft which was agreeable to them both and the Lord Pagolo took it away to show it to the captains with the understanding that if they agreed to it he would do likewise on behalf of the Duke, who gave him his power of attorney. But when he had started the Duke examined the document again and it seemed to him that an article should have been included which took into account the interests of France."

Machiavelli had been listening with impatience, for he wanted to see the agreement, if possible get hold of it, and be gone; but now he gave the speaker all his attention.

"The article was duly drawn up and the Duke ordered me to ride after the Lord Pagolo and tell him that unless it was accepted he wouldn't sign. I caught him up and he flatly refused to accept it, but after some discussion he said that he would take it to the others, but he didn't think they would accept it either. And so I left him."

"What is the point of the article?"

There was laughter in Agapito's voice when he answered.

"If it is accepted it opens a window through which we can slip out of the agreement, and if it is not accepted it unlocks a door through which we can stride with our heads in the air."

"It looks as though the Duke had more desire for revenge on those who have endangered his state than for peace."

"You may be quite sure that the Duke will never allow his desires to interfere with his interests."

"You promised to show me the agreement."

"Here it is."

Machiavelli read it eagerly. By its terms the Duke and the rebels were thenceforward to live in peace, concord and union: they were to retain their commands under him with the same pay as before and as a sign of good faith each one of them was to deliver into his safe keeping one of his legitimate sons as a hostage; but they stipulated that not more than one of the captains at a time should encamp with the Duke, and then for no longer than suited him. On their side they agreed to restore to him Urbino and Camerino and in return he undertook to defend their states against anyone, with the exception of His Holiness the Pope or His Majesty the King of France, who attacked them. This was the clause that Il Valentino had insisted on and which, as Agapito had said, even a child might see made the treaty worthless. Bentivoglio of Bologna and Petrucci of Siena were signing a separate agreement with the Pope. With a frown Machiavelli read the document a second time.

"How can they expect the Duke to forgive the injuries they have done him?" he exclaimed when he had finished. "And how can the Duke be expected to forget the perils in which they have put him?"

"*Quem Jupiter vult perdere dementat prius*," quoted Agapito with a cheerful smile.

"Will you allow me to take this document away to make a copy of it?"

"I couldn't let it out of my hands."

"I promise to return it tomorrow."

399

"It's impossible. The Duke may ask for it any minute."

"The Duke never ceases to assure me of his sincere friendship for Florence. It is of the greatest importance that my government should be made acquainted with this agreement. Believe me, you will not find them ungrateful for any service you are able to render them."

"I have been concerned with affairs of state too long to count on the gratitude of princes or governments."

Machiavelli continued to press him and at last he said:

"You know that I would do a great deal to oblige you. My respect for your intelligence is only equalled by my admiration for your integrity. I do it with misgiving, I will allow you to make a copy of the agreement here."

Machiavelli gasped. It would take him half an hour to do this and time was passing. Was ever lover placed in such a predicament? There was nothing to do but to submit. Agapito gave him his place at the table, a sheet of paper and a new quill. He lay down on the bed while Machiavelli scribbled away as fast as his task would let him. As he wrote the last line he heard the night watchman cry out the hour of the night and immediately afterwards the church clock struck. Midnight.

Agapito went downstairs with him and, when they came to the court round which the Palace was built, called for two men of the guard to light Machiavelli back to his lodging. A chill rain was falling and the night was raw. When they arrived at his house Machiavelli dismissed the soldiers with a gratuity and unlocked the door. He waited within till he could no longer hear their steps and, locking up behind him, slipped out again. He crossed the alley and gently knocked in the prearranged manner. There was no reply. He knocked again. Twice, a pause, once, a pause and then twice more. He waited. A bleak wind blew down the narrow alley, gusts of rain splashed his face, and though he was well wrapped up, with a muffler to keep the noxious air of night out of his lungs, he shivered in the cold. Was it possible that the women had grown tired of waiting? But where was Piero? He had told him to stay in the yard till he came, and Piero had never failed him before. Piero must have explained why he was delayed, and after all, though for different reasons, it was as essential to them, those two women, as it was urgent to him that the opportunity should not be lost. On the walk from the Palace he had noticed on passing the front of the house that no light showed, and it occurred to him now that it would be well to see if there was a light at the back. After knocking once more, again to no purpose, he went back into his own house and up to his bedroom, since from there he could see into the yard of Bartolomeo's house and the windows that faced it. Nothing. He looked into impenetrable darkness. It might be that Piero had gone in for a moment to drink a cup of wine and to warm himself and by now was back at his post. Machiavelli went out again into the cruel night. He knocked, he waited, he knocked, he waited, he knocked, he waited. His feet and hands were like ice; his teeth were chattering.

"I shall catch my death of cold," he mumbled.

Suddenly he was swept by a gust of anger and he

401

was on the point of thundering on the door with both his fists. But prudence restrained him; he would be no further advanced if he aroused the neighbours. At last he was forced to conclude that they had given him up and were gone to bed. He turned away, and miserably let himself into his own house. He was cold, hungry and bitterly disappointed.

"If I don't catch my death of cold, I really shall have the colic tomorrow."

He went into the kitchen to find something to eat, but Serafina bought the day's food every morning and if there was anything left over kept it under lock and key, so he found nothing. The brazier had been taken out of the parlour, which was cold as death, but Machiavelli had not even the solace of going to bed; he had to sit down and write a report of his conversation with the Duke. It took him a long time, because he had to write the most important parts in cypher. Then he had to make a fair copy of the articles of agreement to enclose in his letter. He did not finish till the small hours of the morning. The missive was urgent and he could not afford to wait till he found a casual messenger who could be trusted to deliver a letter for a gold florin or two, so he clambered upstairs to the attic where his two servants slept, woke them and told the more reliable of the two to get his horse saddled and be ready to ride out of the city as soon as the gates were opened. He waited till the man was dressed, let him out of the street door, and then at last went to bed.

"And this should have been a night of love," he muttered savagely as he pulled his nightcap well over his ears.

XXIII

HE SLEPT RESTLESSLY. He woke late in the morning and found his worst fears realised. He had caught cold and when he went to the door to shout for Piero his voice sounded like an old crow's. Piero appeared.

"I'm sick," he groaned. "I've got fever. I think I'm dying. Get me some hot wine and something to eat. If I don't die of fever I shall die of starvation. Bring a brazier. I'm chilled to, the bone. Where the hell did you get to last night?"

Piero was about to speak when Machiavelli stopped him.

"Never mind about that. Later, later. Get me some wine."

He felt a little better when he had drunk and eaten. He listened sullenly when Piero explained that he had waited in the yard for more than an hour as Machiavelli had told him to do. He had waited though the pouring rain soaked him to the skin. He had waited though Monna Caterina begged him to come in.

"Did you tell them what had happened?"

"I said exactly what you told me to say, Messere."

"What did they say?"

"They said it was a pity."

"They said it was a pity?" croaked Machiavelli wrathfully. "My God! And to think that the Almighty created woman to be a helpmate to man. They said it was a pity. What would they have said to the death of Hector and the fall of Troy?"

"At last they forced me to take shelter. My teeth

403

were chattering. They said we could hear your knock from the kitchen. They made me take off my coat and dry myself by the fire."

"And the fish and the capons?"

"We kept them hot a long time and at last Monna Caterina said they'd only spoil so we'd better eat them. We were hungry."

"I was starving."

"We left something for you. Some fish and half a chicken."

"Considerate."

"We heard the clock strike once and we heard it strike a second time and Monna Aurelia went to bed."

"She did what?" Machiavelli spluttered.

"We tried to get her to wait a little longer. We said you'd be coming in a minute. She said that two hours was enough to wait for any man. She said that if business meant more to you than pleasure there wasn't much pleasure to be expected from any intimate relations with you."

"A *non sequitur*."

"She said that if you loved her as much as you pretended you'd have found some excuse to break off your interview with the Duke. We reasoned with her."

"As if one could reason with women!"

"But she wouldn't listen. So Monna Caterina told me it was no good my waiting, she gave me another drink of wine and sent me away."

It occurred to Machiavelli then that Piero had no key to get in with.

"Where did you spend the night?"

The boy gave him an arch, complacent smile.

"With Nina."

"You spent your night more profitably than I did, then," said Machiavelli grimly. "But I thought she'd gone to stay with her parents."

"That's what she told Monna Caterina. We'd arranged it beforehand. She got La Barberina to let her have a room in her house and I was to join her as soon as I could get away."

La Barberina was a procuress with a well-established and respectable business in Imola. For some minutes Machiavelli was silent. He was not a man to accept defeat.

"Listen, Piero," he said when he had well considered: "that old fool Bartolomeo will be back before night. We must act quickly. Let us not forget that when Jupiter wished to gain the favours of the beautiful Danae he approached her in the likeness of a shower of gold. Go to the merchant Luca Capelli where I bought the gloves I sent to Monna Aurelia and get him to let you have the scarf in blue silk with the silver embroidery that he showed me. Say I'll pay for it as soon as the money I'm expecting from Florence arrives. Then take it and ask to see Monna Caterina; give her the scarf for Aurelia and tell her that I'm dying of love and the cold I caught waiting at the door, but that as soon as I'm better we'll meet and I will devise a new plan to satisfy Monna Aurelia's desires and my own."

He waited impatiently for Piero to execute the commission and return with a report of his reception.

"She liked the scarf," said Piero. "She said it was pretty and asked how much it cost. When I told her she liked it still more."

"Very natural. What else?"

"I told her that it had been impossible for you to get away from the Palace and she said it didn't matter at all and not to give it another thought."

"What!" cried Machiavelli, outraged. "Really women are the most irresponsible creatures in the world. Doesn't she see that her whole future is involved? Did you tell her that I stood out in the rain for an hour?"

"Yes. She said it was very imprudent."

"Who expects a lover to be prudent? You might as well ask the sea to be calm when it is assailed by the angry winds of heaven."

"And Monna Caterina said she hoped you'd take care of yourself."

XXIV

MACHIAVELLI WAS LAID UP for several days, but by dint of purging and blood-letting recovered, and the first thing he did then was to seek out Fra Timoteo. He told him the tragic story. The monk was sympathtic.

"And now," said Machiavelli, "let us put our heads together and think out some way to get rid of our good Bartolomeo again."

"I have done my best, Messere; I can do no more."

"Father, when our illustrious Duke attacked the city of Forlì he was repulsed, but he did not for that reason raise the siege; he used every stratagem his intelligence suggested and eventually brought about its surrender."

"I have seen Messer Bartolomeo. He did exactly what I told him to do and he is persuaded that the intercession of San Vitale was efficacious. He is convinced that Monna Aurelia conceived on the night of his return from Ravenna."

"The man is a fool."

"Though a religious I am not so ignorant as to be unaware that a certain time must elapse before it can be known whether he is right or wrong."

Machiavelli felt some irritation. The friar was proving less helpful than he had expected.

"Come, come, father, do not take me for a fool too, Whatever miraculous powers the saint's relics may possess, we know that to make a sterile man fertile is not one of them. I invented the story myself and you know as well as I do that there isn't a word of truth in it."

Fra Timoteo smiled blandly and there was unction in his voice when he replied.

"The operations of Providence are mysterious, and who can know the ways of the Eternal? Have you never heard the story of St. Elizabeth of Hungary? Forbidden by her cruel husband to succour the necessities of the needy, she met him in the street one day when she was carrying bread to the poor. Suspecting that she was disobeying his orders he asked her what she had in her basket and in her fright she told him it was roses. He snatched the basket from her and when he opened it found that she had told the truth: the loaves of bread had been miraculously turned into sweet-smelling roses."

"The story is edifying," said Machiavelli coldly, "but the point escapes me."

"May it not be that San Vitale, hearing in Paradise the prayers that the pious Bartolomeo addressed to

407

him, was moved by the simple faith of this good man and performed for him the miracle which you had assured him it was in the saint's power to do? Does not Holy Scripture tell us that if we have faith we can move mountains?"

If Machiavelli had not possessed great self-control he would have given rein to his anger. He knew very well why the monk was refusing his further aid. For twenty-five ducats he had done what he had agreed to do and it was not his fault if the plan had miscarried. He wanted more money, and Machiavelli had no money to give him. The chain he had given Monna Caterina, the gloves, the attar of roses he had bought for Aurelia, had taken all his spare cash; he owed money to Bartolomeo, he owed money to several merchants, the money he was receiving from the Signory only sufficed for his current expenses. He had nothing to offer now but promises and he had an inkling that promises would mean little to Fra Timoteo.

"Your eloquence and your piety, father, bear out the good report I have heard of you, and if my letter of recommendation to the Signory has the effect we both desire I am sure it will be to the spiritual benefit of the people of Florence."

The monk bowed with a grave dignity, but Machiavelli saw that he was unmoved. He went on.

"A wise man does not put all his eggs in one basket. If a plan miscarries he tries another. Do not let us lose sight of the fact that if Bartolomeo is disappointed in his hopes he will adopt his nephews to the injury of his wife and his mother-in-law and to the loss of your church."

"It would be a misfortune which it would be my Christian duty to persuade all concerned to bear with resignation."

"We are told that God helps those who help themselves. You have not found me ungenerous in the past, you will not find me ungenerous in the future. It is to your interest as well as to that of the two ladies that Bartolomeo's hopes should not be disappointed."

A faint smile for a moment lit Fra Timoteo's Roman features.

"You know that I would do much to oblige a person of your distinction, but supposing that the good Bartolomeo's hopes are disappointed, how do you propose that we should gain God's help by helping ourselves?"

Machiavelli suddenly got an idea. It amused him so much that he nearly burst out laughing.

"Father, like the rest of the world you have doubtless from time to time to take a purge, and suppose you take a dose of aloes at night, you have certainly discovered that its action is more satisfactory if you take a dose of salts in the morning. Does it not occur to you that the efficacy of Bartolomeo's pilgrimage to San Vitale would be increased if he made another to Rimini, for example, which would oblige him to absent himself from this city for another twenty-four hours?"

"You are a man of so many devices, Messere, that I cannot refuse you my admiration. But this one comes too late. Messer Bartolomeo may be a fool, but I should be more of a fool than he if I counted on his being more of a fool than he is."

"Your influence over him is great."

"That is all the more reason for my not losing it."

"Then I can't count upon your aid?"

"I do not say that. Wait a month and then we will talk of it again."

"To a lover a month is a hundred years."

"Let us not forget that the patriarch Jacob waited seven years for Rachel."

Machiavelli saw well enough that the monk was mocking him. He was going to do nothing until Machiavelli could make it worth his while. He was seething, but he knew it would be fatal to show his irritation. Controlling himself he parted from the monk with a pleasantry: he begged him to accept a florin for a candle to be burnt at the altar of the miraculous Virgin so that Bartolomeo's wishes might be fulfilled. There was no sting in a defeat accepted with spirit.

XXV

HIS ONLY HOPE NOW of having his way with Aurelia was to enlist the aid of Monna Caterina. It was obvious that her concern at the misadventure which had frustrated their well-laid scheme must be great, greater than his indeed, for with him it was only a matter of satisfying his desire for a pretty woman; but her very security was at stake. He could no longer rely on the monk, but in her he had a self-interested ally, and that was an ally you could count on. He had a firm belief in the ingenuity of her sex; to deceive was food and drink to it, and it was to her manifest advantage to do everything she could to bring their plan to a successful issue. He decided to arrange a meeting with her. The secluded life the two women led made it none too easy, but fortunately Piero was there to act as a go-between. He congratulated himself on his foresight in urging the boy to make love to Nina.

Next day he bought a beautiful fish at the market and sent it by Piero to Bartolomeo's house at a time when he knew the fat man would be about his business in the city. It would be very unlucky if he could not get an opportunity to see her alone and make an appointment. Piero carried out his commission with his usual competence and returned to tell his master that Monna Caterina after some hesitation had agreed to meet him at such and such an hour, three days from then, at the church of St. Dominic. Her choice of place was adroit. It was evident that with her feminine intuition she had realised that Fra Timoteo could be trusted no longer and it was just as well that he should not see them together.

Machiavelli went to St. Dominic's without an idea in his head, but he was untroubled, for he was confident that Monna Caterina would be able to suggest something; his only fear was that it would cost too much money. Ah, well, if the worst came to the worst he would have to borrow once again from Bartolomeo; after all, it was only just that he should pay for the service Machiavelli was prepared to render him.

There was not a soul in the church. Machiavelli told Monna Caterina how it had happened that he had not been able to keep the appointment and how he had stood knocking at the door in the rain and how he had caught a dreadful cold.

"I know, I know," said Monna Caterina. "Piero told us and we were greatly distressed. Aurelia kept on saying: 'The poor gentleman, it would be on my conscience if he died.'"

"I had no intention of dying," said Machiavelli. "And if I had been at the gates of Paradise the thought of Aurelia would have brought me back."

"It was all very unfortunate."

"Let us not think of the past. I have recovered my health. I am full of vigour. Let us think of the future. Our scheme has miscarried, we must devise another; you are a clever woman, and I find it hard to believe that you cannot arrange some way whereby all our wishes may be satisfied."

"Messer Niccolo, I did not want to come here today; I only came because of your Piero's entreaties."

"He said you had shown hesitation. I could not understand."

"No one likes to be the bearer of ill tidings."

"What do you mean?" cried Machiavelli. "It is impossible that Bartolomeo should have conceived any suspicion."

"No, no, it is not that. It is Aurelia. I have argued with her, I have gone down on my bended knees, I can do nothing with her. Ah, my poor friend, girls are not what they were when I was young; then it never occurred to them that they could disobey their parents."

"Don't beat about the bush, woman. Tell me what you mean."

"Aurelia refuses to go on. She will not do what you desire."

"But have you put the consequences before her? Haven't you shown her what her position will be, and yours, if Bartolomeo adopts his sister's sons and

412

Monna Costanza becomes mistress of your house?"

"I have said everything."

"But the reason? Even a woman must have a reason for what she does."

"She believes that by a special interposition of Providence she has been preserved from mortal sin."

"Sin?" shouted Machiavelli, in his agitation forgetting the decorum due to the sacred building in which they were thus conversing.

"Do not be angry with me, Messer Niccolo. It is not for a mother to persuade her daughter to act contrary to the dictates of her conscience."

"Saving your presence, Madonna, you are talking stuff and nonsense. You are an experienced woman and she is but an ignorant girl. It is your duty to point out to her that of two evils not only reason but heaven itself commands us to choose the lesser. Who in his senses would refuse to commit a little sin, and one to which considerable pleasure is attached, in order to gain a great good?"

"It is no use, Messere, I know my daughter, she is as stubborn as a mule; she had made up her mind and I can do nothing with her. She wishes me to tell you that in memory of the interest you have taken in her she will always treasure the elegant gloves and the silk scarf you gave her, but she will accept no more presents from you and desires you to offer none. She desired you further to make no more attempt, either direct or indirect, to see her. For my part I shall always remember your kindness with gratitude and I only wish I could make up to you for the disappointment you have suffered."

413

She paused for a moment, but Machiavelli made no reply.

"I need not tell a man of your wit and worldly wisdom that women are capricious and uncertain. If he chooses the right moment even the prude will accept the embraces of a lover, but if he misses it even the wanton will refuse them. I bid you a very good day."

Monna Caterina gave him a curtsy in which according to his perspicacity an observer might have seen derision, resentment or civility, and was gone.

Machiavelli was confounded.

XXVI

NOTWITHSTANDING ALL HIS ATTEMPTS during the next month it was not till he was about to leave Imola that he saw Aurelia again. Fortunately his work kept him too busy to brood over his disappointment. The rebels were reported to be at loggerheads. At last, however, all signed the agreement which Agapito had shown Machiavelli except Baglioni of Perugia, who told them they were fools and dupes to put their hands to such a document, and when he found them determined to make peace at any cost strode in a passion out of the church in which they were meeting. The Duke appointed Pagolo Orsini governor of Urbino, which by the terms of the treaty he recovered, and to reward him for persuading the captains to sign it made him a present of five thousand ducats. Vitellozzo wrote humble letters in which he sought to excuse his actions.

"The traitor stuck a knife in our backs," said

Agapito, "and now he thinks he can undo the harm with soft words."

But Il Valentino appeared to be well pleased. It looked as though he were prepared to let bygones be bygones and restore the repentant rebels to his confidence. His amiability seemed suspicious to Machiavelli and he wrote to the Signory that it was hard to guess and impossible to know what the Duke had in mind. He had now large forces at his disposal and it was evident to all that he would make use of them. Rumours were current that he was making preparations for his departure from Imola, but whether he intended to march south and attack the Kingdom of Naples or north to wage war on the Venetians was more than anyone could tell. Machiavelli was disturbed to hear that influential persons from Pisa had come to offer him their city. Florence had spent time, money and lives in the attempt to recapture it, for its possession was necessary to their commerce, and if it was held by the Duke their position, both from the economic and the military standpoint, would be hazardous. Lucca was close, and the Duke, speaking of it, remarked in a way that Machiavelli thought ominous that it was a rich territory and a mouthful for gluttons. If after gaining possession of Pisa he seized Lucca, Florence would be at his mercy. In an interview with Machiavelli the Duke brought up again the matter of the *condotta,* and the wretched envoy was hard put to it to explain the Signory's hesitation to grant him the command he wanted in such a way as not to offend him. The plain fact was that they were determined not to place themselves in the power of an unscrupulous man whom they had

415

every reason to distrust. But whatever sinister plans he turned round in that handsome head of his, the Duke was evidently not ready to resort to more than veiled threats to induce the Florentines to accede to his demands, for he listened to Machiavelli calmly enough. He ended by telling him that he was about to set out for Cesena with his army and once there would do what he decided was necessary.

He started for Forlì on the tenth of December and reached Cesena on the twelfth. Machiavelli made arrangements to follow him. He sent Piero with one of the servants ahead to make sure of a dwelling, and having taken leave of certain persons who had obliged him during his sojourn at Imola, empty now that the Duke, with his court and all the hangers-on, had left, finally went to say good-bye to Bartolomeo. He found him at home and was ushered into his study. The fat man received him with his usual boisterous cordiality. He had already heard of Machiavelli's approaching departure and expressed his regret in very handsome terms. He said how greatly he had enjoyed the acquaintance of such a distinguished visitor and how much he deplored that he would no longer have the opportunity to play with him those too infrequent games of chess and to entertain him at his house with music and such poor fare as he could provide. Machiavelli on his side paid him appropriate compliments and then with some embarrassment entered upon a matter which was on his mind.

"Listen, my dear friend: I am come not only to thank you for all your kindness to me, but to ask you to do me one more kindness still."

"You have only to mention it."

416

Machiavelli gave a slightly bitter laugh.

"I owe you twenty-five ducats. I haven't the money to pay you. I must ask you to wait a little longer."

"It is a matter of no consequence."

"Twenty-five ducats is a considerable sum."

"Let it wait, let it wait, and if it's inconvenient for you to pay there's no reason why you should. Look upon it as a gift rather than a loan."

"There is no reason why you should make me such a present. I couldn't possibly accept such a favour at your hands."

Bartolomeo leaned back in his chair and burst into a great booming laugh.

"But didn't you guess? It is not my money. Our good Duke knew that with the rise of prices and the necessary expenses of your mission your circumstances were embarrassed. Everyone knows that the Signory is niggardly. I received instructions from His Excellency's treasurer to provide you with any sum you might need. If you had asked me for two hundred ducats instead of twenty-five I should have given them to you."

Machiavelli went pale. He was dumbfounded.

"But if I had known the money came from the Duke nothing would have induced me to take it."

"It was because the Duke knew your scruples and admired your integrity that he chose me to be the go-between. He respected your delicacy. I am betraying his confidence, but I do not think you should remain ignorant of so generous and disinterested a gesture."

Machiavelli stifled the obscenity that rose to his lips. He had little belief in the Duke's generosity and none in his disinterestedness. Did he think to buy his good will for twenty-five ducats? Machiavelli's thin lips tightened so that his mouth showed as no more than a bitter line.

"You are surprised?" smiled Bartolomeo.

"Nothing the Duke may do can any longer surprise me."

"He is a very great man. I have no doubt that we who have enjoyed the privilege of being useful to him shall on that account be remembered by posterity."

"My good Bartolomeo," said Machiavelli, "it is not the great deeds men do that make them remembered by posterity, but the fine language with which men of letters describe their deeds. Pericles would be no more than a name if Thucydides had not put into his mouth the speech that has made him famous."

While saying these words he got up.

"You mustn't go without seeing the ladies. It would grieve them not to bid you farewell."

Machiavelli followed him into the parlour. There was a certain constriction in his throat and it seemed to him that his heart was beating at an unaccustomed rate. The women had not expected a visitor and they were in their everyday clothes. They were taken aback to see him and perhaps none too well pleased. They rose to their feet and curtsied. Bartolomeo told them that Machiavelli was leaving for Cesena.

"What shall we do without you?" cried Monna Caterina.

Since Machiavelli had the conviction that they would do perfectly well without him, he merely smiled a rather sour smile.

"Messer Niccolo will doubtless be glad to leave a

418

place which offers so little to divert a stranger," said Aurelia.

Machiavelli could not but think there was a hint of malice in her tone. She resumed her work and he noticed that she was still busy with the elaborate embroidery of the shirts the material for which he had brought from Florence.

"I hardly know which to admire most, Monna Aurelia," he said, "your patience or your industry."

"They say the devil finds work for idle hands to do," she replied.

"And pleasant work, too, on occasion."

"But dangerous."

"And hence more attractive."

"Yet discretion is the better part of valour."

Machiavelli didn't much like having his remarks capped, and, though he smiled, his retort was acidulous.

"They say that proverbs are the wisdom of the multitude, but the multitude is always in the wrong."

Aurelia was not looking her best. The weather had been bad for some time and she had waited too long to dye her hair. The roots showed black. One might have thought that she had made-up that morning in haste, for the natural olive of her skin was not quite disguised by the cosmetics she had applied.

"By the time she's forty she'll be no more desirable than her mother," said Machiavelli to himself.

After a decent interval he took his leave. He was glad he had seen Aurelia again. He still desired her, but his desire was not so importunate as it had been. He was not a man who because he was disappointed of the fat quails he had promised himself for his dinner was disinclined to eat the pig's trotters that were set before him; and when he saw that to pursue Aurelia further was fruitless, he had on occasion assuaged his urgent passions in the arms of sundry not too expensive young women whose acquaintance he made through the good offices of La Barberina. Now when he looked into his heart he could not but see that, so far as Aurelia was concerned, he was suffering as much from wounded vanity as from the pangs of unrequited love. He came to the conclusion that she was rather stupid; otherwise she would not have gone to bed in a pet because he had kept her waiting a mere three hours; otherwise it would never have occurred to her that in going to bed with him she was committing a sin, at least till after she had committed it. If only she knew as much about life as he did, she would know that it is not the temptations you have succumbed to that you regret, but those you have resisted.

"Well, it'll serve her right if Bartolomeo adopts his nephews," he said to himself. "She'll be sorry then that she was such a fool."

XXVII

TWO DAYS LATER he arrived at Cesena. The Duke's artillery was approaching the city, his army was at full strength, and he was well provided with money. It was evident that something was afoot, but none knew what. Notwithstanding the activity that prevailed there was in the air a stillness like that which they say obtains before an earthquake: men are uneasy and restless, they know not why, and suddenly, without warning, the ground under their feet shakes and the houses come tumbling about their ears. Machiavelli twice requested the Duke to receive him, and the Duke, thanking him for his courtesy, returned the message that he would send for him when he had need of him. He could get no information from the secretaries. They repeated that the Duke told nothing till he was ready to act, and he acted as necessity dictated. It was obvious that they were as ignorant of his plans as anyone else. Machiavelli was sick and sore and he had no money. He wrote to the Signory asking for his recall and advised them to send in his place an ambassador with fuller powers than they had been willing to grant him.

But Machiavelli had not been in Cesena a week before an unexpected event occurred. Going one morning to the Palace, which the Duke had requisitioned for his own use, he found all the French captains there. They were angry and excited. It appeared that they had on a sudden received the order to take themselves off within two days, and they were deeply affronted by their abrupt dismissal. Machiavelli racked his brains to think of a plausible explanation for this step. His friends at court told him that the Duke could no longer stand the French, since they caused him more trouble than they were worth; but it seemed the height of folly to send away so important a part of his armed force when the troops left to him would not be superior to those under the command of the captains, Orsini, Vitellozzo, Oliverotto da Fermo and the rest, in whose loyalty, after their recent rebellion and unwilling submission, he could certainly place small trust. Was it possible that the Duke had so much confidence in himself that he wanted to show the King of France that he no longer needed his help?

The French went away and a few days later another occurrence took place which Machiavelli, a student of human nature as well as of politics, found of quite peculiar interest. Ramiro de Lorqua was summoned to Cesena. He had remained faithful to the Duke, he was a good soldier and an able administrator. He had been for some time governor of Romagna. But his cruelty and dishonesty had made him hated and feared by the people, and at last, driven beyond endurance, they sent representatives to lay their complaints before the Duke. When Ramiro arrived he was arrested and thrown into prison.

On Christmas Day, Piero woke Machiavelli early.

"Come into the Piazza, Messere, and you will see a sight worth seeing," he said, his young eyes sparkling with excitement.

"What is it?"

"I will not tell you. There is a great crowd assembled. Everyone is amazed."

It did not take Machiavelli long to dress. It had been snowing and the morning was raw. In the Piazza, on a mat on the snow, lay the headless body of Ramiro de Lorqua, richly dressed, with all his decorations, and gloves on his hands. At a little distance was his head stuck on a pike. Machiavelli turned away from the shocking sight and slowly walked back to his lodging.

"What do you make of it, Messere?" asked Piero. "He was the Duke's most valiant captain. They always said the Duke trusted him and relied on him as on nobody else."

Machiavelli shrugged his shoulders.

"It has so pleased the Duke. It shows that he can make and unmake men at his pleasure according to their deserts. I suppose that the Duke had no further use for him and was not displeased to show by an act of justice that he had the interests of his people at heart."

It was generally believed that Ramiro had been the lover of Lucrezia Borgia, and it was dangerous to be either the husband or the lover of Cæsar Borgia's sister. He loved her. Her first husband, Giovanni Sforza, escaped death only because she warned him that Cæsar had given orders for him to be killed. He threw himself on a horse and rode for dear life till he reached the safety of Pesaro. When the Duke of Gandia was fished out of the Tiber with nine wounds in his body, common report ascribed his murder to Cæsar, and the reason given was that he also had loved Lucrezia. Pedro Calderon, a Spaniard and a chamberlain of the Pope, was killed at Cæsar's command "because of something offending the honour of Madonna Lucrezia". She was in point of fact, it was said, with child by him. Her second husband Alfonso, Duke of Bisceglie, was equally unfortunate. One day, a year after his marriage, when he was only nineteen, he was set upon by armed men as he was leaving the Vatican and desperately wounded; he was helped back to the papal apartments, where for a month he hovered between life and death; then, refusing to die of his wounds, Burchard relates, he was strangled in bed one hour after sunset. Alfonso of Bisceglie was the handsomest man in Rome and Lucrezia had made the mistake of loving him too fondly. No one in Italy

423

doubted that he owed his death to Cæsar Borgia's jealousy.

Machiavelli had a good memory and he had not forgotten something that the Duke had said to him at Imola. Pagolo Orsini had complained of Ramiro's brutality and the Duke had promised to give him satisfaction. It was unlikely that he cared anything for the complaints of Pagolo, whom he despised, but was it not possible that by his execution of Ramiro he would dissipate the last of the suspicions harboured by the rebellious captains? How could they fail to rely on his good faith when to gratify one of their number he had sacrificed the most competent and highly trusted of his lieutenants? Machiavelli laughed within himself. It was just the kind of thing that would appeal to Il Valentino, at one stroke to placate the outraged people of Romagna, assure his false friends of his confidence in them, and wreak his private vengeance on one who had enjoyed the favours of Lucrezia.

"At all events," he said to Piero cheerfully, "our good Duke has rid the earth of one more rascal. Let us find a tavern and drink a cup of hot wine to get the chill out of our bones."

XXVIII

THERE WAS A VERY GOOD REASON why Machiavelli had not been able to discover Il Valentino's projects, and that was because they were still unsettled. Something had to be done, for there was no sense in having an army and not using it, but it was not so easy to

decide what. The captains sent representatives to
Cesena to discuss the matter with the Duke, but no
agreement was reached, so after some days they dispatched Oliverotto da Fermo with a concrete proposition to put before him.

This Oliverotto da Fermo was a young man who
not long before had got himself much talked about.
Having been left fatherless in early childhood he was
brought up by his uncle, his mother's brother, called
Giovanni Fogliati, and on reaching a suitable age was
sent to learn the profession of arms under Paolo
Vitelli. After Paolo's execution he joined his brother
Vitellozzo, and in a short while, because he was intelligent and vigorous, became one of his best officers. But
he was ambitious. He thought it base to serve when he
might rule, and so concocted an ingenious plan to
better himself. He wrote to his uncle and benefactor
that, since he had been away from home for some
years, he would like to visit him and his native town
and at the same time see to his paternal estate. And
because his only concern had been to gain renown,
so that his fellow-citizens should see that he had not
spent his time in vain he desired to come in an imposing way with a hundred horsemen, his friends and
servants, in his train; and he begged his uncle to see
that he was received in an honourable manner, which
would be not only a credit to him but to his uncle,
whose foster child he was. Giovanni Fogliati was
gratified to see that his nephew was not forgetful of
the care and affection with which he had treated him,
and when Oliverotto arrived at Fermo very naturally
took him to live with him. But after some days
Oliverotto, not to be a burden on his uncle, moved

into a house of his own and invited him and all the most important personages of Fermo to a solemn banquet.

When they had feasted and made merry, Oliverotto, broaching a topic that was of concern to all of them, spoke of the greatness of the Pope and his son Cæsar and of their undertakings; but getting up on a sudden with a remark that these were matters that must be discussed in private, he led his guests into another room. They had no sooner seated themselves than soldiers came out of their hiding-places and killed them one and all. Thus he gained possession of the city and, since all were dead who might have resisted him, and the regulations he made, both civil and military, were efficient, within a year he made himself not only safe in Fermo, but formidable to his neighbours. This was the man, then, whom the captains sent to Il Valentino. The proposition he brought was with their combined forces to invade Tuscany or, if that did not suit him, to seize Sinigaglia. Tuscany was a rich prize. The capture of Siena, Pisa, Lucca and Florence would provide great spoil to all who took part in the enterprise, and Vitellozzo and the Orsini had old scores with Florence which they would be glad to settle. But Siena and Florence were under the protection of the King of France and the Duke was not prepared to anger an ally of whom he might yet have need. He therefore told Oliverotto that he would not join in an attack on Tuscany, but would be well pleased to have Sinigaglia taken.

Sinigaglia was small, but not unimportant, for it was on the sea and had a good port. Its ruler, the widowed sister of the unfortunate Duke of Urbino, had signed the compact at La Magione along with the rebel captains; but after the reconciliation, in which she would have no share, she had fled with her young son to Venice, leaving Andrea Doria, a Genoese, to defend the citadel. Oliverotto marched on the city and occupied it without opposition. Vitellozzo and the Orsini advanced with their troops and quartered them in the vicinity. The operation had been conducted with only one hitch: Andrea Doria refused to surrender the citadel except to Il Valentino in person. It was strong, and to take it by storm would cost time, money and men. Common sense prevailed. Now that the Duke had sent away his French contingent the captains could no longer regard him as formidable, and so, informing him of Andrea Doria's demand, they invited him to come to Sinigaglia.

When he received this summons he had already left Cesena and was at Fano. He sent a trusted secretary to tell the captains that he would come to Sinigaglia at once and to request them to await him there. Since the signing of the treaty they had shown no inclination to encounter the Duke in person. Anxious to dispel the mistrust which their neglect indicated, he instructed the secretary to inform them in a friendly manner that the estrangement they persisted in maintaining could only prevent the pact they had agreed on from being effective; and that for his part his one and only desire was to avail himself of their forces and their counsels.

Machiavelli was astounded when he heard that the Duke had accepted the captains' invitation. He had closely studied the treaty and it was evident to him that neither side put the smallest trust in the other.

On learning that the captains had asked Il Valentino to join them at Sinigaglia because the commander of the citadel refused to deliver it to one of his officers, he was convinced that they were setting a trap for him. The Duke had dismissed his French men-at-arms and so considerably diminished his strength. The captains had all their men at Sinigaglia or near at hand. It seemed obvious that the commander had made his condition with their connivance, and that when the Duke arrived with his mounted men they would attack him and cut him and them to pieces. It was incredible that he should hazard himself almost defenceless among his mortal enemies. The only explanation was that he trusted in his star and, blinded by arrogance, thought to cow those brutal men by the power of his will and the force of his personality. He knew they were afraid of him, but perhaps he had forgotten that fear may well make brave men out of cowards. True, fortune hitherto had favoured the Duke, but fortune was inconstant. Pride goeth before a fall. Machiavelli chuckled. If the Duke walked into the trap laid for him and were destroyed it would be to the great advantage of Florence. He was the enemy; the captains, held together only by their dread of him, could be separated by skilful manœuvres and disposed of one by one.

Machiavelli chuckled too soon. When the Orsini made the commander of the citadel an offer of money to refuse to deliver it except to the Duke in person he already had the gold the Duke had paid him to do exactly that. He had guessed his captains' design and foreseen what they would do to induce him to come among them. He was a secret man and it was not his habit to discuss his plans till the moment arrived to put them in execution. On the night before leaving Fano he called together eight of his most trusted followers. He told them that when the captains came to meet him one of them was to place himself on each side of each one of them and, as though to do him honour, accompany him till they reached the Palace which had been chosen as his residence. He bade them take care that none of them made his escape. Once in the Palace they would be at his mercy. None of them would leave it alive and free. He had scattered his troops about the country so that none should know how great a force he disposed of, and now he gave orders that they should assemble in the morning at a river about six miles on the way to Sinigaglia. As a sign of good faith he had sent his baggage wagons on ahead of him, and he smiled as he thought how the captains must lick their chops when they contemplated the great booty that awaited them.

All being settled, he went to bed and slept soundly. He started betimes in the morning. It was the thirty-first of December, 1502. The distance between Fano and Sinigaglia was fifteen miles and the road ran between the mountains and the sea. The advance guard of fifteen hundred men was headed by Lodovico della Mirandola; then came a number of Gascons and Swiss, a thousand of them; after them the Duke in full armour on a richly-caparisoned charger; and then the rest of his cavalry. Machiavelli was not highly susceptible to æsthetic emotion, but he thought he had never seen a prettier sight than this army winding its slow way between the snow-capped mountains and the blue sea.

The captains were waiting at a point three miles from Sinigaglia.

Vitellozzo Vitelli, till his health was ruined by the French sickness, was a man of powerful physique, big and strong, but spare, even gaunt, with a sallow, clean-shaven face, an aggressive nose and a small, receding chin. His eyelids drooping heavily over his eyes gave them a strange, brooding expression. Ruthless, cruel, rapacious and brave, he was a fine soldier and had the reputation of being the best artilleryman in Europe. He was proud of his possession, Città di Castello, and of the fine palaces, adorned with frescoes, bronzes, marble figures and Flemish tapestries, with which he and his family had enriched it. He had loved his brother Paolo whom the Florentines had beheaded and he hated them for it with a hatred time could not lessen. But owing to the mercury with which the doctors dosed him he suffered from attacks of intoler-able depression, and was but a shadow of his old self. When Pagolo Orsini at the time they were negotiating a reconciliation brought Il Valentino's terms to the assembled captains, Gian Paolo Baglioni, Lord of Perugia, would not accept them, and though for a time Vitellozzo, mistrusting the Duke's offers, sided with him, he had not the strength to withstand the nagging arguments of the others and in the end agreed to sign. But he signed against his better judgment. True, he had written humble letters of submission and apology, and Il Valentino in return had assured him that all was forgiven and forgotten; but he was uneasy. His instinct told him that the Duke had neither forgotten nor forgiven. One of the articles of the agreement had been that only one of the captains at a time should be on service in the Duke's camp, and there they were, all of them, gathered together. Pagolo Orsini reasoned with him. He had visited the Duke several times, they had talked together long and often, openly and frankly, as man to man, and it was impossible not to be convinced of his sincerity. What better proof of it could there be than that he had dismissed his French lancers and so could only conduct an enterprise without their assistance? And why had he executed Ramiro de Lorqua if not to show that he was prepared to listen to their demands?

"Believe me, the rebellion has taught the young man a lesson, and there's good reason to believe that in future we shall have no cause to be displeased with him."

Pagolo Orsini did not, however, think it necessary to tell Vitellozzo of a certain conversation he had had with the Duke. The Pope was seventy, a man of a plethoric condition who lived the life of a man in his prime, and a stroke might kill him at any moment. Il Valentino could control the votes of the Spanish cardinals and the cardinals his father had created; he was prepared in return for an assurance that his states would be secured to him to ensure the election to the papacy of Pagolo's brother Cardinal Orsini. The prospect was dazzling. Pagolo was the more inclined to trust the Duke, since it seemed certain that he needed the Orsini as much as they needed him.

Vitellozzo was the first of the captains to come forward to greet the Duke. He was unarmed, dressed in a shabby black tunic, and over it he wore a black cloak lined with green. He was pale and troubled and you might have thought from the look on his face that he

431

knew the fate in store for him. No one seeing him now would have supposed that this was the man who had once thought on his own resources to drive the King of France out of Italy. He was riding a mule and was about to dismount, but the Duke prevented him, and leaning over put a friendly arm round his shoulder and kissed him on both cheeks. Within a few minutes Pagolo Orsini and the Duke of Gravina rode up with their attendants and Cæsar Borgia received them with the courtesy due to their great birth and the happy cordiality of one who has been too long parted from dear friends. But he noticed the absence of Oliverotto da Fermo, and on asking for him was told that he was awaiting him in the city. He sent Don Michele to fetch the young man and while they waited engaged the captains in desultory conversation. No one could be more charming than he when it was worth his while, and to see him then you would have thought that nothing had ever happened to mar the harmony of his relations with the three commanders. He was gracious, as befitted his station, but without hauteur, so that there was no hint of condescension in his manner. He was composed, urbane and affable. He enquired after Vitellozzo's health and suggested sending his own surgeon to treat him. With an amused smile he gaily chaffed the Duke of Gravina about a love affair in which he was engaged. He listened with flattering interest to Pagolo Orsini's description of the Villa he was building in the Alban hills.

Don Michele found Oliverotto drilling his troops in a square beyond the river outside the city walls. He told him that it would be wise to let his men take possession of their quarters or they would be seized by the Duke's. The advice was good and Oliverotto, thanking him for the sensible suggestion, immediately acted on it. Having given the necessary orders he accompanied Don Michele to the spot where the others were waiting. The Duke welcomed him with the same warm friendliness as he had shown to the others. He would not let him do the homage he was prepared to do; he used him as a comrade rather than as a subordinate.

The Duke gave the order to advance.

Vitellozzo was seized with terror. He had seen by now how great was the force that followed the Duke, and knew for a certainty that the plot the captains had made stood no chance of success. He made up his mind to rejoin his own troops, which were camped but a few miles away. His illness offered a convincing excuse. But Pagolo would not let him go. This was no time, he argued, to let the Duke think they were doubtful of his good faith. Vitellozzo was broken in spirit; he lacked the resolution to do what his instinct told him was his only chance to escape. He allowed himself to be persuaded.

"I have a conviction that if I go, I go to my death," he said, "but since you are determined to take the chance, whether it be to live or die, I am ready to face fate with you and with the others to whom destiny has linked me."

The eight men whom the Duke had ordered to escort the captains took up their positions one on either side of each of the doomed men and, headed by their commander, splendid in his shining armour, the cavalcade rode into the city. On reaching the Palace that had been set aside for the Duke's residence the captains wished to take leave of him, but he urged them in his frank and open way to come in so that they might immediately discuss the plan he wished to put before them. He had much to say that could not fail to be of interest to them. Time was important. Whatever they decided to do must be done quickly. They agreed to what he asked. He ushered them through the doorway and up a fine flight of stairs that led to the great reception room. Once there he begged them to excuse him so that he might attend to a call of nature, and no sooner was he gone than armed men burst in and arrested them. Thus he played the same neat and simple trick on them that the graceless Oliverotto had played on his uncle and the chief citizens at Fermo, and it had not even cost him a banquet. Pagolo Orsini protested at the Duke's breach of faith and called for him, but he had already left the Palace. He gave orders that the troops of the four captains should be disarmed. Oliverotto's men, being near at hand, were taken by surprise and those who resisted were butchered, but the others who were encamped at some distance were more fortunate; they got wind of the disaster that had befallen their masters and, combining their forces, succeeded, though with serious losses, in fighting their way to safety. Cæsar Borgia had to content himself with putting to death the immediate followers of Vitellozzo and the Orsini.

The Duke's soldiers, however, were not satisfied with plundering Oliverotto's men. They set about sacking the city. They would have spared nothing but for the Duke's stern measures; he did not want a ruined city, but a prosperous one from which he could get revenue, and he had the looters hanged. The city

was in a turmoil. The shopkeepers had put up their shutters and honest citizens cowered in their houses behind locked doors. Soldiers broke into the wine-shops and forced their owners at the sword's point to give them wine. Men were lying dead in the streets and mongrel dogs lapped their blood.

XXIX

MACHIAVELLI HAD FOLLOWED THE DUKE to Sinigaglia. He spent an anxious day. It was dangerous to go out alone or unarmed and when obliged to leave the wretched inn where he had taken refuge he was careful to be accompanied by Piero and his servants. He had no wish to be killed by excitable Gascons the worse for liquor.

At eight o'clock that night the Duke sent for him. On all other occasions on which Machiavelli had had audience with him it had been in the presence of others, secretaries, churchmen or members of the suite; but on this occasion, to his surprise, the officer who ushered him into the room in which the Duke was seated immediately withdrew, and for the first time they were alone.

The Duke was in high spirits. With his auburn hair and neat beard, his cheeks flushed and his eyes shining, he looked handsomer than Machiavelli had ever seen him. There was assurance in his mien and majesty in his bearing. He might be the bastard of a wicked priest but he bore himself like a king. As usual he came straight to the point.

"Well, I have done your masters a great service in ridding them of their enemies," he said. "I desire you now to write to them to collect infantry and send it with their cavalry so that we can march together on Castello or Perugia."

"Perugia?"

A cheerful smile lit up the Duke's face.

"The Baglioni refused to sign the treaty with the others and he left them, saying: 'If Cæsar Borgia wants me he can come and fetch me at Perugia and come armed.' That is what I propose to do."

Machiavelli thought that it had not done the others much good to sign the treaty, but contented himself with smiling.

"To crush Vitellozzo and destroy the Orsini would have cost the Signory a lot of money, and then they wouldn't have done it half so neatly as I have. I don't think they should be ungrateful."

"I'm sure they are not, Excellency."

The Duke, a smile still on his lips, but his eyes shrewd, held Machiavelli with a steady gaze.

"Then let them show it. They haven't stirred a finger, and what I've done is worth a hundred thousand ducats to them. The obligation is not legal, but tacit, and it would be well if they started to discharge it."

Machiavelli very well knew that the Signory would be outraged at such a demand and he had no wish to be the transmitter of it. He was glad to have a way out.

"I should tell Your Excellency that I have asked my government to recall me. I have pointed out to them that they should have here an envoy of more consequence and with fuller powers than mine. Your Excellency could more profitably discuss this matter with my successor."

436

"You are right. I am tired of your government's temporising. The time has come for them to make the decision whether they will be with me or against me. I should have left here today, but, if I had, the town would have been sacked. Andrea Doria is to surrender the citadel tomorrow morning and then I shall set out for Castello and Perugia. When I have settled my business there I shall turn my attention to Siena."

"Would the King of France consent to your taking cities that are under his protection?"

"He wouldn't and I'm not so foolish as to think so. I propose to take them on behalf of the Church. All I want for myself is my own state of Romagna."

Machiavelli sighed. He was filled with an unwilling admiration for this man whose spirit was so fiery and who was so confident in his power to get whatsoever he wanted.

"No one can doubt that you are favoured by fortune, Excellency," he said.

"Fortune favours him who knows how to take advantage of his opportunity. Do you suppose it was a happy accident, by which I profited, that the governor of the citadel refused to surrender except to me personally?"

"I wouldn't do Your Excellency that injustice. After what has happened today I can guess that you made it worth his while."

The Duke laughed.

"I like you, Secretary. You are a man with whom one can talk. I shall miss you." He paused and for what seemed quite a long time looked searchingly at Machiavelli. "I could almost wish that you were in my service."

"Your Excellency is very kind. I am very well content to serve the Republic."

"What does it profit you? The salary you receive is so miserable that to make both ends meet you have to borrow from your friends."

This gave Machiavelli something of a turn, but then he remembered that the Duke must know of the twenty-five ducats Bartolomeo had lent him.

"I am careless of money and of an extravagant disposition," he answered with a pleasant smile. "It is my own fault if from time to time I live beyond my means."

"You would find it hard to do that if you were employed by me. It is very pleasant to be able to give a pretty lady a ring, a bracelet or a brooch when one wishes to obtain her favours."

"I have made it my rule to satisfy my desires with women of easy virtue and modest pretensions."

"A good rule enough if one's desires were under one's control, but who can tell what strange tricks love can play on him? Have you never discovered, Secretary, to what expense one is put when one loves a virtuous woman?"

The Duke was looking at him with mocking eyes and for an instant Machiavelli asked himself uneasily whether it was possible that he knew of his unsatisfied passion for Aurelia, but the thought had no sooner come into his mind than he rejected it. The Duke had more important things to occupy him than the Florentine envoy's love affairs.

"I am willing to take it for granted and leave both the pleasures and the expense to others."

The Duke gazed at him thoughtfully. You might

438

have imagined that he was asking himself what kind
of a man this was, but with no ulterior motive, from
idle curiosity rather. So, when you find yourself alone
with a stranger in the waiting-room of an office, to pass
the time you try from the look of him to guess his business, his calling, his habits and his character.

"I should have thought you were too intelligent a
man to be content to remain for the rest of your life in
a subordinate position," said the Duke.

"I have learnt from Aristotle that it is the better
part of wisdom to cultivate the golden mean."

"Is it possible that you are devoid of ambition?"

"Far from it, Excellency," smiled Machiavelli. "My
ambition is to serve my state to the best of my ability."

"That is just what you will not be allowed to do.
You know better than anyone that in a republic talent
is suspect. A man attains high office because his
mediocrity prevents him from being a menace to his
associates. That is why a democracy is ruled not by the
men who are most competent to rule it, but by the
men whose insignificance can excite nobody's apprehension. Do you know what are the cankers that eat
the heart of a democracy?"

He looked at Machiavelli as though waiting for an
answer, but Machiavelli said nothing.

"Envy and fear. The petty men in office are envious
of their colleagues, and rather than that one of them
should gain reputation will prevent him from taking a
measure on which may depend the safety and prosperity of the state; and they are fearful because they
know that all about them are others who will stop at
neither lies nor trickery to step into their shoes. And
what is the result? The result is that they are more

439

afraid of doing wrong than zealous to do right. They say that dog doesn't bite dog: whoever invented that proverb never lived under a democratic government."

Machiavelli remained silent. He knew only too well how much truth there was in what the Duke said. He remembered how hotly the election to his own subordinate post had been contested and with what bitterness his defeated rivals had taken it. He knew that he had colleagues who were watching his every step ready to pounce upon any slip he made that might induce the Signory to dismiss him. The Duke continued:

"A prince in my position is free to choose men to serve him for their ability. He need not give a post to a man who is incapable of filling it because he needs his influence or because he has a party behind him whose services must be recognised. He fears no rival, because he is above rivalry, and so, instead of favouring mediocrity, which is the curse and bane of democracy, seeks out talent, energy, initiative and intelligence. No wonder things go from bad to worse in your Republic: the last reason for which anyone gets office is his fitness for it."

Machiavelli smiled thinly.

"Your Excellency will permit me to remind him that the favour of princes is notoriously uncertain. They can exalt a man to great heights, but they can also cast him down to the depths."

The Duke gave a chuckle of frank amusement.

"You are thinking of Ramiro de Lorqua. A prince must know both how to reward and how to punish. His generosity must be profuse and his justice severe. Ramiro committed abominable crimes; he deserved to die. What would have happened to him in Florence?

440

There would have been people whom his death would have offended; there would have been people to intercede for him because they had profited by his misdeeds; the Signory would have hesitated and in the end have sent him on an embassy to the King of France or to me."

Machiavelli laughed.

"Believe me, Your Excellency, the ambassador they propose to send to you now is of unimpeachable respectability."

"He will probably bore me to death. There is no doubt about it, I shall miss you, Secretary." Then, as if the idea had suddenly occurred to him, he gave Machiavelli a warm smile. "Why don't you enter my service? I will find work for you to do that will give scope to your quick mind and wide experience, and you won't find me ungenerous."

"What confidence could you place in a man who had betrayed his country for money?"

"I do not ask you to betray your country. By serving me you could serve it to better advantage than you will ever be able to do as Secretary of the Second Chancery. Other Florentines have entered my service and I don't know that they have regretted it."

"Adherents of the Medici who fled when their lords were driven out and were prepared to do anything that gave them a means of livelihood."

"Not only. Leonardo and Michelangelo were not too proud to accept my offers."

"Artists. They will go wherever there is a patron to give them a commission; they are not responsible people."

There was still a smile in the eyes that steadily held

Machiavelli's when the Duke answered.

"I have an estate in the immediate neighbourhood of Imola. It has vineyards, arable land, pasture and woods. I should be happy to give it to you. It would bring you in ten times as múch as the few beggarly acres you own at San Casciano."

Imola? Why had Cæsar thought of that city rather than another? Once more the suspicion crossed Machiavelli's mind that he knew of his fruitless pursuit of Aurelia.

"Those beggarly acres at San Casciano have belonged to my family for three hundred years," he said acidly. "What should I do with an estate at Imola?"

"The villa is new, handsome and well built. It would be an agreeable retreat from the city in the heat of summer."

"You speak in riddles, Excellency."

"I am sending Agapito to Urbino as its governor. I know no one more competent than you to take his place as my chief secretary, but I can see that it would make negotiations with the ambassador Florence is sending to replace you somewhat embarrassing. I am prepared to appoint you governor of Imola."

It seemed to Machiavelli that his heart on a sudden stopped beating. It was a position of importance and one to which he had never dreamt of aspiring. There were cities that had come into the possession of Florence, either by capture or by treaty, but the men sent to govern them were of great family and with powerful connections. If he were governor of Imola, Aurelia would be proud to be his mistress, and by the same token he could easily find pretexts to rid himself of Bartolomeo whenever it suited him. It was almost impossible that the Duke should make this offer without being aware of the circumstances. But how could he be aware of them? Machiavelli felt in himself a certain complacency as he noticed that the double prospect did not for a moment affect him.

"I love my native land more than my soul, Excellency."

Il Valentino was unused to being crossed and Machiavelli thought it certain that on this he would dismiss him with an angry gesture. To his surprise, the Duke, playing idly with his order of St. Michael, continued to look at him reflectively. It seemed a long time before he spoke.

"I have always been frank with you, Secretary," he said at last. "I know you are a man not easy to deceive and I would not waste my time in trying. I will put my cards on the table. I do not ask you for secrecy if I divulge my plans to you; you will not betray my confidence because no one would believe that I gave it to you. The Signory would think you were trying to make yourself important by giving out your guesses as matters of fact."

The Duke paused for a moment only.

"My hold on Romagna and Urbino is secure. In a little while I shall have control of Castello, Perugia and Siena. Pisa is mine for the asking. Lucca will surrender at my bidding. What will be the position of Florence when it is surrounded by states in my possession or under my authority?"

"Dangerous without doubt, except for our treaty with France."

Machiavelli's reply seemed to amuse the Duke.

"A treaty is an arrangement two states make to their common advantage, and a prudent government will disavow it whenever its provisions are no longer advantageous. What do you think the French King would say if in return for his connivance while I seized Florence I offered to join my forces with his to attack Venice?"

Machiavelli shivered. He knew only too well that Louis XII would never hesitate to sacrifice his honour to his interest. He took some time to answer and when he did he spoke with deliberation.

"It would be a mistake on Your Excellency's part to suppose that Florence could be taken at small cost. We should fight to the death to preserve our liberty."

"What with? Your citizens have been too busy making money to be willing to train themselves to defend their country. You have hired mercenaries to fight for you so that you shouldn't be disturbed in your avocations. Folly! Hireling soldiers do not go to war for any reason other than a little money. That is not enough to make them die for you. A country is doomed to destruction if it cannot defend itself, and the only way it can do that is to create out of its own citizens a trained, well-disciplined and well-equipped army. But are you Florentines prepared to make the sacrifices this entails? I don't believe it. You are governed by business men, and a business man's only idea is to make a deal at any price. Short profits and quick returns, peace in our time even at the cost of humiliation and the risk of disaster. Your Livy has taught you that the safety of a republic depends on the integrity of the individuals that compose it. Your people are soft. Your state is corrupt and deserves to perish."

Machiavelli's face grew sullen. He had no answer to make. The Duke drove his point home.

"Now that Spain is united and France, rid of the English, is strong, the time is past when small states could maintain their independence. Their independence is a sham, for it is not based on force, and they maintain it only so long as it suits the convenience of the great powers. The States of the Church are under my control; Bologna will fall into my hands; Florence is doomed. I shall then be master of all the country from the Kingdom of Naples in the south to the Milanese and Venetia in the north. I shall have my own artillery and the artillery of the Vitelli. I shall create an army as efficient as my army of Romagna. The King of France and I will divide among ourselves the possessions of Venice."

"But should all this happen as you desire, Excellency," said Machiavelli grimly, "all you will have achieved will be to increase the power of France and arouse the fear and envy both of France and Spain. Either of them could crush you."

"True. But with my arms and my gold I should be so powerful an ally that the party I sided with would be certain of victory."

"You would still remain the vassal of the victor."

"Tell me, Secretary: you have been in France and have had dealings with the French. What is your opinion of them?"

Machiavelli shrugged a somewhat disdainful shoulder.

"They're frivolous and unreliable. When an enemy

resists the ferocity of their first attack they waver and lose courage. They can stand neither hardship nor discomfort and after a little while grow so careless that it's easy to take advantage of their unpreparedness.''

"I know. When winter comes with cold and rain they slink out of camp one by one and then they're at the mercy of a more sturdy foe."

"On the other hand the country is rich and fertile. The King has broken the strength of the barons and is very powerful. He's somewhat foolish, but well advised by men as clever as any in Italy."

The Duke nodded.

"And now tell me what you think of the Spaniards."

"I have had little to do with them."

"Then I will tell you. They're brave, hardy, resolute and poor. They have nothing to lose and everything to gain. It would be impossible to withstand them but for one circumstance: they have to bring their troops and armaments across the sea. If they were once driven out of Italy it shouldn't be difficult to prevent them from coming back."

Silence fell upon them. Il Valentino, his chin resting on his hand, appeared to be sunk in thought, and Machiavelli watched him at his ease. His eyes were hard and brilliant. They looked into a future of tortuous diplomacy and of bloody battles. Excited as he was by the events of the day and the amazing success of his duplicity, no enterprise seemed too difficult or too dangerous for him to undertake, and who could tell what visions of greatness and glory dazzled his bold imagination? He smiled.

"With my help the French could drive the Spaniards out of Naples and Sicily: with my help the

446

Spaniards could drive the French out of the Milanese."

"Whichever you helped would remain the master of Italy and you, Excellency."

"If I helped the Spaniards, yes; not if I helped the French. We drove them out of Italy before; we can drive them out again."

"They will bide their time and return."

"I shall be ready for them. The old fox, King Ferdinand, is not one to cry over spilt milk; if they attack me he will seize the opportunity of revenge and march his armies into France. He married his daughter to the son of the King of England. The English will not miss the chance to declare war on their hereditary enemies. The French will have more reasons to fear me than I to fear them."

"But the Pope is old, Excellency; his death will deprive you of half your force and great part of your reputation."

"Do you suppose I haven't taken that into consideration? I've provided for everything that may happen when my father dies. I am prepared for it and the next Pope will be of my choosing. He will be protected by my troops. No, I do not fear the Pope's death. It will not interfere with my plans."

Suddenly the Duke sprang out of his chair and began to pace the room.

"It is the Church that has kept this country divided. She has never been strong enough to bring all Italy under her rule, but only to prevent anyone else from doing so. Italy cannot prosper till it is united."

"It is true that if our poor country has become the prey of the barbarians it is because it has been ruled by this multitude of lords and princes."

447

Il Valentino stopped walking and, his sensual lips curling with a sardonic smile, looked into Machiavelli's eyes.

"For the remedy we must turn to the Gospel, my good Secretary, which tells us to render unto Cæsar the things that are Cæsar's and unto God the things that are God's."

The Duke's meaning was plain. Machiavelli gave a gasp of fearful amazement. He was strangely fascinated by this man who could calmly speak of taking a step which must arouse the horror of all Christendom.

"A prince should support the spiritual authority of the Church," he went on coolly, "for this will keep his people good and happy, and I cannot think of a better way to restore to the Church the spiritual authority she has so unfortunately lost than to deprive her of the burden of temporal power."

Machiavelli was at a loss to know how to answer a remark in which there was so brutal a cynicism, but he was saved from the necessity of doing so by a scratching at the door.

"Who is it?" cried the Duke with sudden anger at the interruption.

There was no answer, but the door was flung open and a man entered whom Machiavelli recognised as Don Michele, the Spaniard known as Michelotto. It was he, they said, who had strangled with his own hands the handsome and unfortunate boy, Alfonso of Bisceglie, whom Lucrezia loved. Michelotto was a big, hairy man of powerful build, with bushy eyebrows, hard eyes, a short blunt nose, and an expression of cold ferocity.

448

"Ah, it's you," cried the Duke, his look changing. *"Murieron."*

Machiavelli knew little Spanish, but he could not fail to understand that one grim word. *They died.* The man had remained at the door and the Duke went over to him. They spoke in an undertone and in Spanish, and Machiavelli could not hear what they said. The Duke asked one or two abrupt questions and the other seemed to answer in detail.

Il Valentino gave that curious light, gay laugh of his which meant that he was pleased as well as amused. After a little Don Michele went, and the Duke, a happy smile in his eyes, resumed his seat.

"Vitellozzo and Oliverotto are dead. They died less valiantly than they lived. Oliverotto cried for mercy. He put the blame for his treachery on Vitellozzo and said that he had been led astray."

"And Pagolo Orsini and the Duke of Gravina?"

"I am taking them with me tomorrow under guard. I shall hold them until I hear from His Holiness the Pope."

Machiavelli gave him a questioning glance and the Duke answered it.

"As soon as I had arrested the rascals I sent a messenger to the Pope to ask him to seize the person of the Cardinal Orsini. Pagolo and his nephew must await the punishment of their crimes till I am assured that this has been done."

The Borgia's face grew sombre and it was as though a heavy cloud lurked between his eyebrows. There was a silence, and Machiavelli, supposing the audience was at an end, rose to his feet. But the Duke with a sudden gesture of impatience motioned him to sit still. When

449

he spoke it was in a low voice, but in accents that were hard, angry and resolute.

"It is not enough to destroy these petty tyrants whose subjects groan under their misrule. We are the prey of the barbarians; Lombardy is plundered, Tuscany and Naples are laid under tribute. I alone can crush these horrible and inhuman beasts. I alone can free Italy."

"God knows, Italy prays for the liberator who will deliver her from bondage."

"The time is ripe and the enterprise will bring glory to those who take part in it and good to the mass of the people of the land." He turned his bright-eyed, frowning gaze on Machiavelli as though by its force he thought to bend him to his will. "How can you hold back? Surely there is not an Italian who will refuse to follow me."

Machiavelli stared gravely at Cæsar Borgia. He sighed deeply.

"The greatest wish of my heart is to free Italy from these barbarians who overrun and despoil us, lay waste our territories, rape our women and rob our citizens. It may be that you are the man chosen by God to redeem our country. The price you ask me to pay is to join with you in destroying the liberty of the city that gave me birth."

"With or without you, Florence will lose her liberty."

"Then I will go down to destruction with her."

The Duke gave his shoulders a displeased, peevish shrug.

"Spoken like an ancient Roman, but not like a man of sense."

With a haughty wave of the hand he indicated that the audience was terminated. Machiavelli got up, bowed and uttered the usual expressions of respect. He was at the door, when the Duke's voice stopped him. And now, clever actor that he was, he changed his tone to one of affable friendliness.

"Before you go, Secretary, I should like you to give me the benefit of your advice. At Imola you became friendly with Bartolomeo Martelli. He's done one or two odd jobs for me not too badly. I need a man to go to Montpellier to conduct negotiations with the wool merchants, and it would be convenient if he went on to Paris to do various things for me there. From your knowledge of Bartolomeo, do you think I should be wise to send him?"

He spoke casually as though there were nothing more in the enquiry than the words signified, but Machiavelli understood what was at the back of them. The Duke was offering to dispatch Bartolomeo on a journey that would take him away from Imola for a considerable period, and now there could be no doubt that he knew of Machiavelli's desire for Aurelia. Machiavelli's lips tightened, but otherwise his face betrayed nothing.

"Since Your Excellency is good enough to ask my opinion I should say that Bartolomeo is so useful to you in keeping the people of Imola contented with your rule that it would be a grave mistake to send him away."

"Perhaps you are right. He shall stay."

Machiavelli bowed once more and left.

XXX

PIERO AND THE SERVANTS were waiting for him. The streets were dark and empty. Dead men, most of them stripped to the bone, still lay about, and from a gallows in the main square looters hung as a warning to others. They walked to the inn. The heavy doors were locked and barred, but on their knocking they were examined through the judas and let in. The night was bitter cold and Machiavelli was glad to warm himself at the kitchen fire. Some men were drinking, some were playing dice or cards; others were asleep on benches or on the floor. The landlord put down a mattress for Machiavelli and Piero in his room at the foot of the great bed in which his wife and children were already asleep. They lay down side by side, wrapped in their cloaks, and Piero, tired after the morning's ride from Fano, the exciting events of the day and the long wait at the Palace, fell asleep instantly; but Machiavelli stayed wide awake. He had much to occupy his thought.

It was obvious that Il Valentino knew of his abortive intrigue with Aurelia, and Machiavelli smiled with bitter irony over the mistake that man of tortuous mind had made in thinking that he could use the passion he supposed him to feel to seduce him from the service of the Republic. Machiavelli would have credited him with more intelligence than to imagine that a man of sense could be so besotted with desire for a woman as to allow it to interfere with the serious business of life. Women were a-plenty. Why, when the Duke had kidnapped Dorotea Caracciolo, wife of the captain of the Venetian infantry, and Venice had sent envoys to demand her return, he had asked them whether they thought he found the women of Romagna so unapproachable that he was compelled to abduct transient females. Except to say good-bye to her Machiavelli had not seen Aurelia for several weeks, and if he wanted her now it was because he did not like to be thwarted rather than because his passion was still at fever heat. He knew that, and it would have seemed absurd to him to yield to such a petty emotion. But he was curious to know how the Duke had discovered his secret. Certainly not through Piero; he had tried him and found him true. Serafina? He had been very careful and there was no possibility that she had an inkling of what had gone on. Monna Caterina and Aurelia were too deeply implicated in the plot to have betrayed him. Nina? No, they had taken care of her. On a sudden Machiavelli slapped his forehead. Fool that he was! It was plain as the nose on his face and he could have kicked himself for not having guessed at once. Fra Timoteo! He must be in the Duke's pay; with his close association with Serafina and with Bartolomeo's household he was in a position to spy on the Florentine envoy's movements: and by him the Duke must have known all he did, who came to visit him, when he sent letters to Florence, and when the answers arrived. It gave Machiavelli a peculiar sense of discomfort to realise that he had been under surveillance. But this guess made everything clear. It was no coincidence that, on the night when Bartolomeo was safely praying before the bones of San Vitale, Il Valentino should have sent for him at the very hour appointed for him to knock at Aurelia's door. Fra

Timoteo knew the arrangements and had passed the information on. Rage seized Machiavelli and he would gladly have wrung the sleek monk's neck. Cæsar Borgia, judging Machiavelli by himself, thought the disappointment would exacerbate his passion and so make him more malleable to his own designs. That was why Fra Timoteo had refused to help him further. It was certainly he who had persuaded Aurelia that Providence had prevented her from committing a sin and so she must refrain from it.

"I wonder how much he got besides my twenty-five ducats," Machiavelli muttered, forgetting that he had borrowed them from Bartolomeo and Bartolomeo had got them from the Duke.

But, for all that, he could not but feel a certain complacency at the thought that the Duke was prepared to take so much trouble to inveigle him into his service. It was far from disagreeable to realise that he set so high a value on him. In Florence the Signory thought him an amusing fellow and his letters often made them laugh, but they had no great confidence in his judgment and never followed his advice.

"A prophet is not without honour save in his own country," he sighed.

He knew that he had more brains in his little finger than all the rest of them put together. Piero Soderini, the head of the government, was a weak, shallow, amiable man, and it might have been of him that the Duke was thinking when he spoke of those who were more afraid of doing wrong than zealous to do right. The others, his immediate councillors, were timid, mediocre and irresolute. Their policy was to hesitate, to shilly-shally, to temporise. Machiavelli's immediate

454

superior, the Secretary of the Republic, was Marcello Virgilio. He owed his position to his handsome presence and his gift for oratory. Machiavelli was attached to him, but had no great opinion of his ability. How it would surprise those silly fellows to hear that the agent whom they had sent to Il Valentino just because he was of small consequence had been appointed governor of Imola and was the most trusted of the Duke's advisers! Machiavelli hadn't the least intention of accepting the Duke's offers, but it amused him to play with the idea and imagine the consternation of the Signory and the wrath of his enemies.

And Imola would be merely a step. If Cæsar Borgia became King of Italy he might well become his first minister and occupy the same position as the Cardinal d'Amboise enjoyed with the King of France. Was it possible that, in the Borgia, Italy had found her redeemer? Even though it was personal ambition that spurred him on, his purpose was lofty and worthy of his great spirit. He was wise and vigorous. He had made himself loved and feared by the people; he commanded the respect and confidence of the troops. Italy was enslaved and insulted, but surely her ancient valour was not dead. United under a strong ruler her people would enjoy the security they longed for to pursue their avocations and live in prosperity and happiness. What greater opportunity for glory could any man want than to give that suffering land the blessing of lasting peace?

But suddenly a notion struck Machiavelli with such force that he started violently, so that Piero, asleep by his side, was disturbed and made a restless movement. It had occurred to him that the whole thing might be nothing more than a practical joke that the Duke had played on him. He knew well enough that Il Valentino, notwithstanding his pretence of cordiality, was displeased with him because he felt that he had not exerted himself as much as he might have, to persuade the Signory to grant the *condotta* which would enhance his prestige and augment his resources. This might be his revenge, and Machiavelli felt his whole body prickle as he thought that all that time at Imola the Duke and Agapito and the rest had watched his ingenious moves and guffawed as they devised ways to frustrate them. He tried to persuade himself that this was only an idle fancy which had better be quickly forgotten; but he couldn't be sure, and the uncertainty tortured him. He spent a very troubled night.

XXXI

NEXT MORNING THE DUKE, leaving a small force to garrison the town, set out with his army on the first lap to Perugia.

It was New Year's Day.

The weather was bad, and the roads, poor at the best of times, were converted by the tramping horses, the baggage wagons and the marching soldiers into a slush of mud. The army halted at small towns in which there were no means of accommodation for so great a mass of men and those were lucky who found the shelter of a roof. Machiavelli liked his comfort. It affected his temper to sleep on the bare earth in a peasant's hut cheek by jowl with as many as could find room in which to stretch their weary limbs. One had to eat what food there was, and Machiavelli, with his

poor digestion, suffered miserably. At Sasso Ferrato
news came that the surviving Vitelli had fled to
Perugia, and at Gualdo citizens of Castello were waiting to offer the Duke the town and its territories. Then
a messenger arrived to announce that Gian Paolo
Baglioni, with the Orsini, the Vitelli and their men-at-
arms, abandoning hope of defending Perugia, had fled
to Siena, whereupon the people had risen and next
day ambassadors came to surrender it. Thus the Duke
gained possession of two important towns without
striking a blow. He went on to Assisi. There envoys
from Siena came to ask what reason he had for attack-
ing their city as according to common report was his
intention. The Duke told them that he was filled with
amicable sentiments towards it but that he was determined to expel Pandolfo Petrucci, their Lord and his
enemy, and that if they would do this themselves they
had nothing to fear from him; but if not he would
come with his army and do it himself. He set out for
Siena, but by a circuitous route so that the citizens
might have time to reflect, and on the way captured
various castles and villages. The soldiery plundered
the country. The inhabitants had fled before them,
but when they found any that had stayed behind, old
men or old women too infirm to leave, they hung them
up by their arms and lit fires under their feet so that
they might tell where valuables had been hidden.
When they would not, or could not because they
didn't know, they died under the torture.

Meanwhile good news arrived from Rome. On
receipt of his son's letter telling him what had occurred
at Sinigaglia, His Holiness sent a message to Cardinal
Orsini not, naturally enough, to inform him of what

had happened to his friends and kinsmen, but to impart the glad tidings that the citadel had surrendered; and next day, as in duty bound, the Cardinal went to the Vatican to offer the Pope his congratulations. He was accompanied by relations and retainers. He was conducted to an ante-chamber and there, together with the other members of his family, put under arrest. It was safe then for the Duke to dispose of his captives, and Michelotto strangled Pagolo Orsini, the fool who had been taken in by the Duke's smooth words, and his nephew the Duke of Gravina. The Cardinal was imprisoned in the Castle of San Angelo, where after no long time he very obligingly died. The Pope and his son might congratulate themselves on having crippled the strength of the family that had been for so long a thorn in the flesh of the Vicars of Christ. It was indeed a cause for rejoicing that in disposing of their personal enemies they had done an important service to the Church. They proved thus that it was in point of fact possible to serve God and Mammon.

XXXII

WHEN THE DUKE ARRIVED at a place called Città della Piave, Machiavelli was relieved to learn that his successor was on the point of leaving Florence. Città della Piave was a town of some note, with a castle and a cathedral, and he had the luck to find a decent dwelling-place. The Duke proposed to stay there briefly to rest his troops, and by the time he set forth again Machiavelli hoped that Giacomo Salviati, the new ambassador, would have come. The long journeys on horseback had tired him, the bad food upset his stomach, and he had got little sleep in the wretched lodgings which at the day's end he had been obliged to put up with.

After two or three days it happened that one afternoon he lay on his bed to rest his way-worn limbs, but uneasily, for he was not a little troubled in mind. Though he had written almost daily to the Signory to tell them what it behoved them to know, he had hesitated to inform them of the more important parts of his conversation with the Duke at Sinigaglia. The Duke had offered him wealth and power; the opportunity was prodigious, and it might well occur to the Signory that since he occupied already as important a position as he could ever aspire to he might find the temptation irresistible. They were small men with the low suspiciousness of pettifogging attorneys. They would ask themselves what there was between them to make Il Valentino think him susceptible to such advances. It would be a black mark against him. He would be a man whom perhaps it was wise not to trust too much and it would not be difficult to find a plausible reason for his dismissal. Why, Machiavelli asked himself, should they suppose he would put the interests of Florence above his own when it was just because they did not do that that they were jeopardising her safety? It seemed prudent to keep silence, and yet if somehow the Signory got wind of the Duke's proposals his very silence would condemn him. The situation was awkward. His reflections, however, were rudely interrupted by a booming voice asking the woman of the house whether Messer Niccolo Machiavelli lived there.

459

"Messer Bartolomeo," cried Piero, who had been sitting at the window reading one of his master's books.

"What the devil does he want?" asked Machiavelli irritably, as he got up.

In a moment the burly fellow burst into the room. He flung his arms round Machiavelli and kissed him on both cheeks.

"It's been the very deuce to find you. I've been to house after house."

Machiavelli disengaged himself.

"How is it you're here?"

Bartolomeo greeted his young cousin after the same exuberant fashion and answered:

"The Duke sent for me in connection with some business at Imola. I had to pass through Florence and I came with some of your ambassador's servants. He'll be here tomorrow. Niccolo, Niccolo, my dear friend, you have saved my life."

He once more seized Machiavelli in his arms and again kissed him on both cheeks. Machiavelli once more extricated himself from this embrace.

"I am delighted to see you, Bartolomeo," he began, somewhat frigidly.

But the merchant interrupted him.

"A miracle, a miracle, and I have you to thank for it. Aurelia is pregnant."

"What!"

"In seven months, my dear Niccolo, I shall be the father of a bouncing boy, and I owe it to you."

If things had gone differently Machiavelli might have been embarrassed by this remark, but as it was he was stupefied.

"Calm yourself, Bartolomeo, and tell me what you

460

mean," said he crossly. "How do you owe it to me?"

"How can I be calm when the dearest wish of my heart has been gratified? Now I can go to my grave in peace. Now I can leave my honours and my possessions to the issue of my own loins. Costanza, my sister, is beside herself with rage."

He burst into a great bellow of laughter. Machiavelli gave Piero a puzzled look; he could make neither head nor tail of it; and he saw that Piero was as surprised as he.

"Of course I owe it to you; I should never have gone to Ravenna and spent that cold night praying before the altar of San Vitale but for you. True, it was Fra Timoteo's idea, but I didn't trust him; he'd sent us on pilgrimages to the shrine of one saint after the other and nothing had come of it. Fra Timoteo is a good and saintly man, but with priests you have to be on your guard; you can never be quite sure that they haven't some ulterior motive in their advice. I don't blame them, they are faithful sons of our Holy Church; but I should have hesitated to go if you hadn't told me about Messer Giuliano degli Albertelli. I could trust you, you had only my welfare at heart, you are my friend. I said to myself that what had happened to one of the most notable citizens of Florence might just as well happen to one who is not the least notable citizen of Imola. Aurelia conceived on the night of my return from Ravenna."

His excitement and his flow of speech had brought him out into a profuse sweat and he wiped his glistening forehead with his sleeve. Machiavelli stared at him with perplexity, distaste and vexation.

"Are you quite sure that Monna Aurelia is in this

condition?" he said acidly. "Women are inclined to make mistakes on these matters."

"Sure, as sure as I am of the articles of our faith. We had our suspicions before you left Imola; I wanted to tell you then, but Monna Caterina and Aurelia begged me not to. 'Let us say nothing,' they said, 'until we are certain.' Did you not notice how poorly she looked when I took you to say good-bye? She was angry with me afterwards; she said she couldn't bear you to see her looking so hideous; she was afraid you'd suspect and she didn't want anyone to know until all doubt was removed. I reasoned with her, but you know what women's fancies are when they're with child."

"I suspected nothing," said Machiavelli. "It's true that I have only been married a few months and my experience in these things is limited."

"I wanted you to be the first person to know, since except for you I should never have been the happy father I now shall be."

He gave every indication of being about to clasp Machiavelli in his arms again, but Machiavelli warded him off.

"I congratulate you with all my heart, but if my ambassador is arriving tomorrow I have no time to waste; the information should be conveyed to the Duke at once."

"I will leave you, but you must sup with me tonight, you and Piero, to celebrate the occasion in style."

"It would be hard to do that here," said he ill-temperedly. "There is scarcely anything to eat and the wine, if there is any, will be as bad as it has been all along the way."

"I had thought of that," said Bartolomeo, with a

bellow of laughter, rubbing his fat hands together, "and I brought wine with me from Florence, a hare and a sucking pig. We will feast and drink to the health of my first-born son."

Though he was by now thoroughly out of humour, Machiavelli had fared too badly since leaving Imola to be able to resist the offer of a tolerable meal, and so with what amiability he could muster accepted.

"I will call for you here," said Bartolomeo, "but before I go I want you to give me some advice. Of course you remember that I promised Fra Timoteo that I would give a picture to be placed over the altar of our miraculous Virgin, and though I know I owe my good fortune to San Vitale I don't want to put an affront on her. She undoubtedly did her best. So I have decided to have a picture painted of Our Lady seated on a rich throne with her Blessed Son in her arms and with me and Aurelia kneeling on each side with our hands clasped like this." He put his great paws together and raised his eyes to the ceiling with an appropriate expression of devotion. "I shall have San Vitale standing on one side of the throne, and Fra Timoteo has suggested that on the other, since the church is dedicated to him, I should have St. Francis. Do you like the idea?"

"Very choice," said Machiavelli.

"You're a Florentine and must know about such things: tell me to whom I should give the order."

"I really don't know. They're a very unreliable, dissipated lot, these painters, and I've never had any truck with them."

"I don't blame you. But surely you can suggest some-one."

Machiavelli shrugged his shoulders.

"When I was in Urbino last summer they talked to me about a young fellow, a pupil of Perugino, who they say already paints better than his master and who they expect will go far."

"What is his name?"

"I have no idea. They told me, but it meant nothing to me and it went in at one ear and out of the other. But I dare say I could find out and I don't suppose he'd be expensive."

"Expense is no object," said Bartolomeo with a grandiose wave of the arm. "I'm a business man and I know that if you want the best you must pay for it. And only the best is good enough for me. I want a big name and if I have to pay for it I'll pay for it."

"Oh, well, when I get back to Florence I'll make enquiries," Machiavelli answered impatiently.

When he had gone Machiavelli sat down on the edge of the bed and stared at Piero with a look of complete bewilderment.

"Did you ever hear the like?" he said. "The man is sterile."

"It is evidently a miracle," said Piero.

"Don't talk such nonsense. We are bound to believe that miracles were performed by our Blessed Lord and by His apostles, and our Holy Church has accepted the authenticity of miracles performed by its saints, but the time of miracles is past, and in any case why in the name of heaven should San Vitale go out of his way to do one for a fat stupid fool like Bartolomeo?"

But even as he spoke he remembered that Fra Timoteo had said something to him to the effect that even though San Vitale's singular power was an invention of Machiavelli's, Bartolomeo's absolute belief in it might effect the miracle he expected. Was it possible? At the time he had thought it only a hypocritical excuse on the man's part to avoid giving him more assistance till he received more money.

Piero opened his mouth to speak.

"Hold your tongue," said Machiavelli. "I'm thinking."

He would never have described himself as a good Catholic. He had indeed often permitted himself to wish that the gods of Olympus still dwelt in their old abode. Christianity had shown men the truth and the way of salvation, but it asked men to suffer rather than to do. It had made the world feeble and given it over a helpless prey to the wicked, since the generality, in order to go to Heaven, thought more of enduring injuries than of defending themselves against them. It had taught that the highest good consisted in humility, lowliness, and contempt for the things of this world; the religion of the ancients taught that it consisted in greatness of spirit, courage and strength.

But this was a strange thing that had happened. It shook him. Though his reason revolted he was aware within himself of an uneasy inclination to believe in the possibility of a supernatural intervention. His head refused to accept it, but in his bones, in his blood, in his nerves, there was a doubt that he could not still. It was as though all those generations behind him that had believed took possession of his soul and forced their will upon him.

"My grandfather suffered from his stomach too," he said suddenly.

Piero had no notion what he was talking about. Machiavelli sighed.

"It may be that if men have grown soft it is because in their worthlessness they have interpreted our religion according to their sloth. They have forgotten that it enjoins upon us to love and honour our native land, and to prepare ourselves to be such that we can defend her."

He burst out laughing when he saw the blankness of Piero's face.

"Never mind, my boy, pay no attention to my nonsense. I will get myself ready to announce to the Duke the arrival tomorrow of the ambassador, and in any case we'll get a good supper out of that old fool."

XXXIII

THEY GOT IT. Under the influence of the first decent meal he had eaten since leaving Imola and the good Chianti that Bartolemeo had brought from Florence, Machiavelli expanded. He made indecent jokes, he told obscene stories, he was lightly ribald, grossly coarse and gaily lewd. He made Bartolomeo laugh so much that his sides ached. All three of them got a little drunk.

The events at Sinigaglia had caused a stir in Italy and a multitude of imaginative Italians had related the story in their different ways. Bartolomeo was eager to hear the facts from an eye-witness, and Machiavelli, pleasantly mellow, was very willing to oblige him. He had written his account three or four times to the Signory, in part because of its importance and in part because at least one of his letters had not reached its

466

destination. He had reflected upon the various incidents, he had had the opportunity to gather details from one or the other of those close to Il Valentino, and he had by now got to the bottom of much that at the time had puzzled him.

He made a thrilling story of it.

"When Vitellozzo left Città di Castello for Sinigaglia he bade farewell to his family and friends as though he knew it was for the last time. To his friends he left the charge of his house and its fortunes and he admonished his nephews to remember the virtues of their ancestors."

"If he knew the danger he was running why did he leave the safety of his walled town?" asked Bartolomeo.

"How can man escape his destiny? We think to bend men to our will, we think to mould events to our purpose, we strive, we toil and sweat, but in the end we are nought but the playthings of fate. When the captains had been arrested and Pagolo Orsini was complaining of the Duke's perfidy, the only reproach that Vitellozzo made him was this: 'You see how wrong you were and in what a plight my friends and I have been placed by your folly.'"

"He was a scoundrel and he deserved to die," said Bartolomeo. "I sold him some horses once and he never paid me for them. When I demanded the money he told me to come to Città di Castello and get it. I preferred to pocket my loss."

"You were wise."

Machiavelli asked himself what had been the thoughts of that ruthless man, old, tired and sick, during the hours that passed between the time of his arrest and the time when tied to a chair, back to back with Oliverotto, Michelotto's cruel hands had wrung the life out of him. Michelotto was a pleasant fellow to meet, he would drink a bottle of wine with you and crack a lewd joke, play strange Spanish tunes on a guitar and by the hour sing wild, sad songs of his country. It was hard then to believe that he was the murderous brute you knew him to be. What fearful satisfaction did he get out of doing his foul work with his own hands? Machiavelli smiled as he thought that one of these days the Duke, having finished with him, would have him killed with no more compunction than when he had killed his trusted and loyal lieutenant Ramiro de Lorqua.

"A strange man," he muttered, "perhaps a great one."

"Of whom are you speaking?" asked Bartolomeo.

"Of the Duke, of course. Of whom else could I have been speaking? He has rid himself of his enemies by the exercise of a duplicity so perfect that the onlooker can only wonder and admire. These painters with their colours and their brushes prate about the works of art they produce, but what are they in comparison with a work of art that is produced when your paints are living men and your brushes wit and cunning? The Duke is a man of action and impetuous, you would never have credited him with the wary patience that was needed to bring his beautiful stratagem to a successful issue. For four months he kept them guessing at his intentions; he worked on their fears, he traded on their jealousies, he confused them by his wiles, he fooled them with false promises; with infinite skill he sowed dissension among them, so that the Bentivogli in Bologna and the Baglioni in Perugia deserted them. You know how ill it has served Baglioni: the Bentivogli's turn will come. As suited his purpose he was friendly and genial, stern and menacing; and at last they stepped into the trap he had set. It was a masterpiece of deceit which deserves to go down to posterity for the neatness of its planning and the perfection of its execution."

Bartolomeo, a loquacious fellow, was about to speak, but Machiavelli had not yet said his say.

"He has rid Italy of the petty tyrants that were its scourge. What will he do now? Others before him have seemed to be chosen by God to effect the redemption of Italy, and then in the full current of action have been cast off by fortune."

He rose to his feet abruptly. He was tired of the party and did not want to listen to Bartolomeo's platitudes. He thanked him for his entertainment and, escorted by the faithful Piero, went back to his lodging.

XXXIV

NEXT DAY BARTOLOMEO, his business transacted, set off for Perugia on his way home. Later on, Machiavelli, with Piero and his two servants and a number of the Duke's gentlemen, rode out to meet the Florentine ambassador. After Giacomo Salviati, for such was his name, had changed from his riding clothes to the dignified garb of a Florentine of rank, Machiavelli accompanied him to the castle to present his credentials. Machiavelli was eager to get back to Florence, but he could not leave till he had made known to the ambassador the various persons with whom it was necessary for him to be acquainted. Little was done at the Duke's court for love, and Machiavelli had to inform his successor what services such a one could render and what payment he expected. He had to give his opinion of the trustworthiness of one and the unreliability of another. Though Giacomo Salviati had read the letters that Machiavelli had written to the Signory, there was much that he had not ventured to say, since the danger was constant that letters would be intercepted, and so he had to spend long hours recounting by word of mouth a multitude of facts that it behoved the ambassador to know.

It was in consequence six days before he could set out on the homeward journey. The road was long and bad and none too safe, and so that he might get as far as he could before nightfall he had decided to start early. He was out of bed by dawn and it did not take him long to dress. The saddle-bags, packed the night before, were taken down by the servants, and the woman of the house in a few minutes came up to tell him that all was ready for him to start.

"Is Piero with the horses?"

"No, Messere."

"Where is he?"

"He went out."

"Out? Where? What for? Tiresome fellow, doesn't he know yet that I hate being kept waiting? Send one of my servants to find him and be quick about it."

She hurried to do his bidding and had hardly closed the door behind her when it was opened again and Piero came in.

Machiavelli stared at him in amazement: he was dressed not in his own shabby riding clothes, but in the scarlet and yellow of the Duke's soldiers. There

470

was a mischievous smile on his lips, but it somewhat lacked assurance.

"I've come to say good-bye to you, Messer Niccolo. I have enlisted in the Duke's army."

"I did not imagine you had put on that gaudy costume just for fun."

"Don't be angry with me, Messere. During the three months and more that I've been with you I've seen something of the world. I've been witness to great events and I've talked with men who were concerned in them. I'm strong and young and healthy. I can't go back to Florence and spend the rest of my life driving a quill in the Second Chancery. I wasn't made for that. I want to live."

Machiavelli looked at him reflectively. The suspicion of a smile hovered on that razor-blade which was his mouth.

"Why didn't you tell me what you had in mind?"

"I thought you would prevent me from doing it."

"I should have looked upon it as my duty to point out to you that a soldier's life is hard, dangerous and ill-paid. He takes the risks and the commander gets the glory. He suffers from hunger and thirst and is exposed to the rigour of the elements. If he is captured by the enemy he is robbed of the very clothes on his back. If he is wounded he is left to die, and should he recover and be useless for combat little is left him but to beg his food in the streets. He spends his life among coarse, brutal and licentious men to the ruin of his morals and the peril of his soul. I should have felt it my duty to point out to you that in the Chancery of the Republic you would have a position at once respectable and secure in which by industry and subservience

471

to the whims of your superiors you could earn a salary just enough to keep body and soul together, and after many years of faithful service, if you were adroit, slightly unscrupulous and very lucky, you could count on advancement if the brother-in-law or the nephew by marriage of an influential person did not at the moment happen to want a job. But having done my duty I should have taken no further steps to prevent you from doing what you wished."

Piero laughed with relief, for though he was attached to Machiavelli and admired him, he was not a little afraid of him.

"Then you are not vexed with me?"

"No, my dear boy. You have served me well and I have found you honest, loyal and energetic. Fortune favours the Duke and I can't blame you for wanting to follow his star."

"Then you will make it all right for me with my mother and Uncle Biagio?"

"Your mother will be broken-hearted. She will think I have led you astray and will blame me, but Biagio is a sensible man and will do his best to console her. And now, my dear boy, I must be off."

He took the boy in his arms to kiss him on both cheeks, but as he did so noticed the shirt he was wearing. He pulled up the heavily-embroidered collar.

"Where did you get that shirt?"

Piero flushed to the roots of his hair.

"Nina gave it to me."

"Nina?"

"Monna Aurelia's maid."

Machiavelli recognised the fine linen he had brought Bartolomeo from Florence and he stared

frowning at the elaborate needlework. Then he looked into Piero's eyes. Beads of sweat stood on the boy's forehead.

"Monna Aurelia had more material than she needed for Messer Bartolomeo and she gave Nina what she didn't want."

"And did Nina do that beautiful embroidery herself?"

"Yes."

It was a clumsy lie.

"How many shirts did she give you?"

"Only two. There wasn't material for more."

"That will do very well. You will be able to wear one while the other is washed. You are a lucky young man. When I sleep with women they do not give me presents; they expect me to give them presents."

"I only did it to oblige you, Messer Niccolo," said Piero, with a disarming smile. "You urged me to make advances to her."

Machiavelli knew very well that Aurelia would never have dreamt of giving her maid several yards of costly linen, and he knew that the maid could never have drawn that intricate design; and Monna Caterina herself had told him that only Aurelia could do that delicate handiwork. It was Aurelia who had given the boy the shirts. And why? Because he was her husband's third cousin? Nonsense. The truth, the unpalatable truth, stared him in the face. On the night of the assignation, when Machiavelli had been sent for by the Duke, it was not with the maid that Piero had slept, but with her mistress. It was by no miraculous intervention of San Vitale that Bartolomeo's wife was about to bear a son, but by the very natural instru-

473

mentality of the young man who stood before him. That explained why Monna Caterina had given him ridiculous excuses for not arranging another opportunity for him to meet Aurelia, and why Aurelia had avoided all further communication with him. Machiavelli was seized with cold fury. They had made a pretty fool of him, those two abandoned women and the boy whom he had befriended. He stepped back a little to have a good look at him.

Machiavelli had never set great store on masculine beauty; he considered it of small importance compared with the pleasant manner, the easy conversation and the audacious approach which had enabled him to get all the women he wanted; and though he had recognised that Piero was a personable fellow he had never troubled to look closely at him. He examined him now with angry eyes. He was tall and well-made, with broad shoulders, a slim waist and shapely legs. The uniform set off his figure to advantage. He had brown curly hair that covered his head like a tight-fitting cap, large round brown eyes under well-marked brows, an olive skin as smooth and clear as a girl's, a small straight nose, a red, sensual mouth, and ears that clung close to his skull. His expression was bold, frank, ingenuous and engaging.

"Yes," reflected Machiavelli, "he has the beauty that would appeal to a silly woman. I never noticed it or I'd have been on my guard."

He cursed himself for having been so stupid. But how could he suspect that Aurelia, cousin though he was of her husband, would give a thought to a lad who after all was no more than an errand-boy just out of school? Machiavelli had used him to fetch and

474

carry, to run hither and thither at his beck and call; and if he had treated him with an indulgence he now regretted, it was because Biagio was his uncle. Piero was not unintelligent, but he had none of the graces you learn by living in the great world, and, having little to say for himself, for the most part kept quiet in the presence of his betters. Machiavelli knew very well that, as for himself, he had a way with women; he had never failed to charm when to charm was his object, and he thought there was little anyone could teach him in the art and science of gallantry. Piero was no more than a callow youth. Who in his senses could have supposed that Aurelia would cast so much as a glance of her fine eyes on him when she had at her feet a man of distinction, worldly wisdom and urbane conversation? It was preposterous.

Piero suffered his master's long scrutiny with composure. He had recovered from his embarrassment and there was a wariness in his manner which suggested that he was alert.

"I've been very fortunate," he remarked coolly, but as though he were somewhat inclined to take good luck as his due. "Count Lodovico Alvisi's page fell ill on the way from Sinigaglia and had to go back to Rome, and he's taken me in his place."

This Count Lodovico, an intimate of Il Valentino's, was one of the Roman gentlemen who had taken service under him as a lancer.

"How did you manage that?"

"Messer Bartolomeo spoke to the Duke's treasurer about me and he arranged it."

Machiavelli faintly raised his eyebrows. Not only had the boy seduced Bartolomeo's wife, but he had

475

used him to get a sought-after position with one of
the Duke's favourites. If he had not himself been so
intimately concerned he would have found the
situation humorous.

"Fortune favours audacity and youth," he said.
"You will go far. But let me give you some advice.
Take care that like me you do not get a reputation
for wit, since if you do no one will think you sensible,
but notice men's moods and adapt yourself to them;
laugh with them when they are merry and pull a long
face when they are solemn. It is absurd to be wise
with fools and foolish with the wise: you must speak
to each one in his own language. Be courteous; it
costs little and helps much; to be of use and to know
how to show yourself of use is to be doubly useful;
it is idle to please yourself if you do not please others,
and remember that you please them more by
ministering to their vices than by encouraging their
virtues. Never be so intimate with a friend that he
may injure you should he become your enemy, and
never use your enemy so ill that he can never become
your friend. Be careful in your speech. There is
always time to put in a word, never to withdraw one;
truth is the most dangerous weapon a man can wield,
and so he must wield it with caution. For years I
have never said what I believed nor ever believed
what I have said, and if it sometimes happens that I
tell the truth I conceal it among so many lies that it
is hard to find it."

But while these old saws and homely common-
places tripped off the end of his tongue Machiavelli's
thoughts were intent on something much more
important, and he scarcely listened to what he said.

476

For he knew that a public man can be corrupt, incompetent, cruel, vindictive, vacillating, self-seeking, weak and stupid, and yet attain to the highest honours in the state; but if he is ridiculous he is undone. Slander he can refute; abuse he can despise; but against ridicule he has no defence. Strange as it may seem, the Absolute has no sense of humour, and ridicule is the instrument the devil uses to hinder aspiring man in his arduous quest of perfection. Machiavelli valued the esteem of his fellow-citizens and the attention that was paid to his opinions by the heads of the Republic. He had confidence in his own judgment and was ambitious to be employed in affairs of consequence. He was too clear-sighted not to see that in this abortive affair with Aurelia he cut a comic figure. If the story were told in Florence he would become a laughing-stock, the helpless victim of brutal jest and cruel innuendo. A cold shiver ran down his spine at the thought of the pasquinades, the epigrams, that his misadventure would suggest to the malicious wit of the Florentines. Even his friend Biagio, the easy butt of his jokes, would welcome the opportunity to pay off many an old score. He must stop Piero's mouth or he was ruined. In a friendly way he put his hand on the lad's shoulder and smiled pleasantly; but the eyes he fixed on Piero's, the bright darting little eyes, were cold and hard.

"There is only one more thing I would say to you, dear boy. Fortune is inconstant and restless. She may grant you power, honour and riches, but also afflict you with servitude, infamy and poverty. The Duke also is her plaything and with a turn of her wheel she may plunge him to destruction. Then you will need friends in Florence. It would be imprudent of you to make enemies of those who can help you in distress. The Republic is suspicious of those who leave her service to enter that of those whom she mistrusts. A few words whispered in the right ear might easily lead to the confiscation of your property so that your mother, driven from her house, would have to live on the unwilling charity of her relations. The Republic has a long arm; if she thought fit, it would not be hard to find a needy Gascon who for a few ducats would drive a dagger into your back. A letter might be allowed to fall into the Duke's hands which would suggest that you were a Florentine spy, and the rack would force you to confess that it was true, and you would be hanged like a common thief. It would distress your mother. For your own sake, then, and as you value your life, I recommend you to be secret. It is not wise to tell everything one knows."

Machiavelli, his gaze fixed on Piero's brown, liquid eyes, saw that he understood.

"Have no fear, Messere. I will be as secret as the grave."

Machiavelli laughed lightly.

"I did not think you were a fool."

Though it would leave him with only just enough money to get back to Florence, he thought this was a moment to be generous even to excess, so taking out his purse he gave Piero five ducats as a parting gift.

"You have served me well and faithfully," he said, "and it will be a pleasure to me to give Biagio a good account of your zeal in my interests and in those of the Republic."

He kissed him affectionately and they went downstairs hand in hand. Piero held the horse's head while Machiavelli mounted. He walked by his side till they came to the city's gate and there they parted.

XXXVI

MACHIAVELLI GAVE HIS HORSE a touch of the spur and it broke into an easy canter. The two servants followed close behind. He was in a vile temper. There was no denying it, they had made a perfect fool of him, Fra Timoteo, Aurelia, her mother and Piero; he didn't know with which he was most angry. And the worst of it was that he didn't see how he could settle his account with them; they had had a lot of fun at his expense and there was no way by which he could make them pay for it. Of course Aurelia was a fool, sly as all women were, but a fool; otherwise she wouldn't have preferred a smooth-faced pretty boy to a man in the flower of his age, a man of affairs who was entrusted by his government with important negotiations. No intelligent person could deny that the comparison was all in his favour. No one could call him repulsive; Marietta had always told him she liked the way his hair grew on his head; it was like black velvet, she said. Thank God for Marietta: there was a woman you could trust; you could leave her for half a year and be certain that she would look neither to the right nor to the left. It was true that she had been rather troublesome of late, complaining through Biagio that he didn't come back and didn't write and had left her without money. Well, in her condition one must expect women to be peevish. He had been gone three and a half months, she must be getting quite big, he wondered when she would be delivered; they had already made up their minds that the boy should be called Bernardo after his own father now with God. And if she grumbled at his long absence it was because she loved him, poor slut; it would be well to get back to her; that was the advantage of a wife, she was always there when you wanted her. Of course she wasn't the beauty that Aurelia was, but she was virtuous, and that was more than you could say for Monna Caterina's daughter. He wished he had thought of bringing her back a present, but it hadn't occurred to him till that moment and now he simply hadn't the money.

He wished he hadn't spent so much on Aurelia. There was the scarf, and the gloves and the attar of roses, and the gold chain—well, no, not gold, silver gilt—that he'd given to Monna Caterina; if she'd had a spark of decency she'd have returned that, it would have done very well to give to Marietta and would have pleased her. But when did women ever return the presents you made them?

An old procuress, that's what she was, and not even honest. She knew quite well that the chain was the price he was paying her to arrange things for him, and when she didn't deliver the goods surely the least she could do would have been to return the purchase price. But she was an abandoned old wanton, he'd guessed that from his first glance at her, and she got a filthy satisfaction out of helping others to the debaucheries which she could no longer herself indulge in. He was prepared to bet a ducat that she'd put Piero and Aurelia to bed herself. They must have had a fine laugh when they ate the capons and the pastries he'd sent in by Piero and drunk his wine while he was standing at the door in the pelting rain. If Bartolomeo hadn't been the fool he was he'd have known it was madness to entrust a woman like that with the charge of his wife's fidelity.

For a moment Machiavelli's thoughts turned on that gross and stupid man. It was his fault that all this had happened.

"If he'd looked after her properly," said Machiavelli to himself, "it would never have occurred to me that there was anything doing and I shouldn't have tried."

Bartolomeo was to blame for the whole thing. But what a fool he'd been, he, Machiavelli, to send her that expensive scarf to excuse himself for not having kept the appointment; and he'd sent it round in the morning, by Piero of all people, when he was feeling like nothing on earth and his voice was a croak, so that she should get it before Bartolomeo's return. How they must have sniggered! And did Piero take the opportunity to . . . they were a nice pair, he wouldn't put anything past them.

And the exasperating thing was that he'd not only lavished presents upon her, he'd told his best stories to amuse her, he'd sung his best songs to charm her; he'd flattered her, in short he'd done everything a man can do to ingratiate himself with a woman; and then—then that wretched boy came along and just because he was eighteen and good-looking got for nothing what he'd spent a month's time to get and much more money than he could afford. He would have liked to know how Piero had gone about it.

481

Perhaps it was Monna Caterina, with her fear that
Bartolomeo would adopt his nephews, who had
suggested it. He invented her conversation.

"Well, what are we going to do about it? We can't
wait all night for him. It seems a pity to waste the
opportunity. In your place, Aurelia, I wouldn't
hesitate. Look at him with his sweet face and his
curly hair; he's like the Adonis in that picture in the
Town Hall. I know if I had to choose between him
and that Messer Niccolo with his sallow skin and his
long nose and those little beady eyes—well, there's
no comparison, my dear. And I dare say he can do
what you want much better than that skinny
Secretary."

A bad woman. A wicked woman. And why she
should prefer that boy to father her daughter's son
rather than an intelligent man of the world was something he would never understand.

But perhaps there had been small need for Monna
Caterina to put her word in. It's true the boy looked
so innocent and seemed even a trifle shy, but appear-
ances were deceptive. He had a pretty power of
dissimulation, for never had he given the smallest
indication that there was anything between him and
Aurelia; and he was a cool, brazen liar; the only
embarrassment he had shown was when Machiavelli
had noticed the shirt; but how quickly he had
recovered himself and with what effrontery met his
master's unspoken accusations! He was quite impudent enough just to have kissed Aurelia frankly on
the mouth and when he found she did not object,
slip his hand down her open bodice between her
breasts. Anyone could guess what would happen then

and Machiavelli's angry imagination followed them into Bartolomeo's bedchamber and into Bartolomeo's bed.

"The ingratitude of the boy!" he muttered.

He had taken him on this trip from sheer good nature, he had done everything for him, he had introduced him to persons worth knowing, he had done his best to form him, to show him how to behave, to civilise him in short; he had not spared his wit and wisdom to teach him the ways of the world, how to make friends and influence people. And this was his reward, to have his girl snatched away from him under his very nose.

"Anyhow I put the fear of God into him."

Machiavelli knew that when you have played a dirty trick on your benefactor half the savour of it is lost if you cannot tell your friends about it. He found some small comfort in that.

But all the anger he felt for Aurelia, Piero, Monna Caterina and Bartolomeo amounted to nothing compared with that which he felt for Fra Timoteo. That was the treacherous villain who had upset all his well-laid plans.

"Much chance he has now of preaching the Lenten sermons in Florence," he hissed.

He had never had any intention of recommending the friar for that office, but it was a satisfaction to think that if he had had the intention he would now without hesitation discard it. The man was a rascal. No wonder Christianity was losing its hold on the people, and they were become wicked, licentious and corrupt, when there was no honesty, no sense of right and wrong in the religious profession. Fooled,

fooled, he'd been fooled by all of them, but by none so monstrously as by that rascally friar.

They stopped to eat at a wayside inn. The food was bad but the wine drinkable and Machiavelli drank a good deal of it, with the result that when he got into the saddle again to continue his journey the world looked a trifle less black to him. They passed peasants leading a cow or riding on the rump of a heavy-laden ass; they met travellers on foot or on horseback. For a while he pondered over the Duke's participation in his disappointment; if it was a joke, he had kept it to himself as he kept his designs to himself, and if it was part of a scheme to get him in his power, he knew by now that it had failed. Then his thoughts reverted to Aurelia. It was no good crying over spilt milk. Four months ago he had never seen her; it was silly to make such a fuss over a woman whom he had only seen half a dozen times and with whom he had only exchanged as many sentences. He wasn't the first man whom a woman had led on only to let him down when it came to the point. That was the kind of thing a wise man took philosophically. Fortunately it was to the interest of the only people who knew the facts to say nothing about them. It was a humiliation certainly to have been made such a fool of, but anyone can put up with a humiliation that only he is aware of. The thing was to look at it from the outside as though it had happened to somebody else, and Machiavelli set himself deliberately to do this.

Suddenly with an exclamation he jerked his reins, and his horse, thinking he was meant to stop, pulled up so sharply that Machiavelli was thrown forward in his saddle. His servants rode up.

"Is anything the matter, Messere?"

"Nothing, nothing."

He rode on. Machiavelli's exclamation and the instinctive movement had been caused by an idea that had flashed through his mind. At first he thought he was going to vomit and then he knew he'd had an inspiration: it had occurred to him that there was a play in the story. That was how he could revenge himself on those people who had mocked and robbed him; he would hold them up to contempt and ridicule. His ill-humour vanished and as he rode along, his imagination busy, his face beamed with malicious delight.

He would place the action in Florence, because he felt his invention would be more at home in those familiar streets. The characters were there and all he had to do was to emphasise their qualities a little in order to make them more effective on the stage. Bartolomeo, for instance, would have to be even sillier and more credulous than he was in fact, and Aurelia more ingenuous and more docile. He had already cast Piero for the pimp who was to engineer the deception by means of which the hero would achieve his ends, and a pretty scamp he proposed to make him. For the general outlines of the play were clear in his mind. He would himself be the hero and the name he would give himself came to him at once —Callimaco. He was a Florentine, handsome, young and rich, who had spent some years in Paris—this would give Machiavelli the chance to say some sharp things about the French, whom he neither liked nor esteemed—and having come back to Florence had seen and fallen violently in love with Aurelia. What

should he call her? Lucrezia. Machiavelli sniggered
when he decided to give her the name of the Roman
matron distinguished for her domestic virtues who
had stabbed herself to death after having been outraged by Tarquinius. Of course the play would end
happily and Callimaco would spend a night of love
with the object of his desire.

The sun was shining from a blue sky, there was
still snow in the fields, but the road was crisp under
the horses' hooves and Machiavelli, well wrapped up,
was pleasantly exhilarated by the activity of his
invention. He felt strangely exalted. There was in
his mind as yet no more than a theme; the facts were
too tame for his purpose, and he was aware that he
needed to think of a comic stratagem that would give
him a coherent plot on which he could string his
scenes. What he was looking for was a fantastic idea
that would make an audience laugh and not only lead
naturally to the resolution of his intrigue, but allow
him to show the simplicity of Aurelia, the foolishness
of Bartolomeo, the rascality of Piero, the wantonness
of Monna Caterina, and the knavery of Fra Timoteo.
For the monk was to be an important character. In
imagination Machiavelli rubbed his hands as he
thought how he would show him in his true colours,
with his avarice, his lack of scruple, his cunning and
his hypocrisy. He would give false names to all of
them, but he would leave Fra Timoteo his own, so
that all should know what a false and wicked man he
was.

But he remained at a loss for the idea that should
set his puppets in motion. It must be expected,
outrageous even, for it was a comedy that he pro-

486

posed to write, and so funny that people would gasp
with astonishment and then burst into a roar of
laughter. He knew his Plautus and his Terence well,
and he surveyed them in his memory to see whether
there was not in their plays some ingenious fancy
that would serve his purpose. He could think of
nothing. And what made it more difficult to apply
his mind to the problem was that his thoughts willy-
nilly presented odd scenes to him here and there,
amusing bits of dialogue and ridiculous situations.
The time passed so quickly that he was surprised
when they arrived at the place where they had
decided to spend the night.

"To hell with love," he muttered as he got off his
horse. "What is love beside art!"

XXXVII

THE PLACE WAS CALLED CASTIGLIONE ARETINO, and
there was an inn which at all events looked no worse
than any of those he had slept at since leaving home.
What with the exercise in the open air and his fancy
running wild, he had developed a healthy appetite
and the first thing he did on entering was to order his
supper. Then he washed his feet, which, being a
cleanly man, he liked to do every four or five days,
and having dried them he wrote a short letter to the
Signory which he sent off at once by a courier. The
inn was full, but the innkeeper told him there would
be room for him in the large bed he and his wife
slept in. Machiavelli gave her a glance and said that
if they could put a couple of sheepskins on the
kitchen floor he would rest comfortably enough,

Then he sat down to a great dish of macaroni.

"What is love in comparison with art?" he repeated. "Love is transitory, but art is eternal. Love is merely Nature's device to induce us to bring into this vile world creatures who from the day of their birth to the day of their death will be exposed to hunger and thirst, sickness and sorrow, envy, hatred and malice. This macaroni is better cooked than I could have expected and the sauce is rich and succulent. Chicken livers and giblets. The creation of man was not even a tragic mistake, it was a grotesque mischance. What is its justification? Art, I suppose. Lucretius, Horace, Catullus, Dante and Petrarch. And perhaps they would never have been driven to write their divine works if their lives had not been full of tribulation, for there is no question that if I had gone to bed with Aurelia I should never have had the idea of writing a play. So when you come to look at it, it's all turned out for the best. I lost a trinket and picked up a jewel fit for a king's crown."

The good meal and these reflections restored Machiavelli to his usual amiability. He played a game of cards with a travelling friar who was on his way from one monastery to another and lost a trifle to him with good grace. Then settling himself down on his sheepskins he quickly fell asleep and slept without a break till dawn.

The sun had only just risen when he set out again, and it looked as though it were going to be a fine day. He was in high spirits. It was good to think that in a few hours he would be once more in his own house, he hoped Marietta would be too glad to have him back to reproach him for his neglect of her, Biagio would come round to visit him after supper, dear kind Biagio, and tomorrow he would see Piero Soderini and the gentlemen of the Signory. Then he would go and call on his friends. Oh, what a joy it would be to be back in Florence, to have the Chancery to go to every day and to walk those streets he had known since childhood, knowing by name, if not to speak to, almost everyone he passed!

"Welcome back, Messere," from one, and "Well, well, Niccolo, where have you sprung from?" from another. "I suppose you've come back with your pockets bulging with money," from a third, and "When is the happy event to be?" from a friend of his mother's.

Home. Florence. Home.

And there was La Carolina, at a loose end now because the Cardinal who'd kept her had been too rich to die a natural death. She was a grand woman, with a clever tongue, whom it was a treat to talk to, and sometimes you could cajole her into giving you for nothing what others were prepared to pay good money for.

How pretty the Tuscan landscape was! In another month the almond-trees would be in flower.

He began once more to think of the play that was simmering in his head. It made him feel happy and young and as light-headed as though he had drunk wine on an empty stomach. He repeated to himself the cynical speeches he would put in the mouth of Fra Timoteo. Suddenly he pulled his horse up. The servants came up with him to see if there were anything he wanted and to their surprise saw that he was shaking with silent laughter. He saw the look on

489

their faces and laughed all the more, then without a word clapped his spurs to the horse's flanks and galloped hell for leather down the road till the poor brute, unaccustomed to such exuberance, slackened down to its usual steady amble. The Idea had come to him, the idea he had racked his brains to invent, and it had come on a sudden, he could not tell how or why or whence, and it was the very idea he wanted, ribald, extravagant and comic. It was almost a miracle. Everyone knew that credulous women bought the mandrake root to promote conception, it was a common superstition and many were the indecent stories told about its use. Now he would persuade Bartolomeo—to whom by then he had given the name of Messer Nicia—that his wife would conceive if she drank a potion made from it, but that the first man who had connection with her after she had done so would die. How to persuade him of that? It was easy. He, Callimaco, would disguise himself as a doctor who had studied in Paris, and prescribe the treatment. It was obvious that Messer Nicia would hesitate to give his life to become a father, and so a stranger must be found to take his place for one night. This stranger, under another disguise, would of course be Callimaco, that is to say Machiavelli.

Now that he had a plot the scenes succeeded one another with inevitability. They fell into place like the pieces of a puzzle. It was as though the play were writing itself and he, Machiavelli, were no more than an amanuensis. If he had been excited before, when the notion of making a play out of his misadventure had first come to him, he was doubly excited now that it all lay clear before his mind's eye like a garden laid out with terraces and fountains, shady walks and pleasant arbours. When they stopped to dine, absorbed in his characters he paid no attention to what he ate; and when they started off again he was unconscious of the miles they travelled; they came nearer to Florence, and the countryside was as familiar to him, and as dear, as the street he was born in, but he had no eyes for it; the sun, long past its meridian, was making its westering way to where it met earth and sky, but he gave no heed to it. He was in a world of make-believe that rendered the real world illusory. He felt more than himself. He *was* Callimaco, young, handsome, rich, audacious, gay; and the passion with which he burnt for Lucrezia was of a tempestuous violence that made the desire Machiavelli had had for Aurelia a pale slight thing. That was but a shadow, this was the substance. Machiavelli, had he only known it, was enjoying the supreme happiness that man is capable of experiencing, the activity of creation.

"Look, Messere," cried his servant Antonio, riding up to come abreast of him. "Florence."

Machiavelli looked. In the distance against the winter sky, paling now with the decline of day, he saw the dome, the proud dome that Bramante had built. He pulled up. There it was, the city he loved more than his soul; they were not idle words that he had spoken when he had said that to Il Valentino. Florence, the city of flowers, with her campanile and her baptistery, her churches and palaces, her gardens, her tortuous streets, the old bridge he crossed every day to go to the Palazzo, and his home, his brother Toto, Marietta, his friends, the city of which he knew

491

every stone, the city with its great history, his birth-place and the birthplace of his ancestors, Florence, the city of Dante and Boccaccio, the city which had fought for its freedom through the centuries, Florence the well-beloved, the city of flowers.

Tears formed in his eyes and rolled down his cheeks. He clenched his teeth to restrain the sobs that shook him. She was powerless now, governed by men who had lost their courage; corrupt; and the citizens, who once had been quick to rise up against those who threatened their liberties, were concerned only to buy and sell. Free now only by the grace of the King of France, to whom she paid unworthy tribute, her only defence faithless mercenaries, how could she resist the onslaught of that desperate, audacious man who thought her of so little danger that he did not trouble to conceal his evil intentions? Florence was doomed. She might not fall to the arms of Cæsar Borgia, but if not to his, then to another's, not that year perhaps, nor next, but before men now in their middle age were old.

"To hell with art," he said. "What is art beside free-dom! Men who lose their freedom lose everything."

"If we want to get in before dark we must push on, Messere," said Antonio.

With a shrug of the shoulders Machiavelli tight-ened his reins, and the tired horse ambled on.

EPILOGUE

FOUR YEARS PASSED and in that period much happened. Alexander VI died. Il Valentino had provided for everything that might occur on his father's death, but he had not foreseen that when it took place he would himself be at death's door. Though ill, so desperately ill that only the strength of his constitution saved him, he managed to secure the election to the papacy of a cardinal, Pius III, whom he had no reason to fear; but the lords whom he had attacked and driven to flight seized the opportunity to regain their dominions, and he could do nothing to prevent them. Guidobaldo di Montefeltro returned to Urbino, the Vitellis recovered Città di Castello and Gian Paolo Baglioni captured Perugia. Only Romagna remained faithful to him. Then Pius III, an old man and a sick one, died, and Giuliano della Rovere, a bitter enemy of the Borgias, ascended the papal throne as Julius II. In order to obtain the votes of those cardinals whom Il Valentino controlled he had promised to reappoint him Captain-General of the Church and confirm him in possession of his states. Cæsar thought that the promises of others were more likely to be kept than his own. He made a fatal error. Julius II was vindictive, crafty, unscrupulous and ruthless. It was not long before he found an excuse to put the Duke under arrest; he then forced him to surrender the cities of Romagna which his captains still held for him, and, that accomplished, allowed him to escape to Naples. Here after a short while by order of King Ferdinand he was again thrown into prison and presently conveyed to Spain. He was taken first to a fortress in Murcia and then for greater safety to one at Medina del Campo in the heart of Old Castile. It looked as though Italy were rid at last and for good of the adventurer whose boundless ambition had for so long disturbed her peace.

But some months later the whole country was startled to hear that he had escaped, and after a hazardous journey, disguised as a merchant, had reached Pamplona, the capital of his brother-in-law, the King of Navarre. The news raised the spirits of his partisans and in the cities of Romagna there were wild scenes of rejoicing. The petty princelings of Italy trembled in their cities. The King of Navarre was at the time at war with his barons and he put Cæsar Borgia in command of his army.

During these four years Machiavelli was kept hard at work. He went on various missions. He was given the difficult task of constituting a militia so that Florence should not be altogether dependent on mercenaries, and when not otherwise occupied had handled the affairs of the Second Chancery. His digestion had always been poor and the journeys on horseback through the heat of summer, in the cold, wind, rain and snow of winter, the extreme discomfort of the inns, the poor food at irregular hours, had exhausted him, and in February—February of the year of Our Lord fifteen hundred and seven—he fell seriously ill. He was bled and purged and took his favourite remedy, a pill of his own concoction, which, to his mind, was a specific for every human ailment, He was convinced that it was to this, rather than to the doctors, that he owed his recovery, but his illness and its treatment had left him so weak that the Signory granted him a month's leave of absence. He went down to his farm at San Casciano, which was some three miles from Florence, and there quickly regained his health.

Spring had come early that year, and the country-side, with the trees bursting into leaf, the wild flowers, the fresh green of the grass, the rich growth of wheat, was a joy to the eye. To Machiavelli the Tuscan scene had a friendly, intimate delight that appealed to the mind rather than to the senses. It had none of the sublimity of the Alps, nor the grandeur of the sea; it was a plot of earth, graceful, lightly gay and elegant, for men to live on who loved wit and intelligent argument, pretty women and good cheer. It reminded you not of the splendid solemn music of Dante, but rather of the light-hearted strains of Lorenzo de' Medici.

One March morning Machiavelli, up with the sun, went to a grove on his small estate that he was having cut. He lingered there, looking over the previous day's work, and talked with the woodmen; then he went to a spring and sat himself down on a bank with a book he had brought in his pocket. It was an Ovid, and with a smile on his thin lips he read the amiable and lively verses in which the poet described his amours and, remembering his own, thought of them for a while with pleasure.

"How much better it is to sin and repent," he murmured, "than to repent for not having sinned!"

Then he strolled down the road to the inn and chatted with the passers-by. For he was a sociable creature and if he could not have good company was willing to put up with poor. When his hunger told him that it must be getting on towards dinner-time he sauntered home and sat down with his wife and the children to the modest fare his farm provided. After dinner he went back to the inn. The innkeeper was there, the butcher, the miller and the blacksmith. He sat down to play a game of cards with them, a noisy, quarrelsome game, and they flew into a passion over a penny, shouted at one another, flung insults across the table and shook their fists in one another's face. Machiavelli shouted and shook his fist with the best of them. Evening drew near and he returned to his house. Marietta, pregnant for the third time, was about to give the two little boys their supper.

"I thought you were never coming," said she.

"We were playing cards."

"Who with?"

"The usual lot, the miller, the butcher and Batista."

"Riff-raff."

"They keep my wits from growing mouldy, and when all's said and done they're no stupider than ministers of state, and on the whole not more rascally."

He took his eldest son, Bernardo, now getting on for four, on his knees and began to feed him.

"Don't let your soup get cold," said Marietta.

They were eating in the kitchen, with the maid and the hired man, and when he had finished his soup the maid brought him half a dozen larks roasted on a skewer. He was surprised and pleased, for as a rule supper consisted of nothing but a bowl of soup and a salad.

"What is this?"

"Giovanni snared them and I thought you'd like them for your supper."

"Are they all for me?"

"All."

496

"You're a good woman, Marietta."

"I haven't been married to you for five years without finding out that the way to your heart is through your stomach," she said dryly.

"For that sound piece of observation you shall have a lark, dear," he answered, taking one of the tiny birds in his fingers and popping it, notwithstanding her remonstrance, into her mouth.

"They fly towards heaven in their ecstasy, their hearts bursting with song, and then, caught by an idle boy, they're cooked and eaten. So man, for all his soaring ideals, his vision of intellectual beauty and his yearning for the infinite, in the end is caught by the perversity of fate and serves no other purpose than to feed the worms."

"Eat your food while it's hot, dear, you can talk afterwards."

Machiavelli laughed. He slipped another lark off the skewer and while crunching it with strong teeth looked at Marietta with affection. It was true she was a good woman; she was thrifty and good-tempered. She was always sorry to see him go on one of his journeys and glad to see him come back. He wondered if she knew how unfaithful he was to her. If she did, she had never given a sign of it, which showed that she was sensible and good-natured; he might have gone farther and fared worse; he was very well pleased with his wife.

When they had finished and the maid was washing up, Marietta put the children to bed. Machiavelli went upstairs to take off the clothes, muddy and dirty, that he had worn all day, and put on what he liked to describe as courtly and regal garments; for it was his habit to spend the evening in his study reading the authors he loved. He was not yet dressed when he heard a horseman ride up and in a moment a voice he recognised asking the maid for him. It was Biagio, and he wondered what had brought him out from the city at that hour.

"Niccolo," he shouted from below. "I have news for you."

"Wait a minute. I'll come down as soon as I'm ready."

Since it was still a trifle chilly as the day drew in, he slipped his black damask robe over his tunic and opened the door. Biagio was waiting for him at the foot of the stairs.

"Il Valentino is dead."

"How do you know?"

"A courier arrived from Pamplona today. I thought you'd want to know, so I rode out."

"Come into my study."

They sat down, Machiavelli at his writing-table and Biagio in a carved chair which was part of Marietta's dowry. Biagio told him the facts as he had learnt them. Cæsar Borgia had established his head-quarters at a village on the Ebro and planned to attack the castle of the Count of Lerin, the most powerful of the insurgent barons. Early in the morning, on the 12th of March, there was a skirmish between his men and the Count's. Cæsar Borgia was still in his rooms when the alarm sounded; he donned his armour, mounted his horse and flung himself into the fray. The rebels fled, and he, without looking round to see if he was followed, pursued them down into a deep ravine, and there, surrounded and alone, unhorsed, he fought fiercely till he was killed. Next day the King and his men found the body, naked, for they had stripped him of his armour and his clothes, and the King with his own cloak covered his naked- ness.

Machiavelli listened to Biagio attentively, but when he had finished remained silent.

"It is good that he is dead," said Biagio after a while.

"He had lost his states, his money and his army, and yet all Italy feared him still."

"He was a terrible man."

"Secret and impenetrable. He was cruel, treach- erous and unscrupulous, but he was able and energetic. He was temperate and self-controlled. He let nothing interfere with his chosen course. He liked women, but he used them only for his pleasure and never allowed himself to be swayed by them. He created an army that was loyal to him and trusted him. He never spared himself. On the march he was indifferent to cold and hunger, and the strength of his body made him immune to fatigue. He was brave and mettlesome in battle. He shared danger with the meanest of his soldiers. He was as competent in the arts of peace as in the arts of war. He chose his ministers with discrimination, but took care that they should remain dependent upon his good will. He did everything that a prudent and clever man should do to consolidate his power, and if his methods did not bring him success it was through no fault of his, but through the extraordinary and extreme malice of fortune. With his great spirit and lofty intentions he could not have conducted himself otherwise than he did. His designs were thwarted only by Alexander's death and his own illness; if he had been in health he could have surmounted all his difficulties."

"He suffered the just punishment of his crimes," said Biagio.

Machiavelli shrugged his shoulders.

"Had he lived, had fortune continued to favour him, he might have driven the barbarians out of this unhappy country and given it peace and plenty. Then men would have forgotten by what crimes he had achieved power and he would have gone down to posterity as a great and good man. Who cares now that Alexander of Macedon was cruel and ungrateful, who remembers that Julius Cæsar was perfidious? In this world it is only necessary to seize power and hold it, and the means you have used will be judged honourable and will be admired by all. If Cæsar Borgia is regarded as a scoundrel it is only because he didn't succeed. One of these days I shall write a book about him and what I learnt from my observation of his actions."

"My dear Niccolo, you're so unpractical. Who d'you think would read it? You're not going to achieve immortality by writing a book like that."

"I don't aspire to it," laughed Machiavelli.

Biagio looked suspiciously at a pile of manuscript on his friend's writing-table.

"What have you there?"

Machiavelli gave him a disarming smile.

"I had nothing much to do here and I thought I'd pass the time by writing a comedy. Would you like me to read it to you?"

"A comedy?" said Biagio doubtfully. "I presume it has political implications."

"Not at all. Its only purpose is to amuse."

"Oh, Niccolo, when will you take yourself seriously? You'll have the critics down on you like a thousand of bricks."

"I don't know why; no one can suppose that Apuleius wrote his *Golden Ass* or Petronius the *Satyricon* with any other object than to entertain."

"But they're classics. That makes all the difference."

"You mean that works of entertainment, like loose women, become respectable with age. I've often wondered why it is that the critics can only see a joke when the fun has long since seeped out of it. They've never discovered that humour depends upon actuality."

"You used to say that not brevity, but pornography was the soul of wit. You've changed your mind?"

"Not at all. For what can be more actual than pornography? Believe me, my good Biagio, when men cease to find it so they will have lost all interest in reproducing their kind, and that will be the end of the Creator's most unfortunate experiment."

"Read your play, Niccolo. You know I don't like to hear you say things like that."

With a smile Machiavelli took his manuscript and began to read.

"A Street in Florence."

But then he was seized with the slight misgiving of an author who reads something for the first time to a friend and is not sure that it will please. He interrupted himself.

"This is only a first draft and I dare say I shall make a good many changes when I go over it again."

501

He flipped the pages uncertainly. The play had amused him to write, but one or two things had happened that he had not counted on. The characters had taken on a life of their own and had diverged a good deal from their models. Lucrezia had remained as shadowy as Aurelia had been, and he had not seen how to make her more substantial. The exigencies of the plot had obliged him to make her a virtuous woman induced by her mother and her confessor to submit to something her conscience disapproved of. Piero, whom he had called Ligurio, on the contrary played a much greater part than he had intended. It was he who suggested the scheme by which the foolish husband was taken in, he who got round Lucrezia's mother and the monk, he in short who staged the intrigue and conducted it to a happy conclusion. He was astute, ingenious, quick-witted and pleasantly unprincipled. Machiavelli found it very easy to put himself into the rascal's shoes, but by the time he had finished discovered that there was as much of himself in the artful schemer as in the love-sick gallant who was his hero.

Thinking how odd it was that he should play two parts in one play, he looked up and asked Biagio:

"By the way, have you heard anything lately of your nephew Piero?"

"In point of fact I have. I meant to tell you, but with all the excitement of Il Valentino's death I quite forgot. He's going to be married."

"Is he? Is it a good match?"

"Yes, he's marrying money. You remember Bartolomeo Martelli at Imola? He was some sort of relation of mine."

Machiavelli nodded.

"When Imola revolted he thought it safer to get away till he saw how things were going. You see, he'd been one of the Duke's chief partisans and he was afraid he'd have to pay for it. He went to Turkey, where he had a business. The papal troops got to the city before there were any real disturbances, and as luck would have it Piero was with them. It seems he was well liked by some influential men who had the ear of the Pope and he managed to protect Bartolomeo's property. But Bartolomeo was banished, and lately the news has arrived that he died in Smyrna, and so Piero is going to marry the widow."

"Very right and proper," said Machiavelli.

"They tell me she's young and good-looking; evidently she needed a man to protect her, and Piero has a head on his shoulders."

"That was the impression he gave me."

"There's only one fly in the ointment. Bartolomeo had a little boy, between three and four years old, I think he is, and that won't improve the prospects of any children Piero might have."

"I think you may be sure that he will cherish the little boy as if he were his own," said Machiavelli dryly.

He returned to his manuscript. He smiled with some complacency. He could not help thinking that he had succeeded with Fra Timoteo. His pen had been dipped in gall and as he wrote he chuckled with malice. Into that character he had put all the hatred and contempt he felt for the monks who fattened on the credulity of the ignorant. By that character his play would stand or fall. He began again.

503

"A Street in Florence."

He stopped and looked up.

"What is the matter?" asked Biagio.

"You say that Cæsar Borgia suffered the just punishment of his crimes. He was destroyed not by his misdeeds, but by circumstances over which he had no control. His wickedness was an irrelevant accident. In this world of sin and sorrow if virtue triumphs over vice it is not because it is virtuous, but because it has better and bigger guns; if honesty prevails over double-dealing, it is not because it is honest, but because it has a stronger army more ably led; and if good overcomes evil it is not because it is good, but because it has a well-lined purse. It is well to have right on our side, but it is madness to forget that unless we have might as well it will avail us nothing. We must believe that God loves men of good will, but there is no evidence to show that He will save fools from the result of their folly."

He sighed, and for the third time started reading *"A Street in Florence."*

*This book was designed
by William B. Taylor
for Heron Books, London*

Printed in Switzerland